Watched

Cindy M. Hogan

Summary: When fifteen-year-old-Christy witnesses the
murder of a Senator's aide, she finds herself watched not only by
the killers and the FBI but also by two hot boys

Library of Congress Number

2011909217

ISBN: 0615493386
ISBN-13:9780615493381

For Hensley and Hannah, whose eager requests for
"the next chapter" pushed me to complete it.

Watched

Sydnee

Be unpredictable

M. Hogan

CHAPTER ONE

I plastered a smile on my face, trying in vain to stop the shiver that traveled with slow determination up my spine.

None of the other seven in my student tour group seemed to have a problem with the Hotel Norton's dark gray stone exterior. Six sat on its wide steps, chatting away, while one, the boy who made my heart all but stop, ventured inside the hotel to see if the bathrooms were "suitable" for us to use. No one seemed ready to walk the four or five blocks back to our hotel just to use the bathroom and no one wanted the fun night to end.

"Get over here, Christy," Marybeth called from the steps, her extra long, brown hair blowing lightly in the cool breeze as she patted the empty spot next to her.

"In a minute," I said, unsure if I would be able to keep that promise and hoping Alex would come out and tell us the bathrooms in that hotel had dripping faucets, doors that didn't close and those awful cloth towels that went round and round in the dispenser, getting dirtier and dirtier with each pull. At least then we'd have to go to another hotel. And maybe, just maybe, the hot rock in my stomach would go away.

I kept my eyes fixed on the hotel door, wanting Alex to appear so I could feel the soft tingles he always gave me. It had been five long minutes since he'd gone inside, and the sprinkling of goose bumps on my arms seemed to grow with each passing one. It didn't make any sense, but something felt wrong.

Sneaking out of our safe, inviting hotel at ten at night to explore Washington, D.C. had been the scariest thing I'd ever done. I may have come from a small town, but I still knew that D.C. boasted one of the highest crime rates in the U.S. Unfortunately, I had this maddening drive to be accepted by this group of kids and I wasn't going to let a few statistics prevent it. So, I had ignored the warning voice in my head and snuck out with them, down the back stairs of the hotel and into the cool, sticky, night D.C. air.

I had no interest in politics. I had come to get away from home to change who I was. Was I asking too much of a high school student political trip? Could my life change in two short weeks? I was counting on it, praying for it.

Nothing bad had happened to us as we roamed around the last two hours, but that little voice, not so little now, screamed at me to head back to our hotel. It felt like that voice had the power to root me to my spot. I couldn't even go over to my new friends, a mere twenty steps away. Instead, I leaned against a "no parking" sign in the grassy strip next to the street.

An eternity seemed to pass before Alex slinked back out the massive, dark wooden doors of the hotel. Right on cue, my heart started pounding.

"This place is perfect," he called out, walking toward the others, a roguish look dominating his face and sending a speeding freight train barreling through my chest. "It's a bit creepy inside, too," he said, flashing a perfect set of teeth. I hadn't met anyone who could resist Alex's charm and all six on the steps stood, as if in a trance, to follow him inside. I, on the other hand, despite the butterfly wings tickling my stomach, still couldn't seem to move.

Book after book I'd read told this exact story: unsuspecting girl loses her brain when perfect boy enters her life. I always considered the girls in those stories weak or silly, until Alex happened to me. Heck, my heart skipped a few beats just looking at him, and my mind turned to jelly. There was no rational explanation. After only a few days in D.C., I'd already learned that feelings could easily control the mind if you let them. I felt helpless…and an unknown part of me liked it—a lot.

To get my feet to move, I tried to convince myself it was the Ritz inside that dark, foreboding hotel. It didn't help. A desperate panic filled my gut as all seven went in without me. Any hope I'd dredged up the last four days of becoming a new person, accepted and liked, drowned in a flood of horrible memories: sitting alone at lunch, being taunted, being picked last for teams and never being invited to anything. None of the others even noticed I hadn't gone in with them.

I tried to slow my frantic heart by taking deep long breaths, leaving my mouth dry. No one but adults ever noticed anything good about me at home, and I'd been determined not to repeat that cycle here in D.C. Yet here I stood, the forgotten one, in front of a horrible hotel. I didn't want to be that person again. I willed my legs to move, but like my feet were encased in cement, I couldn't. As the seconds ticked by, I felt more and more alone. Then, Rick and Marybeth opened the door and came to my rescue.

"Are you crazy?" Rick said, his arms out to his sides, palms up as he walked toward me.

"Yeah," Marybeth said, her dark brown eyes creased with worry. "You can't stay out here by yourself. It's too dangerous."

I heard an odd chuckle escape my lips. Relief or perhaps renewed fear. I felt liked, but not safe.

I sighed, glad that I hadn't looked like a total loser. Rick and Marybeth had this insane idea that I was being brave, just waiting outside for everyone to get back. Were they out of their minds? Who would do that in this city?

They each looped an arm through mine and led me to the door, my legs no longer protesting. Inside, the large foyer split into two wide sets of stairs that wound around a huge center column that housed an elevator in the middle. I couldn't see where the stairs ended. They seemed to go on forever. Dark wood and stone lined the walls from floor to ceiling, reinforcing the ominous feel of an old medieval castle.

"Alex said to hug the wall while going up the stairs," Marybeth whispered. "The girls' bathroom is on the left at the top. Once you reach the last step, peek around the corner. If no one's looking, go on in. Just follow me. Okay?"

"Yeah, but why are we sneaking in anyway?" I whispered, touching her arm. "Why can't we just ask to use the bathrooms?"

"Alex thinks it's more fun this way, I guess," Rick said, rolling his eyes, a tone of disbelief in his voice.

"I'd rather just ask," Marybeth said. "All this sneaking around gives me the creeps."

"Me, too," I said. It had escaped my lips even though deep down I knew Alex's adventurous side was a large part of what attracted me to him. I felt a bit hypocritical but still said, "I can't wait for this to be over."

I watched Rick's sandy blonde hair disappear around the curve of the stairs. Marybeth followed him, and I followed her, all the while that voice in my head screamed for me to stop. I took a deep breath, focusing on Rick and Marybeth coming out to get me and how great that had felt. Besides, I couldn't turn back now. Not after they'd come back out after me. I had to watch my breathing; it seemed too loud. I felt warm, the chill from outside melting away. The pungent smell in the air, however, made me want to hold my breath. Marybeth rounded the

4

corner and disappeared. I was certain that if she could make it to the restroom, I could as well.

I took the last step up the stairs, taking one last deep breath, and peered around the corner. A shallow gasp escaped my lips looking at the scene before me. Shiny black barrels of large guns poked below the dark leather coats of two men standing next to the front desk. They seemed relaxed, talking to the tall, wickedly pretty receptionist. They weren't like regular guards with handguns in a holster on their hips, though. They had serious firepower.

Were they the reason Alex had had such a mischievous look on his face or was it just the medieval feel of the hotel that attracted him? I suspected both. I felt a tension in the air that wouldn't allow me to quickly draw my eyes away. Maybe some important people were staying here and needed protection. On the other hand, maybe all hotels in D.C. had similar armed guards. I hadn't seen any at our hotel, but then again, I'd never been in the lobby past eight o'clock at night, either.

Why hadn't the guards or receptionist noticed eight high school kids dashing for their restroom? Perhaps most, or all of their guests would take one look at the long staircase and take the elevator instead. I would have. If they didn't hear the ding announcing the arrival of the elevator, they wouldn't pay attention to what was going on around them. Or, maybe they were simply distracting each other and we had been lucky. My heart thudded against my ribcage urging me to move. Despite the massive twinge of fear I felt, I headed for the door marked, "Ladies", busy ants filling my stomach.

Wow! This was one elegant bathroom. Alex had chosen well. No wonder they didn't want just anyone to use it. Real towels and miscellaneous personal products like cologne and powder sat neatly on the marble counter next to the old fashioned looking faucet. There were two large stalls inside, kind of like office cubicles with walls of marble that didn't go all the way up to the ceiling, but with real doors—no peeking sides like stalls in normal public bathrooms. I waited my turn with Marybeth, playing with the products on the counter, until both Summer and Kira came out. As I was about to use the toilet, I heard muffled voices above me.

Remembering that some guy had been caught taking pictures of girls in bathrooms near my hometown, I glanced up to see if I could find an offending camera. I couldn't see any, but I still heard voices. That's when I noticed a large vent just below the ceiling on the wall. I couldn't even think of using the toilet until I'd taken a look, just to ease my mind. My heart started to pound again as I climbed onto the back of the toilet, prepared to catch some pervert on the other side of the vent.

I stood on tip-toe, straining to keep myself up high enough to see through the vent. I looked down onto some sort of large ballroom, the glossy wooden floor shining up at me, although the scene below had nothing to do with dancing. The same type of guns the men in the lobby carried were in the hands of six men whose bodies and heads were draped in flowing robes like middle easterners'. They surrounded a rectangular table where four other men sat. The two facing me wore the same type of robes as the guards that surrounded them, but the other two looked like American businessmen with suits and short cropped hair, their backs turned toward me.

These people were way below me—at street level—I guessed. We had climbed all those stairs to get to the bathroom. I was concentrating so hard, trying to make out what was happening down there, that I almost fell when Marybeth asked, "Are you almost ready, 'cause I don't want to go out there alone."

"You startled me!" I whispered back down at her.

"What are you doing up there?" she asked, brushing strands of light, brown hair over her shoulder, her soft, pretty face looking up at me in surprise.

"I heard voices and wanted to make sure some perv wasn't trying to look at us or take pictures of us while we're in here," I whispered.

"Perv?" she asked, crinkling her perfectly shaped nose.

I guessed in Iowa there weren't any pervs. I climbed down and opened the stall door.

"Take a look. Something weird's happening."

"No, that's okay."

"No, really, you've got to see this."

I pushed her toward the toilet until she relented and climbed up to look. "What's going on?" she whispered after looking.

"You've got me."

"Let's get out of here," she said.

"Wait," I said, as I climbed up next to her. "Let's just find out what they're saying. Can you hear them?" My stomach flipped.

We both looked through the vent, squished against each other, trying not to fall off the back of the toilet.

Not one minute had passed before Marybeth whispered, "I know that voice! It's Senator Randolph—on the right."

"Senator Randolph?"

"He's one of Iowa's Senators," she explained. "My dad says he's going to save the farmers in our state and is a blessing from heaven. We listen to his every last word every time he speaks."

"He doesn't look like he's in heaven right now," I said, my stomach now a roiling ocean.

"Shhh! I can't hear." She urged me to silence.

7

This was the most forceful I'd ever seen Marybeth, and so I listened as hard as I could. Slowly, the words started to make sense.

"You failed...Senator," the robed man on the right, who appeared to be the leader, said. "What... to impress on you the absolute ...of a favorable result in this matter? The news...tell only of ...death of the bill...told you had the votes." I had to concentrate on their mouths to help make out the heavily accented words and the man's large crooked nose kept distracting me, twitching every time he started a new sentence.

"We do!" the Senator said. "...them... bill *will* pass."

"...not want all this attention...it. ..late," the robed man on the right continued.

"No, No!" stammered the man next to the Senator louder than the others. "You'll see. We *have* won."

"...nothing!" The robed man on the right, said.

With those words, another guard, standing behind the Senator, raised his arms into the air. Only then did I realize that instead of a gun, his hands were wrapped around a long, thick shiny sword. The light reflected harshly off it. With a loud "Arhhhh!" the robed man whipped the sword through the air and through the neck of the man sitting next to Senator Randolph. His arms moved like lightning as his body made a complete circle. The man's head now lay beside him on the floor. Blood spurted everywhere, like a geyser. I couldn't believe how far it flew. I jumped back and partially fell onto the seat of the toilet and had to grab the stall wall in order to stop myself from falling all the way to the floor. In a rush, I climbed back up to see if I had really seen what I thought I had. My stomach lurched and I covered my mouth to keep a gasp from escaping as I looked down on the carnage.

Even though the action really only took a few seconds, it felt like it happened in slow motion. Blood sprayed through the air and soaked the Senator's face and side. As the first few drops hit him, he leaned down to try to avoid the flood, which only allowed the blood to spray all over his back, too. No one there escaped the volcano of blood. Unconsciously, I wiped the side of my face and looked for Marybeth.

She no longer stood beside me. I found her in front of the toilet, eyes wide, mouth open, no sound escaping. Then her eyes rolled up in her head, her knees gave out and her head and back hit the stall door, forcing it open as she crashed to the floor. Had they heard? For a few seconds I was frozen in place, my mind wanting me to climb back up and see if the people in the ballroom had heard Marybeth fall, while my heart wanted to help Marybeth. My mind won out. I figured we would be in greater danger if they'd heard.

I climbed back up and looked through the vent and for a split second, I thought I saw the crooked-nosed guy look right at me. I ducked. Had he seen me or was he really only looking at the guard with the sword? Ice spread through my veins as I dared one last look through the vent. No one had moved from their spot except the Senator, who stood behind his beheaded friend, pacing and moaning. Maybe his loud moaning had covered the sounds of Marybeth's fall. I looked back at her. She lay there, out cold.

CHAPTER TWO

"Marybeth, Marybeth," I whispered, climbing down from the toilet. I was terrified, but too busy to be consumed with fear.

I knew I had to get out of there, but I couldn't drag Marybeth out. What if someone saw us, like those guards at the desk? I couldn't think straight. *What should I do?* My head swam. We had to leave, but how? No amount of intellectual smarts, books, competitions, or research could have prepared me for this, and I certainly didn't know what a cool person would do.

Before panic could overtake me, I stepped over her and hurried to the door to crack it open. By luck, Kira was right there, reaching for the doorknob. When she saw me, she looked in the direction of the receptionist and then motioned for me to come out. I shook my head, opened the door further and grabbed her arm before she could walk away. Her gorgeous, dark red hair fluttered across my face as I pulled her in. The soft scent of shampoo lingered in the air, a stark contrast to the musty smell in the bathroom. I pointed at Marybeth, now sitting, with her knees to her chest, rocking back and forth, eyes closed.

"Whew!" escaped my lips. What a relief. She wasn't dead. Kira moved toward her.

"What happened?" she asked.

"We've got to get out of here," I interrupted. "Help me with Marybeth."

We tried to lift her, but she was too heavy and dead weight at that.

"We need one of the guys," Kira said as she reached

for the door. At the same moment, Rick slipped inside. He took one look at Marybeth rocking back and forth and said, "What the… ?" and moved toward her like he alone was responsible for her safety.

"She fainted," I whispered. "Rick, we've got to get out of here…"

"Fainted? How is that…" He knelt beside her, inspecting her head.

"Shh!" I said, pointing at the vent. "Look, I don't have time to explain. Let's just get out of here."

"Slow down and tell me what happened," Rick said, as calm as ever. "Could you hand me some paper towels, Kira…and wet a few of them, please."

Kira, more than happy to help any boy, grabbed some towels and put a few under a stream of water coming from the old fashion looking tap. The door opened, making me jump. The rest of the crew walked in and they didn't look happy.

"What's the hold up?" Alex asked, commanding the room.

"Marybeth fainted," Kira blurted, taking advantage of a chance to have Alex notice her.

"You've got to be kidding," Alex said, looking around.

"Why would she faint in here?"

"That's precisely what I'm trying to figure out," Rick said, staring hard at me.

All eyes fell on me. "Well, Marybeth and I," I stuttered, "just saw a guy's head get chopped off. We've got to get out of here and fast. Marybeth made a lot of noise when she fell and…"

"I don't see anyone with their head chopped off," Josh interrupted with a laugh, his muscle bound body bumping playfully into Summer, her tiny frame swaying with each push.

"Yeah. Where's the body?" Summer said, laughing out loud. "Oh, and the head?"

"Shh!" I said, looking up at the vent. "Do you want them to hear us?"

Alex looked up at the vent. "You saw it through that vent?" he asked, walking toward the marble counter by the sink that also gave access to the large vent.

"No, don't look. Please, let's just go," I said, feeling time tick away with every step he took.

"This I've got to see," Alex said, ignoring me and hopping up onto the counter to look through the vent. He ducked right after looking and whispered, "What the...."

I watched as his beautiful face turned serious.

"Get up here Josh, you won't believe this," he whispered.

I wondered if the counter could hold his weight.

Josh climbed up next to Alex, the counter creaked (but didn't give in) and only a mere second after looking through the vent, he jumped back down, his face white as a sheet. Seeing such a big guy get sick at the sight of blood seemed odd. Summer hurried over to him and rubbed his arm.

"Was it bad?" she asked, showing him her best pouty lips. He didn't answer, instead he leaned over the sink, hands clutching the counter, and took deep breaths.

"No way," Rick said, and then mumbled, "Could you hold this, Kira?" He handed her the paper towels he held to Marybeth's head and climbed up next to Alex, who had pulled out his cell and was snapping pictures of the gruesome scene below.

"We better get out of here." Rick whispered, after his brief look down at the ballroom. He jumped off the counter without a sound and his face paled. He put a hand up to his mouth and heaved a few times.

"Yeah," I whispered. "Let's get out of here!" I moved toward the door.

"Wait," Alex whispered down to us. "I want to get more pictures. Evidence, ya know."

The thought of the details of the gruesome incident being frozen in time on his phone gave me some relief. Maybe justice could be served.

Why I did it, I'll never know, but I walked back into that stall and climbed back up on the back of the toilet. Only the quiet click-click of Alex's camera phone disturbed the silence.

The Senator still paced, his hands in his blood-soaked hair. The two robed men were still seated and the guards stood as if stone, even though the man's blood completely surrounded their shoes.

"Come on, Alex," Josh said. "I'm outta here."

"Don't leave yet," Eugene said, his voice whiny. "I want to see." He climbed up next to Alex, pushing him against the stall divider. As he clumsily struggled for position, he bumped Alex and his phone fell over the stall wall and into the toilet below me. My shoes got spattered.

"You idiot!" Alex whispered as he jumped down to get his phone. It sat at the bottom of the toilet, and Alex cursed as he reached in for it. I watched his every move. He shook it hard, trying to get as much water out of it as possible as Summer handed him a bunch of paper towels. Leave it to Eugene to do stuff that reinforced his social awkwardness.

Loud voices drew me back to the horror scene in the ballroom. The two robed men, who had been sitting, stood, talking to the Senator. My heart drummed unevenly listening to the spotty conversation below me.

"Let this be a warning … make it happen, Senator."

"…mistake!" The Senator cried. "Don't you see? He will be missed. I thought … not want attention…? Jonathan! No…" The Senator sobbed, his eyes fixed on his beheaded partner.

Jonathan? I thought. *His name is Jonathan.*

I could hear, somewhere in the back of my mind, others leaving the bathroom, calling to me, but I was frozen somehow. I had to hear the rest—despite the fact that I could feel the time disappearing. The fear that welled up inside me, held me still as a mountain and knowing the dead man had a name made my insides buzz. Surely he had a family. Would they ever know what really happened tonight?

The execution was so swift, so why was it re-playing so slowly in my mind? I imagined each droplet of blood falling like a red snowflake to the ground. Remembering the brief second that I thought the leader had looked up toward the vent and had looked me directly in the eye, haunted me. My fear escalated the longer I watched and yet I just stood there.

Despite my desire to rid myself of the image, the leader's face was permanently etched into my brain; my photographic memory proving to be a disadvantage in this situation. He hadn't seen me, I told myself. His voice seemed to trail off as my fear intensified. The pure brutality was weighing heavily on me now.

I started to shake as I witnessed the leader and the Senator slip robes over their blood stained clothes and one of the guards wrapped cloth over his head before they headed for the doors. The Senator looked like one of them now, his body and head wrapped just like theirs. He reached into a pocket, pulled out a handkerchief and wiped the side of his face as he continued to walk.

The guards hadn't moved an inch. Even the executioner stood stoically, with his sword point stuck into the wood floor as if nothing had happened. Blood puddled around the two guards' feet—an incredible amount of it. It was nauseating to see a man's head severed from its body sitting several feet away.

"Burn him," the robed leader said in a firm voice to his soldiers. And then, the Senator, glancing back with a worried look on his face, slid through the ballroom doors. My mind screamed for me to run, but it was like being trapped in a nightmare.

The four guards, like robots, began to move.

I heard someone speaking behind me, but couldn't make out any of the words. Everything moved in slow motion. I wished it had all been a dream. Then I could wake up and it would all go away. Why hadn't I listened to the voice and stayed at our hotel? Were friends worth this?

The words, "Burn him" were burning my brain. It was as if I could no longer see anything but a sword swinging downward, and a pompous man exiting a bloody ballroom saying, "Burn him."

Someone wrapped his strong arms around me and brought me down from my perch. Rick's handsome, kind face smiled at me. My feet touched the ground and his grip loosened, but I didn't want him to let me go, so I grabbed him hard.

"Christy, it's over. It's all over. It'll be okay," he said, his voice calm and soothing.

I wanted to believe him, but how could I? My mind raced and nothing made any sense.

"Where's everyone?" I asked, my eyes darting around the room.

"They're outside, waiting for us. Come on. Let's join them," he answered, his firm hand leading me to the door.

"No, they didn't go out did they?" I said in hysterics, vaguely remembering hearing people leave earlier. I should have stopped them. "They could have been seen!

The guards in the lobby! They'll know we saw what happened."

"They were very careful. They're waiting for us outside. Let's go. We've already been here too long. Just keep holding on to me. I'll help you out. It's going to be okay," he said, trying to assure me.

I kept holding onto him, and he led us out the bathroom door. Before reaching the stairs a voice called out to us.

"Can I help you?"

My entire body went ice cold. We'd taken too long. We'd be killed just like that man in the ballroom.

The raven-black haired receptionist stood only feet from us, her eyes large and dark. The two guards stood by the reception desk glaring at us.

"Oh, no," Rick said with a completely steady voice. "My friend just feels a bit sick and so we used your bathroom. I hope that's okay. I just need to get her back to our hotel." We turned and headed down the stairs. How was he being so calm? My insides were full of frozen butterflies, their wings cutting into my stomach.

"Should I call for an ambulance?" the woman asked, her eyebrows raised and her lips thin and somehow threatening.

"No, thank you. Our friends are waiting for us outside," he replied.

I felt the piercing glare of the guards. Did they suspect? Rick practically carried me down the stairs.

My thoughts wouldn't give me any peace, until the cool night air hit my body bringing me back to my senses. The others huddled together at bottom of stairs.

"What happened?" "Did they see you?" "Christy, you don't look very good."

"The receptionist saw us. Let's just get out of here," Rick urged. "I have a really bad feeling about this."

"Me, too," Alex whispered. "Let's go to a different hotel than our own in case they decide to follow us. Let's go this way. I know a hotel we can go into."

Rick tugged at my hand to follow the others, but as terrified as I was of finding those guards behind us, I had to look. No guards-only the receptionist stood just outside the door, arms crossed in front of her chest. I was glad I couldn't make out the expression on her face.

I grabbed Rick's arm, "Oh my gosh, that lady's watching us."

Rick looked back.

"You sure you don't want an ambulance?" she called out with a voice that sounded like deep bells chiming.

"No, no," Rick said, "She's doing better already. Thanks, though."

As I turned to follow the others, I thought I did see some black cloth peek out from the corner of the hotel we had just escaped. I quickly turned my head back to take a better look. It was gone, only the receptionist stood there staring after us.

Once we rounded the corner, out of eyeshot of anyone at the hotel, Alex took off running and we all followed, guilt lacing our steps. We hadn't gone far before he led us into another hotel's lobby. It was so late that it was easy to get past the TV-watching receptionist. I took note that there were no guards. We slipped into an elevator that took us to the fifth floor and then Alex suggested we take the stairs back to the third floor, just in case someone was watching. The hair on my neck stood straight up. I could *feel* that someone. I knew he was there, somewhere. Watching. Waiting.

Alex opened the door to the stairs and listened for footsteps. Apparently he didn't hear anything, because he led us down the stairs and then opened the door to the third floor. We had walked half-way down the hall when he opened a door on our left. The laundry room. A perfect place to hide. Had he been here before?

We crowded in on each other, all finding a place to get as comfortable as we could. I wished I could have been next to Alex, but instead, I was sandwiched between Kira and Marybeth, all three of us sitting up. When Kira made her daring move to wedge herself between Alex and me, hot liquid seemed to fill my stomach. I thought she liked Rick. Josh's massive muscle bound body lay in front of the door, blocking out the light, keeping anyone from getting inside.

Everyone started whispering about what had happened until I said, "You guys, we should probably be super quiet because when I looked back at the hotel, before we rounded the corner, I thought I saw someone peek around the corner of the hotel entrance."

Silence prevailed after that. Only seconds later, we heard quiet footsteps that paused at the door. No one dared breathe. Someone tried the door knob. Luckily, we had locked it. The footsteps moved past the door. A long time later, slow, even breathing told me several of the others had fallen asleep.

Even though it was the last thing I thought I could do, I slept, too. Sometime later, I woke to Josh's foghorn-loud snoring. I was startled at first and wondered where I was. Then the whole awful affair came flooding back. I shivered despite the sweat I felt beading along my hairline. Everyone was dead asleep. The air was stale and I noticed a faint glow a few feet from me and moved toward it. Eugene's watch read five a.m. and my heart sank. We were in so much trouble!

"Get up you guys," I said. "It's five o'clock. We've got to get back to our hotel. Mrs. J. will freak if she finds out we're not there." Mrs. Jackson was not only our chaperone, but she was also in charge of the larger group of fifty students staying in our hotel. I had thought it would make her the strictest chaperone, but it hadn't. Maybe it made her the most lenient because she was stretched too thin. She did like her schedules, though. We were always going here or there with no downtime. Ever. And she would definitely notice if we didn't show up for breakfast.

I could hear people moving about me and even got pushed around a bit as everyone woke up. Once Josh sat up, some light peeked through the bottom crack of the door. I could start to make out some shadows of the people around me. Someone opened the door just a little and peeked out. It was Alex. My heart pounded looking at him all disheveled. He looked awesome even with crazy hair. Would he think the same of me? He left the door cracked open. Light and cool air rushed in.

"Don't look at me," Summer said, breaking the silence. "No one look at me. I can't imagine how I look."

Everyone looked at her, of course. She looked perfect. I reached up and felt my hair. I was sure it was a complete mess. I looked around for a mirror, even though I knew there wasn't one. If only I had perfect, lush blonde hair instead of thin dirty blonde hair. How would it be to be perfect all the time? I sighed.

"What?" she almost hissed. "Don't sigh at me. It wasn't my choice to come here. I didn't want to sleep on a tile floor and have no shower today. Christy, I can't believe you dragged me into this."

I surprised myself by saying, "Hey, I didn't drag you into anything." My face felt hot. I hated Summer and yet longed to be her. Could I somehow extract her good looks, popularity, and wealth but leave the nasty, snottiness behind?

"Listen up guys," Alex said, cutting through the thick air. "It doesn't matter how we got here and it's no one's fault. But, we don't know if anyone's waiting outside to follow us again." There was a glint in his eye. A part of him loved this.

An echo of someone trying to open the laundry door last night reminded me that someone probably was waiting.

"But," he continued, "if they are, maybe they didn't get a good look at all of us and are just waiting for a large group of kids to leave the hotel. We should split up, leave in at least two different groups, catch cabs, go to two different places and then meet back up at our hotel before Mrs. J., or anyone else for that matter, knows we were gone."

"That means," Eugene pointed out while pushing the bridge of his glasses hard against his pointy nose, "we have to be back at the hotel *before* eight, when we're supposed to leave."

He was always right—the man with all the information. It was like looking in a mirror at myself watching and listening to Eugene. No wonder people had tormented or avoided me at home—I had tormented them. It made me cringe to think how similar we were. I always thought I was being helpful having all the answers, but realized now how annoying it must have been. Being the top of my class my whole life had pretty much ended my chances of having a social life.

"That gives us less than three hours to give any possible tracker the slip and be back, ready to go for the day," Alex said. "Just act like you're sight-seeing or something. Okay?"

Everyone agreed. For a split second, I thought about having no money for the cab, but then reminded myself that everyone, except Marybeth and I, was loaded. And even Marybeth was a millionaire compared to me. Money was no object for any of them.

The first group would go East in their taxi, and the second would go West.

I was in the second group.

CHAPTER THREE

Big, old, majestic buildings that screamed tradition surrounded me at Georgetown University. Somehow, the towering trees and green grass brought a stillness that settled softly over me. I took in a deep breath of the clean, fresh air.

Dawn had arrived, bringing a glow to the campus. The four of us were not alone, but almost. I saw a few people walking purposefully past us. The bench I sat on was heavy with dew, but I didn't care. I wanted nature to somehow gently wash me with peace and comfort. With each deep breath, my mind slowed, and I was able to concentrate on nothing for a while. More than anything, I didn't want to think about last night's bloody ballroom.

I could barely hear Kira and Rick's footfalls as they walked along a path in front of me, her arm linked in his. Marybeth lay on the edge of a large fountain, her hair draping over the edge and her eyes closed. She hadn't spoken since she fell to the bathroom floor, yet birds were chirping and singing, oblivious of the horrible thing that had happened.

I started wondering what it would be like to go to school here. I hadn't even considered attending Georgetown before now. It would be a long two years before I could escape high school, though. If only my parents had listened to my counselors last year explaining that I could easily leave high school and go to any university I wanted, I would already be studying somewhere instead of staying in a high school that offered me nothing except torture. Maybe I would have fit in. I only fit in here because of Marybeth's magic.

She had saved me from social suicide my second day in D.C. We'd arrived on Sunday, but it had been so late, we'd gone straight to bed once we got to our hotel. Monday morning I'd pulled my hair into a tight ponytail, and had my most comfy bright pink sweats on, ready for a long day of touring.

As I left the room, Marybeth had called out to me, "Christy?"

I had stopped, holding the door open. "Yeah?"

"We don't have time to work out."

"Oh," I said, looking down at my clothes. "I wasn't planning on it."

"You're not gonna wear that all day are you?" Her tone was not mocking, but concerned.

"Huh?" I said, looking down at my clothes again, feeling my face burn despite feeling her sincerity. What was wrong with my clothes? They were my most comfy ones ever.

"They're sweats!" she almost yelled, exasperation lining her words. "And your hair's in a ponytail—"

"Yeah. We're going to be on the bus a lot of the day, touring, and I wanted to be comfy."

"Comfy? Since when was being a hot girl comfy? You need to shine. Not wilt away."

Did she just call me a hot girl?

"Look at yourself. With a bit of effort, you'll look amazing. What other clothes do you have?" she had asked as she walked over to my closet.

Then she had taken over. With the little she had to work with, she did amazing things for me. Not only did she get me to be as fashionable as possible, using a lot of her own things, too, she had also put my hair down and straightened it with the coolest iron I'd ever seen. I'm sure Kira never would have given me the time of day at

23

breakfast that first day if I'd arrived in my bright, pink sweats. I had been resistant to some of the things she wanted to do, like putting make-up all over my face.

"That's okay, Marybeth," I'd said. "We'll be late."

"You know, Christy, you have the longest, most fabulous eyelashes I've ever seen."

"Thanks."

"The only problem is that I had to be two inches from your face to know they were there. You have to at least wear mascara. You'll love it. I promise. And so will the guys."

That was all she had had to say. If mascara would make Alex notice me, I was in.

When we had come down for breakfast, after she had performed her magic, I couldn't help but notice that everyone *had* dressed perfectly. Most of the girls had worn high heels and skirts and fancy jewelry. No one had worn anything remotely like sweats. They'd looked like mannequins in expensive store windows. Shoes matched purses and everyone's faces were flawless. Kira had waved us over to the table where the rest of the six from our group sat. No one had mocked me or made me feel dumb. Could the change I so desperately wanted come from something as simple as changing my appearance? It sure seemed like it.

The last three days she had loaned me a belt here, shoes there, jewelry here…Everyday at least one thing I had worn had come from her.

"That makes the outfit," she had said, as she had put the finishing touches on me each day. And every day, as I had looked in the mirror to see the final product, I had had the same thought, "I look so different."

Watching Marybeth lie there on the fountain made me wish I could do something for her. Maybe I should tell

Mrs. J. what happened. She had been an answer to my prayers.

I couldn't stop my thoughts drifting to the beheaded man named Jonathan, though. Did he have a family? Would they ever know what happened to him? Maybe they wouldn't if I didn't say something to someone. It seemed like the right thing to do, after all, the truth will set you free, right? My stomach twisted and contracted. Would this truth get me killed—just when things were looking up for me and I was becoming somebody?

A man with a backpack, that looked light, not weighted down with books, walked slowly past Kira and Rick and then looked directly at me for several seconds. When I focused on him, I couldn't help but notice how his icy blue eyes contrasted starkly with his dark skin and hair. I stared back, unable to look away. Why was he looking at me like that? My heart would have won a marathon at that moment.

Why would he come to campus with an empty backpack if he were a student? Was I just paranoid?

I tried not to let panic overtake me, focusing on slowing my breathing. I watched as the icy-blue-eyed man turned the corner and went out of sight.

My imagination went crazy. Was he peering from behind the side of that building watching us or was he the first in a string of different tails—all watching and waiting? Would one of them kidnap us and kill us—or worse— torture us to death?

I'd read enough suspense novels to know this couldn't be good. I was afraid to look in the direction the staring man had gone again, but I did it anyway. No one was there.

I stood, but it felt like my legs had turned to stone and it took forever. I clasped my hands together trying to stop them from shaking. Then, wiping sweat from my forehead and walking with deliberation, hoping not to bring attention to myself, I walked over to Rick and Kira. I looked at Marybeth, who had essentially been catatonic since the murder, and I knew that she would freak out if she knew of my suspicions, so I kept them to myself. I also knew it was too early to return to the hotel and meet up with the others, but I didn't feel safe here anymore. I wondered where the other half of our group had decided to go hide out. What if they were being watched, too?

"Hey guys, I read about another really cool fountain over there. Let's go see it," I said, pointing north. It was all I could come up with, lame as it was.

"Really? How far is it?" Kira asked, pushing harder into Rick's side.

"Not that far."

"Whatever," she said. "How much longer do we have to stay, anyway?"

"What time is it, Rick?" I asked.

"It's seven: We still have about an hour before Mrs. J. comes down to breakfast.

"Let's go see the fountain and then grab something to eat," I said, hoping to entice them away from the college. "That way, if someone is following us, we have another chance to lose them."

"I'm not really hungry," Kira said, snuggling into Rick. "And no one's following us."

"It'll make the time go more quickly," I said with a smile, knowing she wanted to get back to the hotel.

"What do you think, Rick?" she asked, flashing her blinding white smile.

I was sure she always got what she wanted, just like she had seemed to have snagged Rick.

"Sounds good to me," he said, his dark blue eyes lingering on me.

"Okay then, let's go," she said.

Sure, she'd go because Rick wanted to…

I walked in the direction of Marybeth to help her up, but Rick beat me there. Kira stood a few feet away sulking, her flawless face drawn out. I had been guiding Marybeth along ever since we left our hideout in the laundry room and Rick's help was a nice bonus. He winked at me when I reached him.

"Thanks," I said.

"No problem," he said, helping her up.

Marybeth didn't seem to be able to do anything on her own ever since the murder. She never said anything or even showed any facial expressions for that matter. Would she ever be herself again? I couldn't help but selfishly wonder if I could get myself ready everyday and not make a fool of myself without her help. We walked in the direction of the made-up "fountain".

If the icy-blue-eyed guy popped up anywhere else today, I would for sure know he was following us. I shivered involuntarily.

There wasn't a fountain. Big surprise. At least we'd made it to a main street where it would be easier to catch a taxi. We hadn't waited more than ten minutes when one dropped off two professor-type men in suits. We asked to be taken to a deli on Connecticut Avenue by Dupont Circle.

It was sad to leave Georgetown University. I would have liked to have stayed longer. It was like a piece of heaven, until that guy cast his shadow over it. I kept looking behind us to see if we were being followed. The streets were packed with cars and taxis but there was no sign of him; I guess I was just being paranoid like Kira said, but the feeling of being watched wouldn't leave me.

The cab driver let us off at a small, packed deli not far from our hotel. Rick, held onto Marybeth, and Kira stood in line to buy some food. I took a table as soon as it became available and looked out the window, searching for the man with icy-blue-eyes. I felt pretty lucky to have snagged the table I did, because it was stuffed into a cozy corner at the front of the deli. I didn't think anyone could see me from outside, but I still had a great view of the sidewalk. The smell of bacon tempted me to eat.

Watching the masses of people on the sidewalk push along, my thoughts drifted back to the horrors of last night. I kept seeing the "leader" in the ballroom with the crooked nose. I pushed away the thought that he had looked me straight in the eyes. I shook my head for all I was worth and forced the image out of my mind. I wasn't being rational. There was no way he could have seen me through that grate. We were way too far away, up that high. There was something so cold about his dark eyes, though, and I shivered despite the warm, stuffy air in the café and my suddenly hot face. I hoped the other three would hurry and get their food and join me. There was definitely a greater sense of safety in numbers. In books and movies, though, people were brave when alone. I wanted to be brave.

Someone with a bright yellow jacket walking by the café caught my attention, reminding me of what I wanted to be doing: looking for the guy I had seen at Georgetown.

I forced myself to watch each person. They were all so different: tall, short, white, black, tan, dark hair, blonde hair, and red hair. I didn't want to miss him in the crowds, so I started to focus on people with blue eyes and dark hair. I questioned my ability to spot him. Everyone with blue eyes and dark hair looked alike. Did I really remember exactly what the guy in Georgetown looked like? For that matter, could I get that leader's crooked nose out of my mind long enough to identify the staring man? I had never had a problem remembering words on a page or pictures of things in books. Could fear prevent me from remembering? Just as I began to believe I wouldn't remember, I saw him, and knew it was him! My brain didn't fail me after all.

Nearly overwhelmed with panic, but at the same time, fighting a very small part of me that wanted to catch him and confront him, I leaned farther into the corner. Could he see me? No. He walked in the direction of our hotel past the café, his view of me blocked. I shuddered at the knowledge that if he had been coming from the other direction, he most likely would have been able to see me through the windows, but he hadn't, and I was safely hidden by a wall when he passed by me. I knew those icy eyes. I was sure. Just before he completely passed the café altogether, he stopped and looked through the windows. I ducked, feeling my eyes grow to the size of golf balls and pretended to tie my shoes. Where were the others? I couldn't see them in the line for food anymore. I looked past the ever-growing queue, past the cash register and finally spotted them. They were behind a divider wall, just to the left of the cash register, and were getting their drinks and some napkins.

I looked back to the door. The staring man from Georgetown was still there, his hand on the door knob until someone wanted inside. He let go, but continued looking as if no one had disturbed him. Would he come in? How could I get my friends to stay where they were, so he wouldn't see them? The divider hid them from his view now, but if they moved even two feet, he would see them. I felt completely useless and at his mercy. I didn't like this feeling—I wanted to grab him, shake him, and tell him to leave us alone. But I couldn't. Just like I hadn't been able to stand up to the bullies at home in Helena.

What could I do to warn my friends? Different ideas flooded my mind, none of which would work. I saw Kira grab a straw and take a step in my direction, Marybeth and Rick behind her. My heart dropped. Thankfully, their progress was slow because people were constantly reaching in front of them for napkins and straws, getting in their way.

I glanced at the door again. I looked harder. He wasn't there! Slowly, I raised my head and looked over the table and out the window at the front of the shop. He wasn't there, either. Where was he? I should have felt relieved that he was gone, but instead, I felt worse. I realized it was almost better knowing where he was. Acid filled my stomach. If he'd kept walking straight, he might have been somewhere between our hotel and this deli. What should I do? Should I tell my friends what I'd seen? At first, I thought I should, but then I wondered if Marybeth could handle it. *"No, she couldn't,"* a voice in my head said.

Kira, Marybeth and Rick walked up to the table, interrupting my thoughts. I let out the long breath I'd been holding. There were only three chairs, and Kira pushed me over so that half of my rear was hanging off mine. Rick set a bagel in front of me, smiling.

"I guess I was hungrier than I thought," Kira said. "It just smelled so good in here, I had to order something."

I was a little envious of the fact that Kira hadn't seen anything in the ballroom. She wouldn't be scarred forever like those who had looked.

Kira opened the container she'd set on the table and dug into her Danish, but Marybeth didn't even open her sack. I knew she must've been hungry, but she only sat and stared at nothing. I couldn't blame her, food wasn't in the forefront of my mind either, but I took small bites since Rick had been nice enough to bring me something.

The last time I heard Marybeth speak was when she hushed me on the toilet in the bathroom in the hotel where the man had been killed. I wondered if she would ever recover from what had happened. She needed a bit more backbone if she wanted to become a Senator. Rick, half-way through his breakfast sandwich, paused only to take a big swig of his drink. I realized my hands were almost dripping with sweat. I had to keep wiping them on my pants. I didn't have a clue how to deal with this. I needed some help. If I told Kira, she wouldn't be able to keep it a secret from Marybeth and I had to keep it from Marybeth if I hoped to get her back. Rick, on the other hand, would know what to do, but how could I tell him without upsetting Kira? Just then, she bumped me with her arm and gave me a menacing look.

"What?" I asked.

"Why are you staring at Rick like that?" she whispered, her mouth so close to my ear, I could feel her hot breath. "Cut it out! He's taken."

"I wasn't staring," I said, even though I knew I had been. "I wasn't even looking at him. I was thinking."

"Oh." Her anger faded, and I thought she was feeling a little foolish. "Guess I was being stupid."

"Yes, you were." I smiled, trying to play it off.

"Were you thinking about *it*?" Kira asked in a normal voice.

"It?"

"You know, *It*," she insisted. "You're sweating like crazy."

I felt my forehead and sure enough, it was even wetter than my hands had been before, and I scrubbed them on my pants.

"Yeah, I guess I was."

"Forget about it Christy. No one's following us. It's really over." She flicked her head back, making her curly auburn hair dance.

"You didn't see *it*, Kira," I said, trying not to sound annoyed.

She turned, her crystal green eyes flashing a look of anger.

"*It* will never be over for me. I'll always wonder if someone's following me."

"I hear ya," Rick said, his face earnest. "I'll never forget it either. Hopefully, no one's following us, though. It's so hot in here and I didn't get you a drink. Are you sure you don't want anything? Can I at least get you some water, Christy? I'll go get you some."

"No, really, I'm okay," I tried to object, but he was already up out of his seat walking away. I tried not to watch him, but he did look good wearing those particular jeans.

Kira huffed. Curiously, I felt some satisfaction. She could be so irritating.

He spoke to the cashier and she handed him a water cup. An idea burned in my mind. This was my chance.

"I'm going to get some more napkins to mop up all this sweat," I said, reaching up and pointing at my forehead. *Pull it together*, I told myself.

I almost tripped over a chair leg on my way there, hurrying to catch Rick before he started back to our table.

"Sorry about that," I called out to the man sitting in the chair.

"No worries," he said.

Rick saw me coming toward him.

"I could've done it for you, Christy," he called. "I know you like to do everything on your own, but—" His look was endearing, but a bit let down.

I signaled him to come around the divider to the drink machine with me.

"What?" he asked, looking confused.

I looked straight ahead in the direction of the drink machine and kept walking, trying to act like I wasn't speaking to him. I knew Kira would be watching us like a hawk and didn't need the added headache, even if it felt a bit nice to make her mad.

"What?" he asked again. He waited for his turn to use the machine, and I waited my chance to get some napkins.

"Don't look at me."

"What?"

"Just listen. Don't look at me," I said quietly, but urgently. "There's something I have to tell you."

"You have my attention."

"Back at Georgetown there was a guy who walked by us with a backpack on."

"There were a couple that I can remember." A playful smile danced across his face. "We were at a University, after all."

"Yeah, but this guy was different. He had icy blue eyes." My heart sped up.

"Icy blue eyes?"

"The way he looked at me was so strange. And his backpack looked empty. It spooked me."

"That's understandable, all things considered." He put his hand on my arm.

"Yeah, well get this," I said, trying to ignore my fluttering heart. "That same guy just walked by the café and was looking through the glass door—like he was looking for something or someone. You guys were over here, and I ducked under the table." I finally grabbed a handful of napkins.

"No way," Rick insisted, his eyes darting to the door. "Your mind is just playing tricks on you."

"No," I said, deciding to hold nothing back. "It was him. I'll never forget those eyes and I never forget a face. I wanted to get us out of there without freaking Marybeth out anymore than she already is. I just said there was a fountain to the north of where we were, but I didn't know if there really was one or not. I needed to see if he would follow us. I'm telling you, he's looking for us right now. He was heading in the direction of the hotel."

"You're serious aren't you? If this "Iceman" really is following us, we are in some deep—"

"I know," I interrupted, not wanting to hear a swear word, but liking the way Rick nicknamed the guy following us, Iceman. "How do we get out of here and back to the hotel within ten minutes without him seeing us or freaking out the girls?"

People started reaching around me for napkins so I moved over to the drink line with Rick. He looked around the café.

"There aren't any other exits are there?" He asked, looking at the door we had come in.

"Not that I can see."

"Hold on a minute." He handed me my cup right as he got to the front of the line, and I filled it.

I peeked around the divider and saw Rick talking to the cashier. She nodded and pointed at some doors behind her.

"Thank you so much. You're saving me a lot of aggravation," I heard Rick say. Then he motioned for Kira and Marybeth to come to us.

I felt Kira's eyes burn me, like hot flames shooting out at me, but she stood and grabbed Marybeth, leading her to us.

"Guys, we've got less than ten minutes to get back," Rick said. "Just in case there's still a tail on us, we're going out the back."

Kira's eyes were again sparkling as she grabbed his arm, letting go of Marybeth. "Great idea, Rick."

Fickle girl. I hated that about girls. I grabbed Marybeth, and we all went through the door to the kitchen and then out the back.

"What did you say to the cashier to let us go out this way?" I asked, once in the alley.

"I told her that my ex-girlfriend was waiting for us outside and that it would be to her advantage if we could go out some other way to avoid the inevitable fight that would happen if we went out the front doors."

"Good one," I said. How had he thought of that?

Give me a debate or an essay and I'll knock it out of the park, but when it comes to real life and common sense, brilliance abandons me. And nowhere was the difference in smarts more apparent than here in D.C. with the murder. I just couldn't find my way through it—I felt totally vulnerable.

I tried not to let anyone see how badly I was shaking. Iceman had really freaked me out.

The back alleyway of the store was just like ones you see in the movies: a long, dark, skinny walkway lined with stinky garbage bags and empty boxes, as well as clothes hanging from lines overhead.

We headed in the direction of our hotel, and I kept repeating in my mind, we won't get caught, we won't get caught. We walked only a short distance before we came upon a brick wall that forced us to go right, down another alleyway, which led to the bright light of the busy sidewalk—the one we were trying to avoid. We all stopped and stared. Rick took a deep breath and so did I. I was scared to death and was so tense, I could feel the pressure in my ears.

"I've got an idea," I said. Where I got it, I didn't know. Was this common sense? "Let's change our appearance as much as we can. You know, to throw them off. If they're there, I mean." I flashed a knowing look at Rick.

"Sounds good to me," he said giving me a half-smile.

I pulled my hair into a pony. Kira pulled up only the front of her hair.

"I'll braid Marybeth's hair," I said. I knew she wouldn't change a thing herself and braiding I could do. She was acting like a zombie. It seemed to take forever to braid her long hair. When I was done, I saw that Rick had turned his T-shirt inside out. We all looked each other up and down, and Kira started to giggle. We'd hardly changed at all. The tension was so high, that I giggled too. It surprised me that I could laugh. Even Rick gave a dry laugh.

"I *really* don't think there's any way we'll be recognized. We don't look like ourselves at all now." Kira's sarcasm was desperately needed to lighten the mood. Could such simple changes really stop them from noticing us? I had to believe they could or that Iceman was long gone. At the moment, I felt like I really could walk out on that sidewalk and not fall apart. I would pretend I was walking onto a stage to debate.

Rick and Kira went first. We waited about two minutes, and then I grabbed Marybeth and we headed out into the crowd. When I hit the sidewalk, it felt like my heart was being squeezed. *This was no debate*, I thought. I couldn't even look up. My heart pounded erratically as I held onto Marybeth's arm and steadily pulled her through the mass of people. I had no idea if Iceman was anywhere around because I didn't look anywhere but at my own two feet. I didn't know what I'd have done if I had seen him anyway.

Out of the corner of my eye, I saw our hotel, and we scrambled up the steps as quickly as we could. Just inside the hotel lobby doors, I let out a long breath—I think I'd been holding the whole way—and glanced around to see if Mrs. J. was anywhere. It looked like all fifty in our group, including the kids from our mini-group, were already in the buffet area eating. I looked out the glass doors of the hotel wanting to celebrate making it to the hotel without being seen, but my heart sank instead.

Icy blue eyes stared up at me. In a flash, Iceman disappeared into the crowds of people on the sidewalk.

"Hurry up girls," Mrs. J. said, walking into the buffet area.

I pulled Marybeth through the buffet room door to listen to Mrs. J., my mind reeling. I had to tell the others.

"We have a full day," she continued speaking, now to everyone. "Today we'll be touring Arlington National Cemetery and the Pentagon. You'll need a jacket and some good walking shoes. The bus leaves in ten minutes."

Marybeth and I hurried and sat down next to Kira and Rick.

"We thought you guys weren't ever going to show up," Summer said. "We've already been here for thirty minutes." She looked perfect, of course. She must have passed on breakfast and gone to her room to get ready.

"We didn't think we'd ever get here, either," Kira said. "You'll never believe …"

"Hey guys, can we hold off on the stories until we're on the bus?" Rick interrupted, his voice serious. Rick's eyes darted around the room, finally resting on mine. It was the first time Rick looked really nervous since leaving the hotel to head for Georgetown. How would he feel when he found out Iceman had been just outside?

CHAPTER FOUR

We all crowded into the back four rows of the bus so we could hear each other talk. Kira made sure I didn't get anywhere near Rick. She told "our" story about how we'd attempted to change our appearance in the alley of the café. She wanted me to look as foolish as possible for thinking we needed to (If only she knew). Rick nudged Alex and I felt the inevitable tingles he always gave me.

Why did he have to be so beautiful? I know people use the word beautiful to describe girls, but Alex McGinnis truly was beautiful. I'd look into his intense brown eyes and be overwhelmed. He smiled easily, showing a perfect set of teeth. His deep brown hair had just the right amount of curl and his tall, tan, muscular body made me forget what I was doing. Charisma emanated from his every pore, drawing, not only me, but everyone in. He had this contagious spark of life that lit up a room as he entered. I wanted to be a part of that life.

"Hey, come over here a minute," Rick said to Alex, pointing to an empty row in front of us.

"Sure, whatever," Alex said, squeezing past Kira and down the aisle.

My face flushed as he passed me. I loved to watch him talk, there was something so soothing about his voice. I thought about him having the presence of mind to take pictures of the murder. He had a cool head in scary situations. Hadn't it affected him at all seeing that blood? I had had to really concentrate to even pretend to be calm.

Rick gave me a smile and a nod before he left. I was sure he was filling Alex in on our "visitor" at Georgetown University and the café—and telling him the whole story—the story only the three of us would now know.

I watched them, trying to see Alex's reaction, but they were bent down low in the seat. I sort of listened to Kira and nodded or said 'yeah' when needed. Alex did raise his head and look my way several times, eyes wide. The butterflies in my stomach went wild. I wished I was a part of their conversation, but I knew that if I were up there too, it would attract too much attention, and others would want to know what was going on. Especially Kira.

After what seemed a long time, Alex, with his head hanging, slightly shaking side to side, took his seat with the group again, and Rick did the same. Summer had just finished her story about their uneventful taxi ride to the Mall and what the four of them had seen there.

I felt Alex staring at me and worked hard not to look at him. I thought my stomach would explode. He'd never really looked at me before.

"I'm sure we're in the clear now. No one could've tracked us back to the hotel," Josh said.

Summer nodded in agreement. "I'm sure we had nothing to worry about from the start."

"We can't think like that," Alex said, looking away from me and giving Rick a knowing glance. "No offense, but you didn't see what we saw, Summer. These are really bad guys. We have to assume they could figure out who we are and are wondering if we saw anything we shouldn't have. The good news is that they must think we didn't see anything—otherwise, we most likely wouldn't be alive."

Someone took a sharp intake of air.

If only they knew.

"We need to act as normal as possible and never discuss it outside of this bus. It's too loud in here for anyone to hear anything even if they tried to listen. We won't give them any reason to suspect we saw what we did. Are we all in agreement?"

I got goose bumps all over.

People nodded, but my stomach only knotted. I didn't know if I could commit to it. Maybe I needed to tell. Maybe for the dead man's sake? Or maybe just out of common decency? I felt guilt coming over me even though I was sure I hadn't done anything wrong.

"Guys, we can't make that promise," Eugene said. "We've got to go to the authorities. We witnessed a crime and we have to report it. *It's* the law." Leave it to Eugene to lay down the law. He pressed his glasses hard against his nose as everyone stared at him.

I let out a deep breath of relief—glad I hadn't been the one who spoke up first.

At home, I would have been eager to debate whether to tell or not to tell, but here, I didn't want anyone to know I was "smart" or really cared. It had become apparent to me that there were many reasons to use your smarts, but making friends was not one of them.

All my smarts at home had given me was a miserable social existence. It hadn't bothered me to be alone with my books, projects and research until social dance class (way out of my comfort zone, by the way) had started second semester. There had been nothing more rewarding to me than perfect scores and winning competitions, but school had gotten old and frankly, easy. Social dance was my way to break free of the monotony.

The first day of class, everyone but three of us had partners. The other two without partners were boys. Instead of choosing me, a girl, the two guys decided to be partners, and I was alone. Everyone had laughed. The sting of that moment still burned when I thought of it. From that moment on, I had seen, really seen, every rejection, every mean comment, every mean action—I truly was a social outcast. Why hadn't I seen that teachers and adults were my only friends before that day?

I was determined, however, to change people's perceptions of me. I watched the cool kids and tried to do as they did and say the things they said. Nothing changed. If anything, I was mocked even more for trying to be someone "I wasn't". For the first time in my life, depressed and alone, I tried to soften the blow by telling myself that I couldn't just decide to be someone different one day and expect everyone around me to forget what I'd said, done and been the last fifteen years and accept the new me immediately. It occurred to me that it must not be in our nature to do so—especially in a small town. I didn't want to believe that it was impossible to escape, though, and this trip gave me hope. I had friends here. I could change things.

To my surprise, no one immediately objected to Eugene. In fact, silence hung in the air for several minutes. Heads bowed, fingers fidgeted, and the sound of bodies shifting on vinyl seats grew louder.

I had to assume everyone felt what I felt, and I couldn't stop myself from blurting out, "I agree." Everyone's eyes turned to me. I was the one shifting in my seat now, the vinyl protesting loudly. Besides, if they knew, really knew we were being followed, they'd want the police involved, too.

"I didn't see anything," Summer said. "And Josh only peeked for a second. We don't need to report anything. Right Josh?"

"Right," he said. His face had returned to the sickly white it held in the hotel bathroom after he had looked down on the bloody scene.

"We were *all* there," Eugene said. "We *all* need to go in. I mean, some guy is dead. Let the authorities decide what to do after that."

I could feel the tension in the group pressing down on me, and I wondered how I would make it through this, too.

The fact that we were being followed was pressure enough.

"Who would we tell?" Josh raved. "The police? Ha! They'd never believe us. We have no proof. That body is long gone, and if I'm not mistaken, burning someone at a high enough temperature leaves no evidence behind."

"We have pictures," Eugene said, looking hopefully at Alex.

"You mean the ones on my *toilet* phone?" Alex asked. His stare could have sliced Eugene in half. Eugene appeared not to notice.

"Maybe someone with a high-tech machine can still get something off your phone. You know, like they do on CSI?" Summer suggested.

"That's a stupid TV show," Alex retorted. "It's all fake."

"We wouldn't go to the police anyway," Eugene pointed out. "It's the FBI we need."

"FBI?" Josh said. "Crap! Crap! Just leave me out of it. Please!"

I wondered if Josh had something to hide or if he was just too afraid.

"How do we even find an FBI office?" Rick asked.

"Every state has field offices," Eugene said. "But the big kahuna FBI building is not far from our hotel."

My stomach sunk.

"Don't you think *they* could be watching for us at the FBI building?" Alex asked. "We could be walking right into their hands and proving we saw something. Let's just forget we saw anything."

Again, I couldn't stop myself. "What about Jonathan?"

"Jonathan?" Rick asked, frowning.

"You know," Eugene said, "the guy who lost his head in the ballroom." The way he said it was so glib that everyone squinted and wrinkled their foreheads at him.

"Sick!" Summer said.

"How do you know his name?" Rick asked me, his tone softer now.

"The white guy whose head didn't get chopped off," Eugene answered before I could, "called out his name several times while looking at him. 'No Jonathan, no.' He said it several times."

Just the facts to Eugene.

"Ughh!"

"Look guys," I said. "I know it seems crazy to tell, but I just can't let it go. Maybe the Feds can catch these guys." I couldn't stop myself from talking. "They said something about a bill passing congress or the Senate or something and Marybeth said the guy in that ballroom, who's still alive, is her state Senator. Maybe we can find out which bill it is they're trying to get passed and stop it. It must really be important to those creeps, and that can't be good. It'll probably cause something terrible to happen to this country. I couldn't live with myself if that happened. Look at Marybeth. She needs some serious help. I can go on my own, but at least Marybeth needs to go with me."

Everyone looked at the back of Marybeth's head. She hadn't moved. Despite the roar of the bus, a silence fell over us that seemed to last an eternity.

"We really should tell someone what we saw," Rick said, quickly becoming my hero in all this. "Wouldn't you want to know if your son or brother or friend was murdered? It would be awful to be left to wonder forever what happened to him. Christy's right. We owe it to the people in Jonathan's life, as well as to our own country." Then he leaned into me and whispered, "Besides, they

43

don't know about Iceman." He raised his eyebrows and then turned to listen to Alex. I wanted to tell him I saw Iceman again, but I let the chance pass.

"This is why I hate politics and politicians," Alex said, adding a few colorful swear words. "Things like this happen all the time in politics. Behind those trustworthy looking faces are lies, death, hatred and more lies. We should tell someone just so that we can blow the lid off this thing, whatever it is. They'll be exposed and maybe we'll have made a tiny difference in politics in America. This trip might turn into something of value after all."

He paused for a moment. "The real question is, how do we tell and not get caught by the bad guys?"

Several minutes more of silence passed. I wanted to yell out that we were already caught, but knew it would only create panic.

"Well, we're on a tour," Eugene finally offered. "Maybe we could tour the FBI building."

"Isn't the FBI building already on our itinerary?" Alex asked. No one seemed to know and I wasn't about to tell them I knew it wasn't, so Alex stood and walked past all the other students and chaperones, to the front of the bus, where Mrs. J. sat.

We watched her shake her head at Alex. Then they talked for a couple of minutes more and both started nodding. He came back, his look triumphant.

"We may have just changed our itinerary to include the FBI building," he said smugly.

"How did you do that?" Eugene asked. "Do you always get what you want?" A look of awe crossed his face.

"Yes," Alex answered, his smile mischievous. "Now, there's no guarantee that we *will* get to tour it, but Mrs. J. is pretty resourceful, so I'm betting on her. We should probably all write down what we saw from that hotel bathroom last night. We could just hand what we write to someone in the FBI building when we go. And if we don't get in, we could always mail it. Then this thing will be over. I don't think we should try and figure out what's going on though. We'll leave it to the FBI to figure that out."

I wanted to clap for him, the man with all the answers.

Everyone agreed to write a statement about what they had seen in the ballroom before going to bed. I usually liked to write, but what I had to write about would be painful and scary. The fact that it could impact so many lives beyond my own, made me even more afraid.

I felt a bit sick.

Arlington cemetery took on a whole new meaning. I couldn't help but think about dying—getting my head chopped off—to be more exact, and being buried there. And yet, the graves of the soldiers also made me grateful to them for giving their lives for me and this country. It made me think of all eight of us dying a slow painful death at the hands of the bad guys. I was freaked, but hid it from everyone. With everyone's silence, an eerie feeling wandered amid the graves. I felt totally unprotected even though it was midday. With the rows and rows of death all around us, I almost suffocated.

We all gawked at the slightly different shade of white brick on the section of newly restored Pentagon exterior as we drove to it—a stark reminder that terrorists had succeeded in causing total chaos on American soil in the not-so-distant-past. Once inside, it offered a slightly lighter feeling, but I would never look at life the same way again. The Pentagon seemed so much more important after last night. I forced myself to listen to the tour guide, but occasionally found myself back in the café looking into

Iceman's cold, blue eyes. I itched to get to a computer and research how secure we really were in America. I had never felt unsafe back home. D.C. held a different story. Did the Pentagon even have a clue about these men? I searched the archives in my brain for all information on the Pentagon. Pages of history books sorted themselves in my mind. But very little on the Pentagon showed up. The pages mentioned the building and its design as well as its general purpose, but nothing to ease my mind.

A low rumble sounded in my stomach and I was almost hyper-aware of what happened around me. The eight of us hadn't gone far from each other at Arlington Cemetery, but here at the Pentagon, more space separated us from each other. It felt good to leave.

Dinner tasted like cardboard, and I found it hard to interact with everyone. I kept to myself as much as possible, looking for an opportunity to tell Rick about Iceman. Truly, I wanted to tell Alex, but my fear, or maybe awe, prevented it.

After dinner, everyone, except Marybeth, crowded into Alex's room to type on laptops. His single room was larger than the double room Marybeth and I shared. Luckily, four in our group had brought laptops from home because they thought they would need them the second half of the trip. Music blared, making it hard to focus. I tried to detach myself from what had happened. I kept having to stop typing while I let the vivid pictures of the murder play across my mind. After typing the last word, I'd had enough. I never wanted to re-visit the ballroom again. I would push the memory into a far corner in my mind and keep it there. I had told and that had to be enough. I slipped out the door after handing Eugene's computer back to him.

"Hey, Christy!"

Did Alex just call me? No. Keep walking. It's just my imagination.

"Christy!" he said, gently grabbing my arm.

I turned slowly, feeling my insides buzz.

"This guy you saw…you really did see him, right?"

"Yeah." I could feel my cheeks burning. This was my chance to tell him I'd seen Iceman again. But I couldn't get my mouth to tell him.

"Freaky. Let me know if you see him again. Okay?"

"Uh huh." I grunted. I stood there staring into his deep brown eyes, unable to turn and walk away.

"Okay," he said again, grinning.

Move, Christy. Move. I screamed at myself—but I couldn't. If you can't tell him about Iceman, get out of here. He chuckled, probably used to this reaction, and then turned to go back into Summer's room. I just stood there, watching him walk away. Then he turned and looked at me when he opened the door to go in. He paused and grinned again, before going inside. He probably thought I was an idiot for still standing there. I did too, especially knowing that the door had been shut behind him for several minutes before I could turn and head for my room.

He had talked to me. Really talked to me. Sure, I was totally embarrassed at my reaction to him, but at the same time, so excited that he had talked to me. Having had almost no sleep in the laundry room of that other hotel caught up to me, and I desperately wanted to get some sleep. Tomorrow was another day. A day that Alex could choose to talk to me again. And yes, I'd tell Rick about Iceman tomorrow. My neck killed me, and I could feel a horrible headache coming on. The room was pitch black, and I could hear Marybeth's even breathing. Thankfully, sleep came quickly.

At seven, the dreaded wake-up call shocked me out of a fitful night's sleep. I'd never had a hard time getting out of bed and always beat my alarm clock at home; but that morning, making my legs slide out of bed was hard. I was beat—like I'd been running all night long.

The curtains on the sliding glass door to our tiny balcony stood open about three inches, letting in the bright sunlight. In a flash, I covered my eyes. A headache came on full bore. I had a lot of headaches, so I always came prepared with prescription meds, but chose to take ibuprofen instead. Heading for the sink in the bathroom to get a drink, I passed Marybeth, who was still in bed sleeping. I thought about nudging her awake, but thought she could probably benefit from a few extra minutes sleep.

A lot of the tension in my neck, that I was sure triggered my headache, started to dissolve once I climbed into the warm shower. The water felt so good flowing over my head and body, I didn't want to get out and simply stood under the delicious, hot stream of water until all the stiffness disappeared.

Coming out of the bathroom, I noticed Marybeth was gone.

Even though the curtains lit up the room a bit, I quickly turned on the lights to have a closer look. Definitely not there. I opened the door to the hallway and looked out, but couldn't see her anywhere. I couldn't leave the room to look for her in my towel, so I headed for my tiny closet to get some clothes. Her bed *was* made. Had she gone down to breakfast without me? I'd just taken too long in the shower. I'm sure she was safe. Maybe she was back to her old self! I couldn't wait to talk to her.

Sliding into my most comfortable jeans and a light blue T-shirt, that I had spent a full four months of my allowance on, felt sweet. I hoped Marybeth would approve. I stared at myself for several minutes, wishing Marybeth stood next to me to help me and say, "Perfect". Returning to the bathroom to brush my hair, I heard a faint voice. I stopped and totally still, focused all my attention on the voice. My heart stuttered and fear crept up my spine. Was someone in the room, watching, waiting for the right moment to grab me? Had they already taken Marybeth?

I looked toward the room. No one could be in there. I was just in there, for heaven's sake. I tried to zero in on the sound, but the drumming beat in my ears made it difficult. Despite the fact that I had already ruled out the possibility that she hid under the bed, I scanned under it again. No Marybeth.

Still hearing the voice, I moved toward the fluttering curtains. Faint, but louder now, the voice sounded like it came from outside, so I peeked around the balcony curtains and saw her. Despite myself, I jumped slightly at the sight of her. Marybeth sat alone on the floor of the balcony, her back facing me, sobbing. My heart dropped. I reached to pull the window open and join her, when I noticed a phone in her hand. Wait. She didn't own a phone. Did she? She hadn't been on it twenty-four-seven, like the others—texting away. I leaned back into the room and put my ear up to the crack in the sliding door.

"Yes. Yes," Marybeth whimpered, but the sobs made it difficult to understand her. "I-I-I will try h-h-harder. I-I-I just miss you so much. I love you, too." She breathed in deeply and then cried all the louder.

Apparently, I wasn't as alone as I'd thought. I wanted to reach out to her and cry with her. We were all alone in our pain, and she had found a way to release some of hers.

Guilt swept over me for making her look down into the ballroom. I caused this pain. She saw the murder because I made her. My heart ached. Friends made me feel more deeply than I'd ever felt. The horrible hurt I'd felt from the rejection of my peers in Helena was nothing compared to this.

It had been two days since a single word had come out of her mouth, and I was glad to hear her voice, even cracked up and sobbing. I reached for the window again, but hesitated at the last moment and pulled my hand back. I had to allow her to have her own private moment. To intrude seemed like the wrong thing to do. We'd been through a lot, and to keep it all bottled up, for someone like Marybeth, must have been incredibly difficult. Besides, I certainly didn't want to send her back into silence.

I decided to wait for her. My first real friend. She didn't want anything from me either. No answers, no help, nothing. She only wanted to help me. She wasn't on the phone anymore, and I was sure she would come in any minute. Maybe I could give her a hug. But, fifteen minutes later, she still sobbed on the balcony. Breakfast would pass us by and Mrs. J. would freak if we didn't get downstairs soon, so I came up with a plan.

I slammed the door to the bathroom and started talking loudly. "Marybeth? Are you already gone? That's weird. She always waits for me," I pretended to talk to myself. "Oh man. No wonder she left. We only have ten minutes till breakfast is over."

I had grabbed a ponytail holder. "Sorry, Marybeth," I mumbled, looking at the holder, wishing I felt confident using Marybeth's flat iron by myself. I grabbed my bag and headed out, slamming the door behind me. I hoped she would hear and follow.

She did. Five minutes later, with a swollen, red face, Marybeth sat next to me, a bagel in her hand. Amazingly, she looked perfect, despite her swollen face.

"Morning Marybeth," I said, hoping she would respond.

"Good morning," she said, staring at my hair, raising her eyebrows.

I bit my lip and gave her a weak smile, pretending not to notice her tear stained face.

I reached back and touched my ponytail and said, "Sorry, you were gone, and I wasn't sure if I should use your flat iron without you."

She giggled. "You're so funny. Of course you can. You should have. If only we had the time…" She looked at the door just as Mrs. J. walked in.

I thought about Marybeth's call, the privacy of it. I mean, of course, it was private, in the sense that she didn't want anyone to know, but also private in the sense that she needed a moment with people she loved and that loved her.

I wished I had someone like that in my life. Maybe Kira and Marybeth would become that way to me. I took a deep breath and genuinely smiled this time, all to myself.

I guess it could have been her parents that she called. It hadn't even occurred to me to call my parents—which is pretty darn weird. Even in real danger I hadn't even thought to call them. My parents didn't pay much attention to me. They didn't have to. I wasn't like some of my brothers and sisters. I always did what I was told, which made me sort of invisible to them. Kira's parents made her call each night at eight sharp to check in. My mom had simply said, "See ya in two weeks. Learn a lot." Not speaking to me for two weeks wouldn't be much different than what normally happened at home. I wondered how many of the others had thought about telling their parents and wished they could. How many of them *had* called their parents and had their own private moment? I searched all of my group's faces.

Josh's square face was mostly hidden behind his large hands shoveling food into his mouth. Surely, he had no intention of mentioning the murder to his parents. It would make him look like a coward.

Alex ate just like I expected someone so beautiful to eat; no shoveling or disgusting noises. I paused for a few seconds to admire his perfect nose and face. I couldn't think of anyone who had a more handsome face. I looked a second too long, and he looked up to catch me staring at him.

I turned back to Marybeth, my face hot. Please, I thought. Let him think I was simply turning my head to Marybeth. Something hit the back of my head and I reached up to feel if something stuck in my hair. I couldn't feel anything, and turned back around. Josh and Alex looked at each other, laughing quietly. My heart flipped. Crap! Alex—making fun of me? Had I misread him? I was such an idiot! Maybe Marybeth's magic make-over hadn't really been magic after all. Or had wearing a ponytail turned me back into the old Christy Hadden?

Alex glanced up and our eyes met for second or so. He didn't turn away and there was a slight smile on his face. His eyes were playful, not hard and mean. I felt my face burn and turned away again. I didn't want him to see my lobster-red face.

"Okay you guys, listen up!" Mrs. J. barked. "We have a slight change in our plans today. My mini-group wanted to get a peek inside the FBI building. As you know, since 9/11, it has been closed to almost all tours. Fortunately, I have connections, and we have an appointment at eight-thirty this morning for a very brief tour. It may not be what you were hoping for, but it's better than nothing. I can only take fifteen of you. That means seven of you, that aren't in my mini-group, can join us. The rest of you will have one hour of free time at The National Mall with the other chaperones. Any questions? Okay, let's load up."

I heard only a few groans. As I stood up, I felt the back of my head to see if I could find what had hit me earlier. I still couldn't find anything. I looked down at the floor and couldn't see anything unusual around me. I felt stupid. Only social things ever made me feel like this. I hated not having control.

"We're in business now," I heard Alex say to Rick as he passed him. "I can't wait for this to be over."

I kept my head down, sure he'd hit me with something. The question was, had he done it to make fun of me or did he simply want my attention? I shook my head. How stupid was I to think Alex would like me?

CHAPTER FIVE

It had been a full day since I'd seen Iceman outside our hotel's doors. I had to tell Rick and soon. I pushed my way to the back of the bus, but Kira had already sat next to him, so, I planted myself next to Eugene. It would have to wait, again.

I thought about the way Alex had looked at me when our eyes met a few minutes ago at the table and I somehow felt he wasn't being mean. I didn't know what the look meant, but his eyes weren't taunting me; they gave me tingles. Maybe Alex and Josh were just playing around with me, like they did with Summer and Kira. At home, when things hit me, the people who did it never hid—they laughed openly. But I just couldn't get Alex's look out of my mind. Was he wanting me to notice he was looking? Mean or nice?

Eugene got on his knees, turned to the back of the bus and pulled out a bunch of papers for us to see. My heart thumped hard as I followed suit.

"The hotel has a great printer," he said smiling, every tooth visible. "It printed these fifteen pages in about fifteen seconds. Just awesome."

"Fold 'em up, Eugene. Now, who's going to pass 'em to the feds?" Alex asked, his eyes perusing all of us.

"Not me." "Not me." "Not me," was all I heard. I looked down and kept quiet, wishing I'd stayed seated. I felt stares, and couldn't help but look up.

Everyone stared at me.

No, not me. I swallowed hard.

"Christy, why don't you do it?" Alex suggested, his voice smooth and convincing. "You look trustworthy. I don't think they would take you for a prankster."

Yep, that was me, miss trustworthy—boring miss trustworthy.

"Yeah! You do it Christy. They'll believe *you*," Kira said.

"Yeah, Christy." "Yeah. You do it." "You can do it." Everyone spoke at once.

I shook my head. I didn't want to do it. Then my eyes caught Marybeth's face, and I knew I had to. My head hadn't stopped shaking 'no', but "okay" escaped in a small whisper. It was like I was being pulled from within, and nothing but the right thing was do-able.

"All right." "You'll be great." "Yeah, you'll be great." "You can do it." Encouraging words filled the back corner of the bus while fear made my stomach clench. And yet, a very slight twinge of excitement at the prospect of giving those papers to someone filled my chest. It would be a true challenge. I would have to remind myself that I was a resourceful, smart girl and could figure it out, even if it involved real life.

The front entrance of the J. Edgar Hoover FBI building was located on Pennsylvania Ave. NW., but we entered on a side road. It looked like a bleak, drab 60's or 70's building, boxy and uninviting. Lots of people packed the sidewalks, but what caught my attention were three men with dark hair and skin that seemed to be looking at our group—none of them Iceman, and I convinced myself that the fear I felt was silly. Just because these guys had dark hair and skin, didn't mean they had anything to do with the ballroom. The guard shack outside the door left me feeling a bit like I was leaving the free-world to enter a militarized zone. I noticed a lot of people milling around and then the three men with dark skin and eyes caught my attention again. They looked out of place somehow, and they stared at us. Were they watching the FBI building to see if we would go there or was their presence just a coincidence? After all our ID's were scanned and confiscated on our way in, I relaxed a little, thinking I couldn't be in a safer place.

In the courtyard area, we were met by two metal detector-like machines. To the side of the first one, long tables stood to put all our contraband on. We couldn't take bags, anything to write with, cameras or anything that wasn't attached to our bodies into the building. I held the papers tightly in my hand, feeling guilty the whole time, waiting for someone to tell me they belonged on the contraband table. No one did.

"Breathe, Christy. It'll all work out," Rick whispered in my ear as he walked past me into the large courtyard.

I hadn't realized I wasn't breathing. My nerves got the better of me. I didn't want to be nervous. I wanted to be confident and in control just by telling myself to be, like before debates and academic competitions. It wasn't working.

I had no idea who to give the papers to or when. I searched the courtyard for anyone that struck me. No one did. In fact, there weren't many people around us at all. A tall, thick man with short, jet black hair, wearing a gun on his hip, walked up to Mrs. J. and shook her hand. They talked for a moment, and then she asked for everyone's attention.

"This is Special Agent Landis," Mrs. J. said. "He's a good friend of mine, and he's the one you have to thank for this tour today. Follow his directions carefully, so that he doesn't regret his decision to let us come."

"Welcome to the FBI building," he said. His voiced boomed in the almost deserted courtyard. "We are under construction and haven't been allowing group tours." I couldn't see any evidence of construction as I looked around. "It's very important for you to follow the directions I give you, just like Mrs. Jackson said. There will be absolutely no talking until I ask for questions at the end of the tour. Do *not* leave the group. Stay together. This will be a short tour and no bathrooms will be available for you to use, so don't ask. Now please, follow me."

We entered the actual building and could see long narrow hallways with door after door jutting off them.

He gave us the general history of the building's odd bi-level construction in about three minutes. Buildings along Pennsylvania Avenue could only be seven stories high when the building was built, but along the backside, on E. Street, they could be eleven. Odd.

I had to find someone to give our letter to and no one was anywhere. We were in the shorter side of the building at the moment, and we walked past a bunch of full classrooms and entered a large amphitheater. It was quite the spectacle, beautiful even. We all sat down while Special Agent Landis went over what the FBI was all about and what it did. Public corruption, espionage, terrorism—I wondered which category our little adventure would fall in to. I scanned the room and saw that our group was alone with Special Agent Landis, no one new had entered the picture. My pulse quickened and I felt my muscles tense.

My mind couldn't focus on his words anymore. I needed to find someone or someplace to leave this letter. After he rambled on and on, everyone stood up to leave.

"The other floors are all offices and interrogation rooms," Agent Landis informed us, as we filed out of amphitheater. "Now we will go see the forensic lab and a firearms demo."

We walked back the way we entered, but continued to some elevators. I was a bit disturbed to see how clean the building was, like it had been sanitized just before we got there. It made me feel like I was under a microscope and I shivered. The longer we were there, the more uncomfortable I got. If only I could turn invisible.

The elevator opened and with a little bumping and jostling, we all fit. My heart jumped when we descended. I had prepared myself to go up, not down. When the doors opened, I understood. It was a firing range, buried deep in the earth, almost like the architects wanted it hidden, knowing what horrible power could be unleashed from its walls. I searched for a new face, anyone to give the papers to—but caged in glass, I could only see a place for one shooter to stand and practice firing. A door opened, and a young man with short cropped hair and sound protection entered the range.

He demonstrated several different weapons with accuracy and finesse. He made it look easy, and his comfort with the various weapons heightened my anxiety. Why hadn't the bad guys just used a gun? The sword was so barbaric. I found myself humming a song, drowning out my thoughts.

Since the shooter stood behind the glass, and I had no access to him, I couldn't give him our letters.

We got back in the elevator and went up this time. No more surprises. We got out and walked into another glass cage to look in on the forensic lab. Everything looked very sterile, all white and silver.

Again, there was no one to pass the letter to.

Panic crept in steadily now.

Fifty minutes of our hour tour had passed, my breathing sped up. I felt dizzy. How would I get this to someone, when there was no one? I frowned hard trying to concentrate and not fall over. National debate championships had never made me so nervous. My confidence came there from knowing what I was doing and that I would succeed. I wanted to feel that way here.

"Hey, Christy," Alex whispered. I jumped about a foot in the air. "Whoa! I guess that answers my question."

"What question?" I asked, my voice croaking.

"I was going to ask you if you were still with us. I can see that you are." He laughed. "You're pretty nervous, huh?" Alex talking to me certainly didn't help my clarity of thought. I trembled inside.

"Yes," I whispered, trying to keep my wits about me. "There's no one to hand this off to."

"There will be, don't worry. You'll know when the time is right. Be patient"

His words always seemed to soothe me, and my desperation faded a bit.

"One last stop," Agent Landis called out. "We'll see the hall of directors."

One? Only one left? I hoped he meant we would be seeing several directors, surrounded by support staff, who would be anxious to take the letter from me.

We climbed in the elevator once more, and when we stepped out, we found ourselves in a clean, narrow, white-walled hall. Hanging on the walls were nicely framed photographs of lots of different men. My heart dropped.

"These are all of the past directors of the FBI," Agent Landis said. "This one here is the first director and it goes down this way until you hit the current director, Mr. Whitmore." He said all of this while sweeping his arm down the hall. "Go ahead and check them out. Please do not open any doors. Thank you."

Again, no accessible people. I caught Alex staring at me with a look that said, good luck. I don't know how you'll manage getting our letter to anyone in this place.

The hall was narrow, so bodies were jostling, bumping with a shove here and a push there.

Again, we squeezed into the elevator. Each time it felt like we had to squeeze tighter together to fit. It dumped us out in a hall near the courtyard.

"Thank you all for coming, "Agent Landis said. "I'm glad that Mrs. J. contacted me, and I hope you learned a lot. Maybe we have piqued your interest in one day joining our team." My interest? Does anyone walk around this building if they work here? The halls were totally empty. "Do you have any questions?" A few kids asked some questions, but the pounding behind my ears kept me from hearing almost anything. He paused for a good three minutes, which seemed like forever, and then continued, "Go ahead through the courtyard here and gather up your belongings from the tables."

We were done. I had failed. I certainly couldn't be blamed for not getting it to anyone, there truly was no one.

Besides, I needed more time. Mrs. J. was right, there wasn't much to this tour. I couldn't count it as an enthralling experience.

"Please, please," I prayed in my head. "Give me someone to give this to."

Our group headed for the exit with all their contraband in hand, and Mrs. J. talked to Agent Landis.

Then it came to me.

He was my last resort. I slowly walked up to Agent Landis trying to give Mrs. J. enough time to finish up with him. I had to get him the papers. He was my only hope. I stood silently to the side of them, waiting. Mrs. J. turned around and headed for the door, seeing me out of the corner of her eye.

"Christy, get your things, we've gotta go," she said.

With my eyes focused on Agent Landis, I pretended not to hear. I'd been repeating what to say to him over and over again and was afraid I would mess up if I talked to anyone else.

"Agent Landis, some of us got together last night and made you a thank-you card, for all your trouble. We are *really* grateful. It was a fantastic experience to get to come in here," I lied, the ease with which it flowed out scared me, but it was necessary.

"Wow," he said, "Thank you. That sure is nice."

"No problem," I replied as I handed the folded pages to him.

Mrs. J. looked surprised at the gesture, raising her shoulders and lifting her eyebrows, telling Agent Landis she knew nothing about it. Of course, she didn't.

"Okay, Christy. Let's go," she said, pushing me along.

I can't even remember what happened between releasing the letter into Agent Landis' hands and clambering onto the bus. I was out of breath, even though I was sure I hadn't run, and went straight to the back of the bus and plopped into an empty seat.

All seven sets of eyes were again on me. As soon as the bus began to move, it felt like the invisible noose around my neck had vanished. I quickly looked out the window, thinking that Agent Landis or some of his buddies would come after the bus, trying to stop it, but no one came.

Only *I* seemed to notice the three dark men watching the bus drive away. What was odd was that the three men I had seen earlier, were still there, just in different spots on the sidewalk. Was I just being paranoid? I turned back around and leaned my head against the seat back and exhaled loudly, closing my eyes and rubbing my face roughly. Only then did I realize that my shirt stuck to me. I must have sweated a whole day's worth in that one hour.

When I dropped my hands and opened my eyes, I found I was still surrounded by anxious eyes. The unspoken question in them made my throat thick.

"I gave it to Agent Landis," I told them hoarsely. "I told him it was a thank-you note from our group."

Their eyes got even bigger.

"Good thinking," Josh said, putting his hand in the air for me to give him a high-five.

"Yeah. Wow, how did you think of that?" Kira questioned.

"I was so scared," I said. "It's crazy, but I said a quick prayer, and then it came to me. I just *know* we did the right thing." I felt proud with the group cheering me. It *had* been exciting, now that I looked back on it. It was nerve racking, but in an odd way, fun. I had done it.

"Now it's over guys. We never have to think or speak of it again," Alex said, giving me a big smile and a nod.

My insides buzzed.

No one said anything the rest of the way to the White House. I felt a deep chill in my bones as the air-conditioning in the White House hit the sweat that had drenched my body and I shivered. I tried not to think about what would happen when Agent Landis read that letter. Was it all over like Alex said? The three men on the sidewalk gave me a sinking feeling that this was just the beginning.

CHAPTER SIX

One bad thing about Mrs. J. was that she didn't want us to miss anything about D.C., so we ended up missing everything. After incessant touring each day, we returned to our hotel at seven for dinner. Today was no exception. What I thought would be another drab night in the rec room turned out to be just the opposite. I had a lot of fun. All eight of us stuck together. I needed that more than I'd realized. Even though giving the letter to the FBI left me lighter, I still felt Iceman's murderous eyes pushing hard on my soul. Maybe I'd have a chance to tell Rick about seeing him again. Maybe I'd even tell him about the guys at the FBI building.

We'd all bunched into the wide open space between the couch and the humungous TV. Summer wanted to play a game again. My first thought was of *Find It,* the last game she'd suggested, the one that had led us to the bathroom vent and a bloody ballroom.

This time she wanted to play, *I've never*. It sounded like fun, except for the fact that I would probably win. Typically, I liked to win, but in this case, I wanted to lose. Despite our recent *adventure*, I wanted to be the most adventurous, not the least, and winning this game labeled you the least adventurous person.

We all had ten of something, paper pieces, jelly beans, coins—anything we could find to hold in our hands. One person would say something he or she had never done. If you had done it, you had to throw an item into the center of the circle. The last person holding an object won the game—and was labeled the least adventurous person there.

Summer started, of course.

"I've never broken a bone," she said.

Alex, Josh, Eugene and Kira all threw something in the circle.

"I bet I've broken the most," Josh said. "Count 'em four big 'uns." Mr. Jock was a shoo-in.

"Well then, I've broken the most," Eugene said, "I've got five breaks to my name."

"Five? No way," Josh said. "I can't believe you beat me, geek. What were you doing to break bones? Playing war on the computer?"

I couldn't help thinking that it was more likely his clumsiness that caused his breaks.

He didn't have a chance to respond before Kira broke in.

"What did you break, Alex?" she spoke in her most sensitive voice.

"My nose."

Everyone laughed. I thought people who broke their noses had large, misshapen ones. Alex's was perfect, and I stared, my heart fluttering.

"I broke my leg skiing," Kira said.

"Where?" Alex asked.

"Colorado," she said, her eyes gleaming. She always seemed to sparkle when she got attention from a good looking guy.

"I love skiing in Colorado. It's the best," Alex said.

Everyone but me and Marybeth nodded and agreed. They were all loaded. I shouldn't be surprised that they would travel all over to ski.

Josh was next. "I've never worn a bra." His look was smug.

"Ahhh!" all the girls said in unison before throwing something in. And then Rick did too.

"What the heck?" Josh said, throwing his head back in cackling laughter.

We all looked at Rick for an explanation.

"Look! I was a cheerleader for Halloween last year, I looked great," he said, not the least bit embarrassed.

"Whatever, dude," Josh said.

Totally cool! Any guy who still dressed up for Halloween was one of my heroes. I bet he'd be a ton of fun to have as a friend. Lost in thought, I found myself staring at him until he winked at me. My face burned.

Eugene, of all people, when it was his turn, said proudly, "I've never kissed anyone outside of my family."

I watched in horror as everyone threw something down except for Eugene and me. Faking the movement of throwing something in crossed my mind, but I'd be lying if I did, so I just couldn't fake it. I didn't want to look like a bigger geek than I was, though. Even Marybeth had thrown something in. I stayed stone still, trying not to bring attention to myself.

"Never?" Alex said, looking directly at me. His shocked look made me want to disappear.

I tried to think of something funny or cool to say, but thought of nothing. I wasn't funny or cool.

So, I held my head high and said, "Never," as proudly as a wounded person could.

"How old are you anyway?" Summer asked, her face lighting up in a mean way.

Great. Everyone was going to know that I was the youngest one here, too.

"Fifteen," I said, feeling my back slump. I wasn't able to fake proud much longer.

"You're just a baby then," Summer snickered. "You've still got some time. But, I got my first kiss when I was twelve."

I wanted to wipe that taunting smile off her fake face. Being kissed at twelve was nothing to brag about.

"I thought you had to be a junior to come on this trip," Eugene said. "Did you lie about your age or what?"

"No," I answered quickly, indignant at the suggestion. "I just wrote the essay and won. I didn't know there was an age limit."

"You won?" Marybeth asked. "Won what?"

"You know, the scholarship to come here on this trip," Eugene said.

Everyone stared at me with squinted eyes and turned down mouths.

"I didn't know there was a contest," Marybeth said.

"There was," Eugene reported. "It was tough to get, too. Out of the fifty kids on this tour, they only gave out one scholarship. You not only had to be a total brain, but you also had to show financial need."

Total brain? Financial need? Kill me, kill me now. I couldn't look anyone in the face. I was mortified. I was a freak. Everyone knew now what a loser I was. The murder and being followed seemed almost insignificant at that moment. Once again, I was the social outcast.

"A brainiac, huh?" Alex said, pausing with his mouth open.

Surprised to hear my own voice, I said, "I thought it might be fun. Besides it was a free trip that I knew I could win." Did I say free? Crap.

"You actually *wanted* to go on this trip?" Alex asked. "I thought this was something that pompous political parents forced on their kids. I would never have come if my parents hadn't made me."

"I wish I'd known about the contest," Marybeth said bitterly, shaking her head. "I saved for two years to be able to come."

Two years? It would have taken me a lifetime to earn that much money, but still, I felt a twinge of guilt, thinking that I might have taken the place of someone like Marybeth, someone who really wanted to be a politician someday and had worked hard to get there.

"That's awesome Christy, only one out of fifty? Good job." Rick said, staring at me. His eyes shining.

A warm feeling flooded my body. Did both Alex and Rick like that I was smart? No way. They must just want something from me.

"You didn't have to pay *anything*?" Marybeth asked, looking like she might get sick.

Everyone still stared at me. I felt hot and uncomfortable, like a leper. Maybe they thought everyone on the trip was rich and privileged.

Loserville claimed me again.

Never kissed, poor and smart. A typical combination that defined a nerd at my age. I wanted to die. My stomach twisted in knots. I would never escape my box.

"It all makes sense now," Summer finally said. She had a wicked glint in her eyes.

"What's that supposed to mean?" Kira asked, scowling.

"Nothing. I'm just saying," Summer said. She tilted her head and raised her eyebrows.

Kira was trying to stick up for me and although slightly comforting, it was like putting a small band aid on a gushing stab wound. I also didn't understand how she could be so mean to me one minute and then turn around and act like I was her best buddy the next.

"There's more to you than meets the eye," Alex added, his stare searching my face.

My heart stuttered and I felt a bit overwhelmed. I wondered what he meant by that. Was it mean? I had always interpreted comments like that as nice, but now I didn't. If only I'd dared ask him. I could feel that my face was on fire, tomato red, without a doubt.

Alex still stared at me with a crooked smile. My heart stuttered again as I looked away.

"Christy," Kira whispered. "Look behind you."

Two hot guys played foosball near the door. They looked great—I had to admit.

Summer looked, too and became more animated and loud the longer she looked at them.

After a few more minutes, she interrupted the game, and said, "Hey, I'll be right back. I've got to go to the ladies room."

Wouldn't you know it. The ladies room was just outside the rec room doors, and she would have to pass the poor schmucks playing foosball. They had no idea what was about to hit them.

We all turned and listened.

"Hey guys. Having fun?" Summer asked, flipping her thick, shiny blond hair over her shoulder.

"Yeah, sure," said the taller of the two. Their voices lowered and we could no longer hear their responses.

I couldn't tell how old they were. I thought college age, even though their faces looked very young. Maybe it was the way they held themselves—really confident— that made me think they weren't in high school.

"Let's get back to the game, guys," Eugene said.

"We can't without Summer," Josh said, his eyes glued to the new guys and Summer. I imagine his self-esteem was taking a hit.

She returned to the group with the two guys trailing her, without going to the bathroom, of course.

"These guys are from New York," she said. "This is Jeremy and he's Nathan. Is it okay if they play too?"

What could we say? After a few moments, "Sure" came from a few mouths and "Whatever" came from a few others. Josh didn't say a word, he just looked at the floor.

"Who has the most things left?" Summer asked, not skipping a beat. Her huge, brilliant smile blinding me.

Everyone looked at me, hello, so I counted my pieces of paper. "Eight," I said, my face hot with renewed embarrassment.

"Eight? Man, Christy, you really haven't ever done anything," Alex said. "No wonder you wanted to come here." He chuckled along with Josh and Summer. I even saw a smile break on Kira's lips.

Alex. I wanted to cry. There was no doubt what he thought about me now. Stupidly, I looked up at him. He looked back at me. Even though I knew someone like him would never be interested in me, it hurt to have the slight glimmer of hope I'd had, dashed.

"Get eight things," Summer told the new guys.

The game didn't last much longer. I won, of course, my humiliation underscored.

The new guys were interesting, even Josh ended up playing nice. They talked sports with him and he jumped on board. It was getting late; Eugene and Marybeth headed up to their rooms. Despite how tired I felt, I knew what awaited me when I closed my eyes: a sword, a bloody head and people chasing me, so I was in no hurry. I sat and listened to the others talk until I didn't hear anymore.

When I opened my eyes, I was thrashing side to side trying to get out from someone's grip when I realized who it was. Jeremy, one of the foosball guys, stood over me, his light brown hair catching the light as he held my arms.

"Wake-up!"he said."Wake-up! It isn't real. It's a dream." His voice gradually grew softer the more alert I became. I noticed that Rick, Kira and Alex were standing right behind him. They all looked really concerned. No one laughed.

"What? What?"I said. "Was I dreaming?"

"Dreaming? No. You were having a wicked nightmare," Jeremy said. "Do you remember it?"

"Not really," I hedged. "Guess I better go to bed." I didn't really want to go, or answer any more questions, and was terrified of closing my eyes again.

"I'll go with you," Kira said.

"No, no, you stay here. I'll be all right. Marybeth's already there, isn't she? You stay, I'll be fine." I really did want her to come with me, but I didn't want to look wimpy. But, what if someone was waiting for me to be alone to snatch me away?

"Okay," she said.

I wished she'd insisted, but fresh, hot college meat had joined the group, and she really wanted to stay and get more of their attention.

I headed for the door, passing Summer and Josh playing foosball, only to find Jeremy on my heels.

"Hey, wait up," he said. "I'm not letting you go alone after a nightmare like that. You must be scared to death."

There was something about the way he talked to me that made me feel like he was a lot older than we were. It made me wary, but at the same time, I sensed he wanted to help me. He was very good looking and seemed nice, so I looked past him to the others, who were deep in conversation again, and slipped through the door he held open for me.

"Hey, do you mind if I grab a Coke?" Jeremy pointed at the door that led to the vending machines.

"No," I said. "Go ahead."

I waited in the hall until he came out, waving a dollar bill. "I hate these machines, they never take my money.

You don't happen to have a buck on you to trade for this one?"

I almost never had money on me. "No, Sorry. Here, let me try."

He handed me his beat up dollar, and I stepped into the vending room. No matter what I tried, it wouldn't take his dollar. I turned around, only to find the door was shut and Jeremy was blocking it.

"No luck," I said. "Sorry." I tried not to think about the shut door and small space we were in.

"Just a sec," he said. He reached into his pocket. Maybe he had another dollar bill. Not even close. He pulled out a black Ipod looking thing and with the push of a button, the room filled with music.

I backed up as far as I could into the soda machines. I was getting creeped out. Music? He leaned in toward me, and I jerked away, slamming the back of my head hard into one of the soda machines. Did he want to make-out in here? There was no way my virgin lips were landing on his. He grabbed my arms quickly, and whispered into my ear. I don't know what he said, because I started to scream. His hand flew up to cover my mouth. His other arm surrounded me, trapping me against the machine, and he whispered, "Don't scream. I'm FBI. I'm here to protect you, not hurt you."

FBI?

I stopped trying to scream. It was useless anyway. His hand held so tight against my mouth that only a muffled, "MMMM", escaped and parts of my lips pinched against my teeth. I opened my eyes to look at the side of his head.

He whispered, "It's okay. Just relax."

After what I'd seen in the ballroom, it was hard to relax, but I *was* trying to. My lips hurt so badly, I squirmed to get his hand away from my mouth. It made him press harder, which increased the pain. I finally gave up, and the pressure of his hand started to lessen. I wanted to move my mouth and check for damage, but his body and other hand held my arms down tight. It did feel good to be able to slide my lips over my teeth and close my mouth.

"Good, Christy, good. Take a deep breath."

I did breathe, but it wasn't deep. He still leaned into me and it was hard to even breathe quick, shallow breaths, let alone deep ones.

"I can't." I pushed out.

I guess he realized he was still squishing me, and he backed up a bit.

I breathed in deeply a few times, my pulse still in stampede mode. I desperately needed some water. The blaring music made me feel even more odd.

"Sorry about that. I meant for this to go differently. I didn't mean to freak you out," he whispered, still right in my ear. "We can't have anyone hear us. Do you understand that?"

"Yes," I said.

"Are you all right?"

"Yes," I answered, gasping.

"Good. Now listen. Ever since you gave us the letter, we've been following you. Other agents have been gathering information about you kids and the things you wrote. You did actually see what you wrote, didn't you? You were telling the truth?"

The letter. He knew about the letter. He must really be FBI. I felt myself relax a bit more and said, "Yes."

"It was really smart, the way you got the letter to us. You were very brave, and Christy, we need you to be brave. We need to get you to our office, so we can get your statement."

"Statement? I already wrote everything down. What else can I tell you?" I lost my calm again. I didn't want to rehash the murder again.

"There are a few things we're unclear about. Sometimes talking it through brings out new things. We need all the information we can get to catch these guys— I'm sure you can understand that."

I started to think about the FBI following us and Jeremy talking to me. What if *they* had been seen by the bad guys? What if *they* were good, but were giving us away to the bad guys on accident?

"No. You said you were here to protect us!" My whisper got louder by the second. "You're going to give us away, they'll see you. They're not stupid, and they probably already know that you're following us. That means they know we told!" Anger was taking over any fear I had. "You can't protect us. Not from them. They're following us. I saw a man with—"

"Shh! Calm down. You have to keep your voice low. There are bugs all over this hotel."

My ear got hot and started to feel a bit wet from him whispering into it. I wanted him to go away. I wanted it to all go away. I certainly did not want to answer a bunch of questions at the "office".

"Why don't you just pick up the people following us?"

"They haven't done anything yet."

"They killed somebody!"

"We need proof."

"They're following us and freaking us out." I persisted.

"Don't let them. Act normal. They're probably just trying to find out what you know. Look. I'll answer all your questions tomorrow. We've been in here too long.

Just understand that we'll be pulling you into the office tomorrow. Don't be scared, you are protected everywhere you go. And Christy, do *not* tell the others about us or this meeting. You all have to continue to act normal. And you can't discuss the murder anymore."

"Are there really bugs all over the hotel?"

"Yes. Be careful what you say. But also know that we have them under surveillance, too."

"What if they spot you? We'll be dead, won't we?" It was hard to keep my cool.

"You won't be dead, and they won't spot us. We're trained to be invisible. You're safe, despite what you might be feeling right now," he said. "I wanted to make contact with you tonight, so that tomorrow would be easier for you. It might have been the wrong choice, but can you help us catch these guys?"

I wanted to shout out, "No!" but, didn't. Those bad men needed to be put away, so I squeaked out a weak, "I think so."

"Look. From what we've heard, they don't know anyone actually saw the murder yet. Really, you're safe. Just follow my lead when we get to your room, okay? You can do this Christy, just be yourself."

The walk to my room was too short. When I opened the door, he said, "Have better dreams. Thanks for trying to get my dollar in that stupid Coke machine. I guess the stars didn't want me to have a Coke tonight." He laughed a quick laugh, his brown eyes expectant.

I stared at him for a few seconds, and he nodded at me, turning his head slightly to the left and opening his eyes wide. I guessed that was my cue to reply.

"Oh, yeah. No problem. I'm just sorry I wasn't any help. I can't wait to crawl into bed. Thanks for walking me to my room, it was really nice of you."

"See ya."

"Bye." I said. "Thanks again."

My bed wasn't as inviting as I'd wished. I still needed to talk to Rick about Iceman and I tossed and turned, afraid to sleep. Terrorists, guns, the FBI, swords, running, and screaming all dominated my thoughts. It was hard to be watched every minute of every day.

"Just be yourself," he had said. What exactly did that mean? I didn't even have a clear picture of who I was, how could I be the person he wanted me to be?

I was both anxious and scared for morning to come.

CHAPTER SEVEN

I kept looking at the clock. 1:00, 2:15, 3:50, 5:23. Would morning ever come? I could see a slight glow around the curtains. Why couldn't I fall asleep? I was so tired.

Should I get up now or wait just a bit longer and then take a long, hot shower? I closed my eyes, choosing the later. Please, Please, let me see something peaceful and beautiful, or nothing at all, I prayed.

I woke to the sound of the shower. I had slept. 6:45.

Thank you, Thank you. I whispered into the air, hoping someone important would hear it.

With the glow around the curtains brighter now, I got out of bed and opened them, quickly closing my eyes to the bright morning light. I smiled and prayed for more dreamless sleep tonight.

"Morning, Christy," Marybeth said, walking from the bathroom. She had a slight smile on her face. I was still getting used to her speaking again.

"Morning!" I said with as much enthusiasm as I could muster. I wondered how she would feel if she knew about what had happened last night with Jeremy.

I took a quick shower, dried my hair straight, then used Marybeth's flat iron, with her help, to make it completely smooth. I could actually do it. If the sun was shining, my hair would stay straight for at least half the day, maybe longer. It was all dependent on the crazy humidity factor. Humidity made my hair curly and frizzy. If only I had naturally straight, sleek hair. I grabbed a pony-tail holder just in case it did turn out to be a normal humid D.C. day. Marybeth wouldn't like it, but frizzy hair wouldn't do either.

Marybeth had waited for me and put the final touches on my outfit before we headed down to breakfast. All my avoidance of food had finally caught up with me. I loaded my plate and headed for the juice.

I stopped short when Jeremy, the handsome FBI guy, walked in front of me. I turned as fast as I could to get away from him. I couldn't deal with him again so early in the morning. I wasn't ready to give my "statement" yet, but the more I thought of it, it was kinda cool to go give a statement to the FBI. Just not right now.

"Hey Christy. Ya hungry?" Alex asked, eyeing the over-flowing plate I had just set down on the table.

I had been so bent on putting some distance between myself and Jeremy, that I hadn't noticed that I was about to sit down next to Alex. I wouldn't have made this mistake otherwise. Then I blurted, "Oh, yeah. I'm starving." I could feel my face burn. My stomach, on the other hand, filled with lovely butterflies—Jeremy forgotten.

"I love a girl with an appetite," Alex said, his smile friendly.

Man, he thinks I'm a pig. I felt the butterflies die in one horrible blast.

I kept my head down, pretending not to hear, and started to eat, feeling stupid.

"No, I'm serious about the appetite thing." I guess he wasn't buying my act. "I hate it when I take a girl out and she barely eats anything. It's not right. Everyone eats, you might as well enjoy it."

I looked at him, to check his sincerity. The moment my eyes met his, the butterflies came back en masse and I couldn't think. He was looking at me, so I smiled. My stomach was doing somersaults now, and I wanted to get up and dance. Luckily, I didn't. At home, I just might have, but not here. I would be in control even if it was curious that he talked to me.

Out of nowhere, orange juice stood in front of me. I looked behind me and saw Jeremy, my very own FBI man.

"My orange juice was all watery," Jeremy said. "They brought some more, so I got you some. You did want some juice didn't you?"

"Yeah, thanks," I said. "How did you know?" My eyebrows crushed together.

Why did I ask that? I didn't want to talk to him any more than I had to. He made me nervous. His good looks made it hard to be too mad, though.

"I thought I saw you going for the juice earlier, so I brought you some."

"Oh," I said. "Thanks."

"Well, enjoy it," he said, walking away. Alex stared at me like I'd just grown horns.

"He brought *you* orange juice?" Summer asked, her face incredulous.

Wildfires lit in my stomach. Why did I let her make me feel bad? Uh, maybe because I wished I were her. Maybe because my whole life no one important socially ever noticed me and I wanted to change that somehow. The attention I was getting here was mostly better than at home, but what did Summer have against me? Maybe my mom was right, that wishes could be dangerous. I certainly didn't want to *act* like Summer. I only wanted her popularity and her money. I would never be snotty or rude. Did money automatically make a person snotty and rude?

I didn't say anything and just looked at her, wishing I could disappear.

"What's the big deal?" Alex asked, his eyes narrowing at Summer. My heart stuttered. Was he sticking up for me?

Mrs. J. interrupted, giving us our ten minute warning to be on the bus, and my group hurried to get the coveted back rows. Just as I climbed onto the bus, I started to feel sick.

"Kira! Kira!" I called out. She was only a few feet in front of me, but it was always hard to hear on the bus.

"What?" she asked, turning to look at me.

"I've got to run to my room," I said. "I'm not feeling so great, don't let them leave without me."

"'Kay!" she yelled back.

I turned around to find Marybeth right behind me.

"I won't let them leave without you," she said, her ultra long, light brown hair, curly and fragrant, made my stomach churn.

"Thanks."

I felt really queasy in the elevator. Afraid I wouldn't make it to my room, I ran as soon as the doors opened. I started heaving as I pushed on my door and barely made it to the bathroom. Some throw-up ended up on the tile floor. The thought of it made me even sicker. I couldn't stop. Everything I'd eaten for breakfast was now in the toilet or on the floor. I wanted to cry, but couldn't because I continued to puke. I puked until there was nothing left. The dry heaves were painful. Hot, sweaty and tired, my hands clutched the seat and my head rested on the front edge of the toilet.

Marybeth walked in on me. "Christy, are you . . . Ooooh, you really are sick. I'll go tell Mrs. J., be right back."

I wanted to tell her not to tell anyone but Mrs. J., but I was once again, heaving.

Please don't let anyone else come. . . please don't let anyone else come.

A bit later, I heard Mrs. J.'s voice. I had finally stopped puking for more than a minute and was lying on the bathroom floor, exhausted.

"Oh, Christy," Mrs. J. said. She flushed the toilet and got a wash cloth wet in the sink and wiped up everything that didn't make it into the toilet. I was mortified, but unable to object.

I sat up dry heaving yet again. When would it end? This time it didn't last long, or at least it didn't seem like it did.

"Would you like someone to stay with you today, Christy?" Mrs. J. asked.

"No, please, no," was all I could get out before lying on the floor.

I didn't want anyone else to witness my embarrassment.

"I'll get one of the other chaperones to stay here with you," Mrs. J. said. "I can't leave the group."

"No," I said with all the force I could muster. "I'll be fine. I don't need anyone to stay with me."

"I shouldn't have asked "if", I should have asked, "who". Tell you what, Christy. One chaperone will stay behind, just in case. She won't come to your room unless you ask her to."

I shook my head, "no."

"You don't have a choice. We can't leave you here all alone when you're sick. Do you have a cell phone?" she asked.

"No," I said.

"Hmm," she said.

"I have one she can use," Marybeth offered. "It's here in my suitcase."

The phone. There it was again. The phone she didn't carry with her.

"Okay. Let's program my cell number into it." Mrs. J. said.

"It's already in there," Marybeth said. Her parents must be ultra-over protective.

"Great. Marybeth, here's Mrs. Dean's cell number," she held her phone out for Marybeth to see the number. "Could you put it into your phone for Christy? Thanks. Do you have water, or soda, or anything like that in here, Marybeth?"

"No."

"Alex, would you please go get some water and drinks for Christy? She's going to need to stay hydrated," Mrs. J. said.

"Sure. Be right back," he said.

Ugghh! Why? Why did he come? What had he seen? Heard?

I thought I couldn't feel any worse than I had, being sick and all, but then my heart started aching, too, discovering that Alex was there, watching. I'm sure he was disgusted. Seriously, I always wanted to puke when others got sick around me. The smell must have been the worst in my little bathroom.

Mrs. J. laid down the law. I was to stay in the room, drink lots of fluids, and call Mrs. Dean with any troubles. At least she wouldn't be *in* my room.

There was no way I was going to call her.

I started heaving again. It felt like my head was going to explode.

Mercifully, they left me to the toilet and bathroom floor.

After what seemed like only a few minutes, I felt a tap on my arm. With effort, I lifted my head from the floor, wondering what Mrs. J. could have forgotten. It wasn't Mrs. J., though. Jeremy held a card, smiling. If I hadn't felt so terrible, I might have laughed in his stupid smiling face. Couldn't he see that I was totally sick and couldn't help them any time soon?

The little card he held read: "FBI. Shhh!"

Then he put the *Shh* card behind more little cards that were in his hands.

"You will feel a prick," the next card read.

A prick? Was he kidding me? I would have kicked him in the face if I'd been able at the time.

He moved toward me and sure enough, a prick. I wanted to scream, but could only moan.

"Moan," the next sign said.

That, I could do, sick moaning sounds were natural for me at that moment. I noticed I was feeling a bit better of a sudden. What was that shot? How had they known to bring it? My mind still swam, but started to clear up.

"Stand up silently," it read. I thought it was a great idea to use those cards to communicate with me. They were completely silent. The bugs wouldn't hear a sound. The FBI was clever.

Jeremy helped me up. I felt a lot better. I saw movement behind Jeremy and jumped. Standing next to my bed, a woman, about my height, fair-skinned with blue eyes looked at me. I guess she was part of this whole thing. Jeremy looked at her and then held up the next card.

"Walk to your bed," it read.

I did, eyeing the lady as I went, my stomach muscles aching, and feeling light headed.

"She'll help you dress and then while we're gone, she'll pretend to be you," the sign said.

I nodded.

"*Quietly, please,*" the sign continued.

The lady pointed to some clothes laid out on the bed and I moved toward them, reluctant to look away from her. Realizing I would have to take the clothes off that I already had on, I turned to look at Jeremy. He gave me a knowing look and turned around to face the opposite direction.

Dressed in my new clothes, the woman walked toward me and put make-up on my face and then a wig over my hair. She smiled at me when she was done. It gave me a weird sensation, like she was my mom, sending me off to Sunday School all clean and pretty. Instead, I was headed for questioning. Without a sound, she tried to get Jeremy's attention, but happily, he still faced away from us. I tapped him on the shoulder and gave a little sick moan. He turned and smiled at me, leading me to the door and pulling it open without a sound. He held up the last sign:

"Go with the man in the hall."

I peeked out and saw a tall, massive, blond-headed guy looking at me, smiling, lips pressed together. What was up with all the smiling? I couldn't *make* myself smile. Maybe they thought it would help put me at ease, but it didn't. It was creepy. I looked back momentarily into the room and saw my decoy climbing into my bed. The door shut behind me. The man in the hall reached his arm out and looped it through mine, pulling me in tight. I felt like I'd been pressed up against a brick wall. With his other hand, my new escort pulled an index card out of his pocket and handed it to me.

It read:

"Stay very close to me. Respond to me when I speak to you. Act like you are enjoying yourself, but don't overdo it. We are a couple who are on vacation in D.C.

We'll be getting into a car out front. Just relax. I'm Lance. You're Susi."

Was he kidding? I couldn't help but stay close to him, his tight hold on me sure to leave bruises. Couldn't he see I was just a kid? I plastered a smile on my face, even though it was the last thing I wanted to do, and let my shoulders fall forward a bit to help me relax.

"Would you like to get something to eat?" Lance asked.

"Sure. I'm starving," I tried not to let sarcasm fill my answer, but a bit seeped in. Of course I was starving, every last particle of food from my stomach was racing through the D.C. plumbing system. A thought raced through my mind—did they drug me? The FBI doesn't drug people, not really, do they?

We got into the elevator after the doors slid open, with four other people inside. They stepped back and pressed their bodies against the walls to make room for the huge mass that was "Lance".

Just like the other four people, we didn't say a word in the elevator and then we all walked out, heading for the front doors of the hotel the second the elevator doors opened. Every step I took made me feel a bit more anxious. What would happen to me? What questions would they ask? Could I answer them? Better yet, would I even make it to the FBI building? Had they drugged me and if so, what else would they be willing to do to me?

As if he could feel my tension rising, Lance started talking to me. I tried to be amiable and answer the questions naturally, which was a stretch to say the least.

I felt a bit better when I sat in the taxi. It felt nicer, roomier than the one Rick, Kira, Marybeth and I had taken to and from Georgetown. We went to a café a few blocks away and had something to eat. We talked about touring

D.C. and what *we* had seen so far. Making things up to answer his questions got easier as time passed.

I ordered a BLT and it truly was the best BLT I had ever had, quite possibly because my stomach was *more* than empty; since I wasn't paying, I decided to try a crème brulee. It was so creamy smooth, that the anger I clung to from my morning date with the toilet seemed to lessen. Instead of murdering the man who most likely drugged me, I'd settle for a hardy punch in his gut and the chance to bawl him out. How had they drugged me? Then it hit me. I remembered the large arms that brought me my orange juice; they were Jeremy's.

CHAPTER EIGHT

Brunch didn't last long enough. I wasn't sure I wanted to head for the FBI building, but I kinda felt excited about the adventure in it. When we walked out of the café, Lance walked over to a sleek, black limo, opened a door, and held it for me. Motioning with his other hand, he encouraged me to climb in. Heck yeah! A real limo sat in front of me! Wow. I was going for a ride in a limo! With a huge grin plastered on my face, I slid across the soft leather seat, taking in every last detail. No one would believe me back home—then again, who would I tell?

We rode in silence for a good half hour, which seemed crazy considering our destination was only a few blocks away. Most of the time, I played with things in the limo, pushing buttons, turning music on and off, eating the food and drinking the bottled water, but I did look out occasionally to see where we were. It was like we made a huge, jaggedy circle all around the FBI building and back. Maybe they were still worried about being tailed, which was strange because with Lance in the car, I felt safe.

Some of the time, my mind wandered to Iceman and I fought to depress it. I wanted to focus on the incredible ride instead. It turned out to be a great diversion from reality.

Forced to stop at a guard shack at the entrance of a parking garage, all four doors of the limo swung open almost simultaneously and four heads peered in. One nodded at Lance, who nodded back, and Lance handed them an ID badge. The one that took the badge left, and the others looked all around inside the car. Once Lance had his badge back, the doors were closed, and we drove into the semi-darkness of the parking garage.

I breathed a sigh of relief, but at the same time, I didn't want my ride in the limo to end. I must have touched everything in it the few short minutes we drove round and round to park. The only thing missing was me sticking my head and body out the sunroof and screaming. I'd always fantasized about doing that.

I felt powerful just being inside this car; it made me sit up taller and feel like I could do anything or be anyone. I imagined I was on an adventure in a book. No one really gets hurt in books. The car stopped again, and I watched Lance get out. Jeremy opened my door from the outside.

A smile stretched across his face. I felt mixed emotions at the sight of him. His face was both familiar and friendly, but I suspected he was the one who had made me so sick. He offered his hand and helped me out. I wanted to crush it, but didn't. I waited until I stood in front of him, then balled up my fist and slugged him in the gut as hard as I could.

"You better not ever drug me again!" I shouted.

Jeremy doubled over, catching his breath. I wasn't prepared for how much it would hurt my hand and pulled it back shaking it while opening and closing my fist. I took a step back, right into Lance's bulky body. He grabbed my arms and jerked them behind my back.

"Now look here…," Lance started to say.

"It's okay agent Miller. I think I deserved that," Jeremy said, still breathing hard. Lance relaxed his grip on my arms.

"You've got quite a punch young lady," Jeremy said, standing up straight and massaging his gut. "I don't intend to drug you again. I'm sorry I had to in the first place. I should've warned you, but I didn't want you to worry about it all night. We needed this to look real. With the hotel being bugged, we couldn't risk—"

"I could've faked it," I insisted. He had drugged me. This was insane.

"Maybe, maybe not. It's over now. Truce?" He held out his hand for me to shake.

I wasn't sure if I wanted a truce. I wanted to be mad just a little longer, so I squinted my eyes, pushed out my lips and said nothing. My stomach still screamed every time I moved.

"Come on. I owe you one. A big one," he said placating me. "What if I made sure you got another crème brulee? Would we be even then?"

I could almost taste the exquisite dessert at the sole mention of it. Could I sell out for something so little, but extraordinary? Apparently, I could, because I felt myself nodding.

"When do I get it?" I blurted out, opening my eyes wide and staring him down.

"Don't worry about it. You'll get it. Now, let's shake on it. No more punching, okay?" There was a fatherly tone to his words and I once again wondered how old he was.

With some hesitation, I raised my hand to his, and we shook on it. The moment our hands touched, I regretted the deal. Maybe I should have upped the ante and not settled so quickly. It had been way too easy for him. I had suffered way more—especially since Alex had seen. It was too late, though. With my handshake, I had agreed; there was no turning back. Bummer.

"This way, Christy," Jeremy said, pointing behind me with one hand and shutting the limo door with the other. "Follow Agent Miller. I'll be right behind you."

The echo of the limo door slamming was so loud, I jumped and followed Agent Miller like a scared rabbit. We walked toward a man who had one hand resting on a gun strapped to his waist. I shivered. This was it. I was going into FBI headquarters to be questioned. There would be no more pretending that I was going to prom or on a fancy date. I was about to face the hotel ballroom head on.

"Identification please," he said, looking us over. The agents offered their badges again and he put them into a slot in the wall. He handed them back just a second later. "And this is?" he asked, staring at me.

"Christy Hadden. Here for questioning," Jeremy answered, sounding very official all of a sudden. I supposed a place like this had to be pretty formal and precise. He handed Jeremy a new ID badge and he clipped it to my shirt.

Next to the guard and to his right, a green light came on. The wall opened up to reveal an elevator. We stepped inside, but nobody turned around to face the doors we had just walked through, like people usually do. Instead, we all stood with our backs to them. Weird. My stomach jumped as we started our ascent, and my heart pounded faster and faster every level we climbed. When we stopped, the whole wall we'd been staring at, moved to its left, revealing a hallway. I'd never seen an elevator open like that before.

We walked down a narrow, non-descript hallway lined with closed doors, just like ones we'd seen on our tour. This time I got to go in one of those doors. It led to a small room with no window and no other door. In the center of the room was a table surrounded by chairs. It looked like a normal meeting room; not what I had imagined. I thought it would be like the ones I had seen so often on TV shows. I was, however, finding out that reality rarely mirrored TV.

"Have a seat, Christy," Jeremy urged, his eyes looking toward the chairs.

They all looked the same, so I picked the one nearest me. It wasn't hard, but soft and giving, with nice arm rests too. I saw no microphone, no tape recorder and no one-way mirror. This was definitely not an interrogation room—at least I tried to convince myself of that.

"I'll be right back," Jeremy said, shutting the door behind him.

I tried to think of nothing while he was gone by staring at the white wall in front of me. I couldn't let myself start replaying the beheading just yet.

Jeremy returned with bottles of water, and a tall, military-looking man followed him.

"Christy, this is Special Agent Durrant," Jeremy said, as they took seats opposite me. "I've read the letters you and your friends wrote. Yours was the most detailed; that is why you are the only one here. I know it will be difficult to relive it all again, but we need you to tell us what you saw. We will stop you and ask clarifying questions along the way. Tell us what you saw."

As I started to talk, I could see myself climbing onto that toilet seat again, both curious and scared. I wasn't simply telling what had happened, I was there. I hadn't actually told the whole story to anyone, and doing so made it seem like it was happening all over again. My clasped hands trembled and turned cold. Instead of running from my memories, I had to face them head on.

Jeremy interrupted me every now and then to ask questions. When he spoke, he seemed oddly far away and quiet. It sounded like I was down a deep well.

"Why were you in the Hotel Norton's bathroom in the first place?" Jeremy asked.

Hadn't I written that part in my letter to them? It hardly seemed relevant.

"Kira needed a bathroom and it was just around the corner. We weren't ready to go back to our hotel because we hadn't finished our game yet.

He nodded, so I continued.

"I climbed on the water tank of the toilet to look through the vent—"

"Why were you climbing up there?" he asked, frowning.

"I heard muffled voices coming from somewhere and saw the vent above the toilet. I was afraid some perv was up there taking pictures of us."

He nodded again, and I plowed forward, words coming from my mouth in a choked whisper.

"Alex took a bunch of pictures with his cell phone—"

"Pictures?" Jeremy interrupted. "You didn't write anything about pictures in your letter."

"I didn't? Oh, probably because the phone got ruined. There aren't any pictures to get now. You see, Eugene bumped Alex and the phone fell into the toilet and it doesn't work anymore."

"Where's the phone now, Christy?" Jeremy asked, his tone very serious.

"I don't know. Alex bought a new phone yesterday. Maybe he threw the broken one away."

Jeremy nodded to Agent Durrant who left the room.

"What did the men's accent sound like?" Jeremy continued after the door shut behind Agent Durrant.

"Sound like?" I paused and thought for a minute. "It was a middle eastern accent as far as I could tell. I've heard people talk like that on the news and on TV shows."

"Are you certain?"

"Yes." I was certain. His voice spoke to me every day. I couldn't get it out of my head.

Agent Durrant, stiff as a board, came back and took his seat once again.

"Why was Marybeth so sure it was her Senator, Senator Randolph?" Jeremy asked.

"She recognized his voice. She said he was a blessing from heaven and would save the farmers."

"Does she still think it was him?"

"I don't know. We've never discussed it." I couldn't believe that three days had passed since the murder, and it was as vivid in my mind as if it had happened moments ago. I was scared, but too busy telling what happened to be consumed with fear until the next question threw me for a loop.

"What did the sword look like?"

I felt cold to the bone, my muscles seemed to lock in place. Only my stomach was left to twist and squeeze. My muscles were already tender and sore from all the puking, and the nausea from earlier returned. My mind was overtaken with the sword, the shiny, thick, curved thing that had sliced through Jonathan's neck like butter. Over and over again, I watched as blood spurted, and his head fell to the floor. Thinking about it had my head spinning and I was losing control. I couldn't get the image of the head, severed from the body, and the blood pooling around it, out of my mind. A dull ache spread through my body. I couldn't help but lay my head on the table and close my eyes. I couldn't face it. I shut down, unable to raise my head. Exhausted, both mentally and physically, I had to give in to nothingness, pushing the memories back into their hiding place. It was like an out of body experience, like I was watching myself disappear into the recesses of my mind, unwilling to deal with the actual beheading again.

The next thing I knew, Jeremy's gentle touch woke me. Reluctantly, I opened my cloudy eyes. How long had I been out? My eyes burned. I shifted in my seat. With no clock in the room, it could have been midnight and I wouldn't have known it.

"Lunch is here," Jeremy said a few minutes later. I heard the door shut. "You'll never believe what I brought you."

I raised my body from the table with care, my stomach muscles protesting as I stretched.

Lunch? Had I been out that long?

"You feel up to eating?"

"Yeah, uh, sorry. How long have I been out?"

"Just a few hours. Don't worry about it. You've had a long few days."

I smiled, wondering what was in the bag he held.

I saw Special Agent Durrant directly across from me. He appeared rough and mean. The contrast of his black hair against his pale skin made him look even more ominous. He never smiled, the corners of his mouth always down, and there was a glint behind his eyes, that was unsettling. He sat straight in his chair, with his arms folded over his chest, scowling the entire time. He hadn't spoken the whole morning, and I couldn't help but wonder why he was there.

Special Agent Jeremy McGinnis was just the opposite, smooth and inviting. His voice calm and his skin tan, paired with his light brown hair, made him very attractive. He sat relaxed in his chair, holding a legal pad that he scribbled on every now and then. Despite the drugging incident, I could actually say that I trusted him for some reason.

"Check this out," Jeremy said, a giant grin on his face. He slid a carton with the logo of the café on it, where Lance and I had brunched earlier that day. In front of me, sat my crème brulee.

I ate it first, savoring each bite. I still felt a bit cheated not demanding ten more of them, but the creaminess of the sweet dessert softened the blow, if only a little. On further reflection, I decided it was pretty smart to drug me. I just needed to be honest with myself. I took my time eating the sandwich, and Jeremy and I talked about nothing in particular. While drinking my lemonade, I finally heard Agent Durrant's voice for the first time.

"Let's get on with it McGinnis," he sneered, his irritation obvious. "We don't have all day. We wasted three hours letting her sleep, and we only have about two and a half left."

Agent McGinnis shot him a look that could kill. I wanted to kiss him for it, figuratively, of course. I mean he was hot, but he must be a lot older than he looks if he is an FBI agent. Agent Durrant didn't even acknowledge the look; he just turned his head and stared at me. It felt like he was boring holes right through me, and I started to sweat. I quickly looked away and found Jeremy's reassuring face.

"In the ballroom, how far away would you say the table was from the vent you were looking through?" Jeremy asked.

"How far away?" I repeated, thinking. I could see the table, the men sitting at it, along with the guards all surrounding it. Once again, it felt like it was happening right in front of me, and I tried in vain to look straight down from the vent and measure the distance mentally. My view was fixed. I couldn't alter it.

"I don't know. I'm so bad with distances," I admitted.

"Just try," Jeremy said.

"Let's take her there," Agent Durrant suggested, sneering like only he could. "Then she can show us exactly where they were."

The nausea came back and the entire event flashed before my eyes, repeating, over and over again. My throat closed, and I couldn't swallow or breathe normally. I closed my eyes and pleaded in my head, show me, please show me the distance. I couldn't go back there. A bead of sweat dripped down one side of my face and then my stomach rolled, darkness loomed again. By sheer grit, I rallied and managed to slow the images flying through my mind. I was determined not to go back to the hotel where Jonathan had been murdered. I watched the leader with the crooked nose and the Senator walk from the table and go out the ballroom doors into the hallway beyond. Over and over they walked.

Why did I keep seeing that? I needed answers. It didn't seem to make sense: then as if some unseen power whispered softly to me, I knew why.

"The table was straight out from the vent," I croaked in a voice that didn't seem to be mine, "I looked straight ahead, and the table was in line with the doors that led to the hallway, the ones the Senator and the leader exited after the beheading." I paused and closed my eyes, thanking the unseen power that had just helped me. My throat loosened, and I took a deep breath and smiled. A real smile too. Someone was watching over me.

I looked at Agent Durrant and his eyes narrowed to slits. I shivered. I wondered why he wanted me to go to the hotel.

"Great," Jeremy said, I'm sure thinking hard. "So, if I were to walk straight out from where the vent is on the wall and Agent Durrant was to walk straight into the ballroom from the northern most doors, we would intersect at the spot where the table stood?"

"Yes," I said, triumphant.

"This next part might be hard for you, but it's essential."

"I'll do my best," I said, trying to take courage.

"A sketch artist will be joining us in about two minutes," Jeremy said, consulting his watch. "We need a sketch of the 'leader'. Can you help us with that?"

I told him I could do it, I could clearly see the leader's twitching, crooked nose. I felt reassured and capable, like when I handed in perfect work at school.

Exactly as predicted, a short, skinny man with friendly eyes entered the room carrying a sketch pad and pencils.

The sketch was done in no time. I was shocked to see the leader's face looking back at me from the paper. What talent. I shuddered and the hair on my arms stood up.

"That's him, huh?" Jeremy asked, looking at the picture.

"Yeah."

Jeremy left the room with the sketch artist, murmuring to him, and then came back to the table. We discussed a few other items, but thankfully, he didn't ask about the sword again.

There was a knock on the door and Jeremy stood to open it while Agent Durrant, eyes still narrowed, continued to scowl at me.

Jeremy brought a photo to the table. "Is this the man?" he asked.

I started trembling as soon as I saw the face of the leader staring out from the photo at me.

"Yes." I didn't know why I was afraid. It wasn't rational. He wasn't following me now. I was safe in the FBI building.

He then pushed another photo across the table toward me. The Senator.

"Have you ever seen this man?"

"That's Senator Randolph, isn't it?"

"Great," he said.

Finally, he slid one more picture across the table.

"What about this guy?"

Jonathan. My throat closed up. I nodded quickly as tears welled up in my eyes. I blinked hard, not able to see, and the tears fell to the table with a tiny splash. To keep my bottom lip from quivering, I clamped it between my teeth.

Jeremy quickly whisked the photos away and set them on his chair before coming around the table to me. I welcomed his strong, firm arms around my shoulders and I gladly buried my face in his shirt.

I had never been comfortable expressing emotion and it pained me to break down twice in one day, especially in front of the same two people. Jeremy's arms were warm and comforting though, and I wanted to stay wrapped in them forever. He understood what I'd seen and could somehow sympathize with me; he was an ally. How I needed him at that very moment. He seemed to never show weakness. Maybe I could fake being strong.

Someone knocked on the door at the same time I heard a watch alarm go off. Jeremy shifted and reached for his wrist, I guess to stop the alarm.

"Christy, are you okay now?" He asked, pulling away and looking into my eyes.

"Yeah, I think so," I said sniffling, but still holding his chest tightly, afraid to let go. He pulled back a bit more and I had no choice.

"We've got to get you back," Jeremy said. "It won't be long before your group returns to the hotel, it's almost six." He looked me directly in the eyes and said, "You were incredibly brave today. Thank you so much. We know who we're looking for now and we'll try to get some evidence from the hotel. But, there's one more thing we need to know." He moved back to his chair and shuffled through the photos he'd set there. "Did the sword look like this?"

I looked at the picture he laid on the table. A curved sword with an intricately decorated handle pierced my eyes. I took a deep breath, closing them after nodding.

"Just so you know. That sword is the typical weapon of this particular terrorist faction. Their leader tends to be on the dramatic side." He emphasized the word dramatic and placed the pictures inside the notebook he'd brought with him, then led the way to the door, saying, "Remember, if you see anyone following you, we have a line on them. We know who they are. Don't be afraid."

I forced a smile and sniffed again, passing him to go into the hallway, thinking about Jeremy calling the bad guys, *terrorists*.

We went out the same way we'd come, and I found Lance waiting for me by the shiny, black limo. I couldn't make myself get excited about the ride this time, though. I was physically tired and mentally spent. On the other hand, I suddenly felt as if my life had become valuable. I was no longer the insignificant smart girl. I also wasn't the girl sitting back watching. I was center-stage and it was terrifying. I wondered why I had ever wished for it. Change hadn't set me free, it had trapped me.

The ride to the hotel was both uneventful and brief. I found it hard to play the part of Lance's girlfriend when we got back to the hotel, but I muddled through it. I was glad to be back in my room even during the silent exchange with my decoy. Jeremy told me back at the FBI building that they would be in touch and to remember that I was safe. Once again I was required to renew my vow of silence about the whole affair. I wondered if I would ever feel safe again.

CHAPTER NINE

Back in my bed, a flood of emotions swept through me. To do what the FBI wanted me to do, to go it alone, seemed impossible. I wouldn't be able to confide in anyone, so no one could help me carry the load; a heavy burden to carry alone.

Couldn't Jeremy see that I was just a kid and not strong like he thought? The pressure of this whole thing seemed to be crushing the life out of me. I wondered if Marybeth had felt this way before finding comfort in her phone call on the balcony. I wished I had someone to call. I resisted crying, not wanting the terrorists to hear.

After only a few minutes, though, my stomach twisted up and unable to hold it back any longer, I started to cry. I tried to whimper quietly, but it didn't take long before I sobbed uncontrollably. I curled up into a tight ball, wishing I could disappear. I didn't want anyone to see or hear me, but at that moment, if anyone had walked up to me, even the most gorgeous guy in the world, I wouldn't have cared or noticed. I thought the tears would never stop. Everything I'd been holding inside escaped all at once and a sweet cleansing took place. Something deep inside me told me I could do this. Something was giving me strength. My chest burned as my load seemed to lighten. Eventually, sleep enveloped me.

I woke to a pitch black room. No faint glow showed itself around the sliding glass doors and the clock by my bed glared at me—4:30 am. I had to squint to not hurt my eyes. I rolled onto my back and rubbed them gently—they felt puffy and sore. When I opened or shut them, it felt like sandpaper stuck to the back of my eyelids, scratching my eyeballs.

I could hear Marybeth's even breathing on the other side of the room and wondered when she had come in last night. Had my group returned at seven o'clock, like every other evening? Did they go to the rec room after dinner? I must have fallen asleep quickly after getting back from the FBI building.

I tossed back the covers and walked to the bathroom on tip toes, shutting the door quietly behind me. Feeling around for the light switch, I closed my eyes before flipping it on. If the clock light had hurt my eyes, I could only imagine what a real light would do. With my eyes still shut, I felt around for the sink and turned the water on, waiting until it wasn't freezing cold before cupping my hands under it. It felt great to wash my face. With each splash, I opened my eyes a bit more, allowing the water to rinse out the saltiness. It burned a little at first, but then the sandpaper under my lids washed away, and I could finally open and close my eyes without pain. I dabbed my face with a towel and took a peek at it in the mirror.

My eyes looked about half their normal size, which was never large anyway. I wondered if mascara would hide any of it. I felt rejuvenated and exhausted at the same time and I leaned my head against the mirror and took a few deep breaths.

"Please, give me strength," I prayed in a whisper. "I can't do this alone." I waited, eyes closed, and a sweet peace returned. I felt strong.

When I lifted my head off of the glass, a large, red circle appeared on my forehead. Rubbing it didn't take it away, and I figured a shower was my only hope.

Even after the shower, my puffy eyes stared back at me from the mirror. *Darn it!*

I carefully opened the bathroom door after turning off the light and waited for my eyes to adjust. There was a slight glow around the curtains now, and I picked out some clothes to wear and put them on. The clock read five-thirty. Luckily, the sliding door opened easily and didn't make a lot of noise. I left the curtains shut but slipped behind them to the balcony. I understood now why Marybeth had escaped to the balcony the other morning. It was a great place to hide.

The calm and cloudless sky gave me exactly the opposite feeling of what I had felt yesterday. Some cars drove on the street below, but not many. I had to remind myself that this was a government town, and the government worked from eight to five. It was a little early for the seven-thirty mayhem on the streets of D.C. A slight wind gently caressed my face.

Tall buildings surrounded me. At home we only had a few slightly tall buildings with hills looming over us. Instead of street after street of hotels and businesses like I saw here, most of our streets had homes on them, even downtown. Thinking of its beauty made me long to return. I missed home in an odd way. I wanted to escape it because of the people at school, not the glorious landscape. What would happen to me when I got back home? Would I have time to change enough for anyone to notice? I hoped any further change I experienced would be minus the pain.

I wondered what my family had been doing. Had they thought about me at all? What would they think if they knew what had happened to me these last few days? Not much probably. They thought I could handle anything and wouldn't worry.

I'd been in D.C. a week now. I couldn't remember what we had planned for today, our last real day of sightseeing. What could we do on a Sunday? Maybe we would relax a bit before the real work of the trip began tomorrow. I kind of wished we'd worked the first week of the trip and played the second. It was odd to do it the other way around. Don't all moms tell kids to work first, then play? If only we *had* done that, we wouldn't have run into the trouble in the ballroom. I really didn't have an interest in politics and it would have been nice just to continue to explore D.C., and not have to worry about "our" political careers.

I heard some noise behind me as Marybeth climbed out onto the balcony with me.

"Hey," she said.

"Hey," I said.

"What ya doing?"

"Couldn't sleep and it's just so nice out here."

"It really is."

"Marybeth, I'm sorry you didn't know about the scholarship."

"That's okay. I probably wouldn't have qualified anyway. My parents make too much."

"Why did you want to go on this particular trip?" I asked. "Why not choose a cheaper one. I saw a lot of cheaper ones advertised on the internet."

"This trip is the best one. The fifty kids in this particular group get special treatment. The ones in all the other groups that combine with us at the last debate, the day before we leave, don't get half of what we do. Look at where we are staying, for instance. All the other groups are in dive hotels, eat crappy food and only get to go see the things that every other sight-seer who comes to D.C. gets to see. Even our bus is cush. This particular group was developed to give political hopefuls the chance to see first-hand, the inner workings of politics in D.C. without getting their hands dirty. This is for the elite. This is partly how they protect their inner-circles of power and keep that power within the same few hands. We get to spend the day with a page, shadow a lobbyist and Congressman's aide or a Senator's aide. We get to be with Mrs. J., who is infamous for setting up future politicians. The people you see eating with us every day, will be the ones leading this country in the years to come. It's all about power and connections. I'm surprised you didn't know all this."

I wanted to tell her that I wasn't interested in politics at all, and I was only here to create a new me, but I figured it would be too big of a pill to swallow, considering the scholarship and all. "It's not like they spelled it out like that on the internet. I just picked the one that had a scholarship."

My stomach growled so loud that I thought it would wake everyone in D.C. We laughed and climbed back into our room. Marybeth told me to go down to breakfast before my stomach disappeared, and she would meet me there as soon as she got ready. I didn't argue. I grabbed my things and took off for the elevator.

Being the only one from our group in the breakfast room felt odd, but I was too hungry to worry about it. Like always, the buffet had everything possible on it; A perk of this tour, I guess. Would our future leaders really come from this group of fifty kids? I loaded my plate high, sat down and dug in. Next thing I knew, Rick sat next to me.

"Wow," he said, looking at my overflowing plate. He rocked into me, his shoulder touching mine, and then his entire arm snuggled up next to mine. I looked up at his grinning face, only inches from me.

"Very funny," I said.

"You beat me, ya know. I've been the first one down here every day until today."

"Slept in, did ya?" I said, turning back to my food. His arm still pressed against mine.

"No. You just got here early. I guess you feel better now, huh? I mean you're eating and everything."

"Yeah," I said. "I thought I was going to die yesterday. I must've eaten something bad." I laughed, but what I really wanted to do was cry thinking about puking my guts out, not to mention having to re-live the worst moments of my life with the FBI agents.

"When we checked on you last night you were sleeping like a baby," he said.

"You checked on me?" I clenched my hands together.

"Yeah. We were all so worried, we checked on you as soon as we got back."

"We?" I hoped against hope that *we* did not include Alex.

"Marybeth, Mrs. J. and I."

"Oh." I was relieved that Alex hadn't come, but at the same time, I wished he had. I looked at my plate and decided I wasn't as hungry as I thought. When I reached for my glass of water, Rick was still touching me.

I looked around him as casually as I could. Yep, no one there. I looked in the other direction, no one there either. There we were at this large table, elbow to elbow, while there was room enough for us to be ten feet apart.

At that precise moment, Kira walked in. Our eyes met. Her eyes narrowed and the corners of her mouth dropped. She started stomping our way. I suddenly felt guilty.

I hadn't done anything wrong, though and didn't need to feel guilty. Sure, Rick was sitting with me, touching me, but I hadn't invited it.

"Hey Kira," I shot out, as the gap between us narrowed.

"Hey, Kira," Rick said casually. "I was just about to tell Christy about yesterday and everything we did."

"Really," she said through clenched teeth.

I finished my water with one big gulp.

"I'll be right back," I said, as I stood up, waving my glass in the air to indicate I needed a refill. After filling my glass with ice, I pressed my cup to the water dispenser and got bumped from behind. Kira.

"What the heck, Christy. I told you he was taken," she said, her face red and her eyes extremely wide open.

One thing's for sure, Kira's direct. She doesn't beat around the bush.

"What are you talking about?" I asked, playing dumb.

"Hello!... Rick, the guy you were all over when I walked in," she hissed.

"All over? Really? Look, for the last time, I'm not interested in Rick and he's not interested in me." The thought of his arm touching mine danced through my mind and I had to look away from her.

"What?" she asked. She stared at me intently.

"I'm truly not interested in Rick, I said. "He's yours, if he'll have you. Have at it." I looked her directly in the eye so that she couldn't misunderstand me.

She let out a breath, and her shoulders sunk a bit.

"You mean it, don't you?"

"Of course," I answered.

She looked at me and then looked in Rick's direction and then back at me again.

"I told you this before," I said. "Believe me, this time. I was all by myself before he joined me. Did you want him to sit way over there?" I pointed to the other end of the breakfast room.

"Well, maybe. I mean, I don't know."

The sad thing was that she really did.

"Stop being so suspicious, Kira. He was just being a nice guy and didn't want me to sit alone. Why in the world would you think he liked me?"

"You looked so cozy together, laughing and talking. He's so cute and nice. You do think he's cute, don't you?"

"Sure, but I'm not interested. Can we drop this? If you get all jealous on me again, I'll have to hurt you. Seriously."

"Fine. I'll keep the claws in for now," she said with a little growl. "But you better watch it." She laughed half-heartedly and went to get some breakfast. What she really meant was that I better stay away. I noticed that the room was getting crowded.

After I'd filled my glass, I headed back to the table. Almost everyone from our group sat around tables now. If my plate hadn't been marking my spot, I would have had to sit that ten feet away from Rick that Kira wanted me to sit. I stopped in my tracks. Alex was sitting next to my empty seat. I was going to be sandwiched between Rick and Alex, and by the looks of it, I would never fit in the small space they'd left me. My heart skipped a beat, and I looked back at Kira and thought about offering the space to her. She hadn't claimed a spot yet and would have to sit far away from Rick and all of us, for that matter, and she wouldn't be happy about it.

"Christy," Rick called out. "What are you looking at? I saved your place. Come on."

I couldn't breathe, thinking about sitting next to Alex. I really, really wanted him to like me, and it was scary. I didn't want the inevitable pain of rejection that always came.

"Uh, there's not enough room for me," I said, motioning with my glass at a different table. "I'll go sit down there."

"Don't be crazy," he insisted. "There's plenty of space." He poked Alex and said something to him that made him look at me.

"Sorry, Christy," Alex said. "Scoot down guys!" he yelled to the left side of the table and everyone moved down.

"There you go, Christy," Alex said, patting the bench next to him.

I tried to smile, but I had no clue if I had been successful. My heart raced and I seemed to have lost my mind. I couldn't think.

"Thanks," I squeaked, more quietly than I'd intended, feeling my cheeks burn.

"No problem," he said, his hand still on the seat.

I looked up to see Kira getting some orange juice. My mind kicked into gear. I wanted to gag at the thought. Think before you drink and only drink what you get yourself, I reminded myself.

"Come on," Alex said again, still patting the seat and looking at me.

Those deep brown eyes got to me, and I hurried to sit down, leaving Kira to her own fate.

CHAPTER TEN

Being sandwiched between Rick and Alex created such a rush of emotions, that I stared at the table, afraid my eyes would betray me. My arm tingled where Alex's arm touched mine, and I felt my temperature rise.

"You must be feeling better," Alex said.

My heart stuttered when he spoke to me, and I almost couldn't look. His stunning face captured me and my throat swelled so that I couldn't speak.

"You are feeling better aren't you, Christy?" he asked again, pulling away a little, his eyebrows pushed together.

"Speak, you stupid girl," my mind screamed. *"He thinks you're going to puke all over him. Or worse yet, give him what you had."*

Somehow I gained power over my tongue, "Of course. Afraid I'm gonna puke on you?" It was like someone else had made me speak—and not my words. Horrified, I looked away.

"No," he said in a quiet whisper. "I just wanted to make sure you were all right. You were pretty sick." He didn't laugh. Him seeing me on the bathroom floor heaving flashed through my mind.

I felt terrible as I met his gaze again. "I'm sorry. I seem to have lost control over my mouth."

He laughed. "Very funny. Like you ever lose control."

"Hey." I couldn't think of anything else to say, so I just stared at him. He stared back, smiling. My heart ran a relay race in my chest. Why was he talking to me? Hadn't the game, *I've never,* sealed my fate as a total loser?

"I was a bit worried you got sick because of all the stress. You know."

He worried about me? No way. "Nope. I'm okay. I mean, it has been stressful, but it must have just been something I ate or drank."

"Hmpf. Well, you didn't miss much yesterday," he volunteered. "We saw the embassies and mansion houses, but once you see one big, stuffy house, you've seen them all. Rock Creek Park was pretty cool, but we couldn't wander, so where's the fun in that? A mass of fifty people moving through a forest kinda defeats its purpose, if you ask me." He touched my arm for emphasis, burning me with his fingertips.

"Yeah," I said.

I would've liked to have seen the mansions, though. It wouldn't have been an everyday thing for me. I grew up without luxury and seeing luxury often motivated me to work hard to escape my inadequate circumstances.

Kira stood at the opposite side of the table glaring at me. After I looked at her, she turned abruptly and sat at another table.

Alex was eating when I looked back at him, so I picked at my food. I could feel the smile on my face in my toes. Alex and I had a conversation.

"Christy, I'll fill you in on what we did yesterday." Rick, taking advantage of the break in our conversation, started to give me the play by play account of what took place the day before.

His version gave a much more detailed account than Alex's. I was a little distracted, wishing it was Alex who talked to me. I did manage to answer Rick at mostly the right times and even asked a few questions. Since he sat only inches from me, I couldn't ignore him or avoid him. I know it sounds mean, I wasn't trying to be, but I just wanted a few moments to revel in the memory of talking to Alex—one I thought I might never have again.

Rick didn't get a chance to finish telling me about everything that had happened, though. Mrs. J. showed up and told us what we could expect for the rest of the day. She said something about a reflecting pool and churches, and while she yammered, I took one last look at Alex and drifted off into la la land. Next thing I knew, two hands, almost simultaneously, touched my shoulders, bringing me back to reality. I looked to my left, it was Alex. My insides buzzed.

"Hey, time to go."

"'Kay," I said, my stomach doing flip flops. His hand lifted off my shoulder, but I willed the pressure to stay there. I noticed he glanced over my head as Rick tapped my right shoulder.

"Let me take your plate," he said—always the gentleman.

"Okay," I said, giving him a quick smile and then turning to look at Alex. He wasn't there. I sighed, looking at the table. When I looked up again, I saw two pairs of eyes staring at me from across the room. The fun flip flops in my stomach turned to agonizing twisting and contracting in an instant. Jeremy and Nathan smiled at me two tables away, but I couldn't smile back. The ballroom scene flashed across my mind.

All of the earlier excitement drained out of me and I felt a weight press down on me. It was difficult to get out of my seat, but Rick was back, waiting, when I managed it. I glanced back at the two FBI agents. They still watched me. Jeremy's grin was so inviting, but I could only return half a smile. Kira, a few feet away, glowered. I shook my head in disbelief. She needed to get a life. Couldn't she see it was Alex that interested me?

The reflecting pool, by the Lincoln Memorial, started our Sunday off right. I couldn't remember a time that I had missed church two weeks in a row. I had missed the first, last Sunday flying to D.C., and then there was today. Come to think of it, I would be missing next Sunday flying back. Mrs. J. did say we would be touring churches, maybe that would take away the odd feeling I had.

Even though church bored me sometimes, I loved the way it made me feel. It wasn't a concrete feeling, in the sense of knowing something from a book, but a feeling that someone was there, from the great beyond, cheering for me. I stole away from the group and found a relatively open spot between two of the trees lining the walkway that flanked the memorial, to sit and think.

Some of our group climbed into the water of the reflecting pool, splashing and playing around. When a guard came and shooed them away, I smiled. I sat on the ground and looked at the calm water.

My mind drifted, and I thought rationally about things that only a week ago wouldn't have crossed my mind.

Why did things like what happened in the ballroom, happen? Why would God allow it? In the far reaches of my mind, I could hear my youth leaders saying, "We all have our agency, and God will never force good upon anyone. Just think if all your choices were taken from you. What kind of an existence would that be?"

Do we have to experience the bad to understand the good? Sometimes it seemed it would all be easier if we didn't have choices—or at least to let someone make the hard ones for me. But, I guess that was someone else's plan, and I certainly didn't want someone telling me what to do every second of my life, even if that meant making mistakes on the way.

But, how could the robed men have been so cold-hearted, and how could Senator Randolph live with himself? What could be so important to these men that they could be so violent, so evil? Was this reality outside my box at home? We all came from the same heaven, so why don't we all just want to be good? I guess it all comes down to who you choose to follow. Happiness follows God and misery follows the devil. While thought provoking, it scared me to think about good and evil in this way.

I felt someone pass behind me, so close that I thought I felt his jeans brush my back, chilling me. I turned to see the legs of a young man walking away from me at a leisurely pace back to the long walkway. My heart drummed unevenly and I froze, every part of my body ice, looking after the young man. What a strange reaction.

I watched him saunter past a bunch of people, take a quick look back and then disappear behind some trees on the other side of the walkway. Was that Iceman? I tried to look away, but couldn't. The muscles in my neck began to ache from being stuck in one position and I wanted to scream out in pain. My neck finally spasmed, sending a chain reaction through my whole body that melted my frozen parts. I could move again.

I jumped to my feet, grabbed the bag Marybeth had loaned me and looked for my group. Some had found their way back into the reflecting pool while others stood bunched in various groups talking. I searched for Rick, needing some comfort, wanting to feel safe. Instead, I found Alex. My heart did flip-flops.

He stood away from everyone else, about ten trees down. Immediately drawn to him, I'd walked more than half way there before I noticed Alex had turned and looked at me. What would I say once I reached him? I looked at my feet. He wasn't Rick. Could he be comforting? I must have looked awfully silly, stopped in mid-stride. I looked back at Alex, who grinned at me. My heart beat wildly and

I had to take a deep breath just to get the courage to go further.

"What are you doing?" he called out, laughing and coming toward me. "You should have seen yourself. It was like someone just lassoed you, stopping you in your tracks."

I pulled my back leg forward so that I didn't look quite so odd. "I just remembered something and …." I trailed off, not knowing how to finish.

"Must've been pretty important. What was it?" He smiled at me, quick and sweet, as he reached me.

"I guess it wasn't *that* important," I hedged, awestruck by his looks.

"What were you doing over there all by yourself?" he asked, nodding toward the place I'd been sitting.

Had he been watching me? "I could ask you the same thing, couldn't I?" Where did that come from? I felt my face flush.

He nodded. "You've got me there…I just wanted some time to myself." He looked at me expectantly, waiting for me to give my excuse.

"Me too," I said. "Things can get a little stifling around here sometimes." My face burned, and I felt the tingle in my arm again where he'd touched me that morning. I unconsciously scanned the area to see if I could figure out who from the FBI was watching. Perhaps that would make me feel safe.

"Looking for something?" he asked.

"Uh," I said, trying to figure out a way not to lie. "No, sorry, I'm…"

"Hey," he said in a low voice. "Do you still have bad dreams about what you saw?"

My shock must have been apparent on my face, because his eyes went a little bigger and he said, "I mean, I do. I can't seem to get it off my mind, and I only saw it after the fact. I can't imagine what it must be like for you, to have seen the whole thing happen."

Could someone hear what he was saying? With my breathing shallow and rapid, my mouth felt like sandpaper. I looked all around, trying to pick out possible bad guys.

"Christy, I'm sorry. I shouldn't have brought it up." With gentle, but firm hands, he grabbed my wrists and moved in closer. A mix of emotions pulsed through me, a thrill of excitement from his touch and a horrible anguish that someone listened to us. His gaze probed, with an amazing intensity that I felt all through my body. I felt a radiating warmth spreading from his hands up my arms. I wanted to reach around him and pull him in tight, telling him everything, but a different kind of fear prevented it. I didn't know if I could trust him with my heart. Closing my eyes, despite desperately wanting to keep them locked on Alex's, I took a deep breath and held it for a few seconds, searching my brain for a solution.

"It's okay," I said, opening my eyes again. The force of his eyes tingled a spot right at the base of my neck. "I thought we'd decided not to discuss it ever again, is all. It's so creepy, that I hate thinking about it."

There, I'd said it and it was the truth. My heart began to really pound as I felt the warmth of his touch continue to spread.

"I'm sorry you've been having nightmares, though. I have too," I confided. I really did feel bad about it. It was my fault he had nightmares after all.

"I won't bring it up again," he said, his face apprehensive. "Sorry. One thing, though. Do you think the FBI believed the letter?"

My hands shook and his hold on my arms tightened.

"I'm sure of it," I said weakly, hardly hearing my own voice. If the terrorists were listening, we were sunk.

They now knew for sure I'd seen everything and that we'd told the FBI.

"You're probably right. I'm surprised the FBI hasn't contacted us about it, though." He stared at me, like he wanted more.

All I could do was stare back and nod.

"I really want those murderers to pay for what they did."

"Me too."

He looked in the direction of the rest of our group and said, "Looks like we're about to leave." He let go of me, his hands falling to his sides. I wondered if he knew how his touch affected me. Did *he* feel anything when he touched me?

I turned to follow the group when Alex called out to me.

"Hey, what's this?" He moved in front of me, holding a small piece of paper.

"I don't know. Where'd you find it?" I asked, reaching for it.

He turned it toward me, grinning, "It fell out of your bag."

It was a photo of the eight of us, eating breakfast. I gasped, my breath suspended. Iceman. He hadn't only brushed up against me, he had put that picture there.

"Who took this picture?" His eyes searched my face. I had no idea what to tell him. I just stared, unable to move. Could I tell him I thought Iceman had done it? My fears multiplied, and I didn't know if I could deal with them alone.

"Christy?"

I needed to slow my racing pulse, and it seemed I had no way out of the situation telling the truth. Could I lie? It would be protecting him. It would be for the "greater good" and surely it wouldn't be called a lie when I had such justification.

"Someone took it the other day," I stammered. "I wanted a picture of all of us together." Both statements were true, but misleading. A feeling of guilt swept over me and my shoulders dropped slightly. I had such conflicting emotions, I wanted to go hide somewhere. I had never outright lied, but now I couldn't say that anymore. I hadn't even been in a situation where I needed to lie before. The guilt wrapped around me, threatening to suffocate me.

"Hmm, it's a pretty good shot. Could I get a copy?" he asked.

"Sure," I squeaked, still feeling horrible.

Man, it was Sunday, and I had lied, on Sunday. I bet that was worse than lying on any other day.

We headed in the direction of our group, who walked toward the bus. I stayed as far away from the reflecting pool as I could, because I couldn't bear looking at myself at the moment. Frustration hit me. Why couldn't I tell him my suspicions? I didn't have to tell him about meeting with the FBI. I could leave that out. Alex walked beside me, without a sound. I looked at the picture and then turned it over. On the back was written,

We know who you are—all of you.

I panicked and my insides were so twisted up from the lie I had told and the fear I felt from Iceman's warning, that I reached out and grabbed Alex's arm.

"Look," I said. "I didn't really ask someone to take the picture. Sorry. I lied." Then I leaned in close to him and whispered, "I'm so afraid that someone is listening and—"

"Hold on. You lied? You didn't ask someone to take the picture?" He smiled like a Cheshire cat.

"Yes. I'm really sorry."

He chuckled, like I was ridiculous to be sorry.

"Listen," I said, trying to clue him in on the seriousness of the situation.

"I'm listening." He covered his mouth with his hand, staring at me, trying to keep a straight face.

"Iceman passed by me a few minutes ago, and I didn't realize it was him or that he'd put this picture there until you saw it. I mean I felt something touch me when a guy passed by, but I thought it was just his jeans rubbing against me. I think it is a warning of some sort. Here, look at this." I showed him the back of the picture.

His eyebrows drew together as he read. "I shouldn't have laughed. I didn't know. How did they know where we were?"

"Iceman knows where we're staying," I said. "I saw him outside the hotel the morning after the murder."

"What? Why didn't you tell me about Iceman being at our hotel sooner?"

"I never had the chance," I whispered.

"I don't get it. Why don't they just kill us if they know? Why would they send a warning like this? It's weird."

"I know. I wondered the same thing. They must have a reason to keep us around." I hoped beyond hope, our discussion hadn't given them what they needed to decide.

"Hey you two," Mrs. J. yelled. "Hurry up! We're waiting!"

Just before getting to the bus, Alex grabbed my arm and whispered, "Let's keep this between you and me for now, okay?"

"Okay," I said, before climbing on the bus.

I pocketed the picture, my heart thudding furiously and not because of the threat.

We had a secret now, just between the two of us.

118

CHAPTER ELEVEN

The Washington National Cathedral made us all feel like little ants once inside. The tour lasted about half an hour, and we learned all about its history. Patterned after the fourteenth century gothic style cathedrals in Europe, with its intricately carved wood and stone, and its detailed and vivid paintings, it tantalized the imagination. How they could build a place like this today let alone in the fourteenth century boggled the mind.

We went up to the observation gallery and looked out at downtown D.C. The beautiful view lifted me. It was so different from what I was used to, especially with the little shops inside it. The lovely took my breath away, but I couldn't find the peace I wanted so badly.

My thoughts kept turning to finding Jeremy. I had to tell him that the terrorists were not only watching us, but were warning me. Why not the others, too? They must know I'd talked to the FBI. But, if they knew, wouldn't I be dead? They must at least suspect. Otherwise, why would they be singling me out? Could there be a mole in the FBI, and no information was safe? Then again, maybe they knew because Alex and I told them all they needed to know at the memorial.

The Northeast section of town, where the National Shrine stood, was considered crime-ridden and dangerous, so I hurried inside and stayed close to the tour guide the whole time, hoping to avoid the possibility of witnessing any more crimes. I know, I know, I used to be all about excitement and change, but I wanted it to be the right kind of adventure, not like the ballroom.

The National Shrine, one of the world's largest churches, hosted a staggering one million visitors a year. Its stained glass windows sparkled beautifully in the light and the enormous building swallowed everything in its path.

I sat in a pew and waited while everyone roamed around the building. It felt nice when Marybeth sat next to me.

"Hey," she said.

"Hey," I answered.

"Ever since you know what, I don't like being alone."

"Me either."

We sat in silence for a while, with Marybeth fidgeting and looking at me until I couldn't stand the suspense any longer and said, "What is it Marybeth?"

"I'm not supposed to tell."

"Not supposed to tell?" My mind went straight for Kira. Had she said bad things about me and told Marybeth to keep her mouth shut? "You can tell me, it won't hurt my feelings."

"Well…" She stared at me intently.

I was getting more mad at Kira as each second passed, and I didn't even know if she had anything to do with the secret.

"Look, if it has to do with Kira, just know that—"

Marybeth interrupted me. "It doesn't have to do with Kira."

I stared at her. All I could do was wait. I desperately wanted to know the secret, but didn't want her to break a confidence.

"I've got to tell someone," she finally whispered. "I'm sure they wouldn't care if I talked to you."

My heart froze. They? I should've told her not to tell me, but I wondered if the terrorists had tricked Marybeth into talking. Then again, she wouldn't be here if they had. Right?

She leaned in close and whispered right into my ear, "The FBI took me to their office yesterday." Then she turned and stared at me, eyes wide.

I'm sure my eyes matched hers. Questions ran through my brain at top speed. She seemed fine, excited even, to have talked to them. How did she hold it together? I thought she would be a total wreck after talking to them; all the scary memories surfacing again. But here she was, telling me about it, like it was some juicy gossip. Maybe talking to whoever she had really did diffuse it all or had I misjudged her? Should I confide in her now? That was the real question.

I looked around, assessing the likelihood of a bug that let the terrorists hear us being in the Cathedral. I decided the probability was pretty low even though the FBI seemed to know our every move. She had broken the promise, not me. Surely, I could tell her. It would be wrong not to. It would be like lying to act surprised at her admission, right?

She bumped me with her arm. "Did you hear me? The FBI read the letter and wanted some more information from me, so they picked me up yesterday. It was so cool. The FBI has been watching us, protecting us, since they got the letter. I feel safer now."

"They took me in, too." I whispered, feeling lighter. I thought I would feel worse because I had broken my promise, but I guess the load of the secret was a heavier burden to bear than telling it.

"No way. When? How?" Her questions gushed out.

"Shhh! Remember, we aren't supposed to talk about it."

"Oh, yeah. Well, I just had to tell you, so you would know, and feel safe and all." She looked ashamed.

"It's okay. I was dying to tell someone, too. I was just too afraid to tell, though."

"I'm glad I told you." Her smile lit up her face.

"We can talk here, but remember, we shouldn't bring it up again. They could be listening." I smiled back.

"Right. But, they know who the bad guys are and they are going to get them. They have a lot of evidence against them."

"Good." I wondered if the terrorists were listening. If so, they had their two eye witnesses wrapped up and delivered. I swallowed hard, hoping they weren't.

I didn't know what to say after that, and we sat in silence, relieved to know that someone else knew. I decided it wouldn't be a good idea to tell her about Iceman and the picture. I wondered if any of the others had been taken to the FBI office too or if they only took Marybeth and me because we witnessed the actual beheading. Then I remembered Alex's question from earlier and wondered if he was trying to find out if they'd contacted me—because they had contacted him.

We hadn't sat long before we headed for the Spy Museum. Everyone was ready for some excitement after visiting the quiet churches. The two hour tour of the museum flew by. We then did this interactive spy operation, where we got to try some of the things that real spies have done. Spying was kinda cool with the right tools. It seemed exciting and made me wonder what the good guys and bad guys were using to disguise themselves and spy on us. But, if I were in the FBI, I would have had the terrorists in custody already. Why were they still out there?

"That was so cool," Rick said as we left the Museum.

"I loved it," Kira said. "What'd you think, Christy?"

She asked me? Wasn't she mad anymore? Maybe she was just playing nice for Rick.

"So much fun," I answered. "Best thing we've done yet."

She rolled her eyes at me. I'd gotten my answer.

Dinner satisfied my hunger, but my gut kept telling me I needed to find a way to tell Jeremy about the picture and seeing Iceman. I came to the conclusion, that it would be better to have them involved, especially if the bad guys were clued into the truth. So, I ate as fast as I could, in order to have time to write a quick note for the "college boys" before we went into the rec room.

I scribbled the note in my room about Iceman giving me the photograph. I folded the note around the picture and put it into a box of Whoppers I had in our room. I took about half of the candy out for myself and left the rest in the box, then I all but ran to the rec room. It was empty though, and I sat on the sofa by the TV and thought about all the ways to get the candy box and its important contents to Jeremy.

A little while later, Kira walked in with Rick, followed by Marybeth and Eugene. I loved having Marybeth back to herself again and having someone to confide in. She was a genuinely nice person, which, in my book, made her unfit for politics. I saw Rick scan the room and pause when he saw me. Kira was talking to him, and he kept nodding and taking small steps in my direction while Marybeth and Eugene played foosball.

Josh, Summer, and Alex came rushing in all of a sudden.

"We're going to play another game," Summer announced, breathing hard. Everyone watched her walk to the center of the room. We couldn't help it, she mesmerized us. "It's called Sardines. Who's played it before?"

Everyone except Eugene and myself raised their hands. Again, I stood with the idiots in the crowd.

"Good," she said, looking at all of us. "It's easy. I'm sure you'll catch on fast. This is how you play. One person is *it* and hides somewhere in the hotel. Everyone tries to find the person who is *it*. When you find him, you smash into him like you were packed in a sardine can and you stay that way until everyone else is smashed in. The last one to get there is *it* the next game. Everyone understand?"

She stood there shining, a large, expectant grin on her face. I had to resist the urge to clap. I had no idea where she came up with all these games. Maybe they were popular people games or maybe they were just games that took more than two or three people to play. I'd never had more than two to three friends to play with anyway.

"Oh," she added, "no hiding in the lobby, and we only have forty-five minutes to find whoever is *it*. It's 8:05 now, so at 8:50 the first round will be over. Home base will be my room. Let's go."

Her room? No. I had to be *here* when the FBI guys came. I might miss them if I left. I had to get them the message today. It couldn't wait.

"You comin'?" Rick asked, holding the door open for me.

I almost said *no*, but couldn't bring myself to do it. I clenched my fists and forced myself to say, "Yeah, I'm comin'."

"Great," he said. "Where were you after dinner, by the way? One minute you were eating and the next you were gone."

"I had to hurry upstairs to my room and write a letter before we came down here, so I ate really fast."

"Oh," he said, nodding his head with a curious look on his face. He probably wondered whom I was writing to, but I didn't offer. Kira stood there, just outside the door, glaring at me again.

I walked as fast as I could to Summer's room, so that I could get back to the rec room as soon as possible. Kira and Rick followed. We crowded into her single room, which, like Alex's, was bigger than Marybeth's and my double room, and it was nicer. The perks of the rich. Josh had volunteered to be the first person to be *it*. He ran off to hide, and Summer shut her door behind him. He only had four minutes.

Four minutes? That was a lifetime to me at that moment, and staring at the clock didn't make the time go faster. If anything, ten minutes must have passed before the clock showed three had passed. Was it working? I asked Eugene how long it had been.

"Three minutes and fifteen seconds," he replied.

I moved toward the door, hoping I could be the first one out of it.

"Time!" Summer yelled.

I scampered out of her room, clutching the Whopper box and heading straight for the rec room. Please, please, I pleaded, don't let Jeremy and Nathan be gone. I took a deep breath as I twisted and pushed on the door knob to the rec room. I looked around. No one was there. Maybe they hadn't come yet. I almost sat on the couch, when I thought I should probably see if Josh was hidden away somewhere in the room. I searched it on the fly and found myself alone. I plopped down on the sofa in front of the TV.

I sunk down into the soft couch; it felt like I was sitting on a feather bed. I tried to relax but couldn't keep my eyes from being stuck on the door. Seeing the door move a hair, and I sat upright. Rick peeked in.

"No one here, huh?" he said lamely, still holding onto the door.

"Nope. Just me."

"Well, I didn't mean no one, I meant—"

"I know what you meant," I interrupted. "It's okay."
Was it my imagination or did he seem out-of-sorts? He
was never like this.

Rick let the door swing shut and moved in my
direction. I half expected Kira to follow him in, but she
didn't. I started to stand up but then he sat beside me,
taking away my momentum, so I stayed seated. He was
touching me again. Could he like me? No one had ever
liked me. Is this how guys act when they like someone?
Was Kira right to be jealous?

His hands curled in his lap, and he fidgeted.
Awkward. I looked at him, then he looked at me. I looked
away and so did he. I wanted the silly, uncomfortable
game to end. I just didn't know how to end it. I didn't want
to hurt his feelings if he did like me, and I didn't want him
to think I thought he liked me when he didn't. What a
mess.

"Christy." He broke the miserable silence. He looked
vulnerable somehow.

"Yeah," I said, eager to move on.

"I was wondering—"

Whatever he wanted to say, I wasn't going to hear it ,
because two handsome college boys entered the room. Just
the guys I had hoped for and needed. The FBI. I heard the
Whoppers move around in their box and looked down to
see that my hands trembled, making the Whoppers jump.

"Where is everyone?" Nathan asked.

"Playing a game," I said. "Do you want to play?"

"Depends. What game?"

"It's called Sardines."

"Sardines?" Nathan snickered and looked at Jeremy.
They both looked at Rick and me and said, "OOOh."

Was there a joke I'd missed? I didn't get it. "Well?" I
finally said.

126

"Sure, we'll play," Nathan said, all smiles.

"Great! Have you played before?" I stood and walked toward them.

"Oh, yeah." Nathan said, his voice was funny, like he knew something I didn't. It bugged me.

"Great," I said, ignoring his tone, still heading in their direction. "Summer set the rules, of course." They both let out a small laugh. "No hiding in the lobby and each round ends at forty-five minutes."

"Forty-five minutes?" Nathan said, his mischievous smile broadened. "Wow, that's the longest I've ever heard a round going."

"Am I missing something?" I finally asked, looking up at them.

Neither one answered; they just smiled, shaking their heads back and forth.

I raised the Whopper box and looked at Jeremy with wide eyes, and then looked at the box of Whoppers. He looked at me and squinted slightly. I repeated my eye movements.

"Whoppers? I haven't had Whoppers in years," Jeremy said.

"Here, have some," I said. He held out his hand and I poured some in. "You too, Nathan?"

"Sure."

"Me too," Rick said.

I'd almost forgotten he was there because I was so focused on getting the box into Jeremy's hands. I gave Rick a few Whoppers, and I saw that Jeremy had finished his. He held out his hand for some more, and I handed him the box giving him "the look" once more.

"There's only a few left. You can have the rest," I said as calmly as possible. The fact was, my insides jumped up and down. I'd finally gotten the info to Jeremy! This spy stuff was fun.

"Guess we'd better go look for the others," Nathan suggested.

"Yeah," I said, feeling much better now.

I watched Jeremy shake the last few Whoppers into his hand and then shake the box as I walked through the door behind Nathan. Then I heard a clunk. What? Did he throw the box away? My head whipped around, and I looked at Jeremy. His hands were empty.

Oh, no! This was not happening! Hadn't he seen my signals? All that hard work for nothing. Maybe I should have been more obvious. I felt like I was walking in quicksand, but Jeremy gently pushed me forward.

Eugene walked toward us from the opposite end of the hall.

"No one in the rec room, huh?"

"Nope," Nathan said.

"Bummer," Eugene said. "Guess I'll keep looking. I've cleared all the floors below this one, so go up, guys."

He turned around and headed back to the stairs. We went for the elevator, Nathan pushing the up button on the wall. I felt Rick's arm against mine. My arm heated up. I forced myself not to look at him.

When the doors to the elevator opened, we all laughed. Alex pressed against Josh. Summer pushed up against both Josh and Alex and only after searching, did I see Marybeth squished between Josh and Alex. Nathan rammed himself against Alex, Jeremy piled on Nathan and Rick grabbed my arm and pulled me into the mix. Rick's arms surrounded me and his body pressed hard against mine. I could hardly breathe, but I sputtered out a laugh anyway. I wondered where Kira was and heard the doors close.

We all heard Summer's stifled voice, "Is everyone here?"

Someone yelled, "Eugene's not, he went up the stairs."

"Then he's it," Summer said. "Game over!"

With those words, the mass of arms and legs started to untangle itself. Rick hadn't loosened his body-hold on me, and I started to wonder if he would. He leaned his chin on my shoulder. Pressure came from behind me and like a bomb exploded, we were shoved against the closed doors. I pried myself loose, turning around, meeting Alex's gaze, which had traveled from my face to Rick's and back again. I turned my head and looked at Rick, who looked past me at Alex, a grin on his face. When I looked back at Alex, he'd turned and moved away.

I wanted to reach out and grab him, but, of course, I was too chicken. Crap! I didn't want Alex to think Rick and I were together. Twice now, it had looked that way. If I'd seen what he had, I'd think we were together, too. Ugh!

"Push the door open button," someone said.

Jeremy pushed it and everyone around me tumbled out and, laughing, headed for Summer's room once more. I was the last one out, but I wasn't laughing.

Mrs. J. came down the hall, obviously headed for the rec room. She stopped when she saw us flood out of the elevator.

"Tomorrow's a long day. You all need your rest. Heck, I need my rest. It's nine o'clock, so, head for bed, please." She didn't walk away like she usually did. She stood there in the hallway waiting for all of us to go back to our rooms. Jeremy and Nathan got back into the elevator. Marybeth and I went to my room and shut the door. While Marybeth sat on her bed, telling about how she had found Josh and Summer first and how they had been making-out in the elevator, I leaned against the door, willing Mrs. J. to leave our hallway quickly. I finally understood why Nathan and Jeremy thought playing sardines was so funny. It was a hook-up game. Duh! I closed my eyes, trying to hear the rest of the story while listening for clues that Mrs. J. was gone. I had to get that Whopper box from the trash.

I placed my ear against the door but heard no sounds, so I reached for the door knob and pushed lightly. "Just a minute, Marybeth," I said. Peeking out the open door, I could see no one. Whew! I pulled the door all the way open and walked out.

"Where are you going?" Marybeth asked.

"I forgot something in the rec room. I'll be right back."

I hurried down the hall as if my life depended on it and pulled the door open. I reached into the trash can. I stopped short when I realized that the can was empty. The box was gone.

CHAPTER TWELVE

I lay in bed, panicked. What had happened to the Whopper box? Did housekeeping take the garbage out? Did Jeremy go back and get it? We hadn't been gone that long, maybe ten minutes. Who else would have taken it? I had so many questions but no answers. Then it struck me. What if the murderers had found it? Was it possible? I suppose anything was possible. How could I have been so stupid? If the murderers had discovered my note and the pictures, they would for sure know I helped the FBI. Then again, maybe they already knew after yesterday. Being a spy wasn't as easy as I'd thought it would be. What's obvious to one, isn't always obvious to another.

I railed on myself most of the night until exhaustion finally got the better of me, and I slept.

"Christy, Christy?"

Marybeth's face was only inches from mine and it startled me. Panicked, I moved my head forward with a jerk and smacked my forehead into Marybeth's nose.

"Oweeee!"she yelled.

I felt dizzy and flopped back down again, rubbing my head gingerly. I tried to blink away the light that pierced my brain. Keeping my eyes tiny slits, I saw Marybeth head for the bathroom to stuff toilet paper against her nose. "I'm so sorry, Marybeth," I managed to say as I slid off the bed, swinging my legs to the floor with caution. When I stumbled toward her, she waved me away, but I kept on going.

"It's seven, Christy. I wanted to wake you up gently."

"I'm so sorry," I repeated, wishing I had the bloody nose and not her. The pressure behind my eyes told me a migraine was on its way. I crossed the floor to the closet and dug into my bag, pulled out my trusty pills and walked to the bathroom. Marybeth had the water on and was wiping blood off her face.

"Could I sneak in there, Marybeth? I need a drink pretty bad," I whispered.

She moved completely out of my way and I shoved the pills in my mouth and took a long drink. I left the water running for Marybeth and headed for my bed. With utmost care, I climbed in.

"Christy, didn't you hear me?" Marybeth said, sounding frustrated. "It's past seven. You won't have time for breakfast. We leave at seven-thirty today, remember?" She still held tissues to her nose.

I knew she was only looking out for me, but I wanted to slug her, to let her know how painful this migraine was. I didn't, of course.

I'll be there in time," I whispered, hoping she would take my cue and whisper, too.

"You're not getting sick again, are you?" she said at full volume, if not a little louder.

"No, no. I have this headache that I'm trying to fend off. I'll be there. Really." I'd have promised her just about anything if she would just leave me in peace at that moment. I couldn't even open my eyes to watch her leave. I could usually keep my migraines from getting unbearable. I just needed time to let my medication work. I pulled the covers over my head and tried to relax every muscle in my body, one by one. I just needed some time.

Without warning, I felt the covers slide over my head. Barely opening my eyes, I saw Kira and Marybeth standing over me, neither leaning close to my head—

probably afraid that I might pop up and slam into them-history repeating itself.

"Time to go," Kira said. "Where are her clothes?" she asked Marybeth.

Marybeth rushed to my closet and pulled out jeans and a T-shirt, then opened her closet to get something else.

"I don't know how I let you talk me into this," Kira said, irritation etched in her voice.

"Hurry, Christy. Get dressed." Marybeth's voice echoed in my head and the light seared my eyes—I tried hard to keep them closed.

"I-I just need some more t-time," I said, so quiet, I almost didn't hear myself.

"You don't have it," Kira said in a pretty mean way.

I didn't move. I couldn't. Then, I felt them stripping my PJ's from my body. I tried to pretend it wasn't happening, until someone pulled my T-shirt over my head and it felt like my head was being ground down to dust. I clamped my mouth shut. Kira yanked my arms through the shirt's sleeves as Marybeth slid my jeans on. Then, they sat me up.

"Look at her hair!" Marybeth said, panicked. "Get a brush and a pony, would ya, Kira?"

"I think she looks just fine," Kira said, chuckling.

"Oh brother! I'll get 'em. Hold her please!" Marybeth said, a bit too loud for my aching head.

"Let me do it," Kira said.

Brushing my hair felt like someone scrapping nails along my scalp. I wanted to die. I couldn't help but moan.

"Be more gentle, Kira," Marybeth said. "You're hurting her. Just pull up the front and sides, it's still pretty straight from yesterday. No ponytail." She spoke in a whisper, which I appreciated. "I've got make-up in my bag. We'll finish on the bus."

Marybeth brushed my teeth, forcing me to drink some water afterwards before they stood and wrapped my arms around their necks, lifting me up. My head throbbed and my stomach turned queasy. I had to keep telling myself that I would be okay, that I *was* okay.

"We forgot her shoes," Marybeth said.

They moved me back to the bed.

"I'll hold her up, you grab 'em," Kira said. "Hurry and put them on Marybeth. She's heavier than she looks."

"Okay, let's go," Marybeth said after slipping my shoes on.

They dragged me out of the room and down the hall. The ding of the elevator sent sharp pains through my skull, and I gasped. Marybeth and Kira held me tighter, dragging me into the elevator. They were kind enough to press their free hands against my ears when we got to the lobby, so that I barely heard the ding this time. As they shuttled me out into the lobby, I heard distant whispers and then someone pulled me out of Marybeth and Kira's hands and lifted me into their arms.

I didn't dare peek to see who was carrying me so effortlessly; the light would definitely bring on the puke. I hoped it was Alex. Could I be so lucky? Truthfully, though, all I really wanted was for the pain to go away. When they finally set me down on the bus bench, I focused again on each muscle, starting with my head and going all the way to my toes, willing them to relax. The jarring and pounding in my head slowed until I could barely feel anything anymore, the meds had finally kicked in. Even the jostling of the bus and getting make-up on my face didn't bother me.

The bus stopped. I could hear whispers that seemed far above me. I tried to make out the words, but they were too hushed. Once again, someone lifted me into their arms and carried me. As we left the bus, I could feel the brightness of the sun hit my closed eyes, and I pulled my hands up to shield them.

"Sorry 'bout that." I heard the faint whisper of whoever was carrying me. I couldn't think clearly enough yet to try and figure out who had spoken. With the meds just kicking in, my mind didn't work properly. We stopped moving and whoever held me gave me to someone else. Next thing I knew I was transferred once more, but whoever held me now, sat.

I dared a peek and saw Alex whispering to Josh. I clamped my eyes shut, then felt my face flush, hoping he wouldn't feel my slamming heart. While embarrassed to be in his arms, somewhat helpless, I couldn't help but feel excited that I was in *his* arms. For the first time in my life, I was truly grateful for inheriting my mother's slim build. He had carried me. The most beautiful boy in the world. I could live happily ever after now.

I closed my eyes. Slowly, but surely, my head began to feel even more normal. Sometimes I only got partial relief with my meds, other times it was like I'd never had a headache. The worst was when they had no effect at all or I was so loopy, I couldn't do anything.

"Christy," Alex said.

Even though I didn't want to open my eyes, afraid I would have to get out of his arms, I looked up at him with one eye, half-closed. I tried to speak, but my mouth wouldn't move. Maybe I was more loopy than I thought.

"How're you feeling?" Only inches from my face, he talked in a whisper. I felt a thrill go through me. He smelled so good. He made me feel alive. "Do you think you can stand? We're about to go into the Capitol, and I don't think they'll let me carry you in."

Both of my eyes locked onto his. I couldn't help it. "Christy?"

"Yeah, I think so," I said, pulling myself together.

"Migraine, huh?" he said. "My mom gets 'em pretty bad. You're lucky your meds worked."

"They don't always," I said. It would have been a long day if they hadn't.

He sat me up on his lap. My heart pounded so fast and hard, I was afraid he could feel it. It felt weird to look at him now, our faces so close together, so I looked away, afraid it would turn out to be a dream. Alex sat on a bench and Josh sat next to him. Summer stood next to Josh. A bunch of kids stood in a line, not far from us, that led to the Capitol building. I could see our group far ahead, almost ready to go into the building. I could make out Rick near the front of the line, waving for us to come.

"We're going to have to hurry," Summer said, her eyes piercing mine.

"Ready?" Alex asked.

"Ready," I said, even though I wasn't. I didn't want him to let me go.

My legs gave a little when I tried to stand, so Alex put his arm around me and helped me walk. I wouldn't have to let him go just yet. We met up with our group right before going through the metal detectors. We were herded into a room where we separated to meet the pages we'd be working with in the Capitol building.

Mine was Jackson Knight. His angular face and body emphasized his small frame and the short tuft of black hair on his head made him look cartoonish. Although nice, he talked a mile a minute and ran around just as fast. Time flashed by. We ran from here to there, made copies, got signatures, and even picked up lunch for some people. Between the meds and his speed, it was all a blur.

Happy to get to the cafeteria at one o'clock for lunch, I looked for anyone in our group. Men in suits filled most tables and I could only see a few kids from our larger group of fifty sprinkled about. Jackson talked on his cell even while he ate. When I finished, he still talked, so I didn't feel bad resting my head on the table for a quick nap.

When I woke up, only a few people sat scattered here and there. I squeezed my eyes shut and opened them again, trying to get my bearings. Where was I anyway? As it all came back to me, I looked for a clock. Four o'clock? No way. Why didn't Jackson wake me up? I rubbed my eyes and then found a note on the table in front of me.

It read,

Call me at 345-375-7869 when you wake up. I'll come and get you. You can't leave the cafeteria without me.

Call him? How? I didn't have a phone. Two men sat together at a table not far from me. Did I dare ask them? At least with them, I would get twice the chance to use a phone. I took a deep breath and walked toward them, praying they would be nice and help me.

"Excuse me," I said. "Do either of you have a cell phone I could borrow? I seem to have lost my page."

The guy on the right with the big red nose and glasses, grinned at me, while the guy on the left openly laughed.

They both reached for their phones and held them out for me to use. I took the phone from the guy on the left. I didn't want to get sick. I dialed the number, but he didn't answer. I left a message.

"Hey Jackson, it's Christy. Sorry I fell asleep on you. I'm awake now. Could you come and get me?" Then I hung up, handed the phone back, and walked to my table.

While walking back, I noticed a man by a far wall hurry behind a pillar. I could have sworn it was that mean FBI guy that scowled at me while I was in the FBI building. I felt a chill go down my neck, but then the thought occurred to me that he was probably there to protect me.

I waited and I waited. Jackson didn't come and get me until five. I had read every piece of literature in the place, which included the ingredients on all the packaged items in the cafeteria. I had time to think about Alex and how unbelievable it was that I kept my cool being so close to him for so long. People filed in for dinner or a snack or something and the room got noisy again, nothing like lunch, but still crazy.

"Man, you must've been pretty tired," he said, when he arrived.

"Guess so," I said. "I'm really sorry."

"No big deal. You'll never be a page anyway. I can tell just by looking at you."

"Really? What gave me away?"

"Maybe it was how hard of a time you had keeping up with me today."

I laughed. "You're just too fast. It was quite amazing watching you work. It was like you could be in two places at once." I didn't mention being on drugs.

Now he laughed. "I've got to get you over to the question and answer session. We're a bit late. By the way, what happened today, didn't happen. I could get in a lot of trouble, and I'm sure it wouldn't look very good for you either."

"I won't say anything."

"Good."

The question and answer session was held in the room where we met our pages. Boring. Squished in the back, I could hardly hear. Other groups, not staying in our hotel, were in the room too, and I couldn't see anyone from my mini group. I just leaned on the back wall and waited.

After it ended, I stood in the lobby area by the metal detectors waiting for people from our group to come out of the session. I saw Kira first. She had attached herself to Rick. I moved back a bit further, hoping they wouldn't see me. I wanted to find Alex and avoid getting trapped by anyone else. I couldn't see him in the mass of people. I sort of hid behind a pillar and peeked out. Then I heard Rick's voice on the other side of the pillar.

"Look, Kira," Rick said, "I do think you're fun and all, but I'm not interested. I thought we agreed we'd just be friends. Why do you keep pushing this? Besides, isn't it Alex you really like? You're all over him every chance you get."

"I like you, too," she said. "And I guess I still hoped we could be more."

"We won't be."

My heart thudded. I shouldn't eavesdrop, but for some reason I did. I couldn't believe what I heard. Kira was so forward. I would never be that way. She was begging him to like her.

"What about friends with benefits while we're here?"

"I'm not into that, Kira. . .Hey Eugene."

"Hey," Eugene said. "Amazing! They are so organized and efficient. Fascinating, really."

I spotted Alex coming out of the room with the last of the group. He, Summer and Josh were talking to a big group of kids and were very excited about something, but I couldn't hear what they were saying. They high-fived each other and headed for the exit doors. I waited a few minutes and then looked around the pillar, Kira and Rick were gone. Last to climb on the bus, I had to sit in the only seat left, next to Eugene. Kira sat next to Rick and talked away. Wow. Persistent. I would've been hiding in shame if I'd been her, which I never would have been in the first place.

Eugene told me all about his "interesting" day and I listened. He was so easy to please. I decided I should be easier to please. I would be a better person if I were. We headed to Georgetown for dinner.

Cafés, restaurants, and bars lined M-Street and Georgetown teemed with young college kids getting a bite to eat or escaping school work. The air was filled with excitement and happiness, and I decided I'd run with the spark in the air and let it consume me. I would be happy tonight. Alex had carried me. It would be a good day.

Long tables lined the restaurant for our large group. Mrs. J. motioned for us to sit at the far table. Rick sat on one side of me and Marybeth sat on the other. I looked around for Alex, and I saw him see me look at him, but didn't stop looking. He walked around the table and was going to sit right across from me, but Mrs. J. sat down first, so he had to sit next to her, making him kiddy-corner from me. I looked down at the table and laughed to myself.

No one could wait to tell about their hilarious experiences with their pages. I didn't think my sleeping experience qualified. Eugene was the only one who found being a page a "fascinating job". Everyone else talked about how relieved they were that they would never have to be a page. Their parents had influence and they would start their careers at a considerably higher level. They did, however, like having first-hand knowledge of what exactly a page did. Maybe so they'd know how to work 'em to death.

The restaurant became very crowded and loud by the time our food arrived. I inhaled my chicken parmesan, my own breadsticks and everyone else's breadsticks. I was amazed at Kira's ability to monopolize Rick at dinner, even after hearing what Rick had to say to her. I hardly spoke to him at all. Marybeth leaned into me at one point and whispered, "Guess what?"

"What?"

"Are you ready to die?"

"Huh?"

"When we walked out of the elevator at the hotel, dragging you along—"

"Yeah."

"Alex was waiting, just inside the lobby. When he saw us supporting you, he hurried over and insisted on carrying you. Insisted, Christy." Her eyes bugged out of her head.

I glanced at Alex. He talked to Josh, who sat next to him. I had crazy butterflies in my stomach. Could he really like me, or was he just being nice when he carried me to the bus? Thinking about it tied my stomach in knots. No one ever liked me, especially not someone like Alex, beautiful Alex. My history had taught me that thoughts like these only led me to pain.

The waitress brought around a dessert platter for all of us to check out. I told Marybeth I'd take ten crème brulees, and we laughed.

"Just remember," Mrs. J. said so all could hear, "dessert is extra. You pay for it yourself."

Crap. Money. I didn't have any. No one had brought my wallet. I'd have to sit this one out. I quietly told the waitress I would pass. I wasn't going to let it get me down. I had told myself I would enjoy the evening, so I would; Alex was nearby; there wouldn't be a Whopper box, icy-blue eyes or girls from school to bully me. Not tonight. There would only be laughing and fun the rest of the evening. I could be in control of myself— rested, well fed and without any fears. For some reason, I felt a confidence I'd never felt before.

I watched as everyone else got amazing desserts: chocolate molten lava cakes, cheesecakes, tortes and soufflés. I saw Alex get his, a crème brulee with blueberries. Heavenly. I watched him take the first bite out of the corner of my eye and imagined I had the brulee in front of me. Alex peeked sideways at me, too. My heart stopped, and there was no question of me looking away.

Eugene talked incessantly to Mrs. J. and Marybeth, keeping their attention away from Alex and me. Josh and Summer picked at each other's desserts. It almost felt like Alex and I were alone.

He took a spoonful of his dessert and brought it slowly up to his mouth. I watched his every movement out of the corner of my eye. Then he stopped and moved the spoon toward me. I pretended not to be aware of it. He moved it around in circles and up and down until I let a laugh slip and looked at him full on.

His too-perfect face pulled me in and made me weak all over. He pushed the spoon further in my direction, and I couldn't help but move toward it. He had to partially stand to get it to reach me. I didn't watch the spoon, I just watched him and he watched me. Somehow that spoon hit its mark and the creamy sweetness slid into my mouth.

He smiled a fun smile, and I wished I knew what he was thinking. He pushed the dish in front of me and held out the spoon for me to take.

I shook my head, but he nodded his. I couldn't help it. I gave in. It wasn't difficult. I took a few bites, enjoying each burst of flavor; and then I really went crazy and scooped some up and held it out for him to take.

I didn't do things like this—especially with boys. Would I be able to live with myself tomorrow? Was I being too forward? It felt great, though, and I'd promised myself not to listen to the little voice of self-doubt that kept me from really enjoying life. At least for tonight. Could something really happen between us?

"It's seven-thirty," Mrs. J. said, "You have until eight-thirty to be back on the bus. Don't be late."

I looked around and saw that we were only one of two groups from our tour that were still there. The other chaperones must have let their kids go already.

"Stay in your group of eight," Mrs. J. added.

I looked back at Alex, but he was already walking out of the restaurant. Shoot. I finally get some real time with Alex and Mrs. J. puts a quick end to it. Outside, the guys started chasing each other down the sidewalk toward Georgetown University. I walked with Marybeth and Kira, taking in all the different smells and sounds around me while they chatted. The sidewalks were alive with all kinds of people and it was fun to weave through them, not caring what anyone thought.

We caught up with the guys at an entrance to Georgetown University. I looked around. Not wanting to give into my fear, I started humming songs from my children's classes at church; looking at all the stars, trying to wipe Iceman's stare from my mind, when suddenly I realized I stood alone. Clouds moved in and hid the stars. It got dark.

Hundreds of newly leafing trees cast eerie shadows in all directions. I felt a drop of cold sweat creep down my spine. Standing alone made it hard to ignore the cold. I took a deep breath and tried not to become frantic. Where had everyone gone so quickly? My legs felt like rubber, so I just stayed still. I didn't want to worry, but I couldn't help it. I wasn't in control after all. Things controlled me. Had the terrorists taken them and were about to take me? My insides felt like jelly.

To my left, I thought I saw movement and took a sharp breath in. I wanted to call out, but my throat was too dry. I couldn't shake the feeling that someone watched me. Then, over my shoulder, I saw Josh and Summer. They sat together, partially hidden behind a big tree making-out. From where I stood, I could just tell who it was. I had to chuckle softly after taking a deep breath. I hated that I'd become so paranoid, afraid to be alone, and raised my head to look at the stars again.

A breeze flitted past as a hand grabbed mine. I screamed out, blood pumping through my veins. Rick bent over laughing and said, "Strung a little tight?"

Without a thought, I drew my eyebrows together and said, "Rick! You scared the crap out of me."

"Sorry, I didn't mean to." He frowned. My heart still thundered. "I just wanted to show you something." He beamed now, unable to hide his excitement. He put on a pouty face, and reached for my other hand and said, "Will you come with me? I really didn't mean to scare you." He breathed hard, smiling again.

I snorted, flicked my head to the side and said, "Okay." His warm hands clasped mine tight, sending a thrill through me. We walked away from Josh and Summer, and my heart skipped a beat. I wasn't the only one nervous. Rick's hand was sweaty, and I wanted to wipe my own.

"Close your eyes," he said, letting go of one of my hands.

"Why? It's dark," I said.

"I know, but you can still see. Just close 'em."

I did and wondered if I'd done the right thing. He pulled me forward, and I could hear a rushing sound in front of us that got louder and louder, drowning out the sound of my shuffling feet. I wanted to peek, but closed my eyes tighter to avoid the temptation.

"Almost there," he said into my ear.

We hadn't gone very far when I felt a light mist hit my face and arms.

"Okay, open your eyes," he whispered.

We stood right next to a large fountain, the water tumbling with such force that it created a halo of mist illuminated by the lights shining up from under the water.

"Wow," I said. "This is breathtaking."

"I thought so too, and I wanted to show it to you."

He stood close behind me. I could feel his breath on the back of my neck as he gently grabbed my hands in his and drew them up in front of me, wrapping his arms around me into a warm and solid hug. He brought his head down so that his chin rested on my shoulder and his cheek pressed against mine. Something fluttered low in my stomach. We watched the water rush in silence, the flutter turning to a warmth that spread through my body. I'd never been hugged like that before.

My heart not only pounded, it crashed, over and over into my ribcage. One part of me wanted to push him away, but it felt so *good* to have someone hold me. Even at home, I was almost never hugged. People just didn't notice me because I always did what I was supposed to. I felt safe and secure with his arms wrapped around me. All the stiffness in my body disappeared and I let my back press snuggly against his chest. The smell of his cologne mixed with the mist in the air settled lightly over me. It felt so right to have him hold me.

"Moments like this are rare," he said.

"They are," I said, not realizing how he might take it.

After a long time, he brought my arms to my sides in a slow, even movement and let go of them for a few seconds as he moved around to face me. Then he took my hands back into his and drew me close.

It seemed my heart would soon crack my ribs, and I almost looked away from his intense gaze when he spoke.

"I really like you, Christy. I was hoping we could maybe hang out the rest of this trip and see where things go." He waited, his eyes intent on mine.

My mind raced, and I couldn't think of anything to say. I hadn't expected this. Especially after over-hearing his conversation with Kira. The pause was a bit uncomfortable, but his eyes never left mine.

"You knew I liked you, didn't you?"

"No." I said in a small whisper. I scrunched up my face in embarrassment, not knowing whether to be happy or sad.

He laughed and stepped back to look up to the darkened sky.

"What about Kira?" I asked, grasping for straws.

"What about her?" he asked.

"She really likes you."

"She only likes me when there isn't a better offer on the table. She smothers me."

I was shocked. I hadn't heard him say anything bad about anyone and he never showed any dislike when around everyone else. He must have seen the surprise on my face because he added, "She's a nice girl, don't get me wrong. I wouldn't want her to think I didn't like her as a friend, I do. I'm just not interested in her romantically."

There, he had said it. *Romantically.* He thought of me romantically. No way. I tingled all over. Someone, no not just someone: A truly hot boy liked me. ME! My chest burst into flames. Suddenly, I wanted to liked him. Did I? I didn't think so, but what *was* I feeling? It felt great. Less than an hour ago, he was nothing more than a great friend. I'd been attracted to Alex all along. Why was I feeling this way about Rick now? He was such a good guy, always doing the right things at the right time and saying the right things, too. Could I like him? Should I like him? I looked into the spray of the fountain, and he moved his head in front of mine and smiled sheepishly.

"Any other objections?" he asked, grinning now.

"I-I don't know. I'm not supposed to date until I'm sixteen," I said, feeling lame.

Where had that come from? That quiet voice in my head talked to me at the most inopportune moments.

He just stared at me, his hands gently moving up and down my arms. It tickled and felt warm. He tilted his head to the side. I couldn't get over the fact that a guy was touching me. I didn't want it to stop.

"Okay. We won't date until you're sixteen, which is...." he prompted.

"In May," I said.

"May? That's only a month down the road. Why sixteen?"

"I don't know, it's just when my parents allow me to date."

"We'll just hang out then."

Was hanging out dating? I wasn't sure. This all felt so good. No, great. I couldn't think straight. He moved in close, and I noticed again how good he smelled. Spicy. I wanted to move in closer to him, but my stomach clenched and then filled with butterflies—so full, in fact, that I thought it might burst, but it felt amazing all the same.

He was cute, just like I'd told Kira. I'd also told her I wasn't interested in him, which I wasn't at the time. Was I now, or was I just responding to him liking me? Did it matter? I mean, *a guy liked me.* Shouldn't I take advantage of that fact? I might never get this chance again.

He pulled in closer, and I let out a nervous laugh pulling back slightly. Then our eyes locked, and he got closer and closer until I had to close my eyes. His lips touched mine, warm and soft, and much to my surprise, I kissed him back.

That voice in my head screamed out, "Whaaat are you doing?"

When I pulled back, Rick's eyes were still closed, I turned and panicked, and ran away.

"Christy!" I heard him call. I kept running, back to where he'd found me, back to where Josh and Summer were, but they weren't there anymore. I ran toward M-Street and found them, standing under a street light, talking, surrounded by the rest of our group.

I could hear footsteps behind me, and so I walked as fast as I could to the safety of the group. I couldn't face Rick right now. What had I done?

I bent over, trying to catch my breath. Alex stood there, and he looked at me and then past me. Rick slowed to a walk before he joined us. His eyes were set on me, questioning. Alex's eyes narrowed as he watched.

Please, I thought, looking at Alex, please don't let Alex think I like Rick. Yet at the same time, the softness of Rick's kiss lingered on my lips, the pleasure of it surrounding me, urging me to turn to him and gather him in my arms and accept him.

I pulled myself together and using Kira's trick, I wedged between her and Marybeth the whole way to the bus, locking my arms through theirs. I made sure I sat by the window and that Marybeth sat next to me, on the aisle. I was safe for the moment, left to feel guilty for my thoughts and actions. My parents would die if they knew.

"What's up Christy?" Marybeth asked. "You look like you've seen a ghost."

"I kinda feel that way," I whispered.

"Why? What happened?"

I debated whether or not I should tell Marybeth. Could I trust her not to tell anyone—including Kira? I had trusted her in the church. Maybe I could trust her now.

"Rick just kissed me." I let the words burst out of my mouth in a small whisper. I left out the part about me kissing him.

"What?" She screamed it so loud that I cupped my hand over her mouth and immediately regretted my decision to tell her.

"Shhh! You can't tell a soul. Swear to me Marybeth." I looked around to find Kira. She sat several seats behind us, with Alex.

Marybeth grinned and looked at me wide-eyed.

"Swear, Marybeth!"

"I swear! Now tell me all about it. I knew he liked you. Kira will just freak out."

"No, she won't freak out, because she'll never know, now will she?"

"Okay, no. I just can't believe it. Tell me everything!"

I told her a shortened version and left out all feelings. I felt weird talking about them to her for some reason.

"Unbelievable, Christy. Unbelievable. You're so lucky."

I felt exposed and stupid and wished I hadn't told her. For some reason, even the Whopper box dug itself out of the corner of my mind, and started harassing me too.

"You idiot," it said. "You should have been more obvious. No one could've known what you were hinting at with your eyes. Even a trained FBI agent had no clue what you meant."

The beating continued and I suffered once again for all my mistakes of this week. By the time the bus reached our hotel, which was only about fifteen minutes away, I was emotionally stretched, like a bug splattered on a windshield.

I dragged myself off the bus and into the lobby, thinking about the possible consequences of telling Marybeth about the kiss, when I was accosted by a conservation group handing out re-usable water bottles and encouraging everyone not to buy bottled water. I had lost

Marybeth. She said she wouldn't tell, I guess I'd just have to believe her. I pushed my way through, trying to make the first elevator ride, and an equally pushy conservationist put a bottle into my hand and said, "Use this tonight and you'll feel great in the morning."

I took the bottle, giving him a pursed smile and got into the elevator with others from our tour group.

When I got to my room, I threw off my clothes, brushed my teeth and climbed into bed. Reaching up to turn my lamp off, I hit the stupid water bottle, knocking it to the floor. I grunted and turned the light out. I was holding back the tears when I started thinking, "What if Marybeth doesn't see your water bottle lying on the floor and trips over it, and breaks her neck?" I turned the lamp back on. "You better leave me alone after this," I shouted into thin air.

I snatched the bottle from the floor and noticed some paper in it. I shook it out of anger—to teach it a lesson somehow. I thought it was probably activist literature, until I saw the initials C.H. handwritten on one corner.

I unscrewed the cap as fast as I could and turned the bottle upside down. What had that activist said? "Use this tonight and you'll feel great in the morning." My hands were shaking so badly, that I almost couldn't unfold the note. It read,

Got it.
Relax.
You're safe.
11:00

I slept well.

CHAPTER THIRTEEN

Ping, five a.m. My internal alarm clock seemed to be working again. Back home, I could never sleep past five no matter what time I went to bed the night before. Sometimes it really irritated me, but most of the time, I loved the peace and quiet of my mornings. I got more done before breakfast than most people did before dinner.

I crept into the shower, trying not to disturb Marybeth. Completely ready for the day by six-thirty, I climbed out on our balcony, but was pushed back in by the rain. Uggh. Rain. I went to the bathroom and looked at my once perfectly straight hair and saw a frizzy mess. I pulled it up into a pony, all I could do on a rainy day. Marybeth would have to be okay with it today. My hair was hopeless.

I stared at myself, remembering Rick's kiss. I had kissed someone before I was sixteen and I wasn't even dating him, not that it really mattered if we were dating or not, but I had always wanted to please my parents and do what I should. I shivered, remembering how the kiss had tickled every inch of my body. They would never approve and a large part of me wanted to take it back, but I knew I couldn't. Another part of me wanted to go back and kiss him again instead of running away. Really, I had failed myself by kissing Rick. I wanted to be better than this and now I couldn't say, "Sweet sixteen and never been kissed." Worse than that, I'd loved it. Who was I becoming? Summer? The thought made me shudder. I needed to figure out what I wanted, what I believed.

I couldn't help but think about how good his lips had felt pressed on mine. Guilt swept over me again, making it seem like a dark, ugly thing I'd done. It had been so exciting and felt great, so why did I have to feel so bad?

The thought of Josh and Summer making out at Georgetown University popped into my mind. They certainly weren't bothered by it. Why? Why were they so different from me? Was the guilt I felt a result of my own beliefs or my parents'? It would be nice to talk to someone about it. I looked over at Marybeth, wondering if I could talk to her about it. Would she understand?

"Marybeth," I said quietly. "It's time to get up." Lying on my bed, I waited patiently for her to get ready, finding it hard not to talk about Rick. I couldn't hold it in any longer and I finally blurted out, "I shouldn't have kissed Rick."

She stopped straightening her hair and said, "Why not? He's aaaamazing!"

"Yeah, but I've just always had this idea that I would be at least sixteen before I kissed anyone. You know, sweet –sixteen-and-never-been-kissed?"

"That's just old fashioned, Christy. No one waits until they're sixteen anymore. You shouldn't worry about it." She finished straightening her hair and held it out toward me. "Get over here. No ponytails allowed."

"It will go crazy frizzy in ten seconds."

"No ponytails allowed," she insisted.

I shuffled my feet as I walked toward her and said, "My parents are really old-fashioned, though, and won't understand." I didn't understand.

"Why would you have to tell them?" Each strand of hair she straightened glistened in the light.

"I don't know. I guess I think they expected me to wait, and I can't believe I let them down. They should know I didn't follow their counsel."

"Parents don't always know what is best for us. You did what was right for you."

"Did I?" She finished straightening my hair and grabbed a spray bottle.

"You make me laugh. You over-analyze everything. The kiss happened. You can't take it back and it was wonderful. Enjoy the moment, girl." She sprayed a mist of whatever was in the spray bottle all over my hair.

That was the real problem. I couldn't take it back. I would never be virgin lips again. I felt a deep chill in my heart, but only for a second. My perfectly straight hair shined. I wished I felt that way inside.

"For once in your life, have fun. Pure and total fun—with no worries."

"I'll try," I said, but felt like it would be impossible. "It's still our secret, right?"

"Right. That spray should hold any frizz at bay."

I stuffed a pony in my pocket just in case. We walked to breakfast together, a knot sitting in my stomach.

When we walked into the breakfast room, I saw Kira chatting with Rick as she ate. Rick didn't look like himself. His short brown hair looked mussed up, like he hadn't bothered to do it today. His almost permanent smile, was nowhere in sight and he looked tired, his back slumped slightly over.

Marybeth and I had timed it just right. There weren't any seats left at our usual table. I dared a glance at Alex, wishing he hadn't sat at the same table as Rick, and walked past to another table. I felt bad, and I knew I would have to face Rick sooner or later, but at the moment, I wanted it to be later.

I scarfed down my food without tasting a thing and dragged Marybeth, bagel in hand, with me to the bus. I wanted to make sure I wouldn't end up with an empty seat next to me. We were the first ones there. Whew!

"Dang, Christy," Marybeth said. "Why were you in such a big hurry just to sit and wait for everyone else to get on the bus?"

"I don't know," I said, hoping she wouldn't press the issue.

"You're so weird sometimes," she said, shaking her head as she looked at me.

"Sorry," I said, motioning to her bagel. "I owe you one." I figured she wasn't the type to ever need a favor, so owing her wouldn't really mean anything, but her response made me wonder if I'd been mistaken.

"Yes, you do, Christy Hadden. Yes, you do. Now out with it. What's up?"

"I just can't face Rick right now," I said. "I feel so stupid."

"Didn't we just clear this up, upstairs?"

"Marybeth, I ran from him."

"So what?"

"I'm totally retarded."

"No you're not. No more pity party! One of the most incredible guys here kissed you. No one has tried to kiss me. So give it a rest. You were lucky to have him want to kiss you. Think of Kira. She's hot on his tail. Don't blow it." I decided not to tell her about the conversation I'd overheard between Kira and Rick.

Rick finally ambled onto the bus, one of the last ones to get on, head hanging, no light in his eyes as he looked at me. I had to look away to ease the pain welling up in my heart. His unhappiness was becoming my unhappiness. I'd have to take care of this tonight, whether I wanted to or not.

"Don't look away from him, Christy," Marybeth whispered. "Go over and sit by him. Just talk to him. It'll all be okay. Oh, he's so sad. Look at him. You've got to go talk to him."

I pushed myself against the window and said, "No way! I'm not ready. I don't know what to say." My brain worked overtime trying to find a solution, trying to find a way to put an end to my guilt and to Rick's unhappiness without deceit or looking like the idiot loser I felt like. It seemed brains couldn't help problems with the heart. At a loss, instead of continuing to think about it, I focused on the note from the FBI. At eleven, something would happen and I wondered what it would be. I tried to convince myself that it wouldn't involve a toilet or drugs, but I couldn't be absolutely sure.

My thoughts kept getting all muddled up with the kiss by the fountain, the note from the FBI and what I should say to Rick. When leaving the bus, I turned to look at Rick and he was looking at me. My stomach churned. He didn't smile. He just looked at me for a second longer and then turned his head and looked out the window. I hurried off the bus.

The buildings that housed the offices of the senators and some of their staff weren't typical, ugly government buildings. They looked more like stately mansions. I had always imagined that senators and congressmen had offices right in the Capitol building, but they didn't. These buildings stood next to it and were connected to the Capitol by underground tunnels. How exciting would it be to explore those tunnels? Would we get the chance?

I dreaded the day shadowing an intern. Following someone around all day, watching them work, seemed ultra-boring. I hoped that whatever happened at eleven would excuse me from the rest of the day with my intern.

I couldn't have imagined having a worse intern. He had a pinched face, light blonde hair and muddy brown eyes. He never spoke to or acknowledged me. I learned quickly to keep a safe distance from him; in a half an hour he had already backed up into me three times and my toes ached. I had to stay so far back or to the side of him, that I couldn't even hear what he said to people. It was going to be a very long two hours with him, so I started watching everyone else and ignoring what he did. Time passed quickly once I did. With everything so new and interesting, I couldn't help but soak it all in.

Amazed at the amount of work that needed to be done for a senator, I focused on the most interesting. The mass of cubicles buzzed with telephone calls, conversations, research, flying papers, and note taking. It was a bit chaotic in my mind, and I wanted to set it in order. Shocked at some of the inefficiencies, I wanted to fix them, but knew I couldn't.

Before I realized it, eleven o'clock rolled around. My heart skipped a beat as I wondered what crazy thing was about to happen. Nothing did. Fifteen minutes later, I started to wonder if the note had meant eleven at night, when a man came and shuttled my intern away. Before he left, he introduced me to Ryan, a bulky, handsome man, whose dark eyes were lightly framed by almost invisible glasses.

Ryan appeared to be just like the FBI men on TV. But, was he FBI? I decided he couldn't be when he told me what I would be doing. He took me into a room made of glass that looked out on everything going on in the large room surrounding it. Ryan had me start researching immigration and taking "brief, concise" notes on what I found on one of the computers that lined the glass walls. I sighed and resigned myself to the fact that the note from the FBI must have meant eleven p.m. Ryan couldn't be FBI. Bummer.

He sat at one of the four computers in the room and worked furiously. If it weren't for the fact that the room was made out of glass, I would have felt trapped in a small claustrophobic box.

The good thing about working with Ryan was that I loved to research. At first, however, all I could think about was my kiss with Rick and what I could possibly say to such a good guy. Why wasn't there the same spark with him that I always felt for Alex? When I forced myself to look at the computer screen, though, I immediately immersed myself in another world. Buzzing through my third website, Ryan asked to see my work. I handed him my notes, and he read for several minutes.

"Wow, this is great work," he said, handing them back to me with a smile.

That, I already knew, but it was nice to have it verified from someone "in the know." I glanced at my stack of papers and saw someone else's handwriting. I reached for it and started to hand it back to Ryan saying, "I think you. . .", when I noticed it was meant for me. A note from the FBI. He was FBI after all.

The note said that I had to pretend to keep researching, but instead of taking notes, I needed to answer the questions on the papers he'd given me. I pretended to read the monitor and take notes, when I was really just answering his written questions. My heart pounded and it was hard not to act suspicious in that room. Anyone could have walked by our glass enclosure and seen what we were doing if they'd only wanted to. I had to work hard not to freak out. A bit sad to think that I wouldn't be talking to Jeremy, all the pain and fear I'd released with my bawling session the night before, stared me in the face once again.

Most of the questions were very specific and about Iceman and what happened after the ballroom and at the Memorial. The easy questions didn't take me long to answer. But it would have been faster if I didn't have to play like I was researching. Some questions had nothing to do with Iceman, though. They addressed my tour group and how we were holding up.

I only wrote one question,

Why haven't the terrorists killed us yet?

I really wanted an answer. It seemed it would all be so much easier if they did just that.

"Could I take a look at your work again?" Ryan asked. It had only been a few minutes since I'd finished, and I wondered how he'd known to ask me for it.

"Great again," he said with enthusiasm after reading through my responses. "Maybe we could change just a few things." He wrote some follow-up questions, which he handed me to answer. He also added a few comments, his writing plain and easy to read.

They had located Iceman, who gave me the photo. He only worked for the head guy that had ordered the kill of the Senator's aide. I shouldn't fear him; he was a little guy in the scheme of things.

I would anyway. He scared me.

Also, they'd gathered some evidence from the ballroom and had rescued the pictures from Alex's toilet phone and were building a strong case against the leader of the terrorists and the Senator. The FBI would wait until we left D.C. to take them all into custody. Everything was going along as planned. They knew what they were doing. I should forget about the photo, and go about the rest of the trip like nothing had happened. I was being protected.

The note ended. He hadn't answered my question. I turned and looked at him until he turned to me. I raised my eyebrows and said, "What about this one right here." I pointed at my question.

"Hmm," he said, taking the paper from me. He wrote a simple sentence.

We don't know.

Great. Just great. They didn't know why they kept us alive.

I also couldn't forget the photo. Its personal nature felt like a serious warning to all eight in my group, not only Marybeth and me. The danger loomed over us all.

I wished I could have talked to Jeremy to calm my fears. He made me feel safe somehow.

Time flew by. I worked hard and did the best I could, but after answering the FBI's questions, I had a harder time losing myself in my work. My mind wandered. I wondered who would read through my notes and what would happen to them. I looked at Ryan. He must have felt me look, and he turned and asked, "Did you have a question?" Could he read my mind?

"Yeah, I was wondering who'd be looking over my research."

"Staffers do that. It slowly works its way up through the chain of power if it is any good,"

"Really?" I asked, not convinced. I wondered if I had been wasting my time. I mean, while interesting, I didn't want to know all about immigration.

He looked me straight in the eye and said, "Really."

I guess I'd have to accept his answer.

My intern, who will remain unnamed because I couldn't remember his name, came at five and whisked me away to the daily question and answer session, with the interns this time. It seemed to go on forever. I wanted to get back to the hotel, and I'd just realized how famished I felt.   I hadn't eaten since breakfast because Ryan hadn't thought to give me a lunch break. The FBI had dealt me another raw deal.

The question and answer period went long, so instead of leaving at five-thirty, we left closer to six. I hurried onto the bus and plopped onto a seat, looking out the window, when I felt someone sit next to me. My heart about failed me when I found Rick staring back at me.

I had been so distracted by my growling stomach that I hadn't taken any precautions against him sitting next to me. My heart thundered at first, and then I looked into his big, sad, blue eyes, and my heart melted.

He took my hands in his and said, "Can we talk later?"

I'd never been so scared in this same way in all my life. This was painful-scary. *I* had hurt someone. My soul ached. I knew how it felt to be on his side of the fence and be hurt, I had hurt like crazy the last three months at high school, but I'd never been the one doing the hurting. I held my breath and nodded.

"I'll come by your room and get you after dinner, okay?"

I nodded again and seeing Alex coming down the aisle, couldn't help but panic. What if he saw Rick holding my hand? My heart pounded thinking about Rick's hand holding mine. I liked it. Maybe I should just let things happen with him. Then another problem walked down the aisle. Kira.

She would freak out just seeing Rick sit next to me, let alone seeing him holding my hand. She got closer. He got closer. I felt sick. I looked around in hopes of finding something I could set on top of our hands. There was nothing. A few more feet and they would be here. I breathed deeply. I had to look at Alex.

Alex looked at us and then said, "Riiickk", his eyes resting on mine while he raised his hand to high five Rick. Rick let go of my hand and slapped Alex's while he smirked. I pulled my hand quickly into my lap and breathed deeply, staring at Alex, hoping he hadn't seen my hand in Rick's. Had he? Did he care? Then, I felt even a deeper guilt for hoping Alex hadn't seen. I had to treat Rick better.

Kira pushed Alex forward, laughing and flirting.

"Keep it moving, Alex," she said.

She didn't even notice us. I remembered what Rick had said about Alex being a bigger fish in Kira's eyes than he. What Rick had said was true. The sad part was that I felt the same as Kira. My face grew hot; and I felt a bit sad, like I'd lost something. I watched Alex and Kira head for the last bench and sit down. My heart burned with jealousy, while my soul ached.

Rick grabbed my hand again. I turned, and we looked at each other for a few seconds, and then I looked away, my heart speeding along. How could I make this right? He didn't release my hand until we reached the hotel. This time it had been my hand that was sweating, and I was exhausted. Why didn't I feel the same way about Rick that I did about Alex? This guy really liked me—the first guy ever. If there were no Alex, would I feel differently about Rick? Would my heart be pounding out of my chest because a great guy was holding my hand?

Herded into a conference room back at the hotel, we sat around big round tables for dinner and apparently, another question and answer period with Mrs. J. Our mini-group barely fit around the one we chose. The tables were set for seven, but Josh, the last one to arrive, grabbed a chair from the table adjacent to ours and crammed it between Summer and Alex's, which forced us all to sit a bit further away from the table than normal.

"As you eat your dinner," Mrs. J. said, "we'll be discussing the issues you heard about as you shadowed your intern. We'll start as soon as everyone has their food."

A bunch of waiters and waitresses brought the food out impressively fast. Food at last.

"You all have paper and a pen on your tables for notes," Mrs. J. continued. "As you know, we'll be debating the same issues on Friday and Saturday with other groups, so pay attention. We'll start with this table over here. Each table has a mic for you to use."

I tried to pay attention to the speakers. It was the polite thing to do, right? But when the fourth person almost bored me to tears, I decided the polite thing was meant for good speakers, and I tuned out. I had better things to do, like concentrating on eating and watching Alex, who conveniently sat directly across from me. I was hyper-aware of Rick, who sat next to me, but who didn't seem as sad now as he had been. I kept picturing Alex walking up to Rick and me on the bus and seeing us holding hands, wishing I could go back in time and change it. Shame burned my cheeks. I had to get a grip.

At last, everyone's attention fell on our table. I looked at the clock. Eight. It seemed like the waiters had cleared our tables hours ago.

Josh started to tell us about the issues he heard about, and was about as interesting as a blade of grass, so I turned off again. I felt a nudge on my arm and looked at Marybeth, "You're up, Christy," she said.

Caught off guard, "Uh, uh…"escaped my lips.

Alex smiled at me, raising his eyebrows.

Mrs. J., who stood at the front of the room, behind Alex, caught my attention, too, giving me a stern look that knocked me back into reality. My natural desire to "please the teacher" took over, and I spoke about immigration and what I'd learned for a full five minutes. When I took my eyes off Mrs. J., it looked like everyone was staring at me, mouths ajar and eyes wide. I felt my face go hot, sure it was cherry red by now.

I swallowed hard and bent my head down.

What had I said that made them all stare?

"Wow, Christy!" Mrs. J. exclaimed. "That was amazing. Everyone, was that not amazing?"

I heard people clapping, and I looked up. Almost everyone clapped and looked at me, except for some at my table. I shouldn't have been surprised. My speeches always received roaring reviews from crowds—but I didn't want that here. I didn't want anyone to know how good I was.

"Christy is a born politician," Mrs. J. continued. "Didn't you all want to stand up and support her?"

I heard a lot of "yeahs", Rick squeezed my knee, and Alex mouthed, "born politician?", and he chuckled. Born politician? I sure hope not.

I felt the red deepen in my face as Marybeth whispered in my ear, "Smarty pants," and then grunted.

It did feel good to get all the positive attention, but the negative sat like a rock in my stomach and it seemed to drown out the positive. I wished I'd done a boring presentation like everyone else. No one would have noticed me and everything would have been normal. Why did I have to be such a great speaker? I didn't want everyone to know I was smart—I just couldn't help myself—a horrible habit.

"If we would've known she'd be so excellent, we would've had her go first." Mrs. J. said, putting the final nail in my coffin. Marybeth huffed this time and turned her body away from me.

It seemed like the past few days I had been on an emotional rollercoaster that took me soaring, only to drop me crashing below where I had begun. I had no time to relish the good, because the bad lurked only seconds behind, ready to pounce if I felt any happiness at all.

Rick's hand still sat on my knee and he pressed it again. I turned and gave him a weak smile. His returned smile genuinely comforted me. Maybe he understood what

I was going through. A part of me really wanted to like him and let him make me tingle again with another kiss.

The rest of the table finished their presentations, and they weren't half-bad. Of course, Alex's was the best, but everyone was anxious to get out of there by the time we were done. Three hours dissecting political issues with this crowd dragged on too long.

"Tomorrow, you'll be with the lobbyists," Mrs. J. said. "You're dismissed to go get some rest….uh, Christy, could I see you a minute?" I was already out of my chair and heading for the door when she called me.

"Teacher's pet," Josh snickered.

I felt so stupid, like I was back home and a total dork. I walked as slow as molasses to meet her.

"I repeat, wow!" Mrs. J. said. "You truly are a natural. You packed so much feeling and information into your presentation. Enthralling. I think I'll put you with someone special tomorrow, if that's okay."

I figured it really wasn't a question and just nodded.

"Great. Go get some rest. Tomorrow will be an amazing day for you."

In no hurry, I walked down the hall toward the lobby, but felt a hand on my arm before making it out of the hall and into the lobby.

"Christy," Alex said. Apparently he had been down the hall in the opposite direction of the lobby. Great. Now he could ridicule me some more.

I met his stare. He looked excited. My heart pounded.

"A bunch of us are going to a club tonight. You wanna come?"

I expelled a puff of air that showed how unbelievable his offer sounded to me.

"A club? Don't you have to be twenty-one to get into clubs?" I asked before thinking. I let my goody-goody side talk.

"Usually," he said with a smile, "but a guy in another mini-group has a connection and can get us all in to a club in Georgetown. What do ya think?"

His look was intense and his brown eyes melted into mine. My whole body felt like it shook, but I don't think it did. How could I refuse? Alex asked me out. I stood there staring, still in shock.

He reached out and took one of my hands in his, which gave me goose bumps all over, and said, "You have to come." I wanted to die. Was this really happening?

"'Kay," I finally sputtered, while a voice in my head screamed for me to refuse. I did need my sleep and I knew bad things could happen at clubs, but *I* would be with Alex, and he would protect me, and everything would be okay. I couldn't refuse.

"Cool. Sneak out front at eleven," he said. "It'll be fun. You won't regret it." He paused, his eyes amazingly soft, then he shouted out, "Race you to the elevator." He flew down the hall.

After a second of pulling it together, I took off and almost caught him.

"You can run. You almost beat me," he seemed to complain, although his eyes shone.

I laughed, trying to catch my breath as we walked into the elevator.

It was only nine when I got to my room and it hit me. He said to sneak out. I took a deep breath, wondering if I could work up the courage. Was Alex worth it? What if something bad happened again? That little voice in my head told me to forget about it and go to bed, when I heard a slight rap on my door.

Crap! Rick! I'd forgotten.

I pulled the door open a crack, hiding my body behind the door. "I'll be right out."

He nodded, and I shut the door with a soft click, trying not to disturb Marybeth. I couldn't even hear her breathe. Already steaming mad at me for getting the scholarship and Mrs. J.'s praise, I didn't want to make it worse by waking her. I got dressed and slipped through the door.

The moment I saw him, the feelings of the kiss under the spray of the fountain took over my entire mind, and I stood there gawking. His face looked so soft and flawless. He grabbed my hand and led me down the hall, his blue eyes piercing my soul.

"Where are we going?" I asked, trying to ignore the fact that he could feel me shake.

"To my room, where we can have some privacy."

I stopped in my tracks and the shaking stopped as I pulled him to a halt. He swung around to face me.

"I'd rather go somewhere else," I said.

"Oh, okay." He was quiet, probably thinking about where to go. "Maybe a conference room is open. Let's go grab the elevator."

Some strange, hunched over old man stood in the elevator. Not the friendly kind of old I was used to, but the mean-old. His beady eyes seemed to bore through me. When we hit the lobby, I hurried out.

Luckily, the first door of the first conference room we tried opened. Rick offered me a chair and pulled another one around and sat, facing me, our knees almost touching. He smiled at me, but I couldn't smile yet, I was too nervous. My heart pounded so hard I was sure it bruised my ribs.

Rick didn't even wait a few seconds before saying, "Why did you run like that? What happened? I don't know what's worse, you running away from me, or you avoiding and ignoring me after we kissed." His eyes looked adoringly at me.

Man, he went straight to the point (Just like with Kira), and the dagger in my heart dug deeper and twisted. Silent, I searched for a way to speak the truth, but I could only think of lies. Not to mention how distracting his lips were; I found it hard to look away from them. He was so genuine and forthright, I didn't deserve the look in his eyes. He tried to lay everything out on the table, and I searched for a way to hide from the truth.

Stop looking at his lips, I kept telling myself. He deserved an answer, but my mouth was so dry now that I couldn't imagine talking. It felt like an hour had passed since he asked me why I had run and yet he still sat across from me, silent.

He didn't break eye contact. I felt exposed and wondered if he knew how much I wanted his soft lips to touch mine again. I had no right to them, no claim, but I still wanted them. Nervous, my mouth felt full of cotton.

I turned my head to try to hide from his searching eyes, but he reached up and with a firm gentleness turned my face back to his. How could such soft hands be so strong? I guess I couldn't hide.

He moved his fingers gently over mine, glancing down at our hands.

"Christy, talk to me please."

Every time I looked at him, my lips tingled and my heart raced. I tried to pull it together, to give him the answers he deserved; but instead, I started to lean ever so slightly into him. Luckily, he was far enough away, that my leaning was not enough to bridge the gap between our lips.

Somehow I pulled back, the voice in my head screaming that I wasn't being fair to him. He hadn't been my first choice, but it felt so good to be with him, and I wanted more of it. He did look good and I loved the way he cared for people. His kindness seemed unshakeable. At that precise moment, he *was* the one for me. I felt tingles deep inside. My chest burned.

I opened my mouth, but nothing came out. Rick straightened up in his chair, expectant. "Christy, just tell me. Talk to me."

I closed my mouth and swallowed, hoping to bring moisture back so that I could speak. I smiled.

"I don't remember the question." I squeezed his hand.

He let out a big sigh.

"Christy."

"I'm sorry," I tried to explain. "I've had so much on my mind, I'm not thinking clearly. I'm so nervous."

All true statements....

"Why did you run?" he repeated.

He looked so vulnerable and my heart broke and yet thoughts of Alex jumped back into my head. Why was I still thinking of Alex? I looked at my knees and just started talking, "I've just never kissed anyone before, and I freaked out. I didn't know if I should be kissing you or not."

When he didn't respond right away, I dared a glance up. He leaned back, laughing softly. I crinkled up my nose and scrunched my eyebrows together pulling my hands from his. He looked at me, and I looked away.

There I was, telling the truth and he was laughing at me. It couldn't have been worse.

"No, no, Christy, stop," he said.

It bothered me that my pain pleased him so much. I started to feel small, and instead of feeling sorry for him, I started to feel sorry for myself.

He reached back over to grab my hand, and I pulled it away.

"No, Christy, you don't understand. I'm not making fun of you." He got a very serious look on his face, all play gone. "When you told me about not dating until you were sixteen, I should've remembered that you hadn't ever been kissed. I probably shouldn't have kissed you, but it was so perfect there; for our first kiss. And you standing there, so kissable and all."

My heart jumped and I felt the kiss all over again.

"I like you," he continued, "and I wanted to show you. It's hard for me to imagine being uncertain about that kiss, because it was amazing in every way, and I can't seem to get it off my mind." His eyes wandered to my lips. "And now, knowing it was your first kiss, makes it even better. I like the idea that I was your first kiss and at this moment, all I can think about is being your last kiss."

Sincerity oozed out of him, and I felt a spark and wanted to push forward and kiss him, but I held back and instead, said, "But we barely know each other." My feelings were a jumbled mess.

"Well, we can start getting to know each other right now. I want you to feel sure, and I'm willing to wait." He stared, eyes blazing. "I will wait for you, Christy, however long it takes. I want you to feel good about us."

Us? There was an us? My stomach flipped at the idea. How could there be an us when he lived in upstate New York and I lived in Montana? I felt nervous and searched for a clock. It was quarter to eleven. I had to get going. Why did I care about Alex when Rick was right here with me?

"What do you think, Christy?"

What could I say? It was all so reasonable and I didn't have any more time. I bit my lip and looked at him.

I couldn't help but wonder why this great guy wanted me. No one had ever wanted me before, so I said, "Okay."

"Let's get out of here. If tomorrow's going to be anything like today, I'm sure we need all the sleep we can get." He could be so practical. Part of me was sad that he hadn't tried to kiss me again.

As we walked back to the lobby, I looked all around, afraid of running into Alex. What would Alex think if he saw Rick and me heading for my room right then?

Luckily, I didn't see anyone on our way. Rick leaned in and kissed me on the cheek, long and soft. I felt heat linger even after he left.

I needed to focus. I was about to be with Alex.

CHAPTER FOURTEEN

My frizzy hair stuck out all over the place. Blasted rain! Why hadn't Rick told me I looked like a freak? How could anyone like me with hair like this? A pony tail would have to do. It wasn't the hairstyle I was sure people wore to clubs, but I had no time. I tried to make it look more stylish, like Kira and Summer always managed to do, leaving strands of hair framing my face.

My clothes were the bigger problem. I couldn't wear long pants and a button-up shirt to the club. In fact, nothing hanging in my closet here would be good to wear to the club. Thanks to TV, I imagined people in clubs wearing skirts for some reason. I thought of waking Marybeth, but I really didn't have time for that, and I'm not sure she would want to help me at the moment, and she could try and talk me out of going to the club. I really didn't want that. A cute skirt and top that Marybeth had worn flashed across my brain. Should I borrow it? I opened the bathroom door slightly, to let in a little bit of light. I looked over at Marybeth, her breathing even. Would she care? She'd loaned me so many things over the last week. Surely, she wouldn't mind. She had so many clothes, she probably wouldn't even notice. But, should I?

A faint voice in my head said, "No."

I could clean it and return it before she even knew.

"Wake her up and ask her," the voice in my head said.

She's sound asleep. I could just tell her in the morning. I took one last look at her and decided she wouldn't care if I raided her closet even though my stomach was on fire. Deep down, I knew it was wrong. But I did it anyway.

With the little bit of light coming from the bathroom, I could barely make out what was in Marybeth's closet. I used my hands to feel for the skirt and shirt she'd worn.

I grabbed two pieces that I thought were them and crept back to the bathroom. What luck! I had grabbed the right skirt, wrong shirt, but I thought it may have actually been a better choice anyway, and I put them on as fast as possible. They fit without any tugging or pulling.

Was I as skinny as Marybeth? No way. I couldn't stop the smile that spread across my face.

I looked at Marybeth's open closet door and felt a pang of guilt. I glanced down at Marybeth's clothes on my body and took a deep breath.

She wouldn't want me to wake her. It'll be okay. She would want me to look good for this, I convinced myself.

I had left the bathroom light on and hurried to turn it off, then reached into Marybeth's open closet and took out a pair of shoes. One more thing wouldn't matter. They'd be back before she even woke up. My face felt hot. I carefully closed the closet door while looking in Marybeth's general direction, and with great care, opened the door to the hallway and stepped out.

I slid the shoes on as I tried to run the short distance to the elevator. I don't do heels. I stumbled the entire way, hoping I wouldn't break an ankle on my lucky day. I tapped my foot impatiently during my descent to the lobby. I was late.

Please let Alex be there still. I tried to look natural leaving the building and felt that by the time I hit the doors, I was walking considerably better, and had found my balance in the heels for the most part. Alex stood at the bottom of the steps, more hot than ever. His eyes sparkled when he saw me, (or I imagined they did) and he walked up a few steps to meet me. I was all fluttery inside, and my mind went blank, so I simply smiled.

"Christy, you made it," he said, as he grabbed my hand. Shock waves spread up my arm from his touch. The warning I'd been feeling, silenced.

Was this really happening? I had to ask myself over and over. Then a terrible thought crossed my mind. Was this a set up? Were they going to take me somewhere and make a fool out of me, like kids at home had done? I pushed the thought out of my mind, remembering the sparkle in his eye and seeing the cab waiting for me.

The back door was open, and Alex held it. I heard that voice in my head saying, "Danger, danger."

"Sorry I'm late," I said, trying to look sincere while blocking out the voice in my head.

"No worries, Christy," he said, leading me to the door. I climbed in, only to find I sat next to Summer. She gave me a crusty look and said, "Ugh!" turning to face Josh, who sat on the other side of her. She immediately started whispering to Josh, who leaned just enough to the side to have one of his eyes peer over at me. Definitely not a set up. She would have been delighted to see me if it had been.

To my relief, Alex opened the front door and climbed in next to the driver. He turned and winked at me. I smiled, sighing quietly.

We drove to the club in Georgetown and a long line snaked its way to the door. I wondered how long we would wait, only to have them deny me entrance. I was only fifteen, after all. I stared at my shoes. What if they didn't let me in? What if I was the only one they didn't let in? I felt all shaky inside.

We didn't stop at the end of the long line, though; we went straight up to the steps that led to the door. A guy with spiky, sandy blonde hair and super tan skin, who was part of another mini-group at our hotel, talked to a very large man with short-cropped brown hair and a stern face, who blocked the door. Josh walked right up to the guy with spiky hair and spoke with him for a minute, giving a him a cool-looking handshake and then glancing at me. He waved us in. The large man stepped to the side, completely ignoring us, scowling over the ever-expanding line before him. Relief spilled over me. They didn't stop me. They didn't even look at me.

Inside, the guy with the blonde hair said, "You guys are late. It's about time." Josh punched Alex as the guy waved to the cashier, who signaled for us to go through a second set of doors. The moment the second set of doors opened, deafening music crashed into my ears. I resisted the urge to cover them. What was I doing here?

I couldn't believe what I saw. It was like walking onto a TV set. The large room felt a bit cramped packed with all sorts of crazy looking people. Don't get me wrong, they were the beautiful people, only they were contorting their bodies in such random ways, they looked almost fake as the multi-colored lights passed over them— like an animated dance video. Most girls were super-skinny with short, short skirts or dresses that had necklines that plunged to their waists in either the front or the back. I could see more skin on a lot of them than clothes. I felt way over-dressed.

The guys, in contrast, were mostly dressed, with jeans and tight T-shirts. The dance floor itself was semi-dark with bursts of light from several spotlights moving about. Instead of going down the few steps needed to get the dance floor, we turned left and climbed some stairs. At the top, round tables surrounded by chairs and even a few couches filled the space. Our tour friend led us to a table with a reserved sign sitting in the middle of it. He smiled at us and then moved on to the next table, joining five others that I recognized from our question and answer sessions with Mrs. J.

Alex offered me a chair. The one couple already sitting at our table, hit knuckles with Alex, while Josh leaned over to the guy and punched his arm in a playful gesture. I guess they came from the tour too, I just couldn't remember them.

Alex leaned into me, putting his lips next to my ear and said, "Isn't this great!" My heart skipped a beat.

I nodded, trying to convince myself that it was. I had really gotten myself into a jam. What was I thinking when I said yes to going to a club? I never thought I would ever go to a club my whole life and here I was.

Alex started talking and my worries vanished. I couldn't help but notice how good he smelled. I breathed in to capture as much as I could. His cheek, resting on mine, sent tingles throughout my body.

"The owner of this club is Zach's Uncle," he said. "Zach's the guy who met us at the door with the spiky hair. We're pretty lucky to be here. Encha is playing here tonight, so they'll have a packed house."

I wondered who Encha was.

"Cool," I said. I felt like I had to scream for him to hear me. Then I felt him take my hand. At the feel of his touch, I had to take a quick breath in.

A waitress bent over to talk to Josh and Summer, and write their orders on a small piece of paper. She came over to Alex, they talked, and then she scribbled something down and walked away. I felt hot and needed something to drink. Summer leaned over to Alex, and they talked and laughed for a few minutes. He held my hand tight as he leaned into her.

The next thing I knew, the waitress set everyone's drinks on the table. She placed a skinny glass filled with a red liquid in front of me, and Alex had what looked like a beer, amber colored liquid with foam on top. It must have been fake beer or something, I told myself. What was the red stuff in my glass? It couldn't be alcohol, could it? No way. We're minors. Sure, I could see them letting us in to the club, but to serve us alcohol would be going too far. Wouldn't it? I stared at my drink, not daring to ask what it was.

Summer's glass was the same as mine, skinny, with red liquid. She lifted her glass toward the middle of the table, and Josh and Alex brought theirs up to meet hers. Alex motioned for me to do the same. My heart raced. What should I do? I picked up the glass, trying not to visibly shake, and softly tapped my glass against theirs. My insides burned.

They all took a sip from their drinks. I had never drunk before, and stared at the red liquid, still wondering if it was alcohol. The voice in my head warned me not to drink. I shouldn't have come. How could I get out of this? The others looked at me, as if they were watching to see if I would drink it. Alex even nodded at me.

Here's the thing: I'd promised myself that I would never drink. No one in my family drank alcohol, and it scared me. I didn't want to lose control of myself or become an alcoholic; but they were watching me. How could I not? I also knew that if I drank, my choices after that would be limited forever, just like the kiss that I could never take back. I would never be able to say that I didn't drink. I would be a drinker forever. My stomach burned.

In a last second decision, I pulled the glass to my lips, but instead of drinking, I pursed my lips against the glass and pretended to drink, tipping the glass up and pretending to swallow. I put the glass on the table, and they all smiled and took another drink. I mimicked them, except I didn't really drink any of it. It smelled sickly sweet, yet somehow fermented. Yuck! My lips were sticky and I didn't want to lick them, but after a few minutes, I had to. They tasted sweet. Great. I'd tasted alcohol. I wished I had some water. I never should have come here, but I couldn't leave now, Summer would have a heyday with that.

Everyone at our two tables stood, in unison it seemed, and headed for the stairs. I stood as quickly as I could, trying not to look out of place. Alex stood behind me with his hands on my waist, pushing me gently forward. It tickled and made all my nerves hyper-active.

The dance floor was more than crowded, it was packed now. Alex crammed us in the middle of a bunch of people we didn't know, and we could barely move. So much for worrying about how I danced. I was being pushed and bumped on every side, and I wondered why people thought this was fun. Alex wrapped his arms around me and grinned. He loved this. I felt his whole body against mine, and I blushed. Our heads leaned together, and we just sort of swayed, like dancing to a slow dance, without the slow music. I now knew why people liked this. It felt amazing to have him so close to me.

Sweat dripped down my back, which intensified the fact that my mouth was incredibly dry. We danced, or rather moved to a few more songs and then I couldn't take it any longer, my tongue even felt dry. I didn't want to go back to the table and the alcohol, and I certainly didn't want to ask him to buy me water. I felt trapped. Then I thought of a way around it—the bathroom. I told him I needed to go the bathroom, and he responded by grabbing my hand and leading me off the dance floor.

Uber-cool. He took me there, like a perfect gentleman. He opened doors, ordered for me, and watched out for me. I couldn't have asked for more. I entered a stall and made myself go. I looked around, while washing my hands, to see if anyone from our group was in there. No one was. I cupped my hands, catching water in them and drank until I couldn't drink anymore. I patted my face dry with a towel and hurried out, feeling much better.

Alex stood, in all his glory, looking at the dance floor, and I decided to be bold and walked straight up to him and took his hand in mine, giving him a big smile when he looked at me. He smiled back, and my heart raced faster. He pulled me back onto the floor and put his hands on my waist, holding me close. After a few minutes in that spot, he grabbed my hand and threaded me through the crowd in the direction of the stage. I had to really hold tight not to lose him.

We joined the kids from the tour-group right in front of the small stage, and I felt the excitement in the room suddenly skyrocket, with more yelling, jumping, pushing and even more crowding, if that's possible. At the end of the song, the disc jockey screamed into the mic, "Show 'em how much you want 'em here. Everybody, heeeere's Encha."

The crowd went wild, with everyone screaming and jumping. The stage lit up with a mini-firework show including lots of smoke, and then Encha ran on singing some song I'd never heard before. The cacophony was mind-numbing. I wondered if I would be able to hear tomorrow. Alex looked down at me, puzzled, and I realized I wasn't moving. The dizzying noise had frozen me. I smiled and put my hands into the air and started screaming, too. I couldn't believe I was able to get rid of all the tension and fear that wound up inside me from being at the club. How I could reconcile this in the morning with what I believe, I couldn't imagine. It must have been what he wanted me to do, because a grin slid across his face, and he turned and started screaming, too. Playing along turned out to be a lot of fun. The excitement was contagious and the movement insane.

After a while, I felt my voice crack and my throat dry out and become ragged. I swallowed hard and then just opened my mouth, pretending to scream. No one would notice the difference, anyway.

After being poked, prodded and manhandled by people behind us for a good ten minutes, Alex pulled me in front of him. A wall, protecting me.

How could I be so lucky?

After forty-five minutes of total bedlam, over-heated and more thirsty than I could ever remember being, Alex pulled me through the crowd in record speed. I thought the stairs must've become longer, because I was huffing by the time we reached the top. Before we even sat down, Alex tapped the waitress on the arm and told her something. I hoped he had ordered water.

We'd barely sat down, before she set another one of the slender, red drinks in front of me and a foamy amber one in front of Alex. Then, to my relief, she put two empty glasses and a large bottle in front of us. I saw the word water on the front.

Could it be? I was saved.

While Alex talked to the waitress some more, I took my glass, making sure no one was watching, and poured some of the red liquid into a plant that stood behind us and put the cup back on the table. Almost half was gone. Alex turned and went straight for the water, opening it and pouring it into our glasses. I noticed that it looked carbonated, and I tried to see if my mind had played tricks on me, making me see the word water, when it was really champagne or something. He handed me my glass, just as I saw the word water on the bottle again. So I drank, thirstily. He watched me, smiling, until I pulled it away and made a sour face.

That wasn't water! I grimaced at the bottle. I had failed, I had drunk alcohol.

Alex leaned in, pulling the bottle toward me to read. "It's mineral water, Christy. Haven't you ever had mineral water before?"

I didn't want to look stupid, but I couldn't help it. I took the bottle from his hands and read the ingredients, mineral water. I let a deep burst of air out of my mouth in relief that I hadn't had alcohol after all.

I pulled my eyebrows together, and Alex laughed. I pulled him to me, "That's the worst water I've ever drunk," I said.

He laughed again, leaning his head back and laughing at the ceiling. Then, he pulled me to him and said, "You'll get used to it. It's really healthy."

I stared at my glass of water, carbonated nasty water, and had to drink it. I held my nose internally shut as I drank, preventing the bitter liquid from reaching my taste buds. It was my only option, and it *was* refreshing. Alex filled my glass again, and I drank another whole glass. He did too. He filled my glass again, and I noticed that he gave me the last of the water, so I decided I better drink it slowly.

Alex drank his beer and as everyone trickled back to the tables and ordered more to drink, they began mingling and talking. No one stayed in any one particular spot, except for me and Alex. Constantly bombarded with people coming over to him and chatting, Alex rested his hand on my leg, and it felt like it burned where he touched it. I couldn't do anything but smile. Happiness consumed me.

I didn't know if the music had been turned down after the band left, or if I'd just gotten used to the blaring noise, but I could hear people talking and laughing now, where I couldn't before. I thought about how lucky I was to be there with Alex. Any girl would've died to be with him at this club, and he had chosen me. That dizzying idea made my body buzz with excitement.

Alex turned his chair to face me and then pushed

my chair around so that I faced him. His legs cradled mine and he gently brought my hands in his, moving his face toward mine. My heart pounded hard, and I felt weak. *Not here. Don't kiss me here.* Instead, his cheek pressed against mine and nothing more. Surprisingly, I felt a strange mix of relief and sadness. We stayed like that for several minutes, my heart racing out of my chest.

I'd finished all my water and had to go the bathroom. I didn't want the moment to end, but I couldn't wait any longer and pointing to my empty glass, said, "I've got to go to the bathroom."

He nodded and stood up with me, twirling me around as I stood. So cute! We walked side by side, holding hands. Everything was good; Alex McGinnis was holding *my* hand.

The dance floor seemed empty compared to before, but a lot of people still danced out there. Moving about was a ton easier. When I came out of the bathroom, Alex waited right there, his mischievous smile taunting me. He held his hand out, and I took it, saying, "What?"

"You'll see," he said, pulling me down a hall past the bathroom. It was lined with doors on one side that had signs reading, no admittance. My heart pounded. He stopped and took my other hand in his, pushing my back against the wall. A dropping feeling filled my stomach. He moved in close to me and pulled my hands and arms above my head. My heart stuttered as I watched his face come closer and closer.

Wait. This wasn't how I'd imagined it. He pushed me hard into the wall and it kind of hurt. His hot breath smelled bitter. I stiffened as his lips pressed hard against mine. This wasn't really happening was it?

My first instinct was to pull away, but *he* was kissing me. His fingers moved over mine, and his kiss softened. He coaxed my hands back down to my sides and grabbed my waist, pulling me in closer to him. Despite his breath, I couldn't believe how good he still smelled after all that dancing. I just wished he tasted good.

I felt his lips trace my jaw bone, all the way to my ear. It sent shivers up my spine, causing all the hairs on my arms to stand up.

His hot breath hit my ear as he said, "Now you can't say you've never been kissed."

My forehead crinkled. Had I heard him right? His touch felt tenuous-empty. What did he mean by that?

His lips found their way back to mine, soft and giving, but I didn't want them on mine any longer. Before I could turn my head away, he turned his, letting go of my waist and grabbing my hand. He led me back to our table.

I felt numb. Taking a steadying breath, I looked at him while he talked to a few guys at the other table. I had to find out what he meant exactly. Did he just kiss me to rid me of my virgin lips? Was I some kind of conquest? My teeth ground together, and I sat back and crossed my arms. I felt used somehow, and I didn't like it at all. My stomach ached. I wished I'd pushed him away.

"Time to go," Zack announced.

Everyone grumbled but headed for the stairs.

My stomach felt heavy, like a rock sat in it, preventing me from moving. Alex grabbed me from behind, turning me and pulling me up into his arms, his face only inches from mine. He smiled. I turned away, my head swimming. He tugged me forward.

The fresh air outside seemed to clear my head a bit, I just needed more of it. I leaned against the outside wall of the building and bent over, taking my ankles in my hands and breathing deeply. Questions nagged at me. Questions that would probably never be answered, because I was too chicken to ask them. Why had I come? I should have listened to that voice in my head. Nothing good came from tonight. He only asked me here so he could be the conqueror.

I looked the opposite way of the club, still upside-down and saw a dark-skinned man quickly look away when I looked at him. I felt my heart skip a beat. I pulled up slowly, looking across the street and all around to see if I could spot an FBI agent. Another dark haired Arab-looking guy was across the street. I thought he looked at me, but from that distance, I couldn't be sure. Something crawled down my spine, and I shivered.

Alex, beside me, asked, "You cold?" as if he had seen me shiver. He wrapped his arms around me and rubbed my arms with his hands.

"A bit," I answered. Oddly enough, his warm hands seemed to chill me even more.

He held me until our taxi came. The seating arrangement stayed the same, and I was glad. I didn't want to be next to Alex right then.

Summer said, "You've seen the other side now. Don't expect it to last."

Ignoring her was getting easier, but not knowing what Alex's real intentions were ate at me, and yet a part of me didn't want to give Alex up.

I had to look out the windows to get another look at the two guys I thought watched me. They weren't there. I craned my head all around the areas they had been in and finally saw one jumping into a car. "Hmm," I mused, "I wonder if they really are following us."

Then it hit me. Had the FBI even known that I wasn't in my hotel room asleep? Were they there at the club somewhere, and I couldn't see them? Or had we been on our own? We went through the intersection and heard a loud crash. We all looked out the back window. There had been a huge crash right behind us. Our cab driver kept driving as if nothing had happened. I saw shadowy, dark figures jump out, yelling, pointing at our cab. I looked back again, but we were too far away to see anything anymore. Dread spread throughout my whole body. I had an icy feeling the FBI had been at the club and had just saved us.

When we got to the hotel, we snuck up the back stairs, instead of using the elevator, in hopes that we would lessen the chance of running into any adults from our group. Before going in, I kept looking down the stairs to see if we were being followed. I would tell Rick about the crash tomorrow. I didn't want to tell Alex anything after that kiss.

Josh and Summer went giggling into his room together. I wondered why they did so much in secret. You could tell they were close friends when you were with them, but they never held hands or acted like boyfriend/girlfriend during the day. But, in the dark or in secret, they let it all loose.

Alex stopped at his room, slid in his key, opened his door and started to pull me in. I planted my feet and leaned back. My icy feeling was replaced with a deep heat.

He looked back at me with a puzzled look on his face. "What's up? Aren't you gonna come in?"

"No," I said. "I'm so tired and Mrs. J. has me doing some crazy thing with a senior staffer tomorrow."

"You can sleep here." His smile was soft.

I looked at my feet.

"It's no big deal, Christy, come on in."

"No," I said, jerking my hand out of his and walking toward my room. While I was fishing for my key card, he touched my shoulders.

I kept my back to him and cursed at myself for not being able to find my key card fast enough. My face burned with anger.

"Christy, what gives?" he moved around to face me. "Why are you running from me? I thought we had a great time." His fingers brushed my cheeks and tingles lingered where he had touched it. Why did I have to respond like that? I wanted to be mad.

This felt like bad déjà vu. Hadn't I just heard the same words coming from Rick?

"Alex, I did have a great time, I just want to go to bed, that's all. Forget about it."

"Look, nothing has to happen in my room. We can just sleep. I want to get to know you better, and I thought it would be nice to spend more time together."

I had had enough. While it was tempting, the better part of me pulled away from him, my heart thudding so loudly, I was sure he could hear it. "Why did you kiss me at the club?" I spat, my voice harsh, but low. I glared up at him.

"Why?" he asked. His eyes scanned my face. My glare softened. I couldn't look into his liquid eyes without losing a bit of clarity of thought. "Because I think you're great. Because I liked kissing you. . .Because I wanted to." He touched my hand, and I felt that his was trembling. It caught me off guard.

All I could do was stare. He stared back. I listened for the voice to tell me if he was a good guy or a bad one, but the voice was silent. Maybe ignoring the voice, made it ignore me back. I was alone.

"Did you kiss me only because I had never kissed anyone?" I squeaked, hardly believing I had the guts to say it. Like he would tell me the truth anyway.

"Oh, that's what this is all about—what I said to you after I kissed you?"

I just stared, sure he could feel my heart beating at the sound waves between us.

"That's not why I kissed you. I like you, Christy. You're different from the girls I know. I wanted to spend time with you to see if we clicked. I thought we did, so I kissed you. Being your first kiss was only a bonus."

Should I clue him in that someone beat him to the punch? I finally looked up at him, his eyes gloriously intense. I couldn't remember how to breathe at that moment. Could I believe him? His eyes said yes and my body wanted nothing more than to be in his arms, but I didn't move to him. I stayed back, still unsure, but wanting to believe.

He reached out for my other hand, and now, I was trembling.

"Come on," he said, leaning his head in the direction of his room.

"No," I answered. "I can't. Thanks for tonight. It was a lot of fun." I managed to smile at him, even if it was half a smile. I pulled one of my hands out of his, unable to look away. Where my resolve came from, I'll never know. Maybe it was as simple as having made up my mind a long time ago what was most important to me—that I wouldn't put myself in a position to compromise my core beliefs.

"Please, Christy. I've never been around anyone like you. I don't want to blow it." His fingers slid into my hair and gently pulled me closer, I could smell mint on his breath. "I'm sorry," he said, and kissed my cheek. "I'm sorry." He continued and kissed my forehead. "I'm sorry, he said, and kissed the tip of my nose. "I'm sorry," he said, and I closed my eyes, letting his lips press against mine. *This* was how I'd imagined it.

Still, I would not join him.

CHAPTER FIFTEEN

I didn't even bother to undress before getting into bed. Completely exhausted, I didn't have the energy, even though my insides buzzed with excitement. I had kissed Alex again and it had been great. I decided to pretend the kiss at the club never happened. Unfortunately, just because my body was exhausted, didn't mean my mind was.

My conversation with Rick danced through my mind. What would he think when he saw me holding Alex's hand tomorrow? Would Alex even want to hold my hand in public or was it only a one-time thing? Would he treat me like Josh treated Summer—a behind closed doors relationship? A horrible feeling washed over me, and I tried to ignore it, but it steadily grew until I ached all over.

"I'm sorry, Rick," I mumbled into the night, hoping to release some guilt. It didn't work.

I thought about how I'd acted at the club and wished it had been different. I thought about fake-drinking, and that now everyone at the club thought I had drunk alcohol. I didn't really want them to think that, and yet I did. And, then I thought about kissing Alex, my second mistake. (and kissing him again, my third, and fourth and fifth...)

Guilt overwhelmed me; it was sudden, complete and devastating. Hot tears pushed their way to the surface and flowed freely. I was glad for the darkness. Maybe I didn't know myself. I had never dreamed that this trip would test decisions I had made a long time ago. I never thought I would have kissed two different guys in two days, nor did I think I would go to a club where everyone was drinking and being wild. I also didn't think I would ever steal clothes, fake drink or twist the truth. I never thought the opportunity would arise for me to have a boyfriend before I was sixteen. Now there were two guys wanting me to be their girlfriend. Was nothing sacred to me anymore? Had Marybeth's help made people accept me only while here in D.C. or would it extend to my home? Was my past what made me an outcast back home? Could the people back home forget the old me? Did I want to be the new me?

Really, why had Alex thought I would go to his room? Could it be that because I went to the club, he thought I drank, and I kissed him, that he thought I would do more? Did he think so little of me? Maybe he saw nothing wrong with it, though—maybe he'd never been taught that it was. But, couldn't he *feel* it was?

I gasped, realizing that my seemingly little choice of sneaking out to the club to be with Alex had caused a chain reaction that led to places I had never intended to go. I didn't want people to see me as someone who would go to a club. I definitely didn't want anyone to think I drank, and I certainly didn't want anyone to think I was easy. What had I done? How could I undo what had happened? The answer was easy—I couldn't.

One deception had blossomed into many, with no turning back.

I lay awake all night, trying to find a way to ease my guilt. I'd decided that Alex came from another world, entirely different from mine, and I didn't know how to deal with him. I would have to give him up, as hard as that would be. When I was with him, I compromised a lot of what I thought I wanted out of life and pretended to be someone I wasn't. I let the fact that he made me feel so good override my better judgment.

I would also have to tell Rick that I absolutely couldn't date until I was sixteen. The timing with Rick was just off. I felt hot, thinking of his soft lips. I really had to trust that sixteen wasn't some random age my parents picked, but that something magical happened on your birthday to help you be smarter with guys. On the other hand, maybe I would just have to *choose* to be smarter. But, smarter, I'd found, didn't always feel better—at least at first.

Besides, this little world in D.C. was different from reality. Alex, Rick and the rest of them would probably go home and in two minutes forget I existed.

With a start, I sat up. The clock read six-thirty. I stretched and slid out of bed. I smelled cigarette smoke and looked down at myself. Marybeth's clothes. My heart dropped and nervous flutters filled my chest. I looked over at her. The room was just light enough to see her shadow in bed and without a noise, I grabbed a dry-cleaning bag and some new clothes from my closet, hurrying into the bathroom. I shoved her clothes into the bag and showered as fast as I could. What if she woke up? After getting dressed, I ran the clothes down to the reception desk, asking them to bill me. When I got back to the room, I heard the shower. Did she see me leave with the bag? I sat on the edge of my bed, waiting for her to come out, nervous that she had seen something. This guilty conscience thing was going to kill me.

"Hey!" Marybeth said when she came out of the bathroom.

"Hey!"

"You got in a workout this morning, huh?" She asked.

I looked at myself, wondering what had given her that idea. Maybe she had seen me leave with the bag and thought it was a gym bag of sorts. I just smiled and hurried to get ready. I had dodged a bullet, but I still had one more to dodge. I had to get her clothes back into the closet without her knowing. Why had I been so stupid? I should have asked her if I could borrow them. She would have let me. I'm sure of it. If only I'd asked, I wouldn't have this stress now. Marybeth and I hurried down to grab a bagel and then ran onto the bus. Mrs. J. raised her eyebrows at me.

"Doing okay today, Christy?"

"Yes," I said. "Just running a little late." I had to pull it together and give a good performance for Mrs. J., with whomever she wanted to impress. I couldn't let her down.

She smiled, and I made my way to the back of the bus. Both Alex and Rick had open spots next to them and both looked at me. Acid filled my stomach. It didn't seem right to sit with either one, so when Marybeth sat with Kira, I squeezed onto the seat with them.

"What the…," Kira called out.

"Christy, what are you doing?" Marybeth asked, looking at me.

"I wanted to sit with you guys. It's okay isn't it?"

"Whatever," Kira answered.

"Sure," Marybeth said.

The tight fit was worth not having to face either Alex or Rick. Facing Kira's wrath was easier at the moment. It would also be good to keep an eye on Marybeth—to make sure she didn't tell Kira about the kiss.

I picked at the bagel the whole way to the place we were meeting up with the lobbyists, listening to Marybeth and Kira talk about how excited they were about today. They loved the idea of shadowing a lobbyist and seeing firsthand what they did all day. It baffled me. It was like I wasn't even there. Glad in a way, I didn't want to explain to them that I wouldn't be shadowing a lobbyist. Mrs. J. had something else planned for me.

When I stepped off the bus, several men in suits stood on the sidewalk in a row, students massed around them. One called out names and as he did, the student's whose names he had called, rushed up to stand next to him. I just waited by the bus door. After the first man had everyone on his list, he led them away. Then the next man in the row started calling out the names on his list, and he was swarmed with eager students. Soon, I was the only one left without a leader. I headed for Mrs. J.

I caught sight of Rick, who looked at me with questioning eyes. I smiled and shrugged my shoulders. His group walked away, but he lingered, looking at me until he had to go or be left behind.

"Christy," Mrs. J. said. "There you are. Let's go. They're waiting for you." We walked to a car a bit further down the road, waiting for us. We drove toward the capitol and stopped in front of one of the Senate office buildings. I probably should have asked where we were going—but I didn't.

We walked into a large reception area and a tall, thin, stiff man, with short brown hair and glasses, put out his hand for Mrs. J. to take. He then looked me over and decided to give me his hand, too. I noticed I was slouching, so I straightened up. I had to become a performer. I had to produce for Mrs. J. She had gone out of her way to get me here, and I didn't want to let her down. My brain clicked into action. No matter what had been going on in my life, I had to be amazing in some way, now.

"This is Christy, Mrs. J. said. "She is quite incredible—like I told you on the phone. Put her to good use, Stephan." She smiled at me and then walked back out the large glass doors.

Stephan didn't answer her, he simply nodded in her direction and then put me to work, researching, none other than immigration—the same thing I'd given my speech on the day before. Coincidence, or not? He handed me a stack of papers to go through and then a list of websites to

consult. I looked over the sites; I'd already read and
summarized many of them. I wrote the highlights of those
and then moved on to the stack of papers in front of me.

I loved to do research—the perfect thing for me to do
when I was tired. In no time at all, it was time for lunch. I
didn't stay gone the hour allotted me; I would have fallen
asleep at the cafeteria table. Glad to get back to work, I'd
finished the stack of papers and was starting on a few new
websites, when the tall, stiff senior staff member, Stephan,
joined me.

"How's it going?" he asked.

"Great. It's pretty interesting."

"It's about to get more interesting," he said, grinning.
"We need a five minute report on what you've found at
three o'clock. That gives you one hour. Can you do it?"

"Sure," I answered.

"It needs to be your best work, okay?"

"Sure," I repeated, hating the tone of his voice. I
wasn't a child. "I'll have it for you."

In a flash, he was gone. I looked at the fifteen or so
websites that I hadn't gotten to yet. They stared up at me
from the paper. What if I missed something important,
because I hadn't read through all of them? I decided to just
scan them. A five minute presentation should only take me
fifteen minutes to prepare, which left me forty-five
minutes to research. Time passed quickly, and I only got
through ten sites. Writing the speech was the easy part.

"Ready?" Stephan asked, standing in the doorway.

I handed him a nicely printed copy of what I'd found,
along with the speech, annotated and all.

He stared at me with a crazy look on his face.

"How'd you get through all that material?" he asked.

"I didn't. I missed about five of them," I said,
ashamed.

"Hmm," he said. "Only five? Amazing. Come on."

"Huh?" I said.

He held my papers out for me to retrieve, waving them a bit.

"Oh, didn't I tell you?" he said, in a dramatic voice, all stiffness gone. "You get to present the information to the Senator."

"What? Why don't you just do it?" I asked.

"Your research. Your presentation. Now, get a move on."

I stood up, nervous about the unexpected, and followed him out of the cubicle area, back to the entrance foyer.

I'm sure I was supposed to be ecstatic about this opportunity—but I wasn't. Any of the people, except maybe Alex, from our tour group would be clamoring for such an opportunity. To me, it seemed silly to present what anybody could just as well read.

He had me sit on a bench in the foyer and wait while he went to see if they were ready for me. Then, he opened a door for me. The large room was packed with people sitting around an oval table in large, cushiony chairs. I would be presenting my report to a whole group, not a single person. I looked away from them, hoping it would calm my nerves. It's like a debate, I kept telling myself. Speaking in public wasn't hard for me to do, but thinking that these people probably knew more about immigration than I did, made me feel silly.

Stephan took his place in a seat not far from me and nodded for me to start. The silence in the room slithered over me.

At about the fourth sentence of the speech, my instincts turned on and I became a performer again. I felt like I was flying when I did something well. I got brave when I reached the second page, and looked away from my notes. I knew the talk by heart; I'd written it after all. I started making eye contact with each person in the room. I felt powerful and alive. Reaching the back of the room, my eye caught a very familiar face.

I stammered and sputtered, staring into the eyes of one of the men of my nightmares, Senator Randolph. A monster sat in front of me, and I was helping him in some way. I felt my body sway, and everything went dark.

I woke, my eyes slow to adjust to the bright lights shining down on me. A man with white hair started to come into focus. He talked, but it seemed in slow motion.

"She's coming around," the man said, "She just fainted, locked her knees or something. She appears fit as a fiddle. It's the bump on her head I'm worried about."

I tried to sit up, but the room spun.

"Slow down young lady," the white haired man said, "Give yourself a minute or two."

I couldn't help but lay back down. I wondered how I'd gotten there. I took a few deep breaths and took in my fuzzy surroundings. I was in an office of some sort, but a large elegant one, with books lining the walls, and prominent furniture standing in exactly the right places. I decided the white-haired man must be a doctor by the way he looked me over. Then I saw Stephan standing behind him, and I remembered I'd been giving a report on immigration issues when everything went black. Where had they taken me? How long had I been out?

Stephan moved around the doctor, looking stiff and awkward, as always, not knowing what to say to me. He held out bottled water for me to take and said, "Drink this."

I took it and almost laughed out loud. Lying there like that reminded me that I needed sleep. Like a soft blanket, I felt sleep covering me. I turned my head to snuggle into a pillow and felt a sharp pain in my head and let out a loud, "Ooow".

"Be careful now," the doctor said. "You hit your head pretty hard. We need you to stay awake until your teacher gets here. Can you do that for us? He moved in closer, looking comical, zooming down to me.

I giggled.

They giggled too, but it sounded like it was in stereo, like one laugh came from behind me. I tried to sit up, wanting to know who else was in the room, but decided I didn't care enough to endure the pain that stabbed my head when I moved.

After what seemed a long time, the door swung open and Mrs. J. made quite the entrance. She spotted me right off and ran, seriously, ran the ten feet to me with her arms spread out, only to bring them to her mouth when she reached me.

I pushed deeper into the couch.

She looked me over, her eyes lingering on my head.

"Are you all right, Christy? My goodness, what else could happen to you on this trip? I may need to keep you right by me from now on."

"I'm fine," I said. "Really." The idea of being right beside her from "then on" totally freaked me out.

"You don't look fine. You look pale and your eyes are all red."

"I'm tired. That's all."

"She can't sleep yet, however," the doctor said. "She needs to be watched a good four hours to make sure she's okay." He turned to me. "Concussions are no laughing matter, young lady. You could die if you go to sleep before we know you are okay."

"Oh my," Mrs. J. said, gasping.

"She'll be all right," the doctor said, backpedaling. "You just need to be careful and keep her awake for a while." Turning to me, he said, "I hear you were bringing the house down with your presentation when you decided to give everyone a scare."

"Yes, yes, she was doing an amazing job," Stephan added. "I've never seen anyone work so quickly and so well on a project, ever." He moved closer to me and said, "Don't worry, I finished it for you. We all wish you were on our team already. Your conclusions were quite insightful."

The thin broad smile on his face made him look even more stiff and awkward.

Mrs. J.'s look of concern changed to glee. She smiled now, too. "I knew you would be impressed with her, Senator. She is quite amazing." She looked behind me. Someone was there. Did she say Senator?

I craned my head around to look, ignoring the pain. A smiling, round, pudgy face looked back at me. It didn't look at all cold and cruel, but my teeth clenched, my pulse pounded in my head, and I felt a cold finger creep down my spine. Frozen, I gawked at him, wide-eyed and open-mouthed.

It was an interesting thing to look at him. He didn't look at all how I had imagined him. I had created a tall, fierce, bulky, powerful man, who craved power. This man seemed the exact opposite. His fat fingers held a cup of coffee and suggested a calm, unassuming demeanor, while his squinty eyes and friendly smile were inviting. Was he really the cold-hearted man I'd imagined? Or was he merely a good pretender or was he trapped by the bad men—a pawn in their plans?

I couldn't bask in the sun of my accomplishments this time. Every nerve in my body screamed for me to run, despite my new impressions, but I couldn't. I was stuck in a frozen body.

He walked closer to me, and I couldn't even flinch. My jaw ached from being left open, and all I wanted to do was to close it. He reached out and patted my shoulder, making my skin crawl. Was it possible to mask a dark, black soul or was it impossible to hide evil when it lurks within? He looked so nice, friendly even.

"She reminds me of my daughter, Alyssa," the Senator spoke. "She's top of her class and always works harder than the next guy. She, however, sees the world through rose-colored glasses. Not like this young lady, sharp, realistic, feeling."

Did I see tears in his eyes? I could feel my tongue drying out. I wished I could bring the water bottle in my hands to my lips.

Somewhere, at sometime, this man had a choice to make and he had made the wrong one. I thought of his Alyssa. Even if they had threatened his family, wouldn't it be better to lose your family than your entire country? Your soul? Or maybe, the Senator was more wise than I'd thought. Maybe he saw that the terrorists would simply kill his family and then move on to the next until they found someone to do their bidding. Why sacrifice your family when it wouldn't change anything? Maybe he was petrified inside and looking for a way out. Maybe, in his quiet alone time, he cried out in horror at what was happening. My thoughts went round and round—all too real. Who was he really?

After a few minutes, I could move and drank the whole bottle of water in one breath. My stomach started to churn, and I knew I had to get out of there, and fast. I stood up slowly, holding my hand out to the doctor. "Thank you so much for taking care of me. I didn't mean to be a bother."

"You weren't a bother," he said, his eyes earnest.

"Sorry to have caused you so much trouble," I said to Stephan.

"Not at all, not at all. I enjoyed reading your presentation," he answered. "Maybe in the near future you can become a part of the team permanently."

Not a chance.

I moved steadily toward the door, paying particular attention to my balance. I kept my eyes on the exit, and didn't dare look back.

"Thanks for letting me crash in your office, Senator," I said, trying to leave any derision out of my voice. "Sorry about that."

"No problem at all. Get better," he said. Then spine freezing words tumbled out of his mouth. "I feel like I know you. Do you live in my state?"

My hand stopped turning the door handle, but I didn't look back. "No, I don't. And I don't think we *have* ever met," I said, with all honesty, trembling inside.

"Hopefully, we will meet again under better circumstances, Christy."

I couldn't nod. I pulled the door open and walked out, not sure if my heart would stay in my chest. I wondered how often healthy, almost sixteen-year-olds died of heart attacks.

Where the heck was the FBI? Didn't they see me walk into the lion's den? The Senator could have done anything he wanted to me in there. I had been a sitting duck in that office.

Mrs. J. brought me back to the hotel in a taxi. The humid, thick air seemed to choke me, intensifying my doubts and fears. This time I didn't want to be alone. I wanted someone with guns sitting with me, keeping me awake and safe. I felt completely open and vulnerable. I couldn't get rid of the constant chill I felt since leaving the Senate office building.

"Let me get you a drink," Mrs. J. said, starting to stand up from my bed.

"No," I said, grabbing her arm. "I don't need a drink yet." I didn't let go of her arm.

"Why don't we head down to the rec room, where it will be easier to keep you awake until Mrs. Henry gets here. We can grab a drink on our way down there." I realized then that she needed a drink, probably a stiff one, after all the headaches I'd given her on this trip. I followed her out of the room and down the hall.

It had been days since we'd been able to play in the rec room. Mrs. J. and I sat, watching TV for the most part, only talking occasionally. It was a little weird to be babysat, but I was glad not to be alone. Did the Senator know the men he worked with were following me? Was he faking that he didn't know me or was he letting me know he knew? Either way, it scared me.

Mrs. Henry arrived, and Mrs. J. darted out to meet the rest of the students back at the congressional offices. It was already five, and she only had a half an hour to get there.

Mrs. Henry talked my ear off. She knew something about everything. I wondered if I talked people to death like she did.

I got up to stretch my legs and looked out the window. The bus sat empty in front of the hotel.

"Hey, Mrs. Henry," I said. "I think it's time for dinner. The bus is here."

She walked over to the window to verify what I'd said. I wondered what it must be like for the kids in her mini-group. I wondered if she verified everything.

I opened the door to the hallway to find both Rick and Alex heading my way.

CHAPTER SIXTEEN

Tingles covered my whole body like little kisses as all my fear melted away. Only a small knot in my stomach tortured me. Two awesome guys were coming to my rescue, and *I* had to be the luckiest girl alive. The fear of running into Senator Randolph flitted away. I felt like jumping up and down and clapping. Luckily, my body was too tired to do that, and besides I'm sure Alex and Rick would have turned around and run away in embarrassment, if I had. Geek-a-rama. I imagined splitting in two and running to each of them, kissing their soft lips and holding them tightly—a very strange sensation.

I knew what I needed to do about the mess I found myself in with these two guys, but Alex looked confident and stunning, while Rick looked open and charming. I felt my conviction waver. How could I let them go? Maybe it could wait. We only had a few days left together. Maybe I could just let it slide.

It made me nervous thinking about being alone with the two of them, though. What would happen? What would we talk about?

Kira and Marybeth surprised me by jumping out from behind the guys and running toward me. .

"Surprise!" they yelled in unison. I jumped, drawing in a deep breath. The guys both looked back, as if they weren't aware the girls had been there. Why were they so happy to see me? Just yesterday they were upset with me. Fickle girls.

"Did you really faint in front of all of those people?" Kira mocked me, her eyes darting to Rick and then back to me. My face flashed hot. I guess they weren't happy to see me, after all. They just wanted to make fun of me and try to make me look bad in front of the guys.

If she only knew why I'd lost it in that meeting, she wouldn't have been so smug, and she certainly wouldn't be trying to gain points with Rick by ridiculing me.

Marybeth eyed my bandaged head. "Does it hurt?" Her concern, at least, did seem genuine. I doubted she knew how to be anything but genuine anyway. I just hoped she hadn't told Kira about Rick in a weak moment.

"I'd have to kill myself if that had happened to me," Kira continued, the sharp edge to her comments cutting like a knife. I had been teased my whole life, it wasn't anything new, but I had found something different here on this trip, and Kira was ruining it all.

I knew Kira was insecure because of how Rick treated me in front of her, but I didn't realize she could be so vicious. I thought she was my friend. Then again, I guess I hadn't been the best friend to her, either. Even though kissing Rick hadn't been planned, I had kissed him, after I told her I was totally not interested. Maybe I deserved to be treated poorly.

The spicy smell in the air told me the guys had finally reached me. Rick stood behind Marybeth, looking at my head and then sweeping my whole body with his eyes. I kind of wanted to hide, but I loved the rollercoaster sensation it gave me to have someone look at me that way.

"Are you okay?' he mouthed, without a sound.

I nodded. My heart beat faster at thinking he cared about me.

I felt fingers brush mine and turning the other way, I saw Alex smiling, his eyes sparkling. He could be so mischievous. A waft of his cologne hung in the air. I giggled quietly, enjoying the lingering tingle in my fingertips. His attempt at being sneaky excited me. I was glad he hadn't grabbed my hand in front of everyone. It would have been extremely awkward. The logistics of being liked by two guys were complicated.

Kira rambled on about her intern shadowing experience as we got into the elevator. Rick stood next to me, and I could feel his warm arm pressing against mine, keeping the blood rushing through my veins. I didn't see Alex get in with us. When we stepped out of the elevator, I realized Alex's cologne wasn't in the air any more. Where had he gone?

Unfortunately, we were on our way to sit through another dry, boring question-and-answer session with Mrs. J. Just thinking about it made my whole body shift into low gear. I started feeling fuzzy, like I couldn't and didn't want to try to stay awake. I looked at the huge clock on the wall. Oh, man! I couldn't sleep for another forty-five minutes. This was going to be a long forty-five minutes.

Rick walked behind me, his gentle hand ushering me to our table.

"I'll get you something to eat," he said, pulling a chair out for me.

My head told me to go with him, that it wasn't a good idea for me to rest yet, but all my body wanted to do was sit. My legs felt like rubber and I could hardly feel my hands. The few steps more I took to my seat seemed off, like I was walking on a tilted floor. I hadn't realized that not sleeping last night and hitting my head could produce such silly feelings. I wanted to bust out laughing, but chose to sit instead.

As I leaned forward to rest my head, a familiar, spicy smell returned. Alex! I sat as upright as I could. He carried two trays, stacked high with all sorts of food. I guess he had hurried downstairs to get me dinner. He was too much. He unloaded the trays onto our table and then walked away. I looked at the food and heard my stomach rumble, but I didn't know if I wanted to eat. I decided it would take too much energy and pushed my plate to the side and laid my head on the table, closing my eyes. Having no sleep last night was catching up to me. I felt strange, fuzzy all over. My body buzzed now, almost asleep. I really wanted more of Alex, but was too tired to go for it.

"Hey, sleepy head." Alex's voice sounded too far away to be important. He pulled my shoulders up and my head lolled to the side. Somewhere in my mind I heard Alex laugh. "I brought your dinner, Christy. It's time to eat," he said, trying to hold me up and sit down in his seat at the same time.

Someone grabbed my face, moving it gently side to side, and said, "Wake up, Christy. You only have forty minutes left. You can do it."

I peeked and saw Marybeth's face looking down at me. "There you go," she said, "Just open your eyes a little bit further."

I didn't think I could, but then a loud slap jolted my eyes open. Kira, who laughed now, had slapped her shoes together to make the noise. She thought it was so funny. I felt dizzy, like I was about to fall off of a very high mountain, and I swayed to the side. Alex slid his chair closer to me, pushing his side against mine to prop me up. He was so warm but I tried to stay awake, like the doctor wanted me to. My eye lids weighed a hundred pounds, and I didn't have the strength to lift them. Certainly, forty minutes would not make or break me. I'd never been so tired before, so out of control—but then again, I'd never been up all night before, either.

"Christy! Alex said in a loud voice. "Here's some chicken." He held a forkful of chicken in front of me. I moved toward it, my mouth grazing the fork carrying it. I chewed dutifully and swallowed. I could hear distant snickers and laughs all around me, and I wanted to laugh with them, but couldn't.

They soon gave up on force-feeding me and I didn't have a care in the world. The fuzziness I'd been feeling got more intense, and it felt good. I had to laugh. It started with a quiet giggle, and it turned into a full-on loud laugh.

Someone put a hand over my mouth; I tried to swat it away, but never made contact. Next thing I knew, it seemed I was flying and had to laugh some more. The flying stopped and I felt a familiar pillow under my head. I snuggled into it and gave into the blackness.

I bolted upright and looked around the room, breathing hard, like I'd been running for miles. The room was lit, and I looked around like a child who'd lost her toy.

The pattering of water in the shower made me look at the clock. Six-forty, five minutes before our regular wake-up call. I lay back down, my head feeling a bit tender when it touched the pillow. I reached up and felt a bandage and sat up again, memories flooding my mind.

I *did* see the Senator, and I did fall. I *was* taken to his office and there had been a doctor in his lair. It hadn't been a dream. My head spun as I tried to make sense of all the things flashing through my brain.

I needed to talk to Jeremy. Why had the FBI let this happen to me? Gaping holes in their "protection" stared me in the face. Did they even know that I had been in the Senator's office? Couldn't they have kept me from working on the bad guy's team?

It had been a strange thing to see the Senator again. He didn't seem like the cold-blooded killer I had pictured in my mind. He looked kind and even spoke lovingly about his children. He had objected to his friend's murder, but what was he doing with the scary Middle Eastern guys? Was he simply a pawn? He didn't seem to be pressured into passing the bill he'd mentioned. He freaked out only after his friend was beheaded. He hadn't liked the consequences of his choices.

Even I knew at my age, you play with bad guys, you get bad things.

I pulled clothes out to wear for the day when Marybeth opened the bathroom door and walked toward me.

"Christy, you're awake," she stated the obvious.

"Yeah." I said, charging past her to the bathroom.

She reached out for me, "Are you alright?"

"Yeah. I'm super hungry, though and want to hurry." I was super hungry, but that wasn't the whole truth. It seemed to be getting easier for me to lie or tell half-truths, which, I guess, truly are lies, just disguised to make people feel better about telling them. I wanted time with Alex.

"Do you remember last night?" she asked, raising her eyebrows.

I stopped short, holding the bathroom door half open. "Not really."

"Well," she said sighing, "I could fill you in…."

I took a moment to think. Did I make a total fool out of myself? Or what? Did I want to know? Marybeth's eyebrows were still lifted, and she boasted a huge smile, convincing me I wanted to hear. I did want to hear, but I needed a shower. I made a move toward her, but thought better of it. Focus.

"Hold that thought," I said. "Give me ten minutes, and I'm all yours." In my haste, I accidentally slammed the door shut.

"Ooops!" I called out, before jumping into the shower.

I made it out of the bathroom, dressed, still brushing my hair in nine minutes flat.

"Tell me," I said.

"You simply won't believe it," she began. "I couldn't believe it, and I was there. What's the last thing you remember?"

I was sucked into the memory of the Senator that I wanted to forget. A shimmer of panic rushed through me. I decided to start at our hotel.

"Let's see, I was waiting for you to get back. I saw the bus outside and told my chaperone, Mrs. Whatever, that the bus was here. The four of you were walking down the hall when we left the rec room. We took the elevator and then it gets sketchy after that."

"That's where it starts getting good," she said, moving in closer to me, her eyes sparkling. "When I got to the table with my food, Alex was sitting next to you, trying to keep you awake. I tried to help, too, when you started laughing hysterically. I tried to cover your mouth, because everyone was staring at you. The question and answer session had already started. . ."

My stomach lurched into my throat and my cheeks flamed. Why the heck had I been laughing hysterically?

Marybeth must've noticed my red cheeks, because she paused and said, "Don't be embarrassed, Christy. You had a huge trauma, ya know?"

Which was also embarrassing in more ways than you could imagine. Was there a hole I could crawl into?

She forged forward, ignoring my ever brightening face. "Mrs. J. walked calmly over to our table and asked if I would watch over you in our room, until a doctor could get there. She tried to remain calm. You should have seen her face. It was hilarious." She laughed lightly and continued. "Alex said, and I quote, 'Would you like me to carry her up to her room, Mrs. J?' My eyes almost bugged out of my head. Alex was going to carry you to our room."

I was sure my eyes *were* bugging out of my head now, but I swallowed, trying not to show any emotion, even though inside my body, every nerve was on high alert.

Had he carried me again?

"Mrs. J. said that would be great, and then she mumbled something like, 'She only had twenty minutes to go.' She walked away, talking on her cell phone, I guess to the doctor. Alex carried you all the way to our room and stayed, sitting next to you on your bed, until the doc came. Which wasn't long at all. Alex waited out in the hall while the doc checked you out. You were a-okay, by the way. He called someone on the phone, probably Mrs. J., and said you were fine and just needed to sleep it off."

I couldn't help but ask, "Did Alex come back in?"

"Yes!" she almost shouted."He stayed for a few hours and slept, yes, slept next to you, until Josh came to get him, said he needed him for something. Just wait," she paused, making me want the information even more. I found myself leaning even closer to her. My pulse quickening.

"I left to get a drink, and when I came back, he was lying next to you, holding your hand."

I looked at her, speechless. I trembled inside, but tried not to show it. She didn't know about Alex and me, and besides, maybe it wasn't real between us anyway. I couldn't stand her mocking me, because I thought it was. He had kissed me, though. Didn't that mean anything?

"He must like you," she squealed. My mind raced, thinking about the implications of what she had said. After about ten seconds, she added, "And that's not all."

What more could there be? Alex had held my hand. How gentle. How sweet. Why did I have to be totally out of it the whole time?

"Like I said, Josh came about a half-hour later, and Alex left with him."

And…I gave her a so-what look.

"Someone knocked on the door a few minutes after that. I thought it was Alex coming back, but it wasn't." She raised an eyebrow and leaned forward a little. "It was Rick." She paused for several seconds, letting it sink in. I looked at my shoes. I wasn't sure I wanted to hear the rest. My heart beat so fast that I thought I might die.

"He asked how you were, and I told him you were sleeping and then he asked if it was all right if he came in. I said, 'Sure, why not.' and he walked right over to you, looking down at you. He ran his fingers down your arm, very slowly and then he leaned over, right in front of me, without even checking to see if I was looking, brushed your cheek with the back of his hand—I was dyyying— and then he leaned down and kissed you on the forehead." Her mouth gaped and her eyes huge. "Then he held your hand, rubbing the back of it. What's going on, anyway? Did you kiss him again? Are you with Rick or not? "

She wanted answers, but I had none I wanted to give her, so I shrugged my shoulders, trying to act as surprised as she was.

"Kira's going to freak when she hears about Rick," Marybeth said. "Not only did he kiss you, he came to take care of you. She'll be devastated. He is the most decent guy here, after all." She flipped her hair behind her shoulders and put her elbows on her knees, staring wildly at me.

"Please, please, Marybeth," I said, reaching out quickly and taking her arms in my hands. "Please don't say anything to Kira."

Marybeth looked at me like she was going to be betraying Kira if she didn't.

"I don't expect you to lie or anything," I said. "But we only have two more days here and I want them to be fun, not stressful." Her face softened, I could tell she was thinking about it. "If you don't tell her, she'll never know.

I'm sure Rick won't tell her, and I sure as heck am not going to tell her. It's not like there's really anything going on between us anyway. He was just checking on me. It didn't mean anything." To make my words valid, I needed to tell Rick and Alex what I'd decided yesterday.

"Fine," she said. "But if it gets out somehow, I won't lie. And it *did* mean something. Rick's in love with you. I can tell. And maybe Alex, too."

Could she be right? Deep heat settled in my gut. Two guys would never be in love with me. "Thanks," I whispered. It was all that I could hope for.

"How is it that you have two awesome guys after you and you don't seem to even know it?"

Instead of answering, I rushed to finish getting ready. As we were leaving the room, I remembered that I hadn't written a note to the FBI boys about the apparent lack of protection, so I yelled to Marybeth, who was already at the elevator, "Go down without me. I'll catch up."

CHAPTER SEVENTEEN

When I stepped out of the elevator, Mrs. J. met me.

"You feeling all right this morning, Christy?" she asked.

"Yeah," I replied. "One hundred percent better, actually." And I did. I was floating above the ground and nothing could bring me down—not today. Not after hearing about how both Alex and Rick stayed with me yesterday. I smiled and walked past her toward the breakfast room.

"Christy," Mrs. J. called out. "We're in the conference room today. We're eating in there again. We changed our plans slightly, so that we would have more time to practice debating."

I looked through the breakfast room doors wishing I could go in.

"Come on, Christy. You're already late."

I followed her into the conference room. I needed to talk to Jeremy, and I was stuck in the darn conference room. The two FBI agents seemed to come down to breakfast only minutes before we left at eight o'clock each day. I wondered how they always had impeccable timing, almost like they had our schedule. They probably did. I wondered who else had our schedule. A cold chill shook my body.

Everyone was already seated, eating. I looked over at all the other tables and found my mini-group spread out all over the room. When I looked at Rick, I felt my lips tingle and my heart race. I pressed them together and looked away. Trying to deny the truth was a difficult thing. Everyone was talking with the people at their tables, and each table had a list of names in the center, along with the subject assigned to us for the debate. It wasn't hard to find my table. It was the only one with an empty chair. Our subject: immigration. Surprise, surprise. It felt like a conspiracy.

Only then did I notice that no sound came from anyone at *my* table, they all stared at me, mouths closed.

"So, what are we supposed to be doing?" I asked, trying to get things rolling.

One girl with long, brown curly hair answered. "We're supposed to be discussing immigration, the pros and cons, and then decide who is going to argue each side."

"Oh," I said. "What have you discussed so far?"

"Nothing," a red-headed boy said. "We were waiting on you."

I guess my presentation the other night gave them the idea that I knew all there was to know about the subject. They all readied their pens and pencils to take notes and stared hard at me. I guess I did know a lot after all the research I'd done, but, I didn't want to tell them how to think, so I said, "Well, what are some of the problems with immigration that you've all heard about? Let's make a list and dissect them."

After discussing a few things, the ball was rolling, and I wasn't the center of attention anymore. They all loved to talk and argue their points. I was so glad. I glanced at the clock. Seven-fifty-five. Jeremy and Nathan would probably be in the breakfast room by now.

I felt the small piece of paper, intended for the FBI, grow heavy in my hand and decided I should take a trip to the bathroom.

I went straight for the breakfast room, but there was no sign of Jeremy or Nathan. I turned back toward the door and bumped into Jeremy.

Something peculiar happened the moment I saw his face. I remembered how it had felt to hug him and have him hug me and I wanted that again. Somehow, I had to feel that secure and safe feeling of comfort again. When he hugged me at the FBI office, it was like the hug I'd never received from my own dad somehow. I threw my arms around him and squeezed tight. He pulled his arms from under mine and carefully, not completely, wrapped his around me. It wasn't the same as it had been in the FBI office, but there was a glimmer of the security there, in his arms.

"Whoa, Jeremy, someone's missed you," Nathan said, punching Jeremy's arm.

Jeremy was now trying to pry my arms from his waist. I looked up at him. Concern shadowed his face, and I felt a bit silly. I didn't know why I had done that really. Maybe, when I had most needed to feel safe, when I had to recount the murder, he was there. I guess he represented safety and comfort to me.

"Do you have some of that for me, too?" Nathan asked.

I played along and gave him a big hug. There was no safety, no security there.

"Where's everybody?" Jeremy asked, winking at me.

"We're in the conference room all day," I explained. "I don't know if we'll have any free time tonight."

"Bummer," Nathan said.

"You could always come and check," I offered.

"Sure, Christy," Jeremy said.

"Great," I said, and started to walk away, until I remembered the paper in my hand. Seeing Jeremy and hugging him had given me the comfort and assurance I needed and made me almost forget why I had been looking for them in the first place. I fingered the note in my pocket and decided not to give it to him. "Hope I'll get to see you."

I rushed back into the conference room. After we researched and discussed for three hours we ate lunch. Then the debates started. The first addressed the economy.

My group looked at me expectantly and handed me the paper with "PROS" written across the top. I guessed I would be debating today.

The lack of preparation of some of the teams was almost sickening. I hated being bored, but more than that, I hated to feel like I knew more about a subject than a supposed expert speaker/debater.

Most of the room was engaged during the debates. Not me. I was so glad when it was finally our turn to debate. I hoped for some excitement. Unfortunately, my opponent was weak and the debate didn't last long.

By five o'clock, all the assigned topics had been debated and discussed, and Mrs. Jackson had no other choice but to let us go. I was glad to hear that she had been as disappointed with the debates as I had been. She encouraged us to study for the final debate so we wouldn't all look silly.

Heading out of the room, I ran into Alex.

"Hey, we're going to grab something to eat and head over to The Mall. It's really cool to watch the sun set from there. You want to come?" he asked. Butterflies filled my stomach.

Just then Marybeth, Kira and Rick popped up behind me. When I looked at Rick, I felt guilty.

"What should we do tonight?" Kira asked. "We don't really have to prepare for tomorrow's debate do we?"

"Uh…" I stammered, not sure if Alex wanted everyone to know his plans and wanting to tell her everyone should prepare.

"We were just talking about getting a bite to eat and then heading over to The Mall to watch the sun set." Alex offered, no excitement in his voice, eyeing Rick.

I was proud of him for telling them.

"You guys coming?" I asked, kind of hoping they weren't.

"Sure, when are you leaving?" Kira asked, as she looked at both Marybeth and Rick to make sure they wanted to go, too. They both nodded.

"Now," Alex said.

"I need to run to my room right quick," Kira said.

"Me, too," Marybeth said.

"Just meet us at the pizza place at the end of the block," Alex said.

Rick kept moving his eyes between Alex and me until Kira grabbed his arm and pulled him toward the elevator.

"Come on, Rick. You wouldn't let us go by ourselves would you?" she asked, flirtation mode on high.

"Of course not," he said, looking back at me and rolling his eyes.

I felt sorry for him, but he shouldn't let everyone push him around in the name of chivalry. I even felt sorry for Kira. Why would she still be trying to force a relationship with Rick? He obviously wasn't into her. Why did Rick have to be so darn polite? It irritated me. They disappeared into the elevator.

Alex grabbed my hand and led me out the front door. Somehow, his touch made me feel alive. My fingers clung to his. I never wanted to let go; and yet I felt nervous, because I had to tell him about the decision I had made last night. I hadn't made it without a lot of thought. Despite the way I felt every time I saw him or was with him, he and I weren't compatible. I couldn't be my best self with him, even if I wanted to believe I could be and in just a few short days, it would all be over anyway.

Hot tears forced themselves into my eyes as I thought about it. I had to really work to push them back. I was so close to letting it all out, my nose burned. I had to make time to tell both Alex and Rick what I'd decided sometime tonight—no matter how much I didn't want to.

The Pizzeria was almost deserted. Only a few tables near the front of the restaurant had anyone sitting at them, and quiet rock music played in the background. With no hostess near the entrance, we went looking for Josh and Summer, who were already there. It smelled amazing. Pizza always smelled so good.

It seemed to get darker and darker the further into the restaurant we went, though. The walls and tables were bare except for a rare picture and a vase of fake flowers at each table. It spooked me.

Summer and Josh were tucked away in a small booth in the back. One look at me and Summer said, "Did you have to bring her?"

"Knock it off, Summer," Alex said in an extremely mean voice.

She shrunk into Josh's arms.

"We ordered already," Josh said.

"I'll order more. Our whole group is coming. And you will play nice, Summer. I mean it." Alex motioned with one arm for me to slide in next Josh and he walked away. I felt totally out of place and hoped he would hurry. It didn't take long at all. Maybe a few minutes. When he did get back, he pulled a small table from the center of the room, pushed it up against the booth table, and brought three chairs to set around it. I loved it. He thought of the others.

"Feel better?" he asked, letting a big grin spread across his face.

"Definitely!" I said, louder than was necessary.

He slid all the way next to me. His warm arm sizzled against mine. The feelings he gave me were anything but ordinary, and I loved every second of it. I had hoped that once I'd made up my mind to tell him I couldn't ever be with him, that the hold he had on me would vanish. Ha. Ha. If anything, it got stronger.

He turned his head toward me, lifted his right elbow to the table and cradled his chin in his hand. His face seemed to glow in the dim light, self-assured and yet somewhere deep, vulnerable. It was hard to be watched by someone so perfect. My face felt hot, and I wanted to look away, but was captive. His left hand found mine, and I started breathing harder, faster. Even though I felt idiotic, there was no physical way for me to look away. The idiocy was being taken over by a burning, tingling sensation that spread through my entire body.

He nuzzled up to my ear and whispered, "So, tell me about yourself, Christy. Start from the beginning and don't stop until you reach this very moment."

He brushed his cheek against mine, his spicy scent filling my brain with utter nonsense. I couldn't find any words, and I didn't care.

When his cheek left mine, my mind started to clear, and I remembered that he had asked me a question. What was it? I searched my memory, relishing the tingle on my cheek. His eyes held mine with a spellbinding intensity and I wondered if speech would ever come to me again. The decisions I'd made the night before didn't seem important anymore. They could wait.

I heard loud scraping noises of chairs being moved on the tile floor that brought me quickly out of my reverie.

Marybeth, Eugene and Rick took a seat around the little table Alex had joined to ours.

Embarrassment crashed over me. What had they seen? How long had they been standing there?

Kira's eyes were mega-wide and her mouth gaped open, while Rick looked down at me with the look of the betrayed. All the sensations that held me bound moments earlier, vanished. I had to look away from his gaze.

Kira pushed her way past the chairs Alex had set around the table and sat next to Alex, pushing him against me even more. My face flushed as I caught Rick's continuous stare. I liked Alex, but it was all too apparent that I liked Rick, too.

Kira immediately started talking to Alex as the others found their seats. She didn't want to believe Alex was interested in me. Rick sat kiddy-corner to me and we had a perfect view of each other. His hurt expression sawed at my heart.

Back home, I would have considered Rick a ten. If I'd been sixteen, I wouldn't have hesitated dating him—not that he'd have asked me. But, here he was put up against true perfection: Alex. It hardly seemed fair.

"How did you find this place?" Kira asked Alex.

"Uhh," Alex hedged. "My parents used to bring me here a lot when I was younger. The pizza is awesome here."

"So, you did live here," Eugene said, eyebrows raised.

"No," Alex answered a bit tersely. "We just spent a lot of time in D.C."

"Oh," Eugene said, looking at the table.

Kira broke in with a string of questions. "Where did you grow up?"

"All over. We didn't really live in one place for very long," Alex answered.

"That would totally suck to have to change schools a lot," Kira said.

"I didn't go to school," he answered.

That caught everyone's attention, except Rick's. He looked only at me, which prevented me from joining the conversation, because I couldn't think straight.

"You didn't go to high school?" Summer broke in, eyebrows pressed together and her lips parted.

"No," he said. "I was tutored."

A huge debate about the pros and cons of high school education ensued; the best debate I'd heard the whole time I'd been in D.C. Summer and Josh couldn't imagine having a fun life without school and sports. Marybeth felt tutoring was the way to go. Eugene felt school was a non-issue. Kira thought Alex must have been lonely his whole life, and Rick said nothing. I wished I'd been Alex and hadn't had to go to high school. How nice.

Every pre-conceived notion I'd had of Alex no longer seemed valid. I had him pegged as the most popular kid in his school, with girls hanging all over him, having girlfriend after girlfriend with no bounds to his social life. Maybe everything I'd imagined about him was false.

Two of the biggest pizzas I'd ever seen were finally delivered to our table, by a portly, smiling waitress. Pitchers of water and coke sat in the middle of the table.

I had to admit that the pizza tasted great, and it didn't take long for it to disappear.

We were about to head for The National Mall, when all the lights went out.

CHAPTER EIGHTEEN

It was pitch black. I couldn't even see my hand in front of my face. I was scared. I heard Marybeth scream as Alex pushed me under the table. Sitting on the hard tile floor, I brought my knees up hard against my chest, wrapping my arms around them. Alex squished up next to me. What was happening? Why did Alex push me under? Had he seen something that made him think this wasn't just a power outage? My heart pounded, and I could hear the faintest of sounds as if they were on loud speakers.

Out of nowhere a flash of bright light accompanied by the two loudest bangs I'd ever heard, echoed through the pizzeria. My ears buzzed and I covered them.

I felt, but couldn't hear the others at our table push their way under it only seconds after the loud bangs. Squished on all sides, with heavy breathing surrounding me, I felt cramped and hot and found it harder and harder to breathe. I kept seeing the flash of light even though my eyes were shut and my ears filled with a horrible ringing from the bang. After about a minute, the ringing diminished and stars blinded my eyes. At last, I could hear the chaos that had erupted at the front of the restaurant.

A huge crash, like a cabinet with glass had been thrown to the floor assaulted my ears. Unable to see a thing, terror gripped me listening to the loud sounds echoing around us. Had the terrorists come for us? Chairs and tables scraped across the floor and crashed down, glass broke again and again, people shouted, and a roar of gunshots rang through the place. Marybeth whimpered. I wanted to grab a hold of her, but knew it was impossible. With bedlam surrounding us, time suddenly seemed suspended as my thoughts searched for peace.

Instead of peace, a horrible realization washed over me like boiling water. We could die. The men from the ballroom waited for their opportunity to take us out and they'd found it. But, who were they shooting at?

Something hit the wall above us. What I assumed was a bullet, whizzed past. Gasps and shouts of pain filled the air. Every swear word in the book, as well as words in languages I couldn't understand rang out in bursts. Was the FBI here? If not, we would die—or worse, get captured and tortured. A part of me wanted to stand up and turn myself in, but most of me was frozen in fear. *Please don't let anybody get hurt or killed.*

Loud thuds and more shots all seemed to get closer and closer to us.

Summer prayed frantically for someone to save us. Was she crying?

Significant moments of the two weeks flashed across my mind in those desperate minutes and made me pray, too. I'd finally found what I had longed for—I felt like I belonged. People wanted to be with me, cool people, and now I might die.

When feet pounding the tile floor got louder and louder, sounding only feet from our table, I ducked down, pulling myself into a tighter ball. It was a horrible thing to have to rely purely on sound. Thank Heaven for my sight. Gunfire rang out, followed by an "Uhh" and a crash that seemed way too close to us. Feet thudded back to the front of the restaurant. Nothing seemed to get near after that, but it didn't relieve the suffocating fear that had enveloped me. Would they torture us or would they kill us quickly if the FBI didn't succeed?

My mind thought of every horrible torture I'd seen on TV or heard about and brought it to life. I wasn't only trembling anymore, I was shaking. I wanted to live. I wanted us all to live. Even without these new friends, I had discovered I had worth. Alex squished his arm around me and held me even closer, which I hadn't thought possible in that cramped space. Somehow, having his arms around me left me less claustrophobic.

Some lights popped on, casting weird shadows on the floor. I could hear people talking loud and fast as steady footsteps approached us. I held my breath, trying to see what was coming. A feeling of imminent death surrounded me, and I heard someone crying.

Alex whispered softly in my ear, "Christy, I have so much to say to you. I don't know what's about to happen, but I need you to know that I think you're amazing. I've never felt this way about anyone before and—"

"Are you guys okay?" A woman's voice interrupted. Her large, black-booted feet standing at the edge of the table freaked me out a bit.

No one moved or made a noise.

I thought it was so curious that we were hearing a woman's voice.

"It's okay," she said. "I'm with the Drug Enforcement Agency. Come on out. You're safe now."

A sloth couldn't have moved slower than we did as we all shifted and then poked our heads above the tables. A tall, muscular woman wearing a jacket that had the letters, "DEA" on the front, stared down at us, her light brown hair pulled back into a tight bun. We squirmed our way back to our seats, eyes fixed on her.

"Sorry about doing that while you guys were here," she said, a light tone to her voice. "We were hoping you would've already cleared out when we had to move. The good news is, that we got some really bad dudes off the street. You were probably scared to death. Thanks for staying so calm."

Calm? I looked around at everyone's faces, they all showed relief, but my heart wouldn't stop racing, and I'm sure my face didn't show anything like calm. I had to think hard about taking deep breaths to slow the beat. As she continued to talk, I noticed how much I felt like a little kid. The condescension in her voice irritated me, and yet I wanted my dad's arms wrapped around me.

An ambulance's sirens screamed in the distance, and I looked past the large woman to see someone lying on the ground near the front doors, with two others giving him CPR.

I heard everyone around me asking questions and the female officer answering. She told about detonating a flash bang that caused the obnoxious light and noise after the lights went out to distract the drug dealers. The questions from my group seemed to move miles away, while the voices of the men near the front of the restaurant, surrounding the fallen DEA agent, became clear.

"1-2-3-4-5-6"

"Nothing, I'm getting nothing."

"Come on."

"Hang on."

"Stay with us."

A small pool of blood puddled near his chest. Chairs and tables were overturned and scattered and broken glass was everywhere. The sirens rang out and then stopped. Two paramedics rushed into the restaurant with another hot on their heels pushing a gurney. In record time, they put the fallen man on the gurney and rushed him to the hungry ambulance while continuing to do CPR.

A drop of sweat clung to my chin, waiting to fall. Please, let him make it. I brushed the sweat away on my sleeve. Only then did I notice a man, face down on the floor, not ten feet from our table. The large agent talking to us almost completely blocked him from our view. Had he been trying to hide or get away? Or had he been coming for us? Other bodies near the front of the Pizzeria lay still and no one paid them any attention.

Jeremy wasn't here. Nathan wasn't here, and everyone standing around wore DEA jackets. Had the FBI just saved us—or was this merely as it appeared—a drug bust?

Out the front window, a line of officers and agents held the arms of cuffed men. I counted seven in all. I tried to remember if I had seen them when we walked in, but I couldn't recall. I hadn't been paying attention to anything but Alex.

I heard the ambulance's renewed scream slowly soften to a whisper as it drove further away. The cuffed men were taken into a van that pulled up in front of them. After the ambulance disappeared, the doors of the van closed behind them and they were gone. A few agents still milled about the pizzeria, cameras shooting and their notebooks being filled. The medical examiner arrived.

My life suddenly seemed to have meaning. Things finally looked up for me, and my mortality dangled before my eyes. My life could be exciting and I had things to look forward to. Things I didn't want to miss.

Alex's hand grabbed mine, and I turned to him. He smiled, head bent to the side in a playful way. A DEA agent led my mini-group through a back door. Rick glanced back at us, as we climbed out of the booth. I brushed up against the woman agent, who blocked the path to the front entrance, trying to avoid an over-turned chair and noticed a badge on her belt that looked suspiciously like the one Jeremy had worn into the FBI building. Her jacket fell back over it, allowing me only a second or two look. I hadn't had the time to see what was printed on it. I looked her in the eye and she looked back, a pressed smile taking over her mouth.

I forced myself to smile and scooted around the now covered body that lay near our table.

It seemed the incident hadn't fazed anyone else in my group, and it was business as usual to them. Weird. Hadn't they noticed the dead guy right by us, or the severely wounded DEA agent? Didn't they suspect this might have something to do with the ballroom?

Outside, they all talked about going to The National Mall one last time. As we waited for taxis, I did hear Rick comforting Marybeth and pulling her in for a hug. At least Marybeth seemed to be having the right reaction to what had happened. Maybe it would hit them later, when they had time to reflect on it.

Alex helped me into a cab with Summer and Josh again. As we drove, I rested my head back on the seat, closed my eyes and counted my blessings.

Songs I'd learned as a child in church played softly in the background of my mind as I thanked God that I was alive and would live to see another day. My outlook on life had shifted as I had crouched beneath that table—life was worth living—*my* life was worth living. I didn't have to let things around me determine my happiness. No longer would I wait for it to find me, because maybe tomorrow was my day to die. I would no longer live like I had been, scared, lonely and disappointed. Silent prayers of thanks escaped my lips more than once before we arrived at The Mall.

By the time I climbed out of that taxi, I felt great. Nothing but positive things filled my mind. I looked at my mini-group, who had been my existence for almost two weeks, and let myself be happy for my plain Jane life. I discovered I wouldn't trade it for the life of anyone that stood in front of me, not even Summer's. Their lives no longer seemed so inviting.

We played hard at The Mall, laughing, running, and talking. I'd found a freedom I'd never felt before. Running down the stairs to the Reflecting Pool beneath the Memorial should have brought back terrorizing memories of a blue eyed man giving me a picture, but it didn't. I decided not to allow some crazy men to ruin my life and make me live scared any longer. If I was going to die, I didn't want it to be in terror. I wouldn't give them that power anymore. I also wasn't going to let anyone intimidate me again. Summer and Kira's snide comments and dirty looks weren't going to haunt me anymore. I'd wasted the last three months of my life in misery. Now, I was going to be happy.

Some of the time we all walked bunched up, chatting. Other times we splintered into groups of two to six. The ebb and flow was almost musical, and I danced through the various groupings, never staying with one group very long. We made it past the Washington Monument when Eugene let us know we only had half an hour until bed-check.

As we walked to the street to hail taxis, we conspired to act as if we were going to bed, but then meet up at nine-thirty in the rec room, after Mrs. J. hit the sack. I couldn't wait.

Out of nowhere, Rick stood next to me on the sidewalk, and his hand grazed mine. I looked up at him and smiled. His fingers danced across mine and my blood starting racing. It sped up considerably when I felt Alex's hand grab my other hand and pull me to a waiting taxi. Rick tried to grab the one he'd grazed, but Alex had already pulled me too far away and his hand caught only air. Rick's face squished up, and he mouthed the words, "Come with me." I pressed my lips into a frown and let Alex pull me further away. Rick kept his eyes locked on me until my taxi drove away. I know, because my eyes were fixed on his.

In our hotel, Mrs. J. stood at the end of our hallway, telling us to go to our rooms. Like obedient little children, we all did and then waited the long half-hour to escape. Much to my chagrin, as Marybeth and I headed out our door, Mrs. J. stood guard at the end of the hall with a sour face. We hesitated, but only for a moment, and then I grabbed Marybeth's arm, and we headed for the vending machine room. What had gotten into Mrs. J. these past few nights? For almost a week and a half she hadn't monitored us, but now…Could she possibly know something?

Once inside the vending room, we searched our pockets for any change we could find. We were five cents short of the cheapest item. We looked on the floor and in the change slots. Nothing. We stared at each other for a few seconds and then busted up laughing. Why were we trying to keep up the ruse? Mrs. J. knew we were trying to sneak out; she wasn't dumb. We slinked back to our room, waving and saying goodnight to a scowling Mrs. J.

We laughed so hard once the door closed, I was sure my stomach muscles would be sore the next day. It felt good to laugh. No, great. Mrs. J. had beaten us, so we conceded defeat, talking until we fell asleep. I wished I could talk about my problems with Rick and Alex with Marybeth. I didn't want her to think badly about me, though, and I knew she didn't understand the whole no-dating-until-sixteen-thing. Besides that, I wasn't sure I understood it anymore.

CHAPTER NINETEEN

A tapping noise grated on my nerves. I wanted to keep sleeping, but kept hearing, tap, tap, tap… It wouldn't stop, no matter how hard I willed it to. I opened my eyes to tiny slits and realized the tap came from our door. I looked at Marybeth. A light, even breathing came from her direction. With no hope of her getting up, I stomped to the door, but not before checking the clock. One A.M. The idea that danger lurked behind the door didn't even come to mind.

An "Uggh," escaped my lips as I cracked open the door, security latch still in place. Rick stood there.

"It's about time," he said. "You guys must be hard sleepers."

"Maybe that's because it's one in the morning, you dork," I whispered, peering out of the crack with a little smile gracing my lips. My voice croaked, reminding him I'd just woken up.

"Sorry about that. I wanted to talk to you," he said.

"Now?" I asked.

His face gave me the answer.

"'Kay, just give me a few minutes to get dressed."

I shut the door and went to the bathroom to get dressed and brush my teeth, my insides fluttering. I left the room on tip-toe.

The conference room was locked. In fact, all the doors on the main floor were locked and the one security guard sat by the front door half asleep.

"Let's go sit in a hall somewhere," he suggested.

"Okay," I said.

"Did you have fun tonight? I mean after the whole Pizzeria horror?" he asked.

"Yeah. It was a lot of fun. Did you?"

"Yeah, I guess so."

"You looked like you were having fun."

Once we got in the elevator, we decided to get out on fifth floor. We sat near the vending machine doors. My back leaned against the wall, my legs outstretched in front of me. Rick sat to the side of me, cross-legged, knees barely touching the side of my outstretched legs.

He took a deep breath, looking at his legs. His head came up and his eyes met mine. I gave him a slight smile.

"Are you and Alex together?" he asked, his tone serious now.

I felt my eyes turn into saucers at his blunt question. I don't know why. After our last talk, I knew he was a straight-forward kind of guy. I tried to look away, but couldn't.

"No," I finally answered. We weren't together, after all.

"Really? You're not playing me are you?"

"Playing you? No." I couldn't believe he thought I could *play* someone.

"I thought I saw you and Alex... you know, kissing at the pizzeria—"

"You didn't," I interrupted. While we hadn't, I wished Alex had kissed me.

There was an uncomfortable pause before he spoke again.

"You like him though, don't you?"

I wondered what I should say, what I could say and still be truthful and not hurt him. He was really putting himself out there, and I didn't think it was right to mislead him.

"Sure, but I also like you." My stomach dropped hearing me say those words aloud.

He looked so cute sitting there, totally out, exposed and honest. He got cuter by the minute. I loved the way his teeth looked, all perfectly straight and white. I couldn't help but think about our soft kiss near the fountain. I was caught up in staring at those perfect lips and forgot we were having a conversation for a moment. What was happening to me?

"What do you mean, you like me too? Does that mean you like him as a friend and me in a different way? Or do you like us both as friends, or both as more than friends? What does that mean?" His gaze never left me, his look soft and earnest. I swallowed, his boldness making it hard to find the right words. How could I tell him that while he gave me tingles, Alex gave me tingles on steroids?

"Look Rick, this is all so confusing to me. I never thought I would be faced with all of this yet. I'm not even sixteen, so I shouldn't be dealing with it anyway." It took all my power not to look at his lips.

"What does sixteen have to do with my question?"

"I don't know. I mean, because my parents allow me to date when I turn sixteen, I guess I figured it was some kind of a magical age—that at sixteen, we all get some power to be able to deal with dating and driving and all that stuff." I suffered from diarrhea of the mouth. "Maybe that was dumb of me, but I, well, actually, I never even thought that I would have a guy interested in me after I was sixteen, let alone, before I turned sixteen."

"What?" Confusion traced his face.

"What I'm trying to say is," I paused, taking a very deep breath, "at home, no one even looks at me. I'm non-existent. At least to kids my own age. Even though my parents would allow me to date in a month, when I turn sixteen, no one at home would ever ask me out." I couldn't believe I told him. Somehow he made me feel like I could tell him everything—even the sucky stuff. I never would have told Alex this stuff. "It's just stupid. Forget I said anything."

"It's not stupid. Everyone feels invisible at times," he said.

I'd probably made him feel invisible today. I felt horrible.

Having the encouragement I needed, I continued. "Somehow, here, on this trip, people see me. It's crazy. I imagined this happening, but never thought it would. I mean, I wanted this trip to change my life, put a spark into it, but this is more than I ever bargained for. I'm having a hard time dealing with it in the right way. I know you think that me turning sixteen is some artificial line that isn't really important, but it is to me. I've always dreamed about turning sixteen and being able to date. So, for you to ask me who I like and how, is pointless." I breathed deep and hard. First guy down, only Alex left to give the boot. I guess I believed in the sixteen rule.

"Christy, they're only feelings. You don't have to be dating to have feelings."

He was right. His handsome face pleaded with me to be truthful. I didn't know if I wanted the truth, but his look told me I could trust him with more. I was scared to be totally honest.

"Rick, tomorrow is our last real day here. You will go home and within a few hours you will forget that I even exist." I had said it. I didn't want to reveal my feelings, because they would invariably be stepped on in a few short days. I closed my eyes and took a deep breath, trying to keep my composure.

"So, the truth will out," he said in a soft whisper.

I looked at him, and he smiled at me.

"Think about it," I said. "Our group has been in a little mini-world the past few weeks. Things get confusing and we forget that this world isn't real. Then, we go back home and reality sets in. It's like that reality show, *The Bachelor*. People get together, who wouldn't have otherwise, and then, as soon as the show is over and they're back in the real world, they always break up. This isn't the real world. No one wants to be with me in the real world." I felt the burn of tears at the back of my eyes and tilted my head back to prevent their escape.

"That's just crazy talk," he said, moving closer to me. "This feels real to me."

I slumped further down on the wall and pulled my legs to my chest, letting my face rest on my knees, keeping my eyes shut tight, allowing no tears to escape.

"How I feel about you isn't going to change just because we aren't in D.C. anymore." He tried to push my head up, but I resisted. "Christy, look at me," he coaxed.

I peeked out at him.

"Let's just let things go where they will and enjoy the ride. If it ends sooner than we hoped, then at least we had fun while it lasted."

"I don't want it to crash, though." I admitted, pushing my head back down to my knees and losing it.

"Even a crash doesn't make what happened before the crash less real." He reached for my chin and lifted my face, wiping a tear from my cheek.

His warm, gentle touch soothed me. He had a point and I had decided to enjoy life and be happy, to take risks and live every day like it was my last. My legs slid back down to the floor and I nodded.

"You're right," I whispered.

"About Alex," he said, looking me straight in the eye and letting his hands fall to the floor. "I don't think he's the greatest guy for you to get involved with."

"You don't, do you?" I said, teasing him.

"No, really. He doesn't give me a good vibe. I don't really know him, but I know his type."

"And what is his type?" I was starting to get annoyed.

"You know, guys who like the chase and then when they get what they want, they move on."

"You think he's like that?" I hadn't ever talked to Alex about previous girl friends or really anything serious, for that matter. I was shocked at the pizzeria when he said he'd never been to high school. What else didn't I know about him? Really, all I knew was how he made me feel, and I liked that, a lot.

"Just be careful, Christy. That's all I'm saying."

I realized that I didn't know anything about Rick, either. "So, tell me about yourself. What is a typical day, no week, like for you?"

"I'm sure it's like yours. Sundays I go to church..."

"You go to church?" I blurted before I'd thought it through.

"Of course. You do too, don't you?"

"Every Sunday." I was still surprised for some reason.

"Monday through Friday I go to school, have practice, go to lessons, do homework and head home."

"What kind of practice?"

"You know, soccer, lacrosse, basketball. . . ."

"What kind of lessons?"

"Horseback riding, piano, voice, stuff like that. Then Saturdays we attend political stuff and play. We have a lot of dinner parties all week, too."

"Hmpf."

"What's a typical week for you like?"

"Sunday, church and extended family dinner. Monday through Friday I go to school and study. On Tuesday I go to a youth group at my church and on Thursdays I play one of four sports, softball, basketball, volleyball or soccer. Sometimes there's a practice thrown in there somewhere. I'm home most of the time, but I hike and bike a lot." Really, if it was free I did it. If it cost anything, it was out of the question. "What do you love to do?"

Rick moved to lean his back against the wall to sit next to me. We talked more about his family and what he liked to do. After a while, I started to get really tired, and I leaned my head on his shoulder, my eyes closing. My body twitched, and I sat up straight.

"Let's get you back into bed," he said.

"Sorry. I'm just so tired." I complained.

"I know. I'm sorry for keeping you up, but I'm so glad we had some time together to figure stuff out."

"Me, too."

He kissed my hand at the door to my room and waited for me to shut it before walking away. He knew I was a dork back home and didn't seem to care. He had a way of accepting me that was totally foreign.

So excited to have another day in D.C., my internal clock woke me before the wake-up call—even after being with Rick until two-thirty. It was my last real day in D.C. and I wanted to enjoy every minute of it. I still didn't believe that whole shoot-out at the pizzeria last night didn't have to do with the terrorists like that woman wanted us to believe and hoped they had been taken care of last night. Alex had told me he really liked me under the table at the Pizzeria, and I'd worked things out with Rick. Life was good.

After getting ready, I still had some time to kill, so I stepped out onto the balcony. The sky looked overcast, and it felt muggy. I watched as cars drove past and I saw a drycleaners van drive by. Marybeth's outfit. I hadn't gotten it back from the drycleaners yet. I flew through our room and down to the lobby. The receptionist looked at me with pursed lips.

"I sent some things to be dry cleaned two days ago. I still haven't gotten them back, and I leave tomorrow, early. Could you check for them?" I asked.

"Dry cleaning is delivered to your room with maid service," he said curtly. "Are you sure it isn't hanging in your closet?"

"Yes. It isn't there. I was told it would be done yesterday. Please check."

"If it isn't in your room..."

"Just check." I interrupted, trying not to get mad.

"One moment," he said, turning to go into the back room.

What if they lost it? There would be no way to replace it. I hadn't thought of that.

He returned several minutes later, dry cleaning in hand.

Relief washed over me.

"I'm sorry," he said, handing me the hangers. "For some reason, yours was left in the back room."

"Thanks!" I yelled, running to the elevator. I took the plastic off the clothes and removed the hangers. The clothes looked as good as new, and I had to smile. As I chucked the hangers and plastic into a hall garbage, my receipt fluttered to the ground. I grabbed it and stuffed it into my jeans pocket.

What luck! Marybeth was in the shower when I walked into our room. I hung her clothes back on their original hangers and took a deep breath. "Better than when I borrowed them," I whispered to myself and sat on my bed to wait for seven o'clock, guilt burning in my chest.

CHAPTER TWENTY

Alex wasn't in the breakfast room, but Rick was. I was surprised to feel my stomach jump when I saw him.

"Saved ya a seat," he said, gesturing beside him.

"Really?" I said. "Are you sure there's room for me?"

"I think you can squeeze in." He laughed and so did I. We were the only two from our whole group in the room again. But it felt so different this time. I wanted to be with him.

"I'm surprised you're here so early," he said. "It's so unlike you."

"Ha, Ha. Someone even kept me up last night. But, as you know, today is our last real day here. I want to enjoy every minute."

"Ditto."

We laughed about last night and continued our conversation until more of our group joined us. Alex still hadn't showed. Why couldn't I just forget about Alex and give my full attention to Rick? Mrs. J. told us to head for the bus, and Rick took Marybeth's, Kira's and my trash to the garbage. I stood up, watching Rick walk away, when I felt a hand grab mine. Alex's.

I grinned playfully, my stomach tingling, making me feel silly. "Hey," I said. "We missed ya at breakfast." My voice didn't sound like me. It was too perky.

"Yeah, I was so tired, if Josh hadn't woken me, I'd still be sleeping."

"Sorry," I said, wondering why he looked so tired and wishing I'd thought to go knock on his door to see where he was.

He raised my chin up and said, "Hey, why don't we

forget about this thing today and just go roam D.C. together?" His fingers traced my jawbone.

My heart flipped. How I wanted to. "I would love to do that, but I'd lose my scholarship if I did, and I don't know where I would come up with ten grand to pay it back." No fun for me. I guess adventure is hard to come by when you're always trying to do the right thing.

His head dropped slightly to the side. "I'll pay it. Come on, let's go." He motioned with his head toward the exit.

I'll pay it? Did he really just say he would pay it? Good grief, ten thousand dollars down the drain. Just like that. Was ten grand really nothing to him? "That's really tempting, but that would be silly." Oh, how I wanted to go. Why couldn't I say yes?

"I want to spend some time with you. Christy, come on."

"I can't, I'm sorry." A hot rock sat in my stomach.

"Today's the last day." He sighed and wrapped his arm around my waist, pulling me closer.

"I know. So let's make the best of it." I turned out of his arm, grabbing his hand and pulling him toward the door. Rick came into view as I turned. He stood, frozen by the garbage can, staring at us. This morning had been so nice with Rick, why was it so easy to leave him for Alex, now?

Alex saw me look past him at Rick and looked too. I stopped pulling, my stomach burning, only to have Alex turn and pull me out the door.

"Do I need to be worried?" Alex asked, as we boarded the bus.

"Worried?" I asked.

"Yeah, worried."

"About what?" I said, plopping onto an empty seat near the back and sliding toward the window.

"About Rick," he hissed, his face so close to my ear that I felt his breath.

Before I could answer, Rick said, "Hey guys," interrupting us and sitting in the seat just in front of ours as the bus started to move. His breathing was heavy. He must have run. He really didn't want Alex to have me.

Alex turned to face Rick, so slowly that it seemed to take forever. My heart was being squashed, and I held my breath. Rick had known about Alex from the start, but Alex had no clue about Rick. My face burned, and all I could do was stare at Rick. Did I want Rick or Alex? I wanted both.

"Hmm," Alex managed.

I wondered what more Rick wanted to say. He grinned from ear to ear, looking at me. I hoped he would be kind enough not to bring up our meeting last night.

"Our last day here. Can you believe it?" Rick asked.

"Can't," Alex answered in a short burst. The bus moved into traffic.

I tried to answer, but could only shake my head. I looked at Alex, his jaw tight. He stared at Rick with hard eyes. Rick's eyes, on the other hand, were on fire. He was on the attack. *Please, please don't mention last night*, I thought. Rick started to open his mouth to speak again, but I jumped in, unwilling to let Alex know about last night—if that's what he was going to talk about.

"Is the debate going to last the whole day?" I asked, even though I knew the answer.

The fire in Rick's eyes seemed to ebb a bit when he looked back at me.

"I think it gets over at five, but then there's the gala after that," Rick said.

Hmm. The gala. I conveniently pushed it out of my mind.

"I hope they keep us all together," I said. "I can't imagine spending the whole day listening to the unprepared and uninspired."

Alex chuckled and then whispered, "Let's not then."

I'm sure my face was fire engine red at that moment. Did Rick hear? His smoldering voice sent a shock through my body, and I sighed, wishing I could go with him.

Rick's eyes fired up again, he must have heard, but before he could speak, I jumped up, noticing that the bus had stopped.

"Let's get out of here," I said, pushing Alex into the aisle. Rick let us pass and then followed. I smiled at him feeling stupid, ashamed.

Once inside, everyone split up, heading for their registration table that sat under the letter corresponding with their last names. Much to my horror, Senator Randolph was assigned to me. It was too much. It couldn't be a coincidence, could it? Most students would be given names of congressmen, but there were over five hundred students involved in this little experiment and so senators would also have to be used. We were given a little packet that showed where our seat was and what to expect throughout the day. It included a small list of Senate bills and causes that Senator Randolph's campaign was for or against.

I paused as I looked at the list, unable to avoid wondering if the bill the robed man in the ballroom had said must pass was included in the list. Maybe being assigned to Senator Randolph was a blessing after all. Maybe I could figure out what he was up to.

I walked into the huge room. The conference center had been made into a makeshift congressional meeting room—pretty accurately laid out—only on a larger scale.

As I looked for my seat, I smiled sitting in my seat ten rows from the very back on the aisle. Extra space was always a plus to me, but I knew no one around me. I couldn't even see anyone in my mini-group or tour group of fifty. This place was huge.

I thought about what the four bills on Senator Randolph's list involved: immigration, livestock identification, farmers' aid, and energy solutions. I knew the immigration bill forwards and backwards, and in that bill, I couldn't make any connections with the Middle East. That bill had everything to do with boarder immigration from Mexico and Canada. I knew nothing about the other three bills. Then I noticed that Senator Randolph was only sponsoring two of them: immigration and farmers' aid.

I wished I had a computer at that moment; I wanted to research this farmers' aid bill. Looking around, I noticed a lot of students had brought laptops today. A guy three seats down from me had one sitting closed on his desk.

Did I dare ask him to use it? He'd probably think I was a kook, but I really wanted it. I took a deep breath, deciding the information about farmers' aid was more important than my discomfort. I stood up, put my hands together and walked towards this guy, telling myself I could do it. His eyes were closed, head tilted slightly back, hands folded in his lap. He looked harmless enough, so I reached out and tapped his shoulder. He peeked out of one eye, then sat up straight, opening both eyes wide.

"Hi. I'm Christy. I was wondering, could I borrow your laptop for a few minutes, just until we start, I mean?"

"Sure," he blurted, pushing the laptop toward me. It almost fell to the floor, but I caught it. His face was crimson and his eyes almost bugged out of his head.

"Great," I said. "I'm only three seats this way, on the aisle." I gestured with the laptop in the direction I was already walking. He nodded his head but said nothing.

"Twenty minutes to find what I needed," I thought. "Plenty of time."

I was wrong. There was a ton of gibberish on this bill: companies I'd never heard of and couldn't find information on, funding from unspecified sources; lots of nonsense woven into some real stuff.

When the bell chimed, alerting everyone that we would begin in five minutes, I'd barely scraped the surface. I forged on, trying to skim through the slush and find the meat. I looked up and noticed the young man who'd loaned me the laptop looking at me nervously. I gave up and took it to him.

"Thank you so much," I said. "Too bad I didn't have another two hours." I grinned. He kind of lifted his chin a bit, but said nothing.

I wondered if that mess of a bill could possibly have something to do with the Middle East. Then I remembered what Marybeth had said about Senator Randolph. "He's going to save the farmers. He's heaven sent." I tossed around the information I'd seen on the computer for the next three hours of debate—a good distraction until lunch time.

Lunch was 'ala carte, so I grabbed a sandwich and looked for anyone in our group. I would've loved to have found Eugene. He was sure to have his laptop with him, but he was nowhere to be found. There were too many people in too large a space. I would even have settled for some kind of internet phone at the moment.

I sat on a ledge in the corner of the massive room and ate, while cursing the fact that I needed more information and didn't know how I would get it.

A shadow fell over me and I tried not to look up, but the suspense was killing me. After about ten seconds, I did look up. The guy I'd borrowed the laptop from earlier stood in front of me. I gave him a smile and waited for him to speak.

"You could laptop use again?" he stuttered.

"Huh?" I said, trying to focus on him.

He held out the laptop in front of me, paler than before.

"Oh," I said, figuring out what he'd said. "I'd love to use the laptop again. Thanks!"

He managed a grin this time as he handed it over to me.

He reminded me of myself at home. I could never talk to anyone my age one-on-one without sounding like an idiot. This guy was just nervous. I wanted to make him feel comfortable, and so I patted the ledge beside me, and he sat down.

"I'm researching Senator Randolph's farmers' aid bill. Do you know anything about it?" I asked without looking at him, trying to make it easier for him to talk to me.

"Nothing," he squeaked.

"Darn," I said. "There's all this crazy wording in this bill and lots of different companies involved that have no web presence. The bill appears to be a good thing on the surface, but as you dig deeper, more questions appear than answers."

"Humpf," he said. "Sounds like politics to me."

"Does this say that these companies mentioned here," I said, pointing at the screen, "will *own* the land in Iowa, with opportunity to own land in all other states?"

The shy boy, still nameless, looked at the screen with interest.

I read further, trying to disprove my ideas, but they were only strengthened.

"Looks like it to me," the boy said. I was careful not to look at him.

"How could that benefit the farmers?" I said, half to myself.

"That's easy," he said. My looking away seemed to pull him out of his shell. I hoped it would. It would have for me. "If someone else owns the land, there's less risk to the farmers in case of disasters."

I was already four pages further, listening to him, but concentrating on my reading. I had to gasp at what I was reading. Then I remembered I'd been talking to him and needed to comment on what he had said.

"That seems logical," I said. "But what if the land owner owned the crops, too, and the farmers only work for these companies?"

"That sounds great," he said. "Then the farmer has no risk and no loss. Only gain."

"But, they also would get none of the benefits of outright ownership. It would be a job, nothing more. Who are these companies that would have all the power to decide what and when to plant?" I mused.

"There you are," a voice said, interrupting us.

I knew the voice immediately. Alex. I had to smile. I looked up, and sure enough, he smiled down at me.

"What could be so important on that computer," Alex said, "that would keep you from finding me during lunch?"

"I looked all over for you guys," I protested. "I couldn't find you. I was all alone until," I looked toward the unnamed guy and asked, "I never caught your name, I'm sorry."

He dropped his head and said, "Thomas."

242

"Well, Thomas here, was nice enough to let me use his laptop to do some research to figure out this bill I'm supposed to defend today."

"Someone helped you?" he said, sarcasm lining his words. "I didn't know anyone knew enough to help you."

"Ha, Ha," I said. "Have you ever heard of any of these companies?" I asked, pointing to the screen again.

"Never heard of any of them," he answered after looking them over.

"Don't you think that's odd?" I asked. "You know, this bill is sponsored by Senator Randolph." I gave him a knowing look.

"Hmm." Alex said. He looked harder at the screen.

The five minute bell rang, and I felt Thomas, my laptop provider, stand up. He was ready to go back to his seat. I shut the laptop, wishing I could keep it, and handed it over to him.

"Thanks again," I said. "You were really helpful."

He grabbed the laptop and hurried away, head down.

"Alex, I think these terrorists have plans to take over our farmlands, but why? They already control the oil, do they want to control our food supplies, too? It would be impossible. Do you know how many farms fill this country? I can't imagine how they could get control of all of them in less than…. a hundred years."

"Yeah, doesn't seem like a smart move."

I looked up at Alex's too perfect face and had to smile again, my body buzzing. For a moment, Senator Randolph didn't exist and I found myself in shock thinking that Alex might really like me. He had searched for me all during lunch, and he held his sack lunch, still full, his face glowing. Butterflies took over my stomach. I liked this feeling.

He sat down next to me and said, "Let's ditch this place, please."

The force of his eyes melted my heart. I wanted to ditch.

"We've already been over this," I said, smiling.

"Really, Christy," he said. "There are over five hundred kids in there. No one will miss us.... No one will know."

"I'll know," I said. I felt uneasy, unsure about how he would feel about this declaration. Maybe now he would see that I really was a goody-two-shoes.

His head dropped and rolled to the side. He looked at me with only his left eye and clicked his tongue while sighing. His eyes closed and his head hung again. The silence seemed thick as the moments pressed on. I knew he was planning his "farewell to Christy" speech. After all, he could only put up with so much, for so long. I sighed and closed my eyes, trying to prepare for the rejection. I didn't know if I could.

Alex made me feel so good, but I had to let him go. I already knew this but had been putting off the inevitable. Couldn't I bend my own rules to accommodate him, just this once? Just this once? Who was I kidding? I had already bent the rules with him several times and it had only led to heartache. Maybe now he would be saying goodbye, not me. I took a deep breath and opened my eyes.

He looked at me, lips pressed together but slightly up in the corners. He pushed air through his nose as he gave in to a stifled laugh.

"Only you, Christy," he said. "Only you would think like that. Maybe that's why I like you so much. I've never met anyone who had such strong convictions. I surrender."

My eyebrows rose involuntarily, and I gave a big smile—I couldn't help it. He said it again. He likes me.

My insides were all a buzz, and I felt like jumping up and down. It was good, once more, that I didn't. Taking my hand, he pulled me up, all thoughts of telling him goodbye disappeared and we walked back into the debate arena.

Sitting back in my seat, something tugged at my gut. I felt the weight of the murder fall back onto my shoulders like a backpack full of stones. I slumped under the imagined weight of it. Feeling that the answers were just out of reach, made it even harder. I was missing something.

"We'll start with Senator Randolph's bill involving farmers' aid," the Emcee announced.

I sat upright and looked around to see if anyone had heard what I thought I'd heard. "Again, we will be starting with Senator Randolph's bill involving farmers' aid."

All the documents I'd read about this bill sorted themselves automatically in my mind as they always did before a debate and only the important details popped off the page for me to organize into a five minute "rah rah" speech as I walked to the podium. I tried to pull out the points that would cause the most discussion and to voice them in a way that would rile even the softest of competitors. I wanted to hear what this group knew about this bill. Maybe the group could fill in some of the blanks.

Good thing I hadn't skipped out of this place with Alex.

My delivery was flawless, as always, and it appeared to have excited a lot of conversation, especially the idea of letting other countries shoulder the risk for our farmers. The implication that they would also reap the rewards hung out there like a chandelier held up with a cotton thread.

A line of kids assigned to oppose the legislation formed at the bottom of the stage. I sat behind the podium in a seat provided for the people who introduced bills. I closed my eyes and listened intently, for anything I hadn't thought of already. It seemed like forever had come and gone when I opened my eyes and looked at the clock. It had been forty minutes—only five more minutes until I had to stand and give my closing remarks. The ten students who had expressed their opposition had given me nothing. Nothing new that is. I watched a short boy with extremely blond hair and glasses walk up to the podium.

"Please, please, give me something, anything," I said under my breath. I listened, staring at the back of his head. He did give me something. He talked about renewable resources and how our farmland was our only hope for our country's future, especially when it came to energy. Oil wasn't renewable, but things like bio-diesel and ethanol were. That was it. I felt all excited.

Energy—it all had to do with energy. The terrorists didn't need bombs, swords and missiles to bring America to its knees, it only needed its resources. Right as it got interesting, the moderator interrupted him and sent him to his seat.

It was my turn again. I had to tout the bill and couldn't blast it, so I decided to be sly in what I said. I would almost be sarcastic, pretending to sell the bill. Hopefully, the absurdity of what I would say would open the audience's minds to the danger of it. Hopefully, they would go home and discuss what I had to say with their parents and friends and whoever would listen. Hopefully.

My stomach fluttered as my mind finished spinning the tale I was about to put out to the five hundred plus people listening. For the first time in a debate, I had an aching desire to have people really hear what I had to say, and it was late in the day. How could I make them listen?

An amazing thing happened when I stood at the podium. Something incredible—It was like some powerful, unseen force gave me the words to say—like whatever or whoever guided me, didn't want the terrorists to win either. The words flowed without effort from my mouth.

When I finished, I stepped away from the podium and left the stage. Descending the steps, voices rumbled all around me. It seemed everyone was talking to someone. I turned toward the audience and five hundred pairs of eyes stared at me. I smiled despite myself. They had understood. They must have. I murmured my thanks to my unseen helper. The audience's eyes followed my every step, until the Emcee announced the next bill.

As I started up the aisle that led to my seat, I noticed a man by the doors, staring down at me. After what seemed a thousand steps, I could finally make out his face. Iceman. The terrorists were still out there. I guess the sting at the Pizzeria really didn't have to do with them at all. I passed my seat and kept climbing. I zeroed in on his face and didn't let my eyes wander. I sped up. His eyes locked on mine until I was only ten steps from him and he turned and ran.

Something broke inside me, fury took over. If what I suspected the whole bloody ballroom scene was about, was correct, not only would the Middle East continue to tie our hands with their control of most of the oil we used in the U.S., but they would also bring us to our knees with the control of our farmland and our renewable energy sources, even though I didn't know exactly how.

Iceman rushed out the door of the auditorium. I wasn't far behind.

He ran fast. I blasted down the stairs, skipping as many as I could and plowed out the doors to the sidewalk. Out of the corner of my eye, I thought I saw his black jacket turn down an alley some way down the street. I ran flat-out until I turned the corner. He wasn't there. I walked full of purpose down the alley and found I could only turn left.

He stood, facing me at the far end of the alley. Had I trapped him? I hesitated, but only for a second. I refused to be a victim any longer. I had control of my reactions and I would no longer be afraid. My heart stampeded out of my chest, and I pulled hard for air. Fists balled, I flew toward him anyway.

At about the half-way mark, I started to shout at him.

"Why are you following me and my friends? Why? Stay away from us!"

He didn't say anything, his face had a puzzled look on it—a curious look, and then he disappeared down another alley. He wasn't trapped after all. I picked up the pace and tried to follow him. The alley led to another sidewalk and street. He was gone.

I screamed as loud as I could, head back and arms stiff at my sides. I heard doors and windows open and saw faces looking through them at me. I didn't even care. I stood there in all my indignant anger. I let it wash over me and if people hadn't been staring, I probably would have dropped to the ground and bawled. I didn't know what I thought I'd do to him once I got to him, but I hated him for intruding on my last day in D.C. The reality that the FBI hadn't picked up the terrorists, pressed on me like a thousand pound weight and I realized we were still in danger.

I walked slowly out of the maze I had blindly run into, surprised at the distance I'd gone. It hadn't seemed so far moments ago. My pounding heart slowed as I got closer to the conference center I'd fled.

I saw my reflection in the glass doors of the building. Yikes! I needed some touch up. Bathroom, here I come.

I splashed water on my face and dabbed it dry, pulled at my hair and straightened it as much as I could. The hair

next to my neck curled from the sweat that wetted it. I
tried to dry it with paper towels and then fixed my clothes.
My thoughts went wild.

I chased Iceman. He could've killed me. How could I
have been so reckless? Why had he looked at me like that?

Walking out the door, a familiar face met mine.
Nathan's, one of the FBI guys. He swooshed his arms
toward the boy's bathroom.

"Do you want me to—"

He nodded. I pushed the door open and went in.
Jeremy stood there, shaking his head. He pushed a button
on a little pen looking thing and then railed on me.

"What were you thinking just now? Running after a
crazy man, can't lead to anything good. He could have
killed you, you know."

I did know.

"Sorry," I said. "I just lost it. I thought you guys got
the bad guys last night at the Pizzeria and coming up those
steps after discovering what the terrorists were really up
to…. And I saw him looking at me and lost it—

"Pizzeria? What are you talking about?" Jeremy
interrupted.

Was he faking it or did he really not know what
happened at the pizzeria?

"You know, *the raid*. The one you all dressed up like
DEA agents to carry out."

"I don't know what you're talking about."

"Really? I thought for sure it was you guys." I wasn't
sure what to believe. The terrorists had me so paranoid, I'd
never have a moments peace.

"It wasn't."

"Huh… Well, figuring out why they killed that guy
Jonathan made me so mad, something flipped and I had to

go after him. I refuse to be afraid anymore and I wanted answers." My words made me seem braver than I was.

"You figured it out, did you?"

"Yes," I said.

"Are you going to make me drag it out of you?"

"No. Sorry. This bill that the terrorists talked about in the ballroom before they killed the aide, takes farmland and puts it into the hands of corporations, foreign corporations, instead of individuals. About ten companies are mentioned by name as the only possible purchasers of the land. It doesn't seem so bad until you find out that they are companies whose owners are Middle Eastern with ties to their government. If they gain control of our lands, we would lose almost all control of our renewable resources."

"Hmpf," he said.

"It's just a guess, but I bet I'm on the right track. Can you imagine what would happen?"

"Christy, please, don't worry about it, and don't you dare do anything so stupid again."

"Okay. I'll try, but it bugs me so much. We would be impoverished and starve. It would be like going back in time to before the industrial age. America would no longer be a superpower."

"Well, it's a good thing you don't have to worry about it, isn't it? Leave this to us. Okay?"

"But ...."

"Okay?!"

"Whatever, but I know I'm onto...."

"Yes, but you are going to forget about that something and just enjoy your last day here—right? Right?"

"Fine."

"Christy, we have it all under control. As soon as you guys are out of here, we'll move on these guys and they'll be gone for good. It's not your problem anymore. Don't make it one again. And it wasn't our thing at the pizza place."

I just looked at him. I didn't know what to say.

He knocked on the door and waited. About a minute later, a knock came from the other side of the door, and Jeremy opened it for me. I walked out to find Nathan picking up a sign that said, *Closed for cleaning*. Smart move.

"Now," Jeremy continued. "Go have some fun!" He pulled out the pen-looking thing and clicked it again. I wondered if it somehow disabled any bugs near us.

After finding my seat, the girl next to me handed me a note. It read,

Guess you figured it out. Way to go. Thomas.

I looked his way and he smiled at me. I nodded and smiled back. After folding the note, I shoved it into my pocket. As I did, I felt some paper in there and pulled it out.

Pink paper. Oh yeah, the dry-cleaning receipt. How much had it cost me to clean Marybeth's clothes? I smoothed it out on my desk. Twenty bucks. Uggh! That was so much money. I had to lean back in my chair to digest the information. I guess it had been worth it. I wanted to check to make sure I hadn't read it wrong and picked it up to examine it again. Yep, twenty dollars. Unbelievable. Then I noticed something scrawled in the middle of the receipt. I had to look closely to read it with all the wrinkles in the paper. It read,

Be careful what you say and who you say it to.

I gasped.

CHAPTER TWENTY-ONE

Everyone filed out of the auditorium once the final debate ended. The air buzzed with excitement for tonight's gala. How were they going to transform this place into a ballroom in such a short time? It didn't seem feasible.

I'd had almost an hour to digest and fret about the note. What had I been thinking trying to expose the Farmers' Aid Bill here with five hundred plus students and at least one hundred adult political nuts in the audience? I should have just waited and told Jeremy. I'd definitely brought our little group into more danger now.

With no way to erase the huge mistake, I wondered what might happen to us. If only I'd seen the note this morning, maybe I wouldn't have worked so hard to call out the dogs on the Farmers' Aid Bill. I could've talked to Jeremy about it, too.

When I got to the bus, I went straight for the back row. If only I'd kept my mouth shut. If, if, if.

Wait a minute. He ran. Iceman ran from me. He must've heard everything I'd said in the debate, and yet, he ran. Wouldn't he have done something to me in that alley if I'd crossed the line? Maybe I was overreacting. Maybe the weird look Iceman gave me in the alley came from fear. Maybe I put out enough information about them to scare them away.

Rick squeezed past me to sit by the window on the back seat next to me. In a flash, he took the pink paper I still had clutched in my hand and started to open it.

"Hey! That's mine. Give it back," I said. I didn't want him to read it.

"Oh, the way you were holding this little pink slip, made me think it was for me." He smiled broadly, teasing, holding it away from me while continuing to unfold it.

"It's just my dry-cleaning receipt." I insisted, pushing my way over him, my arm completely outstretched, trying to get it back. It was kind of fun to play this way, but I really didn't want him to read the note, and what if Marybeth took notice? She thought she was safe.

"Then it's no big deal, if I take just a quick look." He laughed a little, keeping me back easily with one hand, holding the unfolded receipt with the other, staring hard at it, eyes squinting.

The arm restraining me went lax, and I snatched the receipt from his hand just as the bus started to move. He didn't resist. He merely sat upright and stared at me. He didn't really look at me, though. He looked through me. Until he suddenly focused and asked, "Who wrote that? Was it the FBI?"

I just stared—my insides unsettled.

He moved in close to me, his hot cheek pressed against mine as he talked directly into my ear.

"Was it the bad guys? Have you been getting threats? What's going on?"

I could smell his spicy cologne and imagined we were somewhere else. I thought about when I told him about the guy at Georgetown, he had been masterful in the way he handled it. Maybe he could help me out again. I swallowed hard and took a deep breath before telling him.

"The bad guys have been following us and listening to us since the ballroom. They keep warning me to be silent about what I saw. For the most part, they just make sure I know they're watching." I felt instant relief.

"We've got to tell the FBI. This is crazy," he said.

For a second, I thought I should tell him I'd been talking to the FBI all along, but then I remembered my promise not to say anything.

"No," I said. "The bad guys would know if we contacted the FBI, and we'd be in more danger than we already are. We can't contact them."

"We can get into contact with them," he said. He sat up straight and looked forward.

He sounded so sure that I wondered if the FBI had questioned him too, like me and Marybeth. I looked at him. His blue eyes sparkled with assurance. I leaned back into him and asked him flat out if he had been in contact with the FBI.

"Yes," he whispered.

I took a deep breath and held it, thinking about this "little" revelation. For a moment, time was suspended. Why had they told me not to tell anyone, when it seemed everyone had been questioned? Why did they want to make me feel like I was alone? I felt a little sick. The bus moved into traffic.

"They interviewed me about the murder," he said, matter-of-factly.

I couldn't believe it. I started to feel a tightening heat in my chest. This really upset me. I'd worked so hard to keep my meeting with them a secret, and it weighed a ton, and they let me carry the burden without any help, when I could've had it. The punch in the FBI's parking garage flashed across my mind, and I wanted another shot at Jeremy.

"Did they interview you too?" he asked.

"Yes," I said, feeling no need to keep it a secret any longer. Really, I wanted to tell everyone, I was so mad. "We've met several times actually. They told me I couldn't tell anyone. Why would they do that if they talked to you, too? It makes me kinda mad."

"I don't know. They told me not to tell either."

"I want to punch Jeremy right in the face."

"Jeremy? Was your agent's name, Jeremy?"

I felt my face flash hot. "Yours wasn't?" I asked, wondering what was going on.

"Special Agent Todd Nills, I think."

"Oh. I would've thought they would've used the same agents for all of us." It hadn't occurred to me that there could be other agents questioning everyone else. Maybe there were a bunch of agents hanging out near us all the time, but I only knew Jeremy and Nathan. Maybe they didn't want all of us to draw attention to them. Maybe that's why it was all so secretive. It still made me mad. They should have told me everyone was talking.

"Yeah, weird. Do you think they talked to everyone?"

"Probably," I said, my stomach a ball of fire. "Okay, so how do we let them know about this note? I can't stand the thought of you being in danger."

I chuckled. If he only knew. "I'm not sure. For me, it's kind of the luck of the draw running into them ." I was glad he hadn't made the connection with Jeremy being the "college guy" we'd hung out with the last week and a half.

"Me, too. They just kinda pop up every now and then. Hmm."

"We're leaving tomorrow. Besides, it's too late now, anyway. They meant for me to read the note before the debate today. Me and my big mouth. I just had to prove I was smarter than they were. Now I probably put us all in more danger."

"No, you haven't."

"But I have. If I had seen the note before the debate, I wouldn't have tried so hard to get people to pay attention to their bill. Now they *know* I know. What have I done?"

"Stop it. You figured it out. That's a good thing. We just need to tell the FBI."

I wasn't so sure anymore. They made me mad. Anyway, what could they do now?

"If we get the chance, we'll tell them. But I'm not going to stress about it. Tomorrow we're out of here, and it'll all be a thing of the past." I tried to convince myself what I said was true and took a deep breath, pushing against the back of my seat, looking down the aisle of the bus. My eyes met Alex's. He was two rows forward, legs in the aisle, staring at me.

My face got hot, and I shifted from side to side. I sighed, looking up and seeing Marybeth's face looking down at me, grinning. She moved her eyes back and forth from Rick to me and made a kissing gesture. I wished I'd never told her about Rick kissing me. I shook my head, a minute movement, and narrowed my eyes at her. She gave me a pressed smile and then said, "The gala's going to be amazing. Don't you think, Kira?" Without looking at her, she nudged Kira, who got on her knees and turned around to look down, too. But it wasn't me she wanted to see. It was Rick, and he looked at me.

"My dress is amazing, Marybeth," Kira said, still staring at Rick. "Wait until you see it. And my shoes are to die for."

"My dress makes me feel like a princess," Marybeth said. "I got it from my good friend, Janice back home. She has the most amazing gowns."

Before coming on the trip, I'd decided not to go to the gala. It seemed like such a silly thing, but listening to Marybeth and Kira I got an achy feeling in my gut, wishing I'd brought a dress so that I had the choice. Anyway, an event that would make someone use the word, "gown" probably wasn't a place for me.

"What's your dress like, Christy?" Kira asked me, her eyes never leaving Rick.

"My dress?"

"Your dress for the gala?!" She finally looked at me, smirking.

"Oh, yeah, the gala. I'm not going." My heart pinged a little when I said it.

"What?" You have to go!" Marybeth said.

Kira had a thin smile on her face.

"Yeah, you have to go, Christy," Rick said.

Kira's eyes narrowed.

"I don't *have* to go. Besides, I didn't bring some awesome gown or even shoes for that matter. I'd be totally out of place. It's no big deal." I wanted it to be no big deal, but why did my heart seem to squish at the thought of not going now? I looked forward to avoid the three of them and ran into Alex's gaze again. Why was he staring at me like that? Was it because I was next to Rick? I smiled at him, my nerves on edge, and he stood and made his way to the seat opposite Marybeth and Kira, squishing Eugene against the window as he sat facing the aisle—and me.

I felt Rick sit up tall to look over me at Alex.

"What are ya'all talking about?" Alex said, glancing around at everyone and then back to me.

"Christy's not going to the gala," Kira said in a cheery voice.

"You're not?" Alex asked.

I felt Rick shift in his seat.

"No. I've got some things to do—" I felt my face go hot.

"And, she didn't bring a dress!" Kira blurted.

"Look, it's no big deal. I don't know how to dance all fancy anyway," I said, glaring at Kira and wishing I'd brought a dress.

Alex took a long look at me and then went back to his seat and started talking on his phone. My stomach felt a bit sick. I guess he didn't care if I went or not.

Rick and Marybeth continued to try to persuade me to go.

I refused every time. I didn't want Kira to know how badly I wanted to go. I had to save face. The bus stopped.

"You have two hours, ladies and gentlemen," Mrs. J.'s voice roared. "That is one hundred and twenty minutes and not one longer. Be outside in two hours. Understand?"

After heads nodded, there was a mad dash to get out of the bus. I walked into the hotel last with Rick. Even Alex was long gone. I took a quick look into the buffet room for the FBI. No luck.

Rick tried one more time. "Sure you're not gonna go?"

"I'm sure," I said, feeling a bit sick. "Maybe I should try to get a hold of you-know-who."

"'Kay," he said, as I opened my door. He gave me a crooked smile, eyes gleaming and walked away backwards, looking at me until I looked away and went into my room.

Marybeth hadn't wasted a second. She was already in the shower.

I sat on my bed and tried to clear my thoughts. I'd have to make the best of my evening. Maybe, I'd check the buffet room at about seven for the guys. If they weren't there, I'd check the rec room at eight or eight-thirty if I thought of it. I wrote a note for Jeremy and stuffed it into my pocket. One more note. It was almost over. Tomorrow we'd be gone. Then it would finally be over. I shivered.

I heard the hair dryer and let myself doze off to the hum.

When Marybeth opened the bathroom door, I woke to a gush of sweetly perfumed air.

She looked amazing in a lime green princess dress that made her eyes look even more brilliant.

"You look beautiful!" I said, slinging my legs around and sitting up so that I could feel the fabric of the dress. "Wow! You look just like a princess."

Her hair was pulled up in a loose bun and curls dangled all around it.

I felt another large twinge of regret for not bringing a dress. I'm sure the gala would have been cool. What had I been thinking? I could have danced with Alex. Then again, when I left home, I didn't think there would be an Alex, and he didn't seem concerned I wasn't going, anyway. Rick would have danced with me, though.

There was a knock on the door. Thinking it was Kira, I jumped up, excited to see her "amazing" dress, too. Instead, a hotel guy stood, holding a huge, long pink box with a large white bow on it.

"Delivery for Christy Hadden," he announced, placing the box into my arms.

I squinted, wondering what it could be.

"What in the world," Marybeth said, shutting the door.

She grabbed the envelope from the top of the box as I set the whole thing on my bed. She handed it to me, and I pulled out the card, it read,

I can't wait to see you in this tonight. Alex.

Marybeth, who'd been reading over my shoulder, let out a loud squeal.

My heart pounded hard.

"Hurry, hurry," she said. "Open it, open it."

I fumbled with the bow and finally untied it with the help of Marybeth. I was so nervous, my mind full of

259

questions. How did he do this? When did he do this? Was there really a dress in here? What shoes could I wear? My heart fluttered and tried not to become hysterical.

Lifting off the lid revealed a beautiful pink silky dress with matching shoes in the bottom of the box. He'd thought of everything. I was speechless, mouth open, staring at them.

"Oh my gosh!" Marybeth yelled. "I *knew* he liked you. Now you have to go to the gala. Hurry up, get changed. We only have about thirty minutes to make you stunning. This is a *real* princess story."

As I slid into the dress, I kept thinking this wasn't really happening. It couldn't be. Things like this didn't happen to me. The dress felt weightless and hugged every curve of my body. I felt a bit self-conscious as I stared in the mirror. I clenched my teeth and wondered if I could pull it off.

"Ready?" Marybeth called as she turned the doorknob to the bathroom.

"I guess," I said, as she opened the door.

"Wow! That dress is incredible. Now, let's make the rest of you incredible, too."

Marybeth worked like the wind, pulling my hair up and straightening pieces that fell to my shoulders. In awe, my respect for her grew. I could never have done this to myself and never imagined anyone doing it for me.

"Perfect!" she proclaimed.

Then she put all kinds of stuff on my face. She was done in a flash.

"Are you ready to see yourself?" she asked, grinning from ear to ear.

"Maybe," I said, still unsure about the clingy, sexy dress.

She moved out from in front of the mirror, and I saw a different person. It wasn't me.

"You look gorgeous."

My face looked flawless, and my hair looked professionally done. I could only stare, my heart still pounding as I thought of the possibilities with Alex.

She pushed past me and called me to come put my shoes on. In a daze, I followed her voice, sat on the bed and put the shoes on. Heels again. Yikes. Someone knocked on the door, and Marybeth ran to it. It was Rick—in his regular clothes still.

He stared at me, eyes wide and mouth slightly open.

"You look stunning! But, I…uh…thought you weren't going to go. I figured I'd…."

Marybeth looked at me and then back to Rick.

I didn't know what to say. "Well, I was going to stay and then, uh, um."

"What she's trying to say is," Marybeth said, "She got a package about half an hour ago with that dress in it. So, now she's going."

"Oh! Uh, who sent it?" Rick asked.

Uncomfortable seconds ticked by before Marybeth said, "Uh, Alex."

I clenched my teeth and looked at my shoes. I didn't want him to see my undeniable happiness. I knew it would hurt him. It was so hard to conceal my complete excitement at having a boy buy me clothes and invite me to a gala.

"Hmmpf, smart man," Rick said. "Guess I need to hurry now. See ya there." He rushed from the room, leaving the door to slam shut. I felt bad. I'm sure he was thinking he would stay behind with me. Normally, I would have been swept off my feet, but today was different. Today I was Cinderella and Alex was my Prince.

"Oh, Marybeth," I said. "Is this really real? You've made me into someone I'm not."

"It's you, you just didn't know how beautiful you could be. Oh, one last thing." She reached into a see-through bag from the bathroom, pulled out a glass bottle and sprayed me with it. Now, I even smelled good.

"Let's not make Alex wait any longer," Marybeth said, pushing me out the door, terrorist plots forgotten.

CHAPTER TWENTY-TWO

In front of the hotel, a row of black stretch limos lined the street. A small line had formed in front of Mrs. J., who crossed our names off a list as we climbed into a limo. It was all so exciting we had to share a giggle. Marybeth and I were the only ones from our mini-group in this particular limo, and we were the only girls.

The ride was short, and I figured now was not the time to open the sunroof and scream. Maybe on the way home.

The outside of the conference center was now lit with thousands of lights and a purple carpet flowed down to the sidewalk. Men in tuxes stood at the bottom of the stairs to take tickets and escort the ladies in.

The auditorium was no longer a congressional hall. It had been magically transformed into an enormous ballroom. I couldn't believe they had completed it in only two hours. Tables draped in white and purple were scattered about edges of the room and in the middle was a huge wooden dance floor. My insides buzzed as I looked at all the luxury surrounding me. The yellow, white and purple flowers, that dotted the ballroom, not only looked beautiful, they made the room smell fresh and inviting. I stopped at one large arrangement, felt the tender blossoms, marveling that they were real. This must have cost a fortune to create.

An orchestra played on a stage to our left and several adults and kids were already dancing nearby. In the very center of the room, drinks were being served. I grabbed water and Marybeth drank a Coke. They were served in fancy glasses, not cups. We saw two other stages. From the looks of it, one had a rock band playing and the other a country one, but all I could hear was the ballroom music where we stood. Between the three stages, near the outside edges of the room, were serving areas that had all kinds of food. One area served only decadent desserts, while another had an unimaginable amount of main courses to choose from, and the last had fruits and vegetables galore. Incredible. It seemed every step I took brought me to something new. Lots of people gathered in each area, the numbers growing by the minute.

The room was much larger than I had thought it was during the debate. The stage for the debates must have sat where the drinks were now being served and must have blocked the other half of the room from our view.

"This place is unbelievable, Christy!"

"No kidding," I said. "No wonder this trip cost so much."

"Don't remind me," Marybeth said.

"Come on, this has to make it all worth it."

"I guess you're right. It is beautiful."

I was glad she smiled about it now. "I can't believe I almost didn't come."

"No kidding. Where's Alex anyway?"

I shrugged my shoulders and said, "I haven't seen a soul from our group, yet."

"Me neither. Let's go back by the door. Maybe we'll find them."

We didn't have to go that far. Summer, Josh, Kira and Alex were at the bar. I froze, staring at Alex's perfect profile as Marybeth sailed past me toward them. He looked amazing. His tux made him appear royal.

When Marybeth reached them, Alex turned and looked at me. His eyes widened and then narrowed slightly as a gorgeous smile spread across his face.

My heart raced and my stomach immediately filled with butterflies. I kind of felt sick, too. I couldn't breathe. I'd never felt less invisible than I did at that moment. I had to resist the urge to look at my feet.

His eyes never left mine as he pushed past Kira and Marybeth to get to me. He grabbed my hand and shook his head.

"You look more unbelievable than I'd imagined you would," he said, looking me over head to toe.

A part of me wanted to hide behind something, unsure if I could hold up under the pressure of being looked at in that way. I wasn't used to such scrutiny, and I certainly wasn't used to looking good to anybody. Never before had I felt so naked.

He raised my hand above my head and twirled me around. As I spun, I saw Kira, jaw on the floor, Marybeth, grinning from ear to ear and Josh and Summer talking excitedly as they looked at the two of us.

"You're beautiful," he said, pulling my arms out to the sides like a bird in flight and looking me over again.

Somehow, the way he looked at me really made me feel beautiful.

He pulled me into a hug that I didn't want to end and whispered, "Let's go dance." He led me to the ballroom dance floor.

I tugged on his arm, panicked. I couldn't dance. Sure, I'd taken ballroom dance, but I'd been forced to dance alone—a memory I wanted to forget. He kept pulling me. When we finally stopped, he put one arm around my waist and raised the hand he already held into the air. I frowned up at him, so he bent down and said, "Is there a problem?"

"Just a little one. I don't know how to dance all fancy."

He stood up straight and glanced around us, no expression on his face. Then he leaned back down and whispered in my ear, "Just follow me. I'll go slowly. This is the Waltz. 1,2,3. 1,2,3. Relax."

I tried to relax, let him lead me and remember what I'd learned in class. It was no easy task. Closing my eyes helped. I let myself melt into his motion, and it worked most of the time. At least he never stood on my toes, and I only bumped his a few times. I took a deep breath when the song ended and opened my eyes.

"You're a natural," he said.

"Very funny," I said, giving him a little punch. I know I was stiff and awkward.

"No, really. You were so easy to lead."

The music started up again. "You want to try this one? It's the tango."

"I don't think we should push our luck. Why do you know how to do all these dances anyway?" We'd only focused on the tango for three days in class. I would be lost.

"My parents made me learn them when I was little. They said a true man dances, and dances well."

"Smart parents," I said, laughing.

"Let's move to the side and I'll teach you this one. It's a bit harder than the Waltz."

"Okay, but no guarantees your toes won't be killing you tonight."

My heart hummed the whole time we danced. I tried to stay calm and enjoy myself, but my nerves were on fire.

After slaughtering the meringue and the tango, twice, it was nice to fall back into the Waltz. It made me feel even more like Cinderella. Much to Alex's credit, he never criticized me the whole time—he only cheered me on.

"Let's get a drink and something to eat," Alex said.

"Good idea," I said, a bit relieved. "I'll be right back." I headed for the nearest restroom. I couldn't help humming the music of the last Waltz we danced.

Coming back out of the restroom, looking down at the water spots on my dress, I ran right into someone.

"Oh, sorry," I said.

"Oh, no. I'm so sorry," he said, reaching for me. It was Rick.

When I realized who I'd bumped into, I laughed.

"Fancy meeting you here, Princess Christy," he said with a bow.

"The pleasure is all mine, Prince Rick," I said, with my best curtsey. He was so fun.

"May I have this dance?"

Automatically, I looked in the direction where I'd left Alex, which made Rick look that way too. Alex wasn't there.

"I'm sure he wouldn't mind," he said.

I blushed. "Sorry. It's just that I feel…" I looked at my feet and then back at him. His face was soft and kind even though I'd been so rude looking for Alex. I had to say, "Okay."

He held my hand and took me over to the rock band dance floor. They had just started a slow song. He pulled me into his arms. With no space between us, he rested his cheek on mine and whispered, "You look stunning."

I wondered if he felt the heat in my cheeks when he said that.

"You don't look so bad yourself," I said, trying to play it off. Really, he did look gorgeous. There was something about a tux that made guys look so great. Rick was no exception. My heart beat hard, but I felt comfortable, like I was meant to be in his arms. I loved being with Rick. He made me feel so sure, so right. We danced in silence the rest of the song.

When it ended, I tried to pull away, but he held me tight.

"Just one more," he whispered, as the band started playing another slow song.

"I don't know, Rick. I feel obligated to Alex…"

"I know. But he has you all night. Can't I have you for one more song?"

He moved his face right in front of mine, his eyes pleading.

"Okay. One more." I gave in. It wasn't hard to do.

He pulled me close again and whispered, "It feels so good to have you in my arms."

I sighed, silently agreeing.

When the song was over, he gave me a final squeeze, and kissed my hand before leading me off the dance floor. He put his arm around my waist and said, "You know, I was going to stay at the hotel with you. I almost missed the last limo."

"I thought so. Sorry about that."

"I like Alex's idea better. I wish it'd been mine."

I gave him my best look of understanding, when I noticed Alex, not ten feet from us, leaning back on the bar, looking at us.

I stopped, and Rick looked at Alex, too.

"Don't go, Christy."

"I have to," I said, pulling away. My heart burned and my eyes fell to the floor as I walked toward Alex.

"Where've you been?" he asked when I reached him.

"I ran into Rick by the bathroom, and he asked me to dance."

"I was waiting for you."

"I know. I'm sorry."

"If you don't want to be with me…"

I grabbed his free hand and moved in really close. Looking up at him, I said, "No, I do. I'm sorry. I guess I should've said no to Rick, but…Alex, I'm all yours now, totally and completely."

"Really?" He looked past me now, at Rick, who stared at us.

"Yes," I said, turning back to Alex. "Yes. Come on. Let's dance."

He set his drink on the counter and squeezed my hand. He didn't lead me to the ballroom dance floor this time, though. We went to the country one, our hunger forgotten. I was surprised. Did he like country music? The band sang a popular slow song, and Alex pulled me in to him so tightly, that I almost couldn't breathe. It was uncomfortable, like we were in a vice, being squished together. It reminded me of our "first kiss" and how uncomfortable that had been. We moved in a tiny circle. I was a bit relieved when the music changed to a fast song. His hold on me loosened slightly, and I took a deep breath looking into his eyes.

"I didn't like seeing you in Rick's arms, Christy. Especially, when you stayed for the second song."

He had watched us the whole time.

"Look Alex, he's my friend. What was I supposed to do?"

"Your friend? I'm not blind. He's totally into you. And I saw you leave your room to be with him the other night."

A quick burst of air escaped my lips. He had seen me go with Rick? Is that why he'd been so tired? "Can we forget about it, please?" I said, not wanting to get into it.

He looked at me playfully and said, "Maybe just this once. But you better not be thinking about him tonight." He pulled me in and kissed me, long and hard. Then, his smile wicked, he looked past me. I turned and saw Rick sitting at a table not far from us, a frown on his face. Alex chuckled. I punched him.

"Jerk!" Before I could walk away from him, he pulled me to a different dance floor.

I wasn't prepared for how kissing Alex in front of Rick would make me feel. I didn't think it would bother me. Why did Alex have to act like that?

"Don't ever do that again," I said.

"What?"

"If he does like me, like you said, you were hurting him on purpose, and I don't like that." I pulled my hand hard away from his and turned to walk away.

He grabbed my shoulder and turned me around. "Okay, okay. I won't do it again. I just wanted him to know that you are taken."

"Am I?" I asked, the disgust I felt for him melting away.

Just then, I saw Jeremy, walking toward me at a fast pace and looking around the room with exaggerated sweeps of his head. A huge, bald man doing the same sweeping motions with his head followed him.

"Jeremy," I said, when he was only a few feet away. "What are you doing here?"

"We need to leave right now."

"But, what's—"

"No questions now. Just come with me. Quickly, now." He was already leading me away from Alex. I looked behind me to see the bald guy talking with Alex and taking him away, too. From the looks of it, Alex wouldn't go easily.

I looked over my other shoulder and saw that Rick no longer sat at his table.

My heart raced. He pulled me and I had to run to keep up with him. I realized that my toes and heels had blisters, every step hurt.

Before I knew it, we had run all the way to the back of the conference center and Jeremy pushed me out a door marked as an emergency exit. No alarm sounded. He opened the door to a cab and helped me in. Nathan sat in the cab. He ran some machine over me as the cab began to move. It looked like the wands they use at airports to check you for metal. It squealed three separate times as he scanned me.

"What's going on? What are you doing?"

"Don't miss a single inch of her. They're tricky buggers." Jeremy said to Nathan, ignoring me.

"I won't. Don't worry." Nathan said.

"Hello! Is anyone listening? What's going on?" I asked, enunciating every word.

Jeremy held his finger to his lips. Apparently, I needed to be quiet.

We drove for what seemed forever before we stopped.

When we did, they put me into a large van, and they used a bigger wand to go over my body. Then they handed me some clothes and motioned for me to go to the back of the van.

"Change into these clothes, please."

"Is anyone going to tell me what's going on?" I said.

"Go change, please," the man with the wand said again, insistent.

I moved into a makeshift changing area and was shocked to find they had even given me new underwear and a bra. After changing, one of the men in the van went into the changing area, picked up my beautiful dress and shoes and shoved them roughly into a bag. So much for being a princess. After re-scanning me, they rushed me out of the van and into a black BMW with tinted windows.

"Here's the deal, Christy," Jeremy said, once the BMW sped away. "We overheard some chatter about one of eight packages being picked up at the conference center address. It made us worry that you all were the packages so we had to get you all out of there."

"What?" I said, trying to digest what he had said. "Wait a minute. Did you say they *had* one of the eight? Who?"

"We don't know yet. Maybe no one."

"You don't know yet? When will you know?"

"Soon, Christy, soon."

The car stopped again, and they helped me into an SUV. Neither Jeremy nor Nathan climbed in. Summer and Rick were already inside, fancy clothes gone. Summer's eyes were puffy and red and through her teeth said, "This is all your fault." The door slammed shut.

Rick moved toward me.

"Don't listen to her. She doesn't know what she's talking about."

"Yes she does," I said, dropping my head into my hands and crying. "If only I hadn't looked. If only I had stopped you all from looking."

"I didn't look, and I'm still here," Summer said, sneering now.

"I'm so sorry, you guys," I said through my tears. I had the feeling of being swept along by a dark current.

"It's not your fault, Christy," Rick said. "It's the terrorists' fault. They're the ones who did something they shouldn't have. Don't cry. Please don't cry."

I sunk deep into his chest, taking refuge in his strength and sobbed until I couldn't cry anymore, then let myself drift off to sleep.

I woke up to the sound of tires on gravel and looking out the window, I could see the full moon. We had stopped at a house surrounded by a lot of trees. I stretched and tried to get a kink out of my neck. Everyone else slept until the driver turned around to face us and said, "Everyone up. We're here."

CHAPTER TWENTY-THREE

In the darkness, the huge house reminded me of the spooky houses that were always used for horror movies: two story, painted, wooden houses with wrap-around porches. The only difference was that it showed no signs of aging—no shutters hanging askew and no paint peeling. The light from the windows cast a weird glow on the wooden rockers that moved slightly in the wind. If I weren't so tired and surrounded by FBI agents, I would have been too afraid to go in. We dragged ourselves inside, and were then each taken by our agents to different rooms to sleep. The guys headed upstairs, the girls stayed on the main floor.

Jeremy took me down a narrow hallway, just to the left of the stairs and into a small, plain bedroom with only a twin bed, a nightstand, two token pictures and a dresser. Thick curtains were drawn, and there was a closet and one more door, which turned out to be a small bathroom with a shower. I sat on the edge of the bed, ready to drop over.

"Come here, Christy," Jeremy said, sliding the closet door open.

I stood up and walked over, trying to see what was in the closet before I was actually there. It was lined with wooden slats, and when Jeremy turned the clothes rod, some of the panels of wood slid to the side.

"Now listen. If you get scared or you hear an alarm, turn the rod and jump into this secret spot. See this blanket here?" I nodded, thinking it curious to have only a blanket inside. "This blanket is special. It makes it so that no one can see the heat coming from your body. You must totally cover every inch of you, or else a heat sensor could detect you… And don't forget to slide the closet door closed behind you."

"Okay," I said, wondering how long I could stay in that little spot, covered up with a blanket, without freaking out. Small spaces had never been my friend.

"Nothing will happen—but just in case."

"Can't I just room with Marybeth?" I asked, suddenly feeling alone.

"She's not here."

"Oh my gosh! Is she the one that got taken?" I moved toward him, frantic.

"Whoa, now. The others are at a different safe-house and won't be coming here."

"A different safe-house? But why aren't they coming here?" Despite the fear I felt for Marybeth, I couldn't help thinking about seeing Alex one more time. I wanted to hear what he was about to say at the gala about me "being taken" when Jeremy interrupted him.

"We had to separate you according to what you saw. If this house were to be compromised, which it won't, then we would still have almost the same testimonies available to us at the other safe-house. It guarantees us we will get the bad guys."

"But someone is missing still?"

"Yes."

"Do you know who?"

"It's not important."

"I have to know."

"Well, you're just going to have to trust me when I say this person will be okay. Now, get into bed and go to sleep." He walked toward the door.

"Please, I won't be able to sleep if you don't tell me."

"I'm sorry, I can't. Go to bed. I'll be next door." He shut the door behind him.

"Well, I'm not going to sleep," I yelled after him, as if it would change his mind. I climbed into the bed anyway, with my clothes still on. It was comfortable and warm but did nothing to calm my mind.

What if the terrorists did come? I stared at the closet. The door was open, and I had to climb out of bed to shut it, hoping that would help me stop thinking about having to use that small hideout for real. He hadn't told me how to open the door to the hideout once inside. What if I got stuck in there forever?

I tossed and turned. Who had the terrorists taken from the gala? Had the FBI found whomever they'd taken? At least I knew it wasn't Alex, Summer or Rick.

Finally, after a few hours of incessant worry and fear, I got up and left my room. The empty, long and mostly dark hall seemed to never end. The only light came from small vent-like night lights near the floor. After passing Jeremy's room, I hesitated, feeling a bit scared, but then Jeremy popped out of his room, gun in hand.

When he saw me, he tucked it into the back of his pants.

"You all right, Christy?"

"Yeah. I couldn't sleep." I wasn't sure if I felt safer or less safe knowing Jeremy had a gun.

"I was afraid of that."

"Who did they take?" I asked. "It's driving me crazy. I know you know. Just tell me."

"It's not important, Christy. We have a locator on this person and will bring him back."

"Him? It's one of the guys?"

"I didn't say that."

"You did, too! You said 'him'. It has to either be Eugene or Josh, then."

"No, it doesn't."

"You're driving me crazy! Just tell me."

"No. Don't worry. They will get him *or* her. You all have locators in your clothes: Tiny microchips that send a signal to us so we can keep track of you."

"Really? So you knew where we were every minute of every day?" I had been safe, after all.

"Yes. I told you you were protected. I meant it. Except of course, when we thought you were Marybeth at the club that night. And even then you were protected, just not by us, by her agents."

"No way." I really was safe. "That car that was following our cab....Did you guys cause it to crash?"

"Not me, but other agents. Yes."

Wow!

"Then why did you let me go to Senator Randolph's office?" I felt my face go hot.

"We didn't think you would actually end up with him physically. You just have this way of getting into trouble. It didn't matter that you were with him anyway. We have plants in his office. You were protected in there, too."

"Funny. I didn't feel that way. . . So, was it the FBI at the pizzeria, too?"

"Some of the agents were FBI. But it wasn't our deal. I didn't even know about it until you told me about it. I had to ask at the office what it was all about."

"Really?" It seemed like I'd said "Really" a million times already. My mind was reeling at how safe we'd actually been. Why had I felt so unsafe?

"Really," he said, eyes wide.

"Tell me who. Please."

He shook his head and breathed loudly. "It's not important."

"It is to me. Please tell me." I grabbed his arm hard.

"I have this feeling that I won't be getting any sleep until you know." His pause was long, and I knew from debating at school that the first one to speak would lose. So, I bit my lip to stop myself from asking again.

"Don't worry," he finally said. "Marybeth is a resourceful girl. She'll be fine."

"Marybeth? What? No!" I moved close to him and laid my face on his chest.

"Crap!" he said under his breath. He sighed and then wrapped his arms around me. "Don't worry, we have her signal, and it won't be long before we have her in a safe-house."

"Will I be able to talk to her?"

"Eventually. We've got to round up all the bad guys first. We've already grabbed a bunch of them and are moving in on the others as fast as we can. Once we intercepted the information about the eight packages, we realized we couldn't wait another minute to get the those creeps off the streets. As we speak they are being picked up."

"Hmmm. I just wish I knew she was safe," I said. "Why didn't you tell me everything you were doing so I wouldn't have been so crazy scared and worried if you guys were inept or something?"

"Inept? Are you kidding? We didn't want you guys tipping off the terrorists that we were there watching and protecting you. It only takes one slip of the tongue to blow an operation like this...Now, go to bed and sleep tight."

"You have to realize," I said, "that all I could see was how vulnerable we appeared and how alone I felt."

"I had no idea. Why didn't you just believe me?"

"I guess I'm not the believing type. I have to see to believe." The knowledge that I was this way hit me like a rock. I had always thought of myself as faithful; I didn't have to see to believe. Had I been wrong about myself this whole time? Jeremy didn't respond. He only rushed me back into my room.

After a while of mulling over the information from Jeremy, I fell into a fitful sleep. When I woke up, the edges of the curtains were illuminated with bright light. I couldn't believe my eyes. How long had I slept? It was one? The clock had to be wrong. I yawned and climbed out of bed. The carpet felt good on my feet.

As I passed Jeremy's room, he came out at that instant and met me again.

"Hungry?" he asked.

"Very," I said. The smell of chips and bread called to me.

I guess we had all slept late. A bunch of people sat eating at the table with the notable exception of Summer and her agent. Rick stood up when he saw me.

"You want me to get you something to eat?" he asked.

"No," I said. "I'll get it myself. You finish eating."

The spread of food on the counter looked amazing. Yum.

"How did you sleep?" Rick asked, as I sat beside him, laying my sandwich and drink on the long wooden table.

"Okay. How about you?" I said, looking at the people across the table from us.

"Bad. I think I woke up a million times. I finally just got out of bed. I couldn't stand it anymore."

I turned to look at him, and his blue eyes shined in the light coming from the windows. He didn't look tired at all. I took a deep breath. He made me feel better in this scary house.

"Yeah. After I'd finally slept some, I woke up all startled by the bright sunlight. I feel terrible." We didn't look away from each other until we noticed that the room was suddenly silent.

Sam, Rick's agent, and Jeremy were looking past us toward the stairs, eyes wider than normal. We turned to look, too. Summer stumbled to the table, head bent down, hair all over the place, and she was mumbling to herself like a crazy person—throwing her arms in front of her and then to her sides. Her agent, Mike, held her upper arms, pushing her forward to a seat across from me and down a little, between Jeremy and Sam.

"Sit," Mike ordered, shaking his head and rolling his eyes.

I stifled a laugh as she sat, anger pulsing from her as she folded her arms on the table and plopped her head down on top of them. Her hair was ratted and sticking up all over the place. Unbelievable! Summer a mess? Never. A large grin spread across my face, and I put my hand over my mouth to hide it. What was wrong with me? Why was I happy about someone else's suffering? I thought of the mean girls in my high school and how they seemed overjoyed at my misery, and I felt hot lava rise in my stomach.

Mike walked over to the island, where all of the food was laid out and said, "Summer's feeling a bit out-of-sorts this morning. You want turkey or ham, Summer?"

Everyone looked from Mike to Summer. No answer.

"Turkey it is," Mike said.

We were all still silent. I was sure everyone was unable to believe that perfectly-put-together Summer was anything but put-together today. No one wanted to miss the drama. Why would she come in here like that? I'd never seen her have a hair out of place, even after having slept in that laundry room after the murder.

We watched as Mike put her sandwich and drink in front of her and sat next to her and said, "There you go,

Summer. Eat up. You'll need your strength for the self-defense class today."

"Go away!" Summer yelled into her folded arms. Everyone leaned back a bit, shocked.

"It's your choice, Summer," Mike said. "But you'll regret not eating now. There's nothing else until dinner."

"My choice?" she yelled, lifting her head. "I don't seem to have any choices anymore! Ever since that, that…." Her eyes searched the room until they found me. "That," she said, pointing at me, "had to pull us into this mess. I didn't see *anything,* but I'm still here."

Flames seemed to shoot out of her eyes, and I instinctively leaned further away from her, hoping not to burn.

"I have nothing now! None of my clothes, my make-up. I couldn't even clean my face yesterday." Her eyes now bored a hole through me. "Do you know what that does to your skin—to sleep in makeup?" She sneered. "You don't, do you? Of course not. You stupid backwoods girl."

I couldn't take my eyes off her makeup smeared face, her wild hair and her blazing eyes. She was a total mess and yet, she wasn't ugly, she simply looked like she was posing for a high fashion magazine shoot. Totally unfair—she was beautiful even when she shouldn't have been.

"Look at the clothes they gave me to wear," she continued. "I look like… you," she said, pointing at me again. "This is all your fault." Her teeth were clamped shut like a vice.

The silence was deafening. Rick grabbed my sweaty hand and held it tight.

All I could do was think that she was right. It was my fault that we were here in the middle of nowhere in this safe-house. It was my fault she didn't have her things, and it was my fault her life was in danger. I swallowed hard, trying not to show any expression. I could feel the heat in my neck and face, and I tried to say I was sorry, but my throat closed up around my words.

Rick leaned into me and said, "This is *not* your fault."

He said it loud enough for everyone to hear, and Summer's vengeance was swift and vicious.

"And you Rick," Summer hissed. "Sitting by her, probably holding her hand under the table." She leaned down and looked under the table to verify. "Yep—holding that two-timing b's hand. She looks soooo innocent, doesn't she? She even acts the part. But, you know, she made out with Alex at the club last Tuesday and has been sucking face with him ever since. She's just toying with you."

Now, my face burned. I tried to sit as still as possible, wishing it all away. Wishing I could disappear, but the spotlight was on me. Summer had made sure of it. My mom had been right. Getting what you wanted never turned out the way you thought it would.

"Yes!" she continued. "She's been locking lips and all sorts of other stuff with Alex since then. She doesn't even like you, Rick. She's into Alex. If you can't see that, you're just as stupid as she is. You deserve each other."

His grip on my hand loosened, and I felt his gaze on me. I had to turn to him. His eyes questioned.

I shook my head, looking him in the eye, wishing I had told him the whole truth before. I'd been caught. The truth was out. My stomach felt like cement had just been poured into it. A part of me wanted to rip Summer's head off, but the look in Rick's eyes made me want to cry.

"Is that true?" he tried to whisper only to me, but our audience was too close to miss it.

Justifications filled my mind—all lies. Then shame filled me. I was horrified at the ease the lies had come. All the half-truths I'd told had finally added up and overtaken me. Why hadn't I been honest in the first place? Lying had never been a part of who I was. What had happened to me?

"It's not like that," I said weakly, my head moving side to side. I knew the truth was looking at him through my eyes, and his hand let go of mine. It didn't all have to be true to make me guilty.

"It is like that!" Summer said, cackling now. "Caught ya!" She cackled some more.

I wanted to deny it all, but I couldn't. Would anyone notice if I crawled under the table? I needed to explain it all to him. He just needed to hear my explanation, and he would understand. I reached for his hand as he moved it away, but he quickly jerked it and turned his whole body away from me.

Summer, smiling, started to eat her sandwich, stifling laughter.

I felt all the agent's stares as I tapped Rick and said, "Rick, listen." He didn't flinch. I tapped harder, "Rick, please." I felt my voice catch, but he didn't turn to me.

Being caught was like being punched in the stomach. My throat burned and hot tears pushed their way out. I looked up, trying to fend them off, wrapping my arms around my waist. I wouldn't be able to stop the bawling that was to come. I was about to lose it in the worst possible way—in front of all these people. I lost it at home all the time lately—but I was always alone in my room when I did.

I ran to the stairs and heard Jeremy call out to me, "Christy! Christy!" But I kept running until I hit my room and flung myself onto the bed, sobbing.

I felt so very small. My time in Washington, D.C. was almost over, and I hadn't changed the way I'd imagined at all. I'd wanted to change for the better, and I'd only become worse. I had lost my way and now didn't know how to find it again. I was still a leper. Only now, I was a deceitful one. Why hadn't I been honest—totally and completely? I just wanted to fit in and belong. Now that I had felt what it was like to have people like me, I didn't know if I could live without it.

I felt my bed sink on one side, like someone had sat on it. I jerked up, hoping it was Rick. It was only Jeremy, so I flopped back down on the bed, tears falling freely.

"Hey, Christy," he said, rubbing my back. "We're about to start the defense training. What do you say?"

"I'm not going," I said.

"I'm sorry, but you don't really have a choice. You must be there."

"I can't!" I squeaked. Was he crazy? He was a witness to my humiliation. How could he expect me to join the class?

"You can, Christy. You're stronger than you think. Summer's getting cleaned up, and we'll be starting in about ten. You can clear things up with Rick after the class."

"He'll never forgive me," I said. "I'm such an idiot."

"Christy, for what it's worth, I've seen him around you. He worships you. He's not going to let something like this keep him from you. He's too good a guy. . ."

"Exactly!" I interrupted, turning over on the bed to glare at him. "He is too good a guy to forgive me. I wouldn't forgive me if I were him."

"That's where you're mistaken. You just need to start acting like the good girl your profile says you are." He wiped a tear from my cheek, smiling, pressing his lips together and tilting his head to the side.

"I'm not *that* girl anymore. Haven't you noticed?"

"You are that girl—plus experience," he said. "Experience can be painful."

"No. I've turned rotten."

"Not you," he said. "How you feel does not dictate who you are. You'll see, it will all work out. Next time, stay out of Summer's path. She can be scary." He chuckled, and I smiled weakly. "Go splash some water on your face and come down to the game room. Be the tough girl I know you are and don't let her get to you again." He walked slowly out of the room and shut the door behind him.

What could I do? I had to go down. I had no choice. I would have to face my shame. The cold water burned my eyes, and for a good inch around them, my skin was bright red. How could I go downstairs looking like this? I patted my face dry with a towel, pulled the curtain back and looked out the window at the forest surrounding the house. The naked branches of the trees seemed to shine in the sun next to the dark evergreens. It was like the bare branches were arms waiting to grab me. I shivered. Everything felt wrong here.

I knelt down by my bed and prayed. I asked for forgiveness for all the stupid things I'd done the last two weeks and prayed that I would feel better about myself and have the courage to set things straight with Rick. I said thanks for the chance I'd had to change and for the good parts. I stayed on my knees, my head resting on the bed, letting the comfort I always felt after praying sink in. I felt a warmth cover me, and I promised I wouldn't act like I had been again. Forgiveness really is golden. I realized I hadn't been praying like I usually did and decided that was the reason everything was going wrong, now.

"Christy!" Jeremy called. "It's time."

I closed my eyes and asked God to give me strength one more time and left my room.

Jeremy, smiling, met me at the bottom of the stairs. Putting his hand on the back of my neck, he led me to the game room, renewed.

CHAPTER TWENTY-FOUR

Four Special Agents sat on one side of the room. All the furniture that had been expertly placed earlier in the day, was now pushed together behind them, leaving the other half of the room completely open. Rick stood farthest away from where I stood, and Summer stood next to him. We were all about five feet from each other in an almost straight line. The tension in the room was palpable. I took a deep breath, trying to be brave. I tried to catch Rick's eye, but he only looked straight forward at the agents who looked at all of us.

I took another deep breath telling myself to calm down, and looked at Jeremy, who smiled and nodded. I can do this. I told myself—even alone, I can do this.

"Alright kids," Sam said. "Let's get stretched and chat a bit." Sam's solid body stood in front of us, leading us in stretches and talking about confidence and places of safety as well as how not to look vulnerable. We practiced walking, our heads up, aware of our surroundings. The agents took turns approaching us from all directions, encouraging us to speak with power. Sam even taught us how to identify places of safety if we were on the run.

Jeremy had us stand up and taught us defensive moves. "Forget a man's privates," he said. "He's expecting it. Go for the nose. Hit up and with the ball of your hand." He demonstrated in slow motion with Sam a few times and then showed us full force on a dummy. Funny. I was so stressed when I walked into the room, I hadn't even noticed the four dummies lined up behind us. We practiced on the dummies and the agents tried to take us by surprise and had us practice what we had learned. My favorite move was twisting out of the grip of someone who grabbed me from behind. Every time I faked breaking the arch of someone else's foot, I grimaced. I also wondered how fierce the pain would be if I were to hit someone in the Adam's apple. Would it really be debilitating?

Mike's lesson proved the hardest. We learned how to harness all our strength to hit and kick with power. I realized that without desperate or hateful thoughts, it was hard to be powerful.

I didn't like bringing those emotions to the surface. By the time we could smell the pizza in the kitchen, I was exhausted, mentally and physically. I had no idea how hard it was to defend myself. I gobbled down four slices of pizza before I realized my stomach ached.

"We've got some things to do," Mike said. "So, why don't you guys go relax and watch a few movies before bed. We'll come get ya when we're done." We found we really didn't have a choice in the matter. They all stood, ushering us back into the game room. Someone or several someones had put the room back in order. I wondered how many agents were running around this place. The curtains were drawn and the room took on the feel of a prison.

"Well, let's see," Summer said, as she walked toward the large TV. She fingered through a bunch of DVDs that sat on a shelf next to it. "We'll watch this," she said, taking control and sliding the DVD she had chosen into the DVD player. She grabbed the remote, turned on the TV and backed up into an overstuffed loveseat. Rick sat in an arm chair. The couch was the only place left to sit, so I sat there. Neither of them looked my way.

I spent the first movie staring at Rick. How could I get him to talk to me? Would he listen to me or reject me? Maybe he would simply laugh at me. I imagined him saying, "Oh, you thought I really liked you? I just wanted someone to make-out with while I was here in D.C. and you were an easy mark." But, I knew that would never happen. It wasn't in Rick's nature. Was it in Alex's nature?

When Rick stood up to stretch, I forgot all about Alex, and grabbed the opportunity to talk to him. I took a quick breath, stood up and walked right over to him. Our eyes locked for a mere second, and then he looked away. I almost lost all the courage I'd mustered, but before he could move away from me, I squeaked, "Could we talk, please?"

It felt strange to be the pursuer, but when he didn't acknowledge me, I grabbed his arm with gentle hands and asked again.

He looked at me and said, "I can't think of anything we have to talk about."

Stab, stab, stab. My heart raced so fast I thought I might faint as he moved his arm away from my touch and sat back down. I looked at Summer, for no particular reason, and she was busy picking the next movie, paying us no attention. Looking back at Rick, I noticed he was looking straight ahead at nothing, like he wasn't using his eyes at all.

My heart pounded, bruising my ribs as I pleaded with him. "Please, Rick. I need you to know the truth. Just give me a few minutes—it's all I ask. Please."

He shifted and then stood, without saying a word, he motioned with his arm for me to lead the way. I took him to the opposite side of the room to sit in the window seat. We stared at each other for what seemed forever. How should I start? I didn't know what to say. I had to say the right thing, or I'd lose him forever. I just knew it. I wanted him to accept me again, but how?

I cleared my throat and then forged forward, not exactly sure what was going to come out of my mouth.

"Some of what Summer said was true—but most was not. I did go with Alex to a club, and he did kiss me—"

Rick shifted, ever so slightly in his seat, but kept looking down, so all I could see was the top of his head.

"But, I never made out with him at the club, and the kiss was anything but beautiful. When I got back to the hotel, I was up almost all night thinking about what I should do about you and Alex. I've heard people say they liked two people at one time, and I always dismissed it thinking they were lying to themselves. But, the truth is, I do like both of you. I hated to see that I had become one of those people. I made some decisions that night that I only partially followed through on. I knew Alex wasn't any good for me, but I was so drawn to him. Every time I was with him, though, it seemed he made me lower my standards or at least asked me too. I decided I would tell him I couldn't be with him.

"That's when I also decided I would have to tell you that we would have to wait to date until I was sixteen like I told you that night you woke me up. I did get a chance to tell you that. I'm no fool anymore in thinking that something magical happens at sixteen to make dating easier—especially when for me it's only a month away, but the fact is, a month can make a world of difference.

"If you knew how much I'd changed in the last two weeks here in D.C., you'd flip out. Maybe I'm more mature, maybe I'm just more reckless, but at least I know that I'm trying to do as my parents asked me to do. I know they are more wise than I am and following their advice on this one thing won't kill me. Look at what a mess I've made of my friendships with both you and Alex… on second thought, maybe it does have something to do with not being sixteen, I just don't know.

"Then, things got crazy with me fainting and Alex buying me that dress for the gala and all, and I guess I figured I would only be with the two of you for two more days and you'd forget I existed after that, so I might as well enjoy the time I had with you. I asked myself what could possibly happen. I got side-tracked and let my racing heart lead me.

"When Alex showed his real colors and kissed me at the gala, I was so mad. I hope you saw me punch him. He was being a jerk, trying to rile you up because he was jealous we had danced. Then our agents came and it was all over.

"You're the one that makes me a better person—not him. I love being with you, Rick and want to have that chance again, when the time is right. I'm so sorry for not being totally open with you. It's not like me. Please forgive me. I know it may take time for you to decide what to do, but I'm willing to wait. I guess I have to wait. Maybe, by some miracle, I will be better equipped to deal with the emotional and physical responses that come with dating. When it's time, maybe I'll be smarter."

He didn't move the entire time I spoke. My heart dropped waiting for a response, any response. None came. He simply stood up, after about one minute of silence, walked back over to his seat and sat back down to watch the movie.

Devastated, it took everything I had not to bust out bawling. I curled up on the window seat and closed my eyes. He was right not to forgive me right away. I told myself. He had to digest what I had said—decide if I could be trusted. Maybe I couldn't. Could I really say that I would choose Rick over Alex if I had them both extending a hand out toward me at this moment? I'd already chosen Alex many times over. What made this moment any different?

It was all my fault I had lost him. I had been stupid, straying from what I knew I should have done. After half an hour, the thousand tears I'd shed, stopped. It was time to stop feeling sorry for myself and own up to the natural consequences of my actions. Next time, I would be smarter. Chalk one up for experience. Painful, excruciating experience.

I sat up, looked at my reflection in the window and headed back to the couch. It felt good to curl up into a ball and stare mindlessly at the TV screen. My eyes closed several times, only to pop open when a loud noise from the movie startled me. Then Jeremy came and told us to head for bed. I was glad and ready, wishing Marybeth was here to talk to.

CHAPTER TWENTY-FIVE

Something kept me awake, driving me crazy. I'd been so tired watching the movie, why couldn't I sleep now? This gnawing in my gut ate at me—a worry that wouldn't settle. Was it Rick? Was it Alex? Was it Summer? Was it the terrorists? Or was it that voice in my head that offered protection?

My dry mouth prompted me to get up and get a drink. About halfway down the hall, I had this odd sensation and looked back. My tongue was so dry it stuck to the top of my mouth, so I continued down the hall, to the kitchen—stepping a bit lighter than before, more aware.

Passing the island in the kitchen, I grabbed a cup from the cabinet next to the sink, and reached to turn on the water, but was startled instead. Through the window over the sink, I stared at a man's back His body started to turn, and I crouched down as fast as I could. It was some kind of a reflex. I almost stood back up, thinking I was being silly. He was just there to protect me, after all. He was talking to someone, and said, "Hold on." He must've been talking on a phone. I could hear footsteps heading toward the back door. I scurried behind the island and held my breath as the almost silent sound of the door opening hit my ears.

Something inside me sounded an alarm, so tangible that I couldn't ignore it. I put my hands over my mouth and held my breath. I couldn't hear footsteps or any movement, but I felt someone there—just on the other side of the island. One part of me wanted to run, but something told me to stay still.

I heard the click of the door shutting this time. Then the voice again, through the walls, almost a whisper: "I thought I saw bird one. Birds one to three ready for flight. No alarm."

Then another voice, possibly coming out of a walkie-talkie, "ETA thirty."

"Bird Catcher out."

"Raven out."

I knew one of those voices. From where? It sounded like the cold, harsh voice of the man who helped Jeremy question me at the FBI. The alarm inside of me kept ringing, louder now, more urgent.

Jeremy had said to hide in the closet if I was scared, but this guy had said he thought he saw bird one. Who was bird one? Bird one through three ready for flight. Were we being transferred… or captured?

"Move! Move! Go get Jeremy!" A voice boomed inside my head.

I was scared. Almost frozen. What if he was looking in the window and would see me move? It took all of my will to turn and look around the corner of the island and up at the window. No one was there. My head swam. I left my hiding spot, crawled past the stairs, down the hall, and stood once I reached Jeremy's room.

Wasn't he here to protect me? He couldn't be a bad guy. If it weren't for the constant ringing of warning in my heart, I would have gone back to bed.

I stood outside Jeremy's door for several long seconds, just staring at the white panels on the door, wondering what I would tell Jeremy. Why did I hesitate? My whole body screamed for me to knock, but I just stood, breathing quickly and quietly, afraid to disturb him. I had to be crazy.

"Knock. Now. Knock," the voice in my head urged.

What if someone heard me knock? I tried the door instead. It was locked. I very lightly tapped. No answer. I tapped a bit harder. No answer. I was too afraid to do it harder, so I knelt down and whispered into the door handle, "Jeremy…Jeremy… Jeremy."

I heard the click of the door and jumped back. The door swung open and there was Jeremy, towering over me with a gun pointed right at me. I backed up against the wall behind me, covering my face with my hands.

"Christy?" he said. I peeked through my fingers, and he looked both ways in a flash down the hall and then back down at me, tucking the gun into his back waistband. "What are you doing? How did you—"

I put a finger over my lips and mouthed, "Shhh!"

He rubbed his hands over his face and into his hair then back down over his face again. He waved me into his room. He held his hands out to his sides, palms up. I went to his closet, but there was no panel in there. He followed me and shook his head. I sat cross-legged on the closet floor.

"Are you scared?" he whispered.

I nodded my head over and over again.

He looked around the closet, grabbing some things and pocketing them, only to join me, cross-legged on the floor, closing the door behind him and turning on a small flashlight.

"What's up?" he whispered. "Why didn't you climb into your closet?"

"I went to get a drink, when I saw someone outside the window above the sink. I hid. I just felt like I should, so I did. Then the guy outside said, 'Wait a minute' and I heard him walk toward the back door. I slid around the island so he wouldn't see me. I couldn't even hear him walk, but I knew he was there. Then, he was back outside talking to someone on a radio or something. He said, 'I thought I saw bird one. Anyway, birds one to three are ready for flight.' Then another voice said, 'ETA 30.'

"Then the first guy answered, 'Bird Catcher out.' And the other, 'Raven out.' I thought I knew the voice, and I did. It was Agent Durrant from the FBI building that was with you when I was there, in that room when you asked me all those questions and...."

"Calm down, Christy," Jeremy interrupted. "Take a deep breath. It's only Mack out there. He's supposed to be there."

I did take a deep breath, but it didn't calm my nerves. Something was wrong.

"But you think the guy outside, is Agent Durrrant?"

"I know it's him. It's Agent Durrant."

"Christy, he isn't even assigned to this detail. He's not here."

"He is here. I remember his voice. It's him. He called himself, 'Bird Catcher'."

Jeremy stared at me, obviously thinking.

"Are we being transferred tonight or something?"

"Not that I'm aware of."

"I knew it. We are the birds, aren't we? Rick, Summer, and I—the three birds. They're going to kidnap us in thirty minutes. No, less than thirty minutes now."

"My alarm didn't sound when you left your room," he said quietly, like he was talking to himself. His eyes got big and I knew he finally understood. Jeremy stood up forcefully and opened a metal box on the wall inside the closet. There were all kinds of lights lit up in the box.

He mumbled something like, "No alarm. There's no alarm." Then he turned, slid open the closet door and walked away saying, "Crap! We need to get the others right now. Think Christy, how long has it been since you heard thirty minutes?"

"I- I don't know, maybe five—ten?" I wondered what those lights in the closet meant.

"He set his watch and sent me to Summer's room to wake her while he went to get Rick. Sure. Send me to wake her. I'd probably never survive her wrath. It was pure luck that she was dead asleep and had almost no energy to even get out of bed. I told her to be super quiet, that we were being moved. I helped her put some of her "favorite" clothes on and then Jeremy walked into the room with Rick. Rick carried some blankets, and Jeremy went into Summer's closet and came out with a few more.

"Listen," Jeremy whispered to the three of us, "We're going to go through a tunnel to a secret exit. There's an entrance to the tunnel in the game room. We must move quickly and quietly, but we must crawl. Follow my directions, and we'll make it."

The crawling part was anything but quiet. Every movement we made sounded like we were dragging heavy boxes along the floor.

Once in the game room, Jeremy crawled under the pool table and moved a rug. He yanked on a big metal ring on the floor, lifting a trap door and motioned for us to climb in. One by one we disappeared down the hole. We climbed down for a long time before hitting the ground. It was musty, and I could hear water dripping. We all stood, huddled together, until Jeremy joined us and whispered to quietly follow him. He flipped a switch that lit up little vent-like lights along the floor, like upstairs on the main floor, so we could see a little bit. We walked quite a ways before coming to a door. Jeremy didn't open it. He pulled a cap off of something that looked like the end of a pipe and put one eye up to it, I guessed looking out to see what was on the other side of the door.

He whispered several colorful words and put the cap back on the pipe.

"This is no good. They're watching this exit. We've got to go back."

"Go back?" Summer squealed, looking in the direction we'd come. She was finally awake. "Is it blocked? Did you take us to the wrong place? What's wrong with you?"

"Shh! Listen," Jeremy said. He looked at his watch and continued. "There are men out there who want to take you away. There's only the four of us, standing right here that we can trust. We don't have much time to hide, but we will, and they won't find us. Now, you all need to be more quiet than you have ever been your whole lives and do as I instruct you. No questions. Understand?"

Everyone nodded, even Summer.

"Good, we're going to go back into the house to find a better place to hide. Follow me."

No one was about to stay behind. Everyone was petrified. After climbing back into the game room, he had us take our shoes off and rub them on the backside of the carpet beneath the rug that covered the hole. Then we crawled back through the kitchen and into Jeremy's room. Jeremy shut the door behind us and went to his closet, pulling out several different tools, stuffing them into his pockets. He then led us up the stairs and into Rick's room. He went straight to the window, pulled out some tools and worked in silence for what seemed an eternity.

He sighed and then looked at all of us, motioning with his head to come closer. "We're going to climb out onto the roof. Rick, you will go first and lay four of the blankets on the roof for all of us to lie on. I will bring the other four blankets to cover us. I will come out last. Be careful not to let anything roll down the roof or make a noise. Be as silent as possible."

I was so tense I could feel pressure in my ears. I waited motionless for endless minutes until Jeremy beckoned for me to join Rick on the roof. Please don't let me fall.

CHAPTER TWENTY-SIX

Feeling claustrophobic under the blanket, I wanted to sit and look around instead of laying on the hard, uncomfortable roof. Despite the heavy blanket under and over me, I shivered. I could feel Rick lying still next to me, shifting slightly away every time we accidentally touched each other.

Maybe a minute later, I heard the rumble of gravel. They had arrived. I pushed up against Rick, not caring if he shifted away. Much to my surprise, he didn't. Jeremy pushed against me, too. I guess he didn't want me to go too far.

Rick slid his warm hand under my blanket, down my arm and grabbed my hand. My heart thumped hard, and I really couldn't breathe.

Noisy crunches of gravel sounded like bombs going off, one after the other, getting faster and faster and closer and closer. I wanted to curl up into a ball, but knew it would make a noise in the house. All we could do now was wait. I started breathing again, keeping it quiet and shallow and yet it sounded so loud.

I thought I heard the click of the front or back door. Every sound amplified when gripped with terror. An eerie silence fell over the house. Seconds later, loud, frantic screams met my ears followed by more silence. Gun shots rang through the air. The sounds weren't coming through the roof, they were coming from the front of the house— perhaps through the open front door. A drop of cold sweat crept down my spine and my breathing involuntarily sped up.

This was my fault. People were dying because of me. I should go and let them take me, to save the others. I could end this. Letting go of Rick's hand, I rolled over and bent my legs under my stomach to stand. In a flash, Jeremy's arm came down hard on my back.

"Christy!" he said in a voice that echoed under my blanket. "Don't move."

"I have to go," I whispered. "People are dying because of me. I need to go to them and let them take me. Then it'd be over."

I tried to pull myself up, but I couldn't even wiggle. His arm, like a clamp, held me down. Jeremy was completely under my blanket with me now, both arms holding me tight. My knees ached from being pressed into the hard shingles. I was so uncomfortable that I wanted to scream, but that would give them all away. I couldn't give them away.

"Calm down, take a deep breath," Jeremy whispered. "This is not your fault. We cannot let them win. We will win and you will live. Remember, you are going to save the country." His whisper was so low, I could barely hear it over our breathing. "You figured it out yesterday. Remember. We need you. You are the key to saving our country."

My chest burned and somehow I knew, even though a bit dramatic, he spoke the truth. The terrorists really were trying to get control of all our natural resources, which meant they would eventually control this country.

"You must survive. You will stop countless deaths and misery. You alone."

"What about Marybeth?"

There was silence.

"What about Marybeth?" Fear fluttered in my stomach.

"Everything's going to be okay. We got her."

My heart thudded so hard, I was sure Jeremy could hear it. What was he keeping from me?

"Was she alive?" I asked in a choked whisper.

"Of course," he said.

I sighed.

"Now be quiet," he said.

My knees ached for relief, but I was too afraid to change my position. I kept my ears open for any sound. I could hear faint bumping noises below us and muffled voices from the front of the house.

Suddenly, directly below us, I heard, "There's nothing sir," the middle eastern accent was unmistakable. "No sign of tampering. These alarms haven't been touched."

"Check again!" Agent Durrant's voice boomed with exasperation. "They didn't just disappear into thin air. This house will be checked from the basement up. Every inch of it. We have to find those kids. Now, move!"

"That bastard," Jeremy whispered. "Agent Durrant *is* the mole."

"They're going to find us anyway, Jeremy."

"No they won't. A team will be here soon to rescue us."

"What?"

"I sounded the alarm with Nathan. I figure we've got around five more minutes before this place is crawling with the FBI agents.

"Ones like Agent Durrant?" I couldn't help myself.

"No…like me. Just stay still."

The pain in my knees was sharper than ever, and I wondered how much longer I could hold out.

A distant whir-whir sound filled the air. The distinct sound of chopper blades slicing the air gave me hope even though they didn't seem to get close enough.

Minutes later, I heard the crunch, crunch of footsteps on the gravel as the FBI approached.

I fell from my knees onto my side and cried silently. Jeremy loosened his hold on me and patted my back, keeping me close. He breathed deeply, like he shared my relief.

Loud bursts of gun fire filled the air. I hoped the crystal clear screaming and yelling belonged to the terrorists and not the FBI. I waited motionless for endless minutes, holding back tears in anticipation.

More yelling and crashing noises pushed their way into our ears. The minutes dragged on and on until Nathan's voice screamed out into the night.

"Jeremy, where are you man? Where'd you go? We're secure. You can come out now."

Jeremy let go of me and sat up, the blanket shifting away from us. I didn't move and neither did the others. He stood up and looked around.

"Up here," Jeremy yelled. "I'll come down." Then he spoke to us. "Stay up here, okay guys?"

We could hear people talking, but we were still frozen in place. After a few minutes, that seemed like hours, Jeremy yelled up to us.

"Okay guys, it's safe. Go ahead and get down from there, but wait for me in the room."

I turned onto my back and rubbed my knees.

"You okay?" Rick asked, helping an eager Summer reach the window.

"I think so," I said, looking up at the starry sky and saying a silent thank-you-prayer. Rick sat down next to me.

"I don't think I've ever been more scared in all my life," he said.

"Me either," I said. I looked sheepishly at him, amazed he had talked to me.

"Christy—"

"You guys coming?" Jeremy called out the window, interrupting him.

"On our way," Rick said, standing up and offering me a hand. I climbed through the window, wishing Rick had the chance to finish what he wanted to say to me.

My knees throbbed with pain when I planted my feet on the carpet.

"Listen you guys," he said. "There's a lot of scary stuff down there that you don't want to see. Don't look. I'll go first, you guys follow one at a time and only look at the person in front of you. Do you understand?"

Everyone's eyes were fixed on him and we all nodded.

"Good. Just look straight ahead until we're outside."

Summer pushed her way behind Jeremy. Rick and I followed, down the hall and to the balcony that led to the stairs. Jeremy stopped and yelled down, "Hey guys, kids on their way."

I stood there, staring at the ceiling fan above us, slowly pushing air that smelled like metal and smoke all around.

"Come on, Christy," Rick said, reaching back and taking my hand. I tried to only look at the back of Rick's head, but couldn't. I had to see what happened while we were on the roof. I looked over the railing to see some federal agents staring up at us, with unbelieving gazes, while others milled purposefully about, turning over bodies that lay strewn in unnatural positions, checking for pulses as they went. The color red dominated. Acid burned my throat and my stomach churned. I closed my eyes tightly, trying to forget the images. Why did I look? I breathed deeply through my mouth trying to overcome my growing nausea, but it kept building.

Focus on your breathing, I told myself. You are taking a walk in the mountains. It is a beautiful day, there is a light breeze…We made it to the bottom of the stairs.

Then I smelled it. The sweet, sticky smell of blood. It seemed to fill my lungs and make it impossible for me to breathe. I gasped, looking around, I was surrounded by dead bodies, one of which was staring right back at me, Sam. I pushed past Rick, then Summer, and finally bored past Jeremy into the cold night air. I fell to my knees, only to scream out in pain, trying to get air into my lungs. No air came, I threw up violently. Jeremy kneeled beside me and whispered, "It'll be okay. It'll be okay."

Someone gently held my hair back until I fell to my side, unable to puke anymore. I could hear someone else wretch, too. I shook all over.

"Can we get some blankets over here, please." Jeremy yelled. "I think she's in shock."

Bundling up in the blankets felt heavenly.

Soon, I was tucked away in a warm ambulance on a nice, comfy gurney. Rick held my hand and laid on the bench next to me. I couldn't find words to tell him what I wanted to say.

I wanted to apologize for my behavior with Alex, for the gala—for everything, but it didn't seem to be the right time. Maybe I just wanted to hear what he intended to say on the roof before Jeremy interrupted him, before I bore my soul again.

After a short while, I thought I could actually sleep. Marybeth was safe, we were safe, and the terrorists were gone. I dreamt about walking hand in hand with Rick toward a black sunset when the slide door of the ambulance slid open and Jeremy pushed past Rick to me saying, "We've got to go!" He grabbed my hand away from Rick's and pulled me out from under the covers into the night air. I stumbled, feeling the pain and stiffness in my knees.

"I know your knees are killing you, but you've got to push through it if you want to live."

Shock ran through me as he tugged me forward, dulling the pain. I looked back, the sounds of running and shouting filling my ears. Thanks to the lights from the safe-house, I could make out dark, shadowy figures running about in chaos until the sounds of shooting overtook them.

I saw Rick being led off into the woods in a different direction than we were headed. Then the trees fell in behind us, blocking my view. I kept my ears open for the sounds of pursuit. My pulse pounded in my head. Branches whipped at my face. I tried to hold my hand up for protection, but found I needed it to keep my balance being pulled by Jeremy.

"Faster, Christy, faster."

Flames licked my throat for want of water and air. Then I heard them; footsteps, lots of them, closing in on us. Jeremy must have heard them too, because he propelled me in front of him, whipping his arm to the side to pull me ahead. I ran faster, hearing only the hard footsteps pursuing me and my own ragged breath. Shots rang through the air, making my body scream to keep running. Faster and faster still.

I could feel Jeremy only inches behind me. When suddenly, his body pushed into mine. He fell hard into me with a gasp and the small amount of breath left in me flew out as we slammed into the ground, leaving me to suffocate beneath him, his body heavy and limp. I struggled to free myself; to get the air I desperately needed.

But, I found I had no strength. I couldn't budge him. I tried to shift my head to the side to find an opening to get some air. I could feel the raw cuts in my face burn as they scraped the forest floor until a coolness hit my lips. I pulled hard on the fresh air. My lungs ached as they filled, which interestingly enough, made it harder to get the air I needed. Someone pushed on Jeremy, and I instinctively froze.

Should I play dead or fight? I needed to wake Jeremy. I pinched him, trying to rouse him. I felt a wetness on my fingers and wiped it away. A sickening feeling overtook me. Duh! Jeremy didn't move because he'd been shot. I wanted to cry, my stomach lurching into my throat. Into my heart came a pounding focus. I needed to live. Jeremy's words boiled over in my mind.

"You are the key to saving the country."

As Jeremy's body began to rise, I struggled to make myself stay hidden under him. I got a glimpse of the man's shoes and it somehow gave me more strength to push further under Jeremy.

After hearing several loud shots, the man turning Jeremy fell sideways with a thud. Jeremy's body slumped back onto mine. Only seconds passed before I felt his body being lifted again. I shifted, trying to stay hidden, but it proved impossible. His body flipped quickly, revealing the only face I hoped to see—Nathan's. He brought his hand up to his mouth and rubbed it tightly down his face and neck, revealing a panicked expression that slowly dissolved into a look of relief and sadness.

I gasped, pulling in all the air I could, watching Nathan's attention turn to Jeremy. Everything started moving in slow motion.

I could hear Nathan, but it was like I was in a fog.

"Quick, get help. We need a paramedic," he yelled.

Nathan touched his neck. "Come on, stay with us, Jeremy. Stay with us."

My eyes fixed on Jeremy, my insides thrashed in agony. He ripped Jeremy's coat open, sending buttons flying and exposed his vest, tugging at the Velcro straps on its sides to free it from him. He started breathing for Jeremy and other agents swarmed around.

This wasn't happening. *Live, Jeremy. Live.* I prayed a more honest prayer than I had ever remembered praying. Please, let him live. Take my life, not his.

One of the other agents dropped to his knees to give compressions between Nathan's breathing. Two other agents appeared and grabbed at my arms. I yanked myself away.

"No, no," I cried. "I have to stay. Please, let me stay."

"You don't need to see this, dear," a woman said. The voice was oddly familiar, and I looked up to see the large woman from the pizzeria looking down at me.

"She's bleeding. Get her to the ambulance."

"No, no," I said, shaking my head. The jacket she now wore didn't say DEA, it said FBI.

"That agent in the Pizzeria—"

"He's just fine, dear. He's just fine. Just like this agent will be."

"His name is Jeremy," I yelled, as they tried to pull me away. "His name is Jeremy and he has to live, he just has to. He saved me. Save him, please, save him."

I planted my feet hard, but was no match for the two agents pulling me away. They dragged me all the way back to the ambulance, and I screamed for Jeremy the whole way.

Behind the closed doors of the ambulance, I pressed my eyes shut and sobbed. I sobbed for all the people who would be notified today that their mom or dad would not be coming home. I cried for Rick, and Summer, who would have this memory of death forever. I cried for myself, wondering why I had to be a part of this and cursing my wish for change and adventure. I cried in relief that I was still alive. And I also cried for feeling relieved. And finally, I cried for Jeremy. As I did, I felt my heart break until a torrent of anger unleashed inside me, and I screamed until no more sound would come. My despair consumed me until a man in a paramedic's uniform climbed into the ambulance with me. My eyes burned as I looked at him. He lifted my shirt and looked at my side, wiping it with a wet pad that stung me.

"Oww!" I said.

"Sorry about that," the paramedic said. "You'll be okay. It's only a scratch."

"Jeremy," I said. "Jeremy."

"He'll be okay."

"No. He won't and it's my fault. I have to go to him."

I struggled to sit up, but they had already strapped me in. I pulled at the straps that held me there. The gurney moved and I felt a prick in my arm, a sedative. My worries disappeared.

CHAPTER TWENTY-SEVEN

Feeling someone's warm touch on my hand woke me up. White surrounded me. I couldn't seem to focus. I was in a bed in what looked like a hospital room or a prison, and I wanted to sit up, but couldn't find the strength. My throat, too dry to scream, allowed only a raspy whisper to escape.

"Christy. Christy. It's okay to wake up," a voice said.

Where was I? Help me! Someone help me. I remembered being in a forest running. Run. Run. Scary memories filled my mind.

"Christy, it's me, Rick. You're safe."

Rick? My heart slowed its thundering pace, and I could finally make out splashes of color around the room. I took long, deep breaths.

"Jeremy?" I rasped, looking straight at Rick.

"No, it's Rick. You're safe." He handed me some water, and I gulped it down.

"Where's Jeremy?" I said, looking around the room for him but finding Summer sitting on a chair in the corner instead. A part of me felt relieved. Summer was okay. Rick was okay. But was Jeremy okay? "Is he all right?"

"Jeremy's here, in the hospital," Rick answered.

"He's alive?" I gasped.

"Yes, he's alive." When he said this, he looked at Summer and her eyes rolled, telling me there was more to the story, and it wasn't good.

"I have to see him," I said, trying to sit up again, only to be overcome with dizziness, and having to lie back down. I was scared. It must be bad if they wouldn't tell me.

I heard a door open and a tall, thin woman with hair pulled back into a low ponytail, walked straight toward me. Her face was soft and kind, not a wrinkle anywhere. Her wide eyes never looked away from me. Rick moved aside to let her get close to me.

"I'm glad to see you're awake. I got a bit concerned when you didn't wake up right after taking you off the sedative this morning. But, better late than never." She looked in my eyes and then gently moved her fingers over my face.

"Who are you?" I asked. My face felt stiff.

"Sorry, Christy. I'm doctor Eisen. I've been taking care of you since you got here."

"Why?"

"Well, you had a pretty nasty fall. You had some deep cuts on your face and arms. Luckily, we were able to get a plastic surgeon here quickly enough to patch you up so that you'll have minimal scarring."

"Scarring?" My mind raced. I remembered the trees slapping my face and then my face scraping along the forest floor as I tried to get air. I gulped and touched my face. It felt rough and bandaged.

"I have this antibiotic ointment that you'll need to use on all your cuts and scrapes until they heal. To help them heal, I also got you some cream to go on after the antibiotic ointment. Use it twice a day. If you do this, you will likely have no scarring." She handed me the two tubes of medicine and smiled. "Do you have any questions?"

I said, "No," but wanted to ask a million.

"I'm going to do a few tests to make sure you are able to travel."

She poked and prodded and asked me questions as well as had me do certain movements with my body.

"Ouch!" I said, as she touched a particularly tender spot on my side.

"Make sure you get ointment on that graze, Christy. It could get infected."

"Graze?" I tried to twist and look at what she was talking about.

"Don't you remember how you got these injuries?" Dr. Eisen asked.

"I remember getting whipped by tree branches and falling hard onto the ground, but I don't remember any grazing."

"A bullet grazed your side. You are one lucky girl. You also have three very large, nasty bruises on your body, but you are so young, you will heal nicely."

"Okay."

"That doesn't mean that you won't have to go see your doctor when you get home. Do you understand?"

"Yes."

"Good. Everything I just went over, as well as my private number, is here in your discharge papers. If your doctor at home has questions for me, he must contact me directly. I am the only one who has worked on you, besides the plastic surgeon, and no one knows you are here, except me. The plastic surgeon's private line is also listed here." She pointed to a spot on some papers she was holding.

"Now, a shower will make you feel better. Be careful with your face. Don't get it wet for another few days. We would have liked to have kept you here for those few days, but the FBI is insisting that you get home today. I suppose it will be nice to be surrounded by your family while you heal. Your injuries are hardly life-threatening, but still."

311

"How long have I been here, anyway?" I asked

"Two days."

"Two days?"

"Well, we chose to sedate you, to up the chances that your face would heal correctly."

I didn't know what to say. Would I be a monster?

"I'll be calling you tomorrow to make sure you go see your doctor."

"Okay." Did my parents know what had happened?

"Great. Now you go right ahead and shower. Get yourself ready, but take your time. Don't let the FBI rush you too much—I wish you all the best. And I'll talk to you tomorrow."

"'Kay." Something about her made me feel comfortable and that comfort left when she walked out the door.

"Tell me about Jeremy." I shot at Rick. A horrible feeling gnawed at me.

"We'll go see him. But first, you need to shower and get dressed," he said.

"No…Take me to him now…Please."

Summer chuckled and said, "Yeah. I'm sure he wants to see your blindingly white butt peek through that hospital gown. Let's go. I'm always up for a good laugh."

Unfortunately, she was right. The insanely thin, short and breezy hospital gown I had on revealed much too much. I gasped, my face burning, wondering what Rick might have seen already. The warm fuzzies I'd been feeling knowing Summer was alive began to fade quickly.

Glaring at Summer, I swung my legs around to get off the bed. Every part of my body felt bruised and every move hurt. I stifled a moan.

"I know," Rick said. "You must be totally stiff and sore. There are some clean clothes for you in the bathroom. Take your time." He turned away from me as my feet hit the ground.

I wasn't going to take my time. I was going to be as fast as I could so that I could get to Jeremy. Once inside, I took my clothes off gingerly and noticed the three dark purple, black, gray and yellow bruises the doctor had told me about. The one on my right hip was the deepest shade of black, my right collar bone was not far behind and my left shoulder was a bit lighter gray. I looked in the mirror above the sink and was shocked. My face had a bunch of white strips of tape on it, some exposed long scratches and my left cheek was scraped, red and swollen. I pulled back in surprise, hitting my body into the door, causing a rush of pain from all the bruises.

"You okay in there?" Rick asked.

"Fine," I said, looking at my bruised and battered body one more time. I covered my mouth, remembering Jeremy's body falling onto mine, landing on big roots sticking out of the ground and watching Nathan perform CPR.

I had to see Jeremy.

In the shower, each stream of water stung. I clenched my teeth and worked as fast as I could manage to clean myself. Stepping out of the shower sent stabs of pain in my knees. It did feel good to be clean, though.

I examined my face again after drying off. It looked like I was an actor, playing a part in a horror movie. The only thing I didn't have was black eyes. I wondered how well I would heal. Would I be scarred? Maybe I deserved some scars for causing so many people so much pain.

I didn't have any make-up to hide the mass of scrapes, cuts and stitches and didn't think it would do any good, anyway. I used the antibiotic ointment and then the anti-scarring lotion liberally and kept my hair down, in an effort to hide my face. Mercifully, the clothes they gave me were sweats—fashionable sweats, but sweats nonetheless. Marybeth would die, but I had no choice. I wished she was here.

I took a deep breath before opening the door, giving me courage to face the others. Now I knew what they'd seen when they were looking at me, and it scared me to death.

They sat, watching TV. Rick stood abruptly and said, "How do you feel?"

"Much better, thanks." I looked at the floor, trying to hide my face.

"Good," he said. "Let's go." He walked to me and took my hand. I was sure it was hard for him to look at me—heck, it was hard for *me* to look at me. But, to his credit, he never flinched when he did.

"Where to?" I asked.

"We're going to see Jeremy," Rick said, grabbing my little hospital bag and opening the door. Two FBI agents stepped in front of the door.

"We're ready," Rick said to them.

One agent started walking down the hall, and we followed. The other fell in behind us.

"So, what happened, Rick?" I asked in a whisper.

"We don't have to talk about it, Christy. Really."

"I want to know, I mean, if you can tell me."

"Well, remember the guys Jeremy saw at the end of that tunnel he led us down? You know the one under the pool table in the game room?"

"Yeah."

"After the house had been cleared by the FBI and we were in the ambulance, those people who were outside the tunnel ambushed us."

"No way!"

"There were about twenty of them and they went after us."

"Don't you mean they went after Christy?" Summer interrupted. "No one came after any of us—only her."

"Thanks a lot Summer," Rick said, seeing my eyes fill with tears.

"Well, it's true, and I'm just saying…" Summer continued.

"Well, stop saying it," Rick hissed. "She's been through enough. This isn't your fault, Christy. Don't forget that." He leaned over and whispered, "I'm glad you're safe."

I leaned into him, unable to speak. Had he forgiven me?

"Yeah, we are *all* really glad you're safe," Summer hissed. "We can't wait to go home. The FBI wouldn't let us go home until you could. Thanks a lot! And we have to lie and say we were in a bus crash. We can't even tell our families the truth."

A bus crash. A good explanation. An easy excuse.

Outside Jeremy's room stood two more guards, who hesitantly let us inside. The agents who were outside our hospital room joined them. Jeremy, lying on his bed, looked at me, smiling. I ran to him and hugged him hard, crying.

"You *are* okay. I was so worried about you," I said into his chest.

That's when I noticed he didn't hug me back. I pulled away and looked at him. He still smiled, but didn't move. Was he repulsed by my horrible face? Or was he mad at me?

"I was so worried about you, too," he finally said, his voice catching. His face bore the same wounds, some covered up with white strips, from the slapping branches as mine did, but his eyes sparkled, like always. "You were so brave. I'm proud of you." His eyes glistened with tears and one lone tear slowly fell down his left cheek.

"What's wrong with you Jeremy?" Panic welled up in my heart as I waited for an answer. My heart punched hard against my ribs.

"Not much." He chuckled. "I'm just a little paralyzed."

"Paralyzed? No, no," I said, laying my head on his chest hoping I would feel his strong arms wrap around me and hold me tight. They didn't, and I let the tears flow freely, wetting his shirt. No one spoke for a long time.

I looked him straight in the eye. Tears still spilled easily from his now. "What happened? Paralyzed? How?" I asked even though I knew the answer. He was paralyzed because he tried to protect me.

"Well," he said, trying to hide how his voice cracked with emotion. "A bullet—"

The door to the room suddenly swung open and a man, who was obviously a doctor, said, "Well, well. Who's this?" He looked at me, his deep voice soothing. "I mean, I saw these two kids yesterday and now there's one more." He gestured toward Rick and Summer and then planted his eyes on me.

"This is Christy," Jeremy said.

"Ahhh. Your partner in crime. I should've known. Her face looks as bad as yours. I think she might have more steri-strips than you." He moved over to me and grabbed my chin, looking closely at my face. "I take that back. Her cuts seem to be healing better than yours." He chuckled. "Maybe it's all these tears. Salt water has such a great healing effect. Now, what are these tears for? Are you in a lot of pain?"

"Only every inch of me."

"All bruised up—like someone else I know, huh?" He looked at Jeremy, moving toward him. I stepped away and watched as the doctor gently touched several spots on Jeremy's face. All I could feel was pain for this man who gave his life for me—worse, really. Now he would have a frozen life, unable to do anything that he used to. My insides churned.

"I was just filling Christy in on what happened to me. Could you just tell her?"

There was more? I was going to be sick. I felt hot and looked around for some way to get more air.

"Are you sure, Jeremy? I could leave and come back."

"No. Really, it's okay. Tell her everything. She won't rest until she knows every last detail." He winked at me. How could he do that? He should be mad at me, not playful. He would live a life of sorrow because of me. I tried to hold it together to know the full extent of the damage I'd caused. I leaned on the closest wall to help with the shaking.

"Well, okay…" the doctor turned to me. "Jeremy was shot. The bullet grazed his lower spine and miraculously missed all his vital organs as it exited his left side. His vertebra chipped a bit, but we think this paralysis will be temporary. Once the swelling goes down and some time passes, we hope he will return to normal."

"Oh." I felt a bit of relief. He had a chance to be normal again. I couldn't help but ask, "What are the chances?"

"It's hard to say. Everyone is so different."

"Is it more likely than not?" I whispered.

"Yes."

I expelled a puff of air and relaxed. My urge to puke left me as I moved toward Jeremy again. "Do you hurt or do you feel nothing?" I asked.

"I can't feel anything. Maybe it's a blessing in disguise."

"You always look on the bright side of things. How?"

"It's natural for me," he chuckled.

After checking a few of the machines, the doctor turned and looked at Summer and Rick and said, "Now, you two watch out for Christy here. Don't let her laugh too much. We don't want her cuts to bust open."

Only Rick and Jeremy laughed. Summer sneered.

"I'll be back a little later, Jeremy. And Christy, be good."

"I'll try." I answered, watching him leave, wondering why he hadn't said to "be safe."

"Hey, Jeremy," Summer said. "Why am I still here? It's not like I saw anything. Those goons out there wouldn't explain why *I* had to sit around here waiting for Christy when I could have been home two days ago."

"We didn't know exactly what the bad guys knew, so we had to play it safe to keep you safe. We didn't know if they knew only Christy and Marybeth had seen the whole thing and that you had seen nothing. I think it's pretty clear now that our mole, Agent Durrant, told them about who knew what. When push came to shove and they only had a slim chance of getting rid of one of you back at the safe-house, they went for Christy."

A strange relief washed over me, glad I'd been the target, but glad they hadn't gotten me.

"So, is everyone else safe now?"

"Everyone, including you," Jeremy said, looking at me. The other kids flew home yesterday."

"Why couldn't I go with them?" Summer asked.

"It was easier just to keep the three of you together, that's all."

"I'm so glad everyone's safe," I said. "What about the terrorists?"

"As far as the bad guys go, we think we got them all. They're all either dead or in custody."

"Even the Senator and the guy with the crooked nose and—," I asked.

"All, Christy. You're safe to go home. It's over for you."

The rock in my stomach didn't leave me. I was afraid.

"Don't be afraid, Christy," Jeremy said, as if reading my thoughts. "They got 'em on the run, and besides, I taught you to defend yourself. Just be careful."

Would I ever feel safe again?

"When are we going home?" I asked.

"This afternoon," Rick said, almost whispering. "We go to the airport from here."

"Today? Are you crazy?" I said.

"You mean you want to stay here? All alone?" Jeremy asked.

"I wouldn't be alone. You would be here."

"You need to go home."

The door opened and our "guards" stepped inside. "Time to go."

I leaned back down to Jeremy and hugged him. "Thank you," I whispered. I looked at his dark brown eyes and felt tears well up again.

"Don't cry for me. I'll be out running before your first tear hits the ground."

I smiled and gave him a kiss on the cheek.

"I'll write to you," I said.

"You don't need to do that."

"I want to. Where do I send the letters?"

"Send 'em to FBI headquarters. Nathan'll get 'em to me."

"I will," I said, nodding. "Thank you, Jeremy. Thank you for my life. Promise me you'll get better."

"I will. Don't worry."

"You better!" I said, turning to leave.

CHAPTER TWENTY-EIGHT

Our driver dropped us off curbside at the airport and Summer, Rick, our agents and I headed inside. The masses of people waiting in line at each airline staggered me. People were everywhere.

We snaked through the line to check our baggage. Once we reached the representative, she entered our information and then another airline rep. came and led her away. They disappeared behind a door. Only after several minutes did a completely different rep. come to the counter to help us. Chris, my new Special FBI Agent, complained about the wait and the rep. gave us complimentary hygiene kits for our trouble.

It had only been one hour since they made me put the wig on, and it itched already. Waiting in the long line to check my luggage, I tried to ignore it, but by the time we headed for the security line, I couldn't take it anymore. I pulled hard on Chris' arm and pointed toward the restroom sign.

He rolled his eyes and said, "Hurry up. We don't have a lot of time."

I nodded and hurried in, scratching my head through the wig once I got in a stall. I knew I should be careful not to mess it up and make it obvious that I was wearing a wig, but it itched so bad and I had to scratch so hard to satisfy the itch, I was sure it had moved and didn't look right. I'd fix it on my way out. With the itch gone, I headed for a mirror. The wig had moved, the part sat way left and the long black hair ratted at the top. I flipped the long strands to the back and adjusted the part to the center while tucking in any errant strands of my natural blond hair. It didn't look as good as the make-up artist had left it, but I thought it looked pretty natural.

I had to spend a minute on my face. It looked terrible. The ointment the doc had me put on my scrapes was shiny and oozy now. The make-up artist had been smart putting a long wig on me so that I could look down and hide my face because the ooziness of the ointment made me look like some monster from a sci-fi flick. I turned to get some toilet paper to wipe it away, when I noticed a nun washing her hands at the sink next to me. I smiled at her. She smiled back, turning to grab a paper towel, but finding the dispenser empty, she turned back to the sink.

"Here, use these," I said, handing her the toilet paper I'd just gotten.

"Thank you, dear," she said.

I got more for myself, wiped my face and headed for the exit.

"Young lady," the nun called after me, "here, take this." She held out a necklace.

"No, really, that's okay," I said.

"It's a Patron Saint Christopher charm. He'll watch out for you as you travel." She moved toward me, holding it out to me to take. "Please, you were kind to me and I'd like to return the favor."

Not wanting to hurt her feelings, and knowing that Chris told me to hurry, I took the charm, lifting it up to see a man with a walking staff imprinted on the little gold charm. I said thanks as I hurried out the door.

Chris stood only a few feet from the entrance, looking like he hadn't taken his eyes off the door the whole time I was in there. Before I could tell Chris about the nun, he jumped all over me for taking too much time, grabbed my hand and dragged me to the security line. I slid the charm necklace into my backpack, amused at the idea a patron saint would watch over me and his name was Christopher.

I saw Summer already walking down the aisle for first class ticket holders, and Rick stood at the end of it. He waved his hand at me to go with him. First class would have been nice, but something I could never afford. I pointed at the other line, pulling Chris in that direction, but Chris pulled me toward the first class line.

"This way," he said.

"I don't have a first class ticket," I said.

"You do today," he said, meeting up with Rick and his agent.

Rick smiled and said, "Finally."

I couldn't believe he was being so nice to me after what happened at the safe-house. I thought it was over between us. In fact, he'd been nice to me ever since he took my hand on the roof.

He looked me straight in the eye. I wasn't sure what to make of it. Had he forgiven me? He grabbed my backpack, threw it over his shoulder and then took my hand, leading me into the almost empty first class line to airport security while I tried to open my ticket and see what it said. Was I really in first class?

Both of our FBI agents followed closely behind us, acting like they were traveling, too. It was interesting to see them appear relaxed. I looked around, wondering if there were more agents stashed around the airport that I couldn't see. There were only three people in front of us in line, and Rick turned to me. "Hey, what's the first thing you're doing when you get home?"

I pulled my hand away from his and opened my ticket, ignoring his question. *First class*. Rick bumped into my arm, smiled and said, "A gift from the taxpayers of America." He chuckled.

Awesome.

"So, what are you going to do when you get home?" he asked again.

Home. Unfortunately, we *were* going home. This really was my last day in D.C. My stomach tightened thinking of going back to my ordinary, totally uninteresting, boring life back home. I hoped my parents would let me stay home from school until I didn't have to use the ointment any longer. Fat chance. Would people be able to see that I had changed—that I could be pretty— even with my face a total mess?

I hadn't really thought about what I would do when I got there. All I could think about was what I would miss here in D.C. *Friends.* People who liked me and wanted to be with me. *Guys.* Guys who actually liked me. My heart sank as I thought about the loneliness of home.

I felt a tug at my hand.

"Well?" Rick stared at me.

The playfulness in his eyes made my heart sink even deeper. He was going to go home to his friends and would forget all about me.

"You in there, Christy?"

I forced a smile. "Sorry. I was just trying to figure out what I'm gonna do."

"I know what I'm going to do. After giving my family the biggest hugs ever, I'm gonna make 'em go swimming with me. I'm dying to swim."

This time it was easy to smile as we continued moving toward the security guy. "Swimming's good."

"Yeah. The only thing that would make it better is if you were there with me." He squeezed my hand lightly a couple of times and rocked gently into the side of my arm.

"If only," I said, feeling my skin heat up as he touched it. Truly. If only. Now that I had felt what it was like to have people care about me—how could I live without it? I simply had to make some friends. The thought of going back to everyone treating me the same horrible way for the next two years until I could leave for college crushed me.

When we reached the security check point, I couldn't help but notice how close Rick had gotten to me. I tried to suppress the magical feeling it gave me, but couldn't. If this was the last time I would be with him, I should enjoy it. Why was I being so pessimistic anyway? He *could* call me. He *could* visit. It wasn't out of the realm of possibilities. After all, who would have believed I would have made friends on this trip? Who would've believed I could look pretty? Who would have believed I would kiss someone? Two someones? Even if Rick or Alex didn't call me, maybe guys would notice me and even ask me on a date next month when I turn sixteen. Thanks to Eugene, I could see how annoying I'd been before I came to D.C., and I would never act that way again. My heart raced at the thought.

I handed the security guy my ID and boarding pass. Rick did the same. Our FBI agents followed close behind.

While getting my shoes back on after security, Rick took my backpack again. "We're only a few gates away from each other—but my plane leaves in about ten minutes. You still have a half-hour or so."

I was glad he didn't ask me again about home. He stopped at a gate that had no people waiting in it and led me away from the main walkway, setting our backpacks against a wall.

"Christy—"

"Wait," I said. "Rick, I'm sorry about the gala, that night in the safe-house and—"

"Christy. You don't need to apologize again. I do. I'm sorry for ignoring you at the house. Especially after you explained everything to me. I was rude and mean."

"Stop it. You don't have anything to apolo—"

He pulled me close. I felt his warm breath on my face as he looked straight into my eyes and my heart lit on fire. He moved in even closer. The touch of his body against mine sent tingles to the tips of my toes. He whispered, "Can I kiss you?"

I nodded, wanting nothing more.

He kissed me softly. The kiss by the fountain had been beautiful, but nothing like this. His hand was warm on the back of my neck and his lips were soft and giving. My fingers drifted along his back.

I thought briefly about Alex. My last words to him had been said in anger. In fact, I had punched him. I would never see him again, would I? Not likely. I shouldn't feel guilty for kissing Rick. This kiss was special, like he was gifting me a part of himself. Alex kisses set my body on fire, but that couldn't last forever. Alex was gone. He hadn't meant what he'd said about me "being taken". But why did it hurt so bad to think I'd never see him again? I pushed on the hurt, taking it to the far reaches of my mind, because Rick was here. He was real, and I believed in him. I would kiss him one final time. It couldn't hurt. I was going to enjoy every second. He made me feel safe and secure with who I was, unlike Alex, who always asked me to change in some way. Rick was definitely the right choice. I didn't even hear that voice in my head contradict my thoughts—it was wonderful.

At one point, his arms tightened on the small of my back, and I cringed in pain. He pulled away, ever so slightly, and whispered, "Sorry." I gladly wrapped my arms around him, but he was careful to stay a tiny sliver away so that he wouldn't hurt my bruised body, his hands stopping just before the small of my back. He kissed me until I could barely hold a thought.

"Hey. Hey," a voice called. "You're going to miss your flight, bud. Time to go."

We pulled apart. It hurt to think I would never see him again.

"I'll call you," he said, smiling, pressing his finger against my waiting lips.

I forced a smile, hoping he would.

"We'll get together this summer. Okay?"

"Okay," I said, as he let my hand go, hoping it was true. In one month I'd be legal, too.

"We'd better run," the agent said to Rick. My heart thudded hard as I watched them take off. Rick's gate was only three down, and he handed the boarding agent his pass. Before getting on the plane, he looked my way and waved. I smiled despite myself and waved back, hoping and praying he would call me.

I leaned against the wall, enjoying the sensation of my pounding heart—recording every last detail of my final moments with Rick. I never wanted to forget how I felt at that moment.

My flight to Colorado was leaving in about twenty minutes and I felt my stomach knot up; I felt on edge. I *was* glad to be leaving D.C. and the horror of its memories, but still had reservations about going home. I wished I could stay in Colorado and not continue on to Montana. I looked at Chris, who sat a row away from me.

I stood up and went over to him, sitting in the seat beside him.

"So, you're going with me?" I asked, resigning myself to the idea.

"No," Chris said.

"Will I have to go back to D.C. to testify?"

"Most likely not."

"Why not?"

"They said they got everyone."

"What about justice?" My stomach churned.

"Justice will be served but usually with cases like this, deals are made. This kind of stuff is often kept real quiet. If they can keep it that way, that is." Now my stomach burned at the thought they'd get a sweet deal. I'd have to write Jeremy to find out the details.

"Why are you here if they got everyone?"

"They *think* they got everyone."

My heart pounded with dread. They hadn't gotten everyone after all. Had Jeremy lied to me again? What were his exact words?

"They think? They think?" My voice was shrill.

"Look, we got everyone we knew about. It's only been two days since we started rounding 'em up. It can take months to be sure. Give us a chance to tie off all the loose ends."

I stared at him wide-eyed, panic choking me, while I tried to remember exactly what Jeremy had said. "They're all dead or in custody." Did he just not know because he was in the hospital?

"Don't get all crazy on me now. You're safe, be assured of that." With that, he stood and offered me his hand to help me up.

How could I be assured? I reluctantly took his hand, and we walked to my gate where people were already boarding the plane. But I wasn't ready to board. I needed time to digest what Chris had told me.

"Really," he said, backpedaling, "Don't worry your little head about it. I'm sure we already have everyone involved. I didn't explain it right. You are safe."

I listened with no comment. I didn't know him. Could I believe him? I walked over to get a drink at the drinking fountain and he walked back over to the chairs and took a seat. Jeremy had said more after he said that the terrorists were all dead or in custody. Something about the terrorists being on the run. Why hadn't I *really* heard that while I was with him? I could have questioned him. I walked into the bathroom for no particular reason. I was putting off the inevitable.

I stared at myself in the mirror, washing my hands over and over again. This was it, an end to my ability to change. In a few hours, I would be home. When it came right down to it, I was afraid to go home. Would people see me as a new, different person and accept me? I gently touched a few of the white-strips that dotted my face. I hoped I could make myself pretty like Marybeth had done for me almost every day of the trip.

Would they see that I had more to give than right answers, eloquent speeches, and pristine writing? Would they care about me if they found out what I had witnessed—that I had experienced something horrible? But I couldn't tell. We had just been in a car accident— that was all. My heart hurt thinking about how it would feel if no one saw the new me and liked it. I wanted to be noticed. I wanted to be valued. I wanted to feel included. I looked away from the mirror and that voice in my head came back.

"Remember hope—believe."

The hurt suddenly turned to burning and my despair turned to hope.

I could hope. I could believe. I had to believe that things would be different—better even. I took a deep breath and smiled as I dried my hands. I didn't understand why I felt so uncertain. It didn't make any sense. Like Marybeth had said, I did have two amazing guys vying for my attention in D.C. Why not again? I had made friends, and I could again. The brightness of the hope I felt filled my whole soul.

When I came out, I saw Chris tipping his head to my gate, urging me to board. I looked around one last time and headed for Chris to get my backpack, my mind quieter and yet alert. I bent over to pick up the backpack and something started to buzz in Chris' pocket. He stood up and grabbed my arm, hard, leading me into the family bathroom.

"What's…" I started to say.

He held his free hand up to lips, gesturing for me to be silent. Two large men fell in behind us and stopped at the door to the bathroom while Chris and I went in. He pulled out what looked like a pen and starting at my toes, he moved it over my body. Was it a bug detector? It screamed when he ran it over my backpack. Without talking, he opened my backpack and dumped the contents onto the floor. He ran the detector over it until he singled out the hygiene kit the rep. at the check-in desk had given me. He went to the door and handed it to one of the two men outside the door and then came back to me, moving the bug detector slowly over my whole body and backpack one more time. No buzzing.

"Did anyone else give you anything while here at the airport?"

"No," I said, before remembering the traveler's necklace. "Oh yeah," I laughed. "A nun in the bathroom gave me that St. Christopher's charm," I said, pointing at the charm on the floor.

He shook his head, running the device over it. It didn't chirp, but he picked it up anyway and gave it to the guards outside the door. My insides turned to jelly. I felt so stupid. He'd told me not to accept anything from strangers.

He raised his eyebrows, waiting for me to explain.

I told him about the nun and everything that had happened and what we talked about. He rolled his eyes and sighed.

"We told you not to talk to anybody. I told you not to take anything from strangers. What were you thinking?"

I not only felt two inches tall, I wanted to disappear completely.

"I know it was stupid, but she was a nun. I just didn't know."

"That's the point. You don't know." My face burned and my insides shook.

He put his hand to his ear and gave a description of the nun and rep. to whomever was on the other end.

"What's going to happen now?" My heart battered my ribs. The terrorists were obviously alive and kicking.

"We'll put a decoy with that necklace and kit on the plane to Colorado and then somewhere besides Helena. You're heading for Portland now and then home. Justin, a make-up artist, is on his way to change your look and get you on the plane to Portland."

"I'm sorry. I really am. But you accepted a kit from that rep., too."

"Just do what we tell you from now on." The harshness in his voice made me feel worse.

"I will. I promise." It wasn't fair, though.

He rolled his eyes again and breathed out hard through his nose. He didn't try to make me feel better. He wanted me to feel bad so that I would be more careful.

There would be no question about me being careful. Fear crawled through each and every bone in my body, one by one, slowly chilling me. I wrapped my arms around my middle, hoping I wouldn't start to shiver.

A few minutes later, Justin came in with a bag and had me change into different clothes. Jeans and a t-shirt, along with a hoodie. I wouldn't stand out for sure. Justin was a breath of fresh air. He fitted a short brown wig on me and he sprayed make-up all over my face. He called it airbrushing. If you looked closely, you could see my steri-strips and scrapes, but you really had to look.

"This is the end of the road for us, Christy," Chris said. "Good Luck."

"Thanks," I said, guilt dripping from my voice.

He left the room.

"What's your cover, Anna?" Justin asked.

I was Anna, now? He gave me a quick cover-story about being in a car accident while visiting relatives in Maine. Of course, it became a bus accident for my parents. He had me practice talking with him, just in case someone was insistent on talking to me. He also reminded me to clean up once at the airport in Helena so that my parents wouldn't freak out seeing me in disguise.

I liked Justin and his easy, light-hearted personality. We even joked and laughed while waiting at the gate for my flight. By the time I boarded the plane, I'd almost forgotten that I was a target and that the terrorists were still actively trying to get to me.

I had to believe what Justin had told me. That we had fooled them and I wouldn't be found. What else could I do? I pushed the horror into a corner of my mind and sat back in my nice roomy seat, drink in hand, to watch a movie and escape D.C.

ABOUT THE AUTHOR

Cindy Hogan graduated in secondary education at BYU and enjoys spending time with unpredictable teenagers. More than anything, she loves the time she has with her own teenage daughters and wishes she could freeze them at this fun age. If she's not reading or writing, you'll find her snuggled up to the love of her life watching a great movie or planning their next party. To learn more about the author, visit her at cindymhogan.blogspot.com